THE
MISSING
MORTALS

THE DINSWOOD CHRONICLES

2

ELLEN ALEXANDER

bhc
press™

Edited by Lana King

THE MISSING MORTALS

Published by BHC Press

Library of Congress Control Number:
2018948483

ISBN Numbers:
Hardcover: 978-1-64397-010-3
Softcover: 978-1-947727-84-7
Ebook: 978-1-64397-011-0

Visit the publisher at: www.bhcpress.com

OTHER BOOKS IN THE DINSWOOD CHRONICLES

The Secret of Dinswood

CONTENTS

This book is dedicated to my grandchildren:
Emma, Eli, Owen, James, Adrian,
Elizabeth, Emery, and Liam.
They are truly blessings from God.

THE MISSING MORTALS

PROLOGUE

**DINSWOOD CASTLE
1722 AD**

W
hat is it you're doing, my love?" Darius asked his wife with an affectionate smile.

Rebecca looked over at her husband, her green eyes shining with excitement. "I'm writing a letter to our little one."

"But our baby isn't even here yet," Darius pointed out gently.

"I know, but it's only a matter of days now. I want our baby to know how much we already love him or her," Rebecca added, raising an eyebrow at her husband. Rebecca was convinced that the baby she was carrying was a boy, and Darius was equally certain it was a girl. The sex of the child didn't really matter to either of them. Their only concern was that the baby be healthy.

Darius was watching her from the door of the room they shared. They had been married almost ten years, and Rebecca couldn't help thinking that her husband was just as handsome now as he'd been when she first met him. At forty-four, his dark hair had only a smattering of gray, mostly at his temples. He kept his hair short but long enough so that it lay attractively on his forehead and curled over his ears. His dark brown eyes could still melt her with a glance, and his six-foot-two inch frame was still lean and well muscled.

Darius leaned against the doorjamb and continued to watch his wife as she turned her attention back to the letter she was writing. She was sitting in bed, propped up by a couple of pillows. The pillows were almost completely covered by her long red tresses. Ever since learning of her pregnancy, Rebecca had been positively glowing with happiness, and now that the baby's arrival was only days away, she looked more beautiful than ever.

Darius understood the joy she felt because he was just as happy and excited as his wife. They had been hoping and praying for a child for nine long years. Darius had given up and accepted the fact that they would never have children, but Rebecca had continued to pray. Almost nine months ago, Rebecca had learned that she was pregnant. She had been ecstatic, and Darius had been cautiously optimistic. Not long after learning of her pregnancy, Rebecca began having problems, and her doctors put her on strict bed rest. Normally very active, Rebecca found the sudden inactivity hard, but she endured it without complaint for the sake of her unborn child. Now, they were only days away from the birth of their first child. Darius was extremely proud of his brave wife, and he loved her more than words could say.

Darius remained where he was, watching the poignant scene before him a little longer. There were things he needed to do, but he couldn't seem to drag himself away. Smiling to himself, he thought about the wonderful surprise he had waiting for Rebecca. He planned to give it to her after the baby was born.

With a sigh of regret, he pushed away from the doorjamb and turned to go. As he walked away, seeds of worry and doubt crept into his mind—worry about the impending birth and doubt that he had lived a life worthy of such happiness.

CHAPTER ONE
DISCOVERY

R ay Sutton glanced nervously at his watch for the third time in as many minutes. Then his gaze shifted to the rapidly darkening sky. They were going to have to hurry if they wanted to get the foundation of Dinswood Academy's new gymnasium dug before nightfall. Ray's company, Sutton Construction, had recently been hired by Lord Percival Dinswood to build the new gymnasium. One of Ray's crew, Clint Harris, was currently operating the front-end loader. Ray watched as it dumped its most recent load of dirt. A flash of lightning on the distant horizon had him looking at the sky again. Not only was it going to be getting dark soon, but a storm was on the way. Ray had listened to the latest weather reports on his portable radio earlier that afternoon. This particular storm was bringing with it the possibility of several inches of rain. Flash flood warnings had been issued for the entire area. If they didn't finish digging the foundation now, it might be several days before it would be dry enough to continue. That would put them behind schedule, and Ray was a stickler for schedules. It wasn't only the schedule, however, that had Ray worried. Sutton Construction had won the contract for the job because Ray had put in the lowest bid for the project. If he was going to stay within the budget he'd proposed to Dinswood, the digging needed to be completed today.

A half hour later, Ray breathed a sigh of relief; it seemed as if they would be able to finish the job tonight after all. Clint only had two more loads of dirt to remove, and although it had already gotten dark, the rain had held off. Ray had let the rest of the crew leave over an hour ago, so only he and Clint remained. Ray was just thinking that it might be several days before the ground would be dry enough to set the forms for the foundation when the wind began to pick up. After the heat of the afternoon, the breeze felt good, but Ray knew that it signaled the storm's arrival. Ray glanced anxiously at the loader. Clint was working on his last load when a brilliant flash of lightning lit the sky and the first fat drops of rain began to fall. Ray was preparing to retreat to the castle when he saw it—a glint of light reflected brightly from something in the mound of dirt held in the bucket of the loader. He froze for a moment, curious despite himself, and waited for another flash of lightning so he could get a better look. Ray had heard rumors that some sort of treasure had recently been discovered at Dinswood Academy, and he suspected that it was a part of that treasure that was paying for the school's new gymnasium. Maybe what he had seen was more of the treasure. Ray held his breath and waited. He didn't have to wait long. Another flash of lightning followed quickly on the heels of the first. Although it had been brief, it had been long enough for Ray to see that the glint of light had come from a metal box about two feet long and a foot wide. Driven by a sense of urgency he didn't quite understand, he began frantically waving his arms and shouting to get Clint's attention. But Clint couldn't hear him over the noise of the loader and the storm. Ray began running toward the loader. If Clint dropped that load, he might damage whatever was in the box.

Clint was in the process of turning the loader to dispose of the last load of dirt when he spotted Ray running at him like a madman. *What in the world is wrong with him?* Clint thought. Ray had been driving the whole crew like a man possessed, insisting that they finish digging the foundation for the gymnasium today, and now that they were this close to finishing, it looked like he was signaling for Clint to stop the loader. Unsure of what Ray wanted him to do, Clint let the loader idle and waited for Ray to approach. Ray reached the cab of the loader just as it began to pour.

"Stop the loader!" Ray panted, out of breath from running.

"What are you talking about? This is the last load." Clint was at a loss to understand Ray's strange behavior.

"Set the bucket down and do it gently!" Ray commanded. With his clothes already soaking wet and his hair plastered against his head, he truly looked the part of a lunatic.

Clint hesitated for a moment longer, and then with a sigh and a shake of his head that indicated more clearly than words that he thought Ray had gone off the deep end, he manipulated the levers that would set the bucket down.

"You've unearthed a metal box of some kind. It might have something valuable in it," Ray explained hastily as he ran around to the front of the loader.

Curious now himself and heedless of the downpour, Clint followed. With the help of the loader's headlights and the intermittent flashes of lightning, they quickly located the box and began to dig it out of the pile of dirt in which it was lodged. Once they had it free, they set it on the ground and let the rain rinse off the remaining dirt. Seeing that it was padlocked, Clint shouted, "I've got a crowbar in the cab of the loader." A loud crash of thunder punctuated his statement and had him running around the side of the loader. In moments, he was back with the crowbar and working on the padlock as Ray stood by and watched.

Soon the box was opened to reveal something wrapped in cloth and lying in a bed of straw. Clint reached into the box, but once again Ray stopped him. "I'll do it!"

Reverently, Ray picked up the object and began to unwrap it, all the while licking the rainwater off his lips in greedy anticipation. A perfectly timed streak of lightning revealed the treasure inside. Ray couldn't believe his eyes. He'd finally hit the jackpot. This one piece was probably worth millions, and only he and Clint knew about it. He was about to tell Clint that they would split whatever money they got for it when he happened to look toward the castle. Light shone from a single window on the third floor, and in that window, he could see the silhouette of a man. Someone was watching them, probably the old man himself. He had no choice now but to tell Lord Dinswood about the discovery. Ray shook his head in disgust. It was just his luck. He'd come so close to being able to quit his crummy job and live comfortably for the rest of his life.

Ray looked over at Clint and saw that he was still enraptured by the object Ray was holding. It was apparent that he wasn't aware that they were being observed.

"What do you think it's worth?" Clint asked in awe.

"It doesn't matter. We've got to turn it in," Ray replied.

"Are you crazy? This is our ticket to the good life. No more scratching in the dirt for us."

"Yeah, well, it looks like today isn't our lucky day," Ray said, inclining his head in the direction of the castle.

Clint followed his gaze and swore under his breath. After he'd had a few moments to let his disappointment sink in, he sighed in resignation and said, "You take it to the old man then. I better get the loader out of here while I still can." By this time, Clint was soaking wet too, and water was beginning to pool under his feet. He needed to get the loader up on solid ground before the area around him turned into a muddy swamp.

Ray nodded his agreement and then began rewrapping the object while rain dripped off his forehead and nose. When he had finished, he placed it gently back in its bed of straw and closed the lid of the metal box. Clint had broken the padlock with his crowbar, so Ray made no attempt to relock the box. As Clint restarted the loader, Ray picked the box up and carefully made his way over to the path leading to the castle. As if to add insult to injury, it began to rain even harder. Ray grunted in frustration and anger. It seemed that every time he turned around, that crazy old man was watching him. This job was turning out to be more trouble than it was worth. Then a thought occurred to him. If this box was part of the treasure, there might be more of it buried around the castle somewhere. It was an idea definitely worth pursuing, but it was going to be difficult with the old man around watching their every move. *Well, I'll just have to figure out a way to get Dinswood out of the picture for a while*, Ray thought. There had to be a way short of murder. Ray had no qualms about keeping whatever treasure he discovered, but he was no murderer. He was almost to the castle's back entrance when a solution came to him.

CHAPTER TWO
EARLY RETURNS

mma Higsby was sitting on the bed in her room reading a book when the phone in the hallway began to ring. Without hesitation, she threw the book down, jumped off the bed, and raced to the door, turning the knob and pulling it open in a perfectly timed, well-practiced move. Once through the door, she dashed down the hall to where the phone sat on a small table, managing to grab the telephone receiver just fractions of a second before her five-year-old twin brothers, Taylor and Tyler.

Emma had been half listening for the phone all evening because she was expecting a call from her best friend, Martha Merriweather. Emma didn't have a cell phone, so Martha always called the house phone. All summer long, Martha had called the house at least twice a week so that the two girls could keep each other up to date on all that was going on during their summer vacations. So far, Emma had very little to tell. Her summer had consisted of helping with the household chores and occasionally babysitting her little brothers when Vera and her dad wanted to go out for the evening.

Martha's summer had been a little more eventful and interesting. Her family had spent a couple of weeks in Hawaii and had just recently returned from Paris. The Paris trip had been a business trip for her father, but he had invited the whole family to go along. They had been gone a week, and during that time, Martha hadn't been able to make her usual calls. Emma had been anxious to hear all about Martha's Paris adventure.

Holding the receiver up in triumph, Emma grinned wickedly at her brothers. After a quick, "We'll beat you next time," which was said in unison, the two boys ran off to play. Emma waited until they were gone and then said hello into the receiver.

"Emma, you're not going to believe what just happened!" Martha cried excitedly, not even bothering to identify herself.

"What?" Emma responded somewhat perplexed. She had been expecting to hear all about Martha's trip and couldn't begin to imagine what could be more exciting than that.

"I just got a call from Lord Dinswood and he's going to be calling you next."

Now, Emma was really intrigued. Lord Dinswood was the founder of Dinswood Academy, the most prestigious boarding school in the country. Last year, Emma had won one of the scholarships the school offered. Dinswood Academy was actually a renovated castle set in the heart of the mountains. In his will, Lord Dinswood had left the castle to the state to be used as a school. Emma had fallen in love with the school almost immediately upon her arrival, and it had become like home when she had become best friends with Martha. Then she had met Doug, the dean's son, and his best friend, Sebastian. The four of them had been practically inseparable. Last year they'd had quite an adventure and had eventually discovered that Lord Dinswood was still very much alive. Since that time, they had come to know Lord Dinswood as a kind, compassionate man. Emma couldn't begin to imagine what Lord Dinswood would want from either her or Martha.

Before Emma could respond to this first startling news, Martha continued with another revelation. "He wants us to return to school early. He says he has something important for us to help him with."

Emma's mind whirled with thoughts of what that something important could be. The last task they'd undertaken for the school had nearly cost them their lives. It had been worth it though, and looking back, Emma wouldn't have changed a thing. Her stomach gave an excited flutter at the thought of returning to school early. School wasn't supposed to start for another three weeks. If she was honest with herself, it wasn't just the idea of another adventure that had her insides in a knot; it was the thought of seeing Doug again. She liked Doug a lot and not just because of his dark good looks. She and Doug shared a special bond; both knew what it was like to be without a mother. Emma's mother had died when she was five. Her father had married Vera a year later, and Emma had never been able to look upon her as a mother. In truth, Vera had never encouraged any such feelings from Emma. Emma's relationship with Vera was strained and awkward at best, and it was this in part that had driven Emma to work so hard to win the scholarship to the academy. Doug's situation was a little different but no less painful. His mother had walked out on him and his father when he was only three. She had remarried shortly afterward and, in the years following, had made no attempt to contact Doug. It was as if he didn't exist. Emma had felt an immediate empathy for Doug. Although he tried to hide it, Emma knew his mother's abandonment still hurt him terribly.

Emma was brought back to the present by Martha's exclamation, "Emma, are you there?"

"Yeah, I'm just trying to figure out what Lord Dinswood could possibly need help with."

"I have no idea, but it's kind of exciting, isn't it? Lord Dinswood said he'd be calling Sebastian too, so the gang will all be together again, that is if your parents agree to let you go early. Do you think they will?"

Emma hadn't thought about that. Although her relationship with Vera wasn't the best, Emma still helped a lot around the house and babysat Taylor and Tyler quite a bit as well. Vera might very well refuse to let her go. Emma doubted that her father would care one way or the other. Then Emma remembered that Martha had said Lord Dinswood himself would be calling. Although Vera might say no to her, Emma doubted that she would say no to Lord Dinswood. He could be very persuasive if the situation called for it. Martha's next statement made Emma feel even better about her chances of getting to return to school early.

"Lord Dinswood said he would make all the travel arrangements for us, and since we'll be doing him a favor, he's going to pay our airfare too."

EMMA SAT QUIETLY in the back seat of the car that was taking her up the mountainside toward Dinswood Academy. It had been nearly three months since she'd seen it. As the car drew closer to the castle, Emma sat forward and stared out the window so she would see it the moment it came into view. As eager as she was to see the castle, she was even more excited at the thought of seeing her friends again. Over the summer, she had missed them even more than she'd thought she would. Doug's dad, Dean Harwood, had sent Reverend and Mrs. Palmer down to the airport to pick her up. They had been waiting for her when her plane had landed and had greeted her with a warm hug, making her feel loved in a way she hadn't felt in a long time. After loading her luggage in the silver SUV they were driving, Emma and the Palmers had begun the journey up to the school.

Reverend Palmer conducted services in the school's chapel each week and served as the counselor. His wife, Judy Palmer, was one of the academy's foreign language teachers. During the ride up, Reverend Palmer asked Emma about her summer and filled her in on all that had transpired at the academy in the months she'd been away. With the treasure Lord Dinswood had generously donated to the school, construction of a new gymnasium had begun. The foundation had been dug, and the walls would be going up very soon, Reverend Palmer informed her. Emma was anxious to see for herself. The gym, complete with a weight room and indoor Olympic-size pool, would make it possible for the school to have team sports. It was the hope that this would attract more students to the academy despite its rather rigorous academic requirements.

The academy was unusual, not only because of its high academic standards, but also because of its unique approach. Students at the academy were not allowed to watch television or play video games. Instead, they were encouraged to use any spare time they might have in the pursuit of hobbies or getting some fresh air and exercise outdoors. Each semester, students were given the opportunity to receive instruction in the hobby of their choosing. Last year, Emma had learned to crochet.

Computers were available to the students but were to be used strictly for educational purposes. The school had no Internet access, so research had to be accomplished the old-fashioned way using books. To that end, the school's enormous library was well stocked with the latest and most up-to-date reference materials. Emma's two favorite rooms in the castle were the library and the lounge. Both rooms boasted a fireplace with large comfortable chairs scattered around, giving them a warm cozy feel.

Emma was just thinking that they must be getting close when they rounded a curve and Dinswood Academy came into view. Even though she'd seen it many times, it still took her breath away. The castle, a three-story structure of gray stone, stood proudly in the afternoon sun. The fountain, which was located directly across from the main entrance, was in full operation. An arc of water rose several feet high only to return to the earth as a mist that sparkled in the sun like a million diamonds.

The car was just pulling up in front of the castle when the large twin oak doors of the main entrance were thrust open, and out rushed Martha with Doug and Sebastian close behind. Last year, Emma had learned what a special person Martha was, and she had become more like a sister to Emma than a friend. When the car finally came to a stop, Emma couldn't get out fast enough. Overjoyed at seeing her best friend again, Emma met Martha halfway up the stairs and threw her arms around her. Martha did likewise, and they both laughed out loud as they nearly fell down. Regaining their balance and after another quick hug, the two girls let go of one another, and in their excitement at being reunited, they both started talking at once.

"I've missed you!" Emma exclaimed.

"I was afraid your parents wouldn't let you come," Martha said at the same time.

"They didn't want me to, but they couldn't refuse the offer of free airfare," Emma replied with a wry smile. Then she turned to greet Sebastian who had come to stand next to Martha and froze in surprise. Sebastian was at least two inches taller than when she had seen him last, and he had thinned down considerably. The plump boy she remembered was gone, and if it weren't for the red hair and freckles, she wouldn't have recognized him.

Noticing her reaction, Sebastian said with a sheepish grin, "I know I look different, but it really is me. I had a bit of a growth spurt this summer."

"I should say so," Emma said and looked at Martha to see what she thought of the new Sebastian. Martha gave her a smile that indicated she rather liked the taller slimmer version. Sebastian was growing into a handsome young man. Emma still preferred the dark good looks of Doug, but she could see how a girl could be attracted to Sebastian. Thinking of Doug, Emma now turned to say hello to him. All of a sudden, she felt nervous. It had been three months since she had spoken to Doug. Shyly, she looked up at him and saw that he was watching her with a big smile on his face.

Emma was just as beautiful as he remembered, maybe even more so. It was good to see her again. He wanted to tell her these things, but he lacked the courage, especially with Martha and Sebastian present. Instead, he said, "Hi, Emma. Welcome back."

"It's good to be back," Emma replied with a smile of her own. Doug had changed a bit too. He seemed to have grown as well and was even more handsome, if that was possible.

"The gang's all back together again," Sebastian said happily.

"Yep," Martha agreed. "What trouble can we get into this year?"

Speaking of trouble reminded Emma of the reason for their early reunion and prompted her to ask, "Do you guys know what Lord Dinswood wants us to help him with?"

It was Doug who answered her question. "No, he hasn't told us anything yet. He wants us all to meet with him in his suite after supper. He said he'd fill us in on everything then."

Emma looked at her watch. It was only three in the afternoon, so they had some time to kill before supper. That would give her a chance to get settled in. She and Martha would be sharing the same dorm room they'd had last year along with Clarice and Susie once school started again. At the end of school, they'd been allowed to pick their roommates for the upcoming year. The four girls got along well and had decided to share a suite again. Clarice could be a bit of a snob, but Emma had learned that she really didn't mean anything by it. Susie idolized Clarice, and although she could be a little dim-witted at times, she really was very sweet. At least with Clarice and Susie, she and Martha knew what they were getting.

Reverend and Mrs. Palmer had told her they would have some-one from the school's custodial staff take her luggage up to her room just before they had dropped her off. With any luck, her bags were already in her room. As if reading her mind, Doug suggested, "Emma, why don't you get unpacked, and then we can meet togeth-er in the lounge around four o'clock. I want to show you the progress that's been made on the new gym. Do you think an hour will give you enough time?"

"That should be plenty of time," Emma agreed. In truth, she could probably get unpacked in half that time. She didn't really have that much to put away, but the extra time would give her and Mar-tha a chance to talk and catch up. Emma wanted to get Martha's re-action to the new Sebastian, and Martha still hadn't told her about her Paris adventure. Agreeing to meet again in an hour, the four separated.

The girls' dorm, Brimley Hall, was in the west wing of the cas-tle. As she and Martha walked down the hall leading to the girls' dorm, Emma realized how much she had missed the drafty old cas-tle. It really felt good to be back at Dinswood Academy; it was as if she had come home again. The castle seemed strangely quiet with-out the hustle and bustle of the other students, and Emma realized that the four of them would have the castle practically to themselves for three whole weeks. When they passed the lounge, Emma no-ticed that the doors were open. Peeking inside, she could see that the portrait of Lord Dinswood had been moved from the library, where it had been mistakenly hung after the original renovations, to the lounge where it rightfully belonged. Looking at the picture of Lord Dinswood, Emma wondered yet again what the academy's founder wanted with the four of them. Whatever it was, she had a sneaking suspicion that they were in for another great adventure.

CHAPTER THREE

THE MISSION

An hour later, Emma stood in the back of the castle with Martha, Doug, and Sebastian looking at the foundation of the new gymnasium. Judging from the size of the foundation, it looked like the entire structure would be at least as long as one of the wings when it was completed. The castle and its two wings, which were the boys' and girls' dorms, formed three sides of a square. When completed, the gymnasium complex would form the fourth side. The greenhouse, which now looked tiny in comparison, would sit in the center of the square.

"When will the gym be finished?" Emma asked Doug.

"It probably won't be finished until next year."

As this was their eighth-grade year, Emma realized that they would all be freshmen then. The gym would be completed just in time for them to take part in high school sports. Emma knew that Doug had played basketball before coming to the academy, so he would probably want to be on the school's basketball team. Emma didn't know if Sebastian had taken part in any sports before coming to Dinswood or not, but she was fairly certain that if Doug played basketball, Sebastian would too. Martha had expressed an interest in volleyball, and Emma was hoping that the school would have a gymnastics team. Although she'd never had any training, she'd been told by Martha that she had a gift for it. Her incredible sense of balance had come in handy last spring when they were looking for the treasure.

Emma was brought back to the present by a sudden gust of wind. The sun, which had been shining brightly when she had arrived earlier, was now partially obscured by large white puffy cumulus clouds. The clouds were moving quickly across the sky as if fleeing from the wind. Emma looked to the southwest and saw a thick line of dark blue. A front was moving in, and it looked like they were in for some stormy weather.

Seeing the direction of her gaze, Sebastian said, "I didn't know it was supposed to rain today."

"It wasn't supposed to start until later this evening," Doug replied. "I heard the weather report on the radio earlier. They were calling for some fairly strong thunderstorms tonight."

They continued to wander around the construction area for a while longer with Doug explaining the general layout. He showed them where the gym and girls' and boys' locker rooms would be. Emma couldn't wait to have a real wood floor under her feet and a regular locker room to change in. Currently, the girls had to change in one of the restrooms on the first floor, and PE classes were held in the ballroom. Emma loved the ballroom but felt its marble floor was more conducive to dancing than to calisthenics.

Next, Doug showed them where the weight room and swimming pool would be. He explained that there would be additional locker rooms, complete with showers, adjacent to the pool area. He surprised them all with his next statement. "We're going to have another room with all kinds of exercise equipment too. It's going to be great. It'll have tread mills, elliptical machines, exercise bikes, rowing machines, and a big area for aerobics."

"What a great idea!" Emma said, clapping her hands excitedly. "Miss Krum was the one who suggested the room for aerobics. She said she could use it for her PE classes."

"Well, it will certainly beat jumping up and down on the ballroom's marble floor," Martha said, stating what Emma had been thinking a moment ago.

Just as Martha finished speaking, the sun, which had been peeking out intermittently, disappeared altogether. The puffy white clouds had given way to a solid gray mass. The tree branches began to sway violently, and the leaves made a loud rustling sound as the front approached.

"It looks like it could start raining any minute," Sebastian commented.

"Yeah, we'd better get inside," Doug agreed. Then looking at his watch, he added, "It's almost time for supper anyway."

"What time are we supposed to meet with Lord Dinswood?" Emma asked Doug as they made their way back to the castle.

"Around seven o'clock. He really didn't give a specific time," Doug answered and then cocked his head to listen. "We better make a run for it."

Emma stopped for a second and could hear the rain coming. Martha and Sebastian heard it as well. After exchanging a look of astonishment with each other, they began to run toward the castle with Sebastian in the lead. They made it to the castle entrance just as the first drops of rain began to fall.

"Wow, we made it just in time." Sebastian panted, slightly out of breath.

With one last wary look at the sky, Sebastian pulled open one of the two heavy oak doors that guarded the castle's main entrance. He held the door open for the others and then let it close behind him with a loud thud. They'd only taken a few steps before the heavens opened up, and it began to pour, the rain beating against the castle windows as if desperate to get inside. Emma shivered at the thought and retreated further into the castle. The others must have been spooked as well because without comment they followed.

LATER THAT EVENING, Dean Harwood escorted them up to Lord Dinswood's suite. The faculty residences were on the third floor, so they all crowded into the school's only elevator. On the way up, Doug looked over at Emma. She knew he was recalling the last time they'd ridden in the elevator. It had been installed to give handicapped students access to the classrooms on the second floor, and the faculty used it to get to their apartments. Generally, it was off limits to students. But last year, after a frightening encounter, Doug and Emma had ridden it up to Dean Harwood's suite. Doug and Emma were both standing in the back of the elevator, so no one noticed the look they exchanged. Emma was just beginning to feel a little claustrophobic in the small confines when the elevator came to a stop. Breathing a sigh of relief, she quickly followed the others as they exited the elevator. Dean Harwood led the way down the hall, and soon they were all standing in front of the rather ornate dark cherry wood door of Lord Dinswood's suite. Dean Harwood knocked loudly on the door and was promptly instructed to enter.

When they got inside, they could barely discern the shadowy figure of Lord Dinswood sitting in a brown leather recliner in the far-right corner of the room. Although it was still early evening, the storm clouds effectively obscured the sun, and the meager light coming in through the large latticed window did little to dispel the gloom.

As Dean Harwood closed the door behind him, Lord Dinswood switched on a lamp, and Emma was able to get a better look at the room and its furnishings. In addition to the recliner, there was a good-sized couch with an end table on each side and an armchair opposite the recliner. A hurricane lamp sat on each end table. The floor consisted of tiles, but the area beneath the furniture was covered with a large rectangular rug woven in varying shades of beige and brown. All of the living room furniture was arranged in a semicircle facing a large stone fireplace. On the opposite side of the room, Emma noticed a small square dining table made of oak and a kitchenette complete with a refrigerator, stove, and microwave. Next to the kitchenette was a short hallway, which Emma assumed led to Lord Dinswood's bedroom. The suite was small but cozy, and Emma liked its simplicity.

As Emma moved further into the room, she could hear the rain beating a steady tattoo against the panes of glass. A flash of lightning briefly lit the sky, confirming that the storms weren't over just yet. A chill ran down Emma's spine as she recalled their first trip to the bookstore in Windland last year. It had been storming then too, and it was the first time they had met Lord Dinswood; only he had introduced himself as Cal Thrabek then. He had seemed a bit creepy in the beginning, but later that same day he had come to their aid.

Emma was brought back to the present when Lord Dinswood asked them to take a seat. Dean Harwood sat in the armchair, and the youngsters all found spots on the couch. Emma took the end closest to Lord Dinswood, and Martha sat beside her. Sebastian ended up next to Martha, with Doug on the couch's other end. After everyone was settled, Emma looked up at Lord Dinswood and gasped in surprise. Thanks to the light coming from the lamp on the table next to him, she could see him more clearly now. Even though it had only been three months since she'd seen him last, he looked at least ten years older. Shocked, Emma looked at the others to gauge their reactions. They were all looking at Lord Dinswood expectantly and seemed unaware of her surprise. Emma realized that, unlike her, this was probably not the first time they had seen him since their return to school. At any rate, she made a mental note to inquire about Lord Dinswood's health at the first opportunity.

Emma forgot her worry a moment later when he began to speak. Although his body seemed frail, his voice sounded strong and vibrant, and the story he had to tell was both poignant and compelling.

"I'm sure you are all very curious to know why I've brought you here and what it is I want you to do. To answer those questions, I'll need to take you back in time and tell you a story. Of course, it goes without saying that what I'm about to tell you must remain between us." Lord Dinswood paused and looked at them in that penetrating way of his. Apparently satisfied with what he saw, he continued, "As you discovered last year, I am a descendant of the infamous pirate Bart the Blackheart. What you may not remember is that Blackheart's real name was Darius Bartholomew Dinswood. Darius was a very successful pirate, and after amassing a great fortune, he retired from pirate life and set about the business of finding a proper wife. He was fortunate enough to come across a beautiful young woman named Rebecca McFarland. Rebecca was from a wealthy family in Ireland and was a devout Catholic. Along with the red hair and hot temper the Irish are known for, Rebecca had an adventurous spirit that made her a perfect match for Darius. Knowing nothing about his days as a pirate, Rebecca agreed to marry Darius, and shortly after their marriage, they left Ireland. They spent some time traveling before finally settling here. Darius quickly set about seeing to the construction of a magnificent castle for his bride."

"And that very castle is now Dinswood Academy!" Sebastian blurted out.

"He doesn't need any help, Sebastian. Stop interrupting," Martha said. Sebastian had never been one to sit quietly for very long, and it seemed that this was one area in which he had not changed.

Sebastian gave Martha a sour look but had the good sense not to say anything. Lord Dinswood simply smiled. "You're right, Sebastian. The castle took several years to complete, and during that time, Darius and Rebecca lived in a little cottage not far from here. Miraculously, that little cottage still stands today."

"Were they very much in love?" Martha couldn't help asking.

Seeing a chance to get back at Martha for her reprimand a moment ago, Sebastian said quickly, "Honestly, Martha, let the man talk."

If looks could have killed, Sebastian would have expired that very second. Fortunately for Sebastian, this was not the case. He continued to breathe and proceeded to aggravate the situation further by grinning wickedly at Martha. What Martha would have done next will forever remain a mystery, for at that moment, Dean Harwood cleared his throat and gave both Martha and Sebastian a warning look. Thankfully, they both heeded the warning and said no more.

With the kind of patience that only comes with age and experience, Lord Dinswood smiled kindly at Martha and answered her question. "Yes, my dear. Darius and Rebecca were very much in love. They were two peas in a pod. That is to say they shared many things in common. Rebecca was a vivacious young woman, and Darius loved her more than life itself. She and Darius had many adventures during their years together."

This time, it was Emma who interrupted. "How many children did they have?"

"Ah, now that is where my story takes an unhappy turn," Lord Dinswood replied sadly. "You see, Darius and Rebecca tried for many years to have a child but were unsuccessful. Darius accepted it as penance for the sins he'd committed as a pirate, but it grieved his heart to see how saddened Rebecca was at her inability to conceive. They had both reconciled to the fact that they would never have any children when miraculously, on their ninth anniversary, Rebecca learned that she was pregnant. Of course, she and Darius were ecstatic. The pregnancy, however, was fraught with difficulty, and during her last months, she was confined to bed. Rebecca stoically endured any ills and discomforts that came her way and looked forward to the birth of her first child with a joy matched only by that of her husband. Finally, the time came for her to deliver. Rebecca's labor was long and difficult, and at times, Darius feared that he would lose both Rebecca and the baby. Imagine his joy and relief when Rebecca gave birth to a healthy baby boy. They named the baby Christian, and for a short time all was well, but the long labor had taken its toll on Rebecca. She died three days later from complications."

Lord Dinswood stopped speaking then, and a profound silence settled over the room. Unbidden tears welled up in Emma's eyes. Her heart ached for the Darius and Rebecca of long ago and the little boy who would never know his mother. She looked over at Martha and saw tears glistening on her cheeks. Sebastian had a look of disbelief on his face. He hadn't expected the story to end so tragically. Then Emma risked a look at Doug. It was evident from his expression that he had been equally affected by the story.

How long they sat there like that Emma couldn't say, but the silence was finally broken when Doug asked quietly, "Sir, what is it you want us to do?"

"Well, as I told you earlier, Rebecca was a devout Catholic. Her faith was very important to her. Over the years, she tried to convert Darius, but he was stubbornly set against it. I believe it was because he could never forgive himself for the things he'd done as a pirate. He probably reasoned, as many still do today, that if he couldn't forgive himself, how could God forgive him? Rebecca, not knowing of his pirate days, was never able to understand why he refused to accept God's wonderful gift of grace. Darius, however, understood Rebecca's love for the Lord and supported it. During their ten years of marriage, he commissioned seven pieces from the famous sculptor, Luciano Marnatti. He asked Marnatti to sculpt important women from the Bible—women he knew his wife admired. The first piece was a sculpture of Ruth. Next, Darius commissioned a sculpture of Sarah, then Esther, then Martha, and then Martha's sister Mary. When he and Rebecca learned of Rebecca's pregnancy, Darius asked Marnatti to sculpt Hannah, the mother of Samuel. Hannah, like Rebecca, had been barren. But after praying at the temple, God had granted her request and she had conceived.

"Darius intended to give the seventh and final sculpture to Rebecca after the birth of their child. Reportedly, it was Marnatti's finest work. The sculpture was completed in plenty of time, but Rebecca died before Darius could give it to her."

"Who was the subject of the last sculpture?" Emma asked.

"I'm afraid only Darius and Luciano Marnatti know the answer to that question, and since they are no longer with us, the subject of the last sculpture remains a mystery."

"I don't understand," Emma said.

When Lord Dinswood didn't respond to Emma's comment, Doug asked again, "Sir, what is it you want us to do?"

Lord Dinswood didn't answer Doug immediately but instead looked at the expectant faces of the youngsters sitting before him. The suspense in the room was palpable. Finally, Lord Dinswood was going to reveal why he had called them back to school early. Martha shot a look at Sebastian, clearly warning him not to interrupt. Sebastian, however, had no intention of saying anything. Like the others, he was anxious to hear the reason for their early return.

"After Rebecca died, the sculptures disappeared. It was believed that in his profound grief, Darius went into a rage and destroyed them all. The generations of Dinswoods that followed held to the conviction that the Mortals, as Marnatti called them, were gone forever. I must admit that I believed it myself. Then about a month ago, while the construction crews were digging the foundation for the new gymnasium, a metal box was discovered." Lord Dinswood paused for effect and then continued, "And in that box was the sculpture of Ruth."

An audible gasp arose from the four youngsters seated on the couch. Lord Dinswood sat back to let the information sink in for a moment, but Sebastian couldn't keep quiet any longer. "Do you think the others are still out there somewhere?"

"That is precisely what I believe," Lord Dinswood confirmed.

"And you want us to find them," Doug added.

Lord Dinswood simply nodded.

CHAPTER FOUR
THE STORY OF RUTH

After Lord Dinswood's revelation, everyone began talking at once. It seemed they all had questions. Finally, Lord Dinswood held up his hands to restore some order. When silence reigned in the room once again, he said, "I know you must have a lot of questions, and I intend to answer them all, but one at a time please." Then, seeing that Sebastian was about ready to burst, Lord Dinswood took pity on him and said, "Sebastian, you may go first."

"Why us, sir?"

"That is an excellent question. Why would I entrust a task so important to four young people? The answer is quite simple. First and foremost, I know I can trust you. Last year, you found a treasure unlike anything you could have imagined, and yet you made no attempt to keep any of it for yourselves. Second, you have all proven that you have a great deal of intelligence. In order to find the treasure, you had to solve many riddles. Last but not least, you have shown that you have courage and can maintain your composure even in extreme circumstances. Trust me, I did not choose you four lightly. I gave it a great deal of thought. I have also discussed it at length with Dean Harwood, and he feels that you are very well suited to the task."

"Will it be as dangerous as the treasure hunt was?" Sebastian asked with a nervous swallow.

"I don't foresee any danger. After all, you are simply trying to locate the other six sculptures. Life, however, has a way of presenting us with situations and obstacles we didn't expect, so I can't really say for certain."

At this point, Dean Harwood entered the conversation. "I've agreed to Lord Dinswood's plan only if I'm allowed to accompany you on your searches. I can't, in good conscience, let you proceed without some kind of adult supervision. I told each of your parents that at least one adult would be with you any time you left school grounds. I did not, however, explain the exact nature of the job you would be doing for Lord Dinswood."

"But how are we going to know where to look for the other sculptures?" Sebastian asked quickly before any of the others could pose their questions. Martha frowned at him, but Sebastian appeared not to notice. His attention was fixed firmly on Lord Dinswood.

"Well, now, that's where your intelligence and problem-solving abilities come into play. You see, I believe that Darius may have hidden the other six sculptures in places that were special to him and Rebecca."

"How are we supposed to know what places were special to them?" Sebastian asked again, this time with an apologetic look at the others. Emma, for one, didn't care that Sebastian was asking all of the questions. They were exactly the same questions she would have asked. Martha, however, threw up her hands in exasperation. But because she was eager to hear the answer to Sebastian's question, she said nothing.

"Another excellent question, Sebastian," Lord Dinswood replied with a smile. "You see, Rebecca kept a journal."

"And you have that journal," Martha guessed, raising an eyebrow at Sebastian as she spoke.

"Actually, there's more than one, and they're all in my personal collection in the library," Lord Dinswood confirmed. "You will have full access to the collection. Perhaps you can find clues as to the location of the other sculptures from some of Rebecca's writings."

"Sir, what if the other sculptures no longer exist?" Doug couldn't help asking.

"That would be sad indeed. Of course, the sculptures are priceless, but that isn't why I'm so eager to find them. They are a part of my family's history and thus a part of me. They have a sentimental value that far outweighs their monetary worth, at least as far as I'm concerned. It would give me great pleasure to know that they are all safe and sound before I die."

At this last comment, Emma couldn't help wondering once again if Lord Dinswood was ill, but she didn't want to question him directly. Instead, she asked, "Lord Dinswood, would it be possible for us to see the sculpture that was discovered?"

"I was waiting for someone to ask," Lord Dinswood replied, smiling broadly.

At a nod from Lord Dinswood, Dean Harwood left the room and returned a moment later with a plain gray metal box approximately two feet tall and a foot wide. After setting the box down on the floor in front of Lord Dinswood's chair, he removed the lid. A marble sculpture of a woman was lying in a bed of straw. Gently, Dean Harwood lifted it from the box and raised it high so that everyone could see. The four youngsters gazed at it with expressions of awe. Emma had never seen anything so beautiful. The pure white marble was perfectly smooth, and the lines were clean and bold. Marnatti had given Ruth an angelic face that managed to convey both beauty and strength. The figure was dressed in a flowing robe with a belt that hung loosely around the narrow waist. Her head was covered with a scarf, and her sandaled feet were small and perfectly formed. Emma looked over at Martha to see her reaction. Martha was the artist of the group and would probably appreciate the skill required to produce such a work more than the others.

Martha was staring at the sculpture with a look of rapture on her face. "It's beautiful!" she said on a sigh. "I can't wait to see the others."

"That's precisely what I was thinking," Lord Dinswood agreed. Then with a sigh of his own, he said, "And now if there are no more questions, it's time for this old man to get some rest."

Saying their goodbyes, the youngsters got up and headed to the door while Dean Harwood packed the sculpture of Ruth away. Emma was surprised to see that it was still storming outside. She'd been so engrossed in Lord Dinswood's story that she hadn't even been aware of the thunder and lightning.

Doug was the last one to leave the suite. When he got to the door, he hesitated for a moment. Looking back, he saw the frail figure of Lord Dinswood slumped wearily in his chair, and compassion prompted him to say, "Don't worry, sir. We'll get started first thing in the morning. If those sculptures are out there, we'll find them."

"That's what I'm counting on," Lord Dinswood replied softly as the door closed behind Doug.

The next morning, Emma and Martha were eating breakfast in the dining room. Some of the teachers, including Emma's favorite teacher, Miss Jennings, were also in the dining room at the moment. Emma had been surprised to learn that most of the staff lived at the academy year-round. When she thought about it, however, it made sense. It would be silly to keep a separate residence for only three months out of the year, and the teachers' residences were spacious and modern. The kitchen and custodial staff also remained in house to see to the cooking and cleaning. *It's better than staying in a first-class hotel*, Emma thought.

Emma's thoughts were interrupted by the arrival of Doug and Sebastian. As the two boys took their seats on the bench across from the girls, Emma expressed her concern about Lord Dinswood's health. "Doug, is Lord Dinswood sick? He didn't look well last night."

"I know," Doug said, nodding. "He's been getting weaker all summer long. I asked Dad about it, and he says he's tried to get Lord Dinswood to see a doctor, but he refuses. Lord Dinswood claims it's just old age catching up with him."

"What do you think?" Emma asked, not at all convinced that it was simply a matter of old age.

"I don't know," Doug replied with a sigh. "It seems to me that Lord Dinswood has given up. I mean, now that the treasure has been found and the school is going to be okay, he feels like his work here is done."

"Did he actually say that?" Martha asked in surprise.

"Not in so many words, but I sort of got that impression."

"Maybe if we find the other sculptures, he'll perk up," Sebastian suggested.

"That's just what I was thinking," Doug agreed. "Last night when we left his suite, he said he was counting on us finding the other six pieces."

"Whew," Sebastian said, letting out a big breath. "Talk about pressure. We'd better get to the library as soon as we're done with breakfast and start looking for some clues."

The others agreed and quickly finished eating. When they entered the library, they found that they had it all to themselves. A new librarian had been hired, but as school didn't start for another three weeks, he or she had not yet arrived. Emma's thoughts drifted back to the school's last librarian, Mr. Hodges. He had always given her the creeps. The others had thought she was just being paranoid, but later they'd learned that she'd been right about him. There was no one behind the checkout counter at the moment, and Emma couldn't help giving a little sigh of relief.

"Lord Dinswood's personal collection is on the second floor," Doug informed them.

Behind the counter, a small spiral staircase led up to the library's second story. Lord Dinswood's private collection included some very valuable books, so the second floor was generally off limits to the student body. Only those with special permission were allowed upstairs; and a locked gate, which reminded Emma of prison bars, prevented access to the area in which Lord Dinswood's collection was housed. As Doug's dad had already given him the key, the locked gate would not be a problem for them.

Quickly, they climbed the stairs and went directly over to the gate. A sign next to it read "No Students Allowed." Noticing the sign, Sebastian said, "This is really cool. For once, we aren't going to get in trouble for breaking a school rule." He was thinking back to last spring when they'd broken several school rules during their search for the treasure.

"We didn't really get in trouble last time," Martha reminded him.

"Yeah, thanks to good old Lord Dinswood," Sebastian agreed. Then in an effort to prove his point, he grinned at Martha and added, "But we thought we were going to get in trouble."

Deciding it wasn't worth arguing over, Martha sighed and shook her head, which made Sebastian grin even more. He knew exactly how to push Martha's buttons and seemed to enjoy doing it. Emma had long suspected that Sebastian liked Martha, but at times, he sure had a funny way of showing it. *I'll never understand boys*, Emma thought.

While Martha and Sebastian were debating the issue of breaking school rules, Doug inserted the key in the lock and turned it. It opened easily with a faint click. Doug pushed on the gate, and it swung soundlessly inward. He held the gate as everyone filed past him and, as there was no one else in the library, left it open.

Emma looked around at the multitude of books that comprised Lord Dinswood's private collection and felt a little overwhelmed. There were thousands of books. How were they ever going to find Rebecca's journals? It was going to be like looking for a needle in a haystack. Martha must have been thinking the same thing.

"Unless somebody knows where we're supposed to look, we could be here a very long time."

"Yeah, this could take weeks," Sebastian groaned.

"Well, then, I guess it's a good thing that Lord Dinswood told dad where we could find Rebecca's journals," Doug said, smiling at Sebastian and Martha. "Most of the books have been organized and catalogued according to the Dewey Decimal System, but the journals are in a section marked Family History. It should be pretty easy to find. We'll split up and each take an aisle. Once we find the right section, the journals all have a red binding."

Before the others could start searching, Doug added, "Remember, Lord Dinswood asked us to be really careful with all of the books in here, especially the journals. They're very old, and he doesn't want them damaged. Also, some of the books are first editions and are very valuable."

"I won't touch a thing," Sebastian promised as if Doug's comment had been directed solely at him.

Martha raised her eyebrows in disbelief but wisely said nothing. They all knew from experience what a klutz Sebastian could be at times. He meant well, but sometimes his hands and feet just wouldn't follow the directions they were receiving from his brain. Considering that he'd just grown two inches over the summer, it was very likely that he would be clumsier than ever—at least until his body adjusted to its new dimensions.

"I know you won't, Sebastian," Doug said kindly. It always warmed Emma's heart to see how patient Doug was with Sebastian. No matter how irritating Sebastian could be, Doug never lost his temper with him. Doug had a maturity beyond his thirteen years, and it was particularly evident in his relationship with Sebastian. Sebastian was lucky to have a friend like Doug. Of course, when Emma thought about it, Doug was also fortunate to have a friend like Sebastian. Sebastian was extremely loyal and not at all bothered by the fact that Doug didn't come from a rich family. There were some, namely Bobby Wilcox, who hated Doug for that very reason. Emma had always suspected that Bobby was also jealous of Doug because he was good looking and athletic. Last year at the October Fest, Doug's relay team had beaten Bobby's. Bobby had taken the defeat pretty hard and had vowed to get even. Things had just gotten worse from there. Emma hoped Doug would steer clear of Bobby once school started.

Emma was startled from her thoughts by a nudge from Martha. "Come on. I don't want to spend all day in this library. It's much too nice outside." A glance out one of the windows on the second floor confirmed that Martha was right; it was a beautiful day. The sun was shining, and there wasn't a cloud in the sky. The storms of the previous evening had gone and left behind a vibrantly green and freshly washed landscape.

Nodding her agreement, Emma headed down one of the many aisles. The narrow aisle was bordered on each side by bookcases that seemed to reach all the way to the ceiling. As she proceeded along the towering shelves, the aisle seemed to grow longer and narrower, and she began to feel as if the bookcases were closing in on her. Emma realized that she was experiencing a bout of claustrophobia. Moving more quickly now, she scanned both sides of shelves for the section marked Family History, her breath coming in short gasps. When she didn't find it, she turned and hastily retraced her steps, eager to get out of the small confines. She was just coming out of her row when she heard Sebastian shout, "I found it! I found it!"

Forgetting her claustrophobia for the moment, Emma raced off in the direction of Sebastian's voice. She found him three aisles to the right of the one she had just searched. Martha and Doug were already standing beside Sebastian.

"Where are they?" Emma asked when she reached the others.

"Right here!" Sebastian answered, proudly pointing to a shelf containing a row of books, all with red bindings. There were ten altogether; each was about the size of an eleven by fourteen picture and a couple of inches thick. They all just stood there for a moment—afraid to touch the journals for fear of damaging them.

"Oh, for heaven's sake!" Martha finally blurted out in exasperation. "We're going to have to touch them if we want to find any clues."

"She's right," Sebastian said with a nod, but still he waited. He wanted to see how the others were going to handle the precious journals before deciding if he should attempt it. Lately, he'd been clumsier than usual. His mom had told him that it was because of his recent growth spurt and that it would soon pass. He sure hoped so. What good was it to be tall if you couldn't hang on to a basketball?

"I think we should each take one," Martha suggested, causing Sebastian to frown in consternation. "The journals are probably arranged in chronological order, so we should probably start with the first four." Martha looked around, and seeing that the others were still hesitant, she reached up and carefully pulled the first journal from the shelf.

When the book didn't disintegrate in her hands as they had feared, the others followed suit. As soon as everyone had a journal, they made their way to one of the study tables on the second floor and eagerly began looking through them. As Martha had guessed, the books were arranged by date. Martha's journal covered the first year of Rebecca's marriage to Darius. In it, Rebecca described all of the traveling she and Darius did after leaving Ireland. Although, it was undoubtedly fascinating reading, it couldn't contain the information they were looking for. The other sculptures were most likely hidden somewhere in the vicinity of the castle.

The journal Emma had looked a little more promising. In the first entry, Rebecca spoke of coming to a new land. Carefully, Emma turned the yellowed pages, noting the flowing lines of Rebecca's neat and precise handwriting. Something on one of the pages caught Emma's eye. Rebecca had drawn a picture of a daisy in the top right-hand corner. In the left-hand corner was the date April 21, 1712. Her curiosity piqued, Emma began to read the entry.

Darius and I had the most wonderful day. The grass is a rich green from the recent rains, and the dogwood and redbud trees are in bloom. Everything is coming alive, and we felt like we just had to be a part of it, so we decided to take a picnic lunch and ride up into the mountains. It was a clear day with the sun shining brightly overhead, and the sky as blue as I've ever seen it. A short distance up the mountain, we found a sparkling stream. The snow high up on the mountains has started to melt and fill the streambeds. The water was crystal clear and so cold it nearly took my breath away when I stooped to take a drink. We stopped for a while to water the horses and then continued up the mountain. A while later, we came to a meadow carpeted with a multitude of yellow daisies. I have never seen anything so beautiful, and I said as much to Darius. As we ate our lunch, Darius and I decided that the meadow was the perfect location for our new home.

After she had finished reading, Emma realized that Dinswood Castle stood in the very meadow Rebecca had been describing. Rebecca's entry explained why the meadow was special to Darius and Rebecca and why Darius would have buried one of the sculptures in it. Quickly, she shared what she had discovered with the others.

Doug had found something of interest as well. As soon as Emma finished speaking, he began reading from a page in his journal.

Darius gave me the most wonderful gift today for our third anniversary—a beautiful marble sculpture of Ruth of the Bible. It was sculpted by the famous artist Luciano Marnatti. Darius said he chose Ruth because I am like her in many ways. Out of loyalty and love for her mother-in-law, Ruth left her family and everything she knew. She followed Naomi to her homeland and took care of her. Darius says that I demonstrated my love for him in much the same way. If he only knew how much I love him, he would realize that leaving my family and homeland was no sacrifice at all. I am touched, amazed, and perplexed all at the same time by the nature of his gift. Every time I try to share my faith with him, he refuses to listen, but he obviously has some knowledge of the Bible. How else could he know the story of Ruth? I think it would take a thousand lifetimes to fully understand my husband, but I'll settle for one.

All was silent for a moment after Doug finished reading. It was sad to think that Rebecca hadn't gotten the lifetime with Darius she had desired. At least they had uncovered the story behind the sculpture of Ruth.

CHAPTER FIVE
TAKING A BREAK

They continued to look through the journals until Sebastian sighed loudly and looked pointedly at the clock. "Hey, it's almost time for lunch," he stated as if up until that moment he had been totally unaware of the time. The truth was that he had been getting more and more fidgety as the morning had passed, and for the last hour, he had been looking at the clock every few minutes. He wasn't really all that hungry, but he was tired of sitting in the library. He wanted to spend at least part of the day outside enjoying the sunshine. Lunch was just an excuse to get them all out of the library for a while.

"I'm tired of sitting in here, too, Sebastian," Martha said, not at all fooled by Sebastian's ruse. "I think we could all use a break."

Doug and Emma nodded their agreement. Then Doug said, "Why don't we go outside after lunch and play some badminton. Dad and I set up a net on the front lawn a couple of weeks ago. We can spend some more time going through the journals tonight."

"Sounds great!" Sebastian agreed enthusiastically.

"Sounds good to me too," Emma chimed in as she closed the journal she'd been reading.

With everything decided, they quickly put the journals away and exited the library. As there were no other students currently in residence, Doug left the gate to Lord Dinswood's personal collection and the door to the library unlocked. After a brief discussion in the hall, they split up to go to their dorm rooms and wash up for lunch, agreeing to meet in the dining hall in a few minutes.

Later when Emma and Martha entered the dining hall, they saw that Doug and Sebastian had made it there before them. As they were taking their seats on the bench opposite the boys, Sebastian drew their attention to the teachers' table and said, "The new librarian's here."

Emma and Martha turned as one to get a look. Emma hoped he didn't resemble Dracula like Mr. Hodges had. Her eyes traveled down the teachers' table until she came to a face she didn't recognize. Emma let out a little gasp in surprise. The only thing the old and new librarian had in common was that they were both men. The new librarian was a handsome younger man with light brown hair and bright blue eyes. Because he was sitting down, it was hard to tell how tall he was, but in the light blue polo shirt he was wearing, he looked lean and fit. Emma wouldn't have picked him as a librarian in a million years; he just didn't look the part. Of course, as school hadn't started yet, he was dressed more casually and thus didn't look much like a teacher either. When school started in a few weeks, Emma was sure that the new librarian would be attired in the dress shirt and tie worn by the rest of Dinswood's male faculty. Emma heard Martha's indrawn breath a second later. Apparently, she was just as surprised as Emma at the new librarian's appearance.

"What's his name?" Martha asked, her admiration obvious.

"Good grief, Martha. He's an old man," Sebastian said in disgust.

"I didn't say I wanted to date him. I simply asked his name."

"His name's Mr. Criderman," Doug answered before Sebastian could reply.

It didn't take a genius to see that Sebastian was experiencing a bit of jealousy. Emma decided to see if she could elicit a similar response from Doug. "How old is he?" she all but gushed. She was rewarded by a frown from Doug before he responded.

"I don't really know, but he must be in his thirties." This was stated in a tone that suggested that someone in their thirties was ancient.

Emma gave Martha a quick glance and, when she was sure the boys weren't looking, a conspiratorial wink. Catching on to what Emma was doing, Martha grinned and said, "Oh, he's really young then."

"Is he married?" Emma asked eagerly, trying her best not to laugh.

Both boys frowned this time. Doug was just trying to formulate a suitable response when Emma couldn't stand it any longer. She burst out laughing and was quickly joined by Martha. Realizing that the girls had just been having fun with them, the boys' frowns deepened.

"Very funny!" Sebastian said sourly.

"Honestly, Sebastian, did you really think I'd be interested in a teacher? He's probably more than twice my age," Martha said once she was able to talk again.

Sebastian continued to look angry but wisely said nothing. Doug, on the other hand, was trying to figure out a way to get even. It wasn't long until an idea came to him. Trying to hide his own smile now, he looked directly at Emma and said in a serious tone, "Emma, I can introduce you right now if you'd like to meet him. I'm sure he won't mind us interrupting his lunch when I tell him how eager you are to meet him. Then you can ask him if he's married yourself." Before Emma could reply, Doug stood up like he was going to go over to Mr. Criderman.

Emma stopped laughing abruptly and said more loudly than she'd intended, "Don't you dare! I was just kidding."

"Okay, if you're sure you don't want to meet him," Doug said, slowly taking his seat.

Emma didn't relax until Doug was completely seated. Things had not gone as she had planned, but she had learned a valuable lesson. Douglas Harwood was not someone to toy with.

The rest of lunch was accomplished with little conversation. They quickly downed their meal of pizza and salad and headed outdoors for some fresh air. When they stepped outside the castle, Emma felt as if she had stepped into a sauna. The temperature had risen to the upper eighties, and the humidity was equally high. The air seemed suffocating and close, especially after the conditioned air of the castle.

"Wow, it's hot out here!" Sebastian exclaimed.

"It sure is," Doug agreed. "Do you guys still want to play badminton?"

Emma had to admit that she no longer felt like playing badminton or any other game that required physical exertion. The afternoon heat seemed to have sapped all of her strength. She looked over at Martha who was already shaking her head in the negative. "I don't. It's too hot out here."

"What are we gonna do then?" Sebastian whined. "I don't want to sit in that dusty old library all afternoon."

"Stop whining, Sebastian," Martha said with a groan. "None of the rest of us wants to sit in the library either."

"Why don't we go swimming?" Doug asked, surprising them all.

"Where are we going to go swimming?" Sebastian asked. "In case you hadn't noticed, the pool's not done yet."

Patiently, Doug explained. "We can go swimming in the stream. I know where there are some pretty good swimming holes."

Doug was referring to the stream that ran along the west side of the castle. In the spring, it filled to overflowing as the snows at the higher elevations melted, but at this time of year, the water flow would be at its lowest. There were still, however, areas where the stream would be plenty deep. Last year, when they'd been looking for the treasure, Sebastian had nearly fallen in such a spot.

"Sounds great, but we're not allowed off school grounds unless a teacher goes with us," Martha reminded Doug.

"I'm sure Dad will okay it if I ask him," Doug replied. Before anyone could say anything else, he turned and reentered the castle.

A swim certainly sounded good to Emma. She had already begun to perspire just standing there on the castle steps. Her only concern was that she hadn't thought to bring a bathing suit. There had never been a need for one until today. "Do you have a bathing suit?" she asked Martha.

Martha shook her head in the negative. "No. I'm just going to wear my shorts and a sleeveless shirt."

"I guess that will have to do," Emma replied.

Before long, Doug reappeared. "Dad said it was okay. Why don't you guys go change, and we'll meet back here in a few minutes."

His good humor restored at the thought of a swim, Sebastian grinned happily and held the door for everyone as they entered the castle. "Can you swim?" he asked Martha as she passed him.

"Of course I can swim," Martha replied quickly.

"How about you, Emma?" Doug thought to ask.

"Yeah," Emma said nodding. "I took some free lessons from the YWCA a couple of summers ago."

"Good." Doug knew that Sebastian could swim from past experience. Doug was a good swimmer as well. His dad had insisted that he learn how to swim when he was just a boy, and last summer on vacation in the Bahamas, he and his dad had even done some scuba diving. Doug loved the water and just wished there were more opportunities for swimming and diving around the academy. Thanks to the treasure Lord Dinswood had graciously donated, they would be doing a lot of swimming next year when the pool was completed.

The afternoon went much too quickly as far as Emma was concerned. True to his word, Doug led them to several spots along the stream that were deep enough for swimming. They would walk along the gravel beds that flanked both sides of the stream for a while and then swim when they got hot. The water was refreshingly cool and crystal clear. Other than the oppressive heat, it was a beautiful day. The sun sparkled brightly off the surface of the water as it bumped and bubbled over the stream's gravel bottom on its way to the river. Tall trees lined both sides of the stream bank and, in some places, formed a canopy over the water. Every now and then, the foursome would stop to rest in one of these shady areas and drink some of the bottled water they'd brought along.

All too soon, it was time to return to the castle and get cleaned up for supper. They didn't have time to stop and swim on the way back, so by the time they reached the castle, they were miserably hot once again.

"I never thought I'd say this, but I'm looking forward to a nice cold shower," Sebastian said as they climbed the steps to the castle's main entrance.

The others simply nodded their agreement. They were too hot and tired to summon up the energy required for a reply.

Later in the dining hall, there was little conversation as the four of them hungrily downed their supper of meatloaf, green beans, and mashed potatoes. When they had each eaten their fill, they disposed of their trays. Emma assumed that they would now return to the library to continue looking through Rebecca's journals, but Sebastian had other ideas.

"Do we really have to go back to the library now?" he asked of the group in general. "I hate to waste daylight."

"What'd you have in mind?" Doug asked.

"I was thinking we could play a little badminton. The net's in the shade now, and it's cooled down a little bit."

Doug thought this over for a moment and then turned to the girls. "Well, what do you think? We can play for a while and then go to the library after it gets dark."

Emma and Martha nodded their agreement to the plan, so after Doug had retrieved rackets and a couple of birdies from the storage closet, they headed outside. Although, as Sebastian had predicted it was cooler outside than it had been that afternoon, it was still plenty warm. Several games later, hot and thirsty, they returned to the castle to get some water and cool off. They sat in the lounge and sipped their water for a while. When they felt sufficiently cooled and hydrated, they headed to the library. Emma began to feel a little guilty. Lord Dinswood had brought them all back to the academy early to help find the other sculptures, and they had spent the majority of the day entertaining themselves outside. The others must have been feeling the same way because once they'd retrieved the journals they'd been looking through that morning, there was little conversation as they sat down at one of the study tables and began to read with renewed focus and determination.

They read in silence for several minutes. The only sound was the faint ticking of the grandfather clock on the floor below. The second floor of the library was similar to a loft in an apartment. When on the second floor, one could look over the railing and see the majority of the ground floor of the library including the fireplace and reading area on its east side. The only portion of the library that couldn't be seen from above was that portion directly beneath the loft.

The second floor had its own lighting, which consisted of three rows of relatively modern rectangular fluorescent lights. The lighting for the ground floor was more ornate and consisted of six chandeliers that hung on long chains from the high ceiling of the main library. Anyone on the second floor could look out over the rest of the library and see the tops of the crystal chandeliers.

When they had first entered the library, there had still been a little light coming in through the large windows on the south wall, so they hadn't turned on any of the lights downstairs. Once upstairs, they had only turned on the two small lamps on their table so they could read. In the time they'd been sitting there, darkness had descended outside. Emma paused a moment in her reading and looked around. Except for the small circle of light cast by the table lamps, the rest of the library was in total darkness. She suddenly had the strange inexplicable feeling that they were being watched. Emma felt the hair rising on the back of her neck and shivered. She looked across the table at Doug. He was completely absorbed in the journal he was reading. Her gaze wandered to Martha and then to Sebastian. None of the others seemed to have noticed anything unusual. Deciding that she was just being paranoid and thankful that she wasn't alone, she returned to her reading.

Soon she was once again engrossed in the story of Rebecca and Darius. It was clear from Rebecca's writings that she and Darius were very much in love and very happy together. Every now and then, Rebecca would express her desire to have a child. She expressed regret that she had not yet conceived, but she was hopeful that God would bless them with a child someday soon. It made Emma sad to think that it would be seven more years before Rebecca's prayer for a child would be answered and sadder still that Rebecca wouldn't live to raise the child she'd so desperately wanted. It just wasn't fair.

Emma's thoughts shifted to the loss of her own mother; that hadn't been fair either. Emma felt the familiar sting of tears at the thought of what might have been if her mother had lived. With an effort, she turned her attention back to the journal but not before Doug had noticed tears glistening in her eyes.

He wanted to ask her if she was okay, but he didn't want to embarrass her in front of the others. Besides, he was almost certain he knew the cause of her tears. Rebecca's tragic story had Emma thinking about her own loss. He'd been thinking about his mother too. He couldn't understand how she could leave him like she did, and because he couldn't understand, he couldn't forgive. In an attempt to dispel his own gloomy thoughts, he asked of the group in general, "Has anybody found anything? Remember we're looking for places that would have been special to Rebecca and Darius."

"That's the problem," Sebastian said with a sigh. "How are we supposed to know what was or wasn't special to them?"

"Well, you can sort of tell from what Rebecca says," Martha began, and then she realized to whom she was talking. With a sigh of her own and a brief shake of her head, she decided to try another tack. "Maybe you should just mark the pages where Rebecca mentions going somewhere with Darius. Then we can all look at them and decide if it's a possible location for one of the sculptures."

"Okay," Sebastian agreed, "but what should I mark the pages with?"

"Honestly, Sebastian. Do I have to think of everything? Just tear some pieces of paper to use as bookmarks."

"I don't have any paper."

Martha opened her mouth to deliver what most certainly would have been a stinging reply when Doug broke in. "I think there's some paper behind the counter downstairs. I'll go get it."

Doug had to turn on one row of the second floor's overhead lights so he could see to go down the stairs. Emma was glad for the additional light and hoped Doug would leave the lights on when he returned.

He quickly disappeared from view as he descended the stairs. They could hear him rummaging around behind the checkout counter for a few moments and then the sound of his footsteps on the stairs once again. He reappeared with a grin on his face and a stack of paper in his hand, which he held up in triumph. As Emma had hoped, he left the single bank of overhead lights on and approached the table.

"This ought to do it," he said as he sat down. Then a thought occurred to him. "You know it might not be a bad idea if we all took some paper and marked pages like Sebastian. Then once we've gone through all the journals, we can compile a list of the most likely places."

"And if we don't find the sculptures in those places, we'll start looking in the unlikely places," Emma added.

"That sounds like a good idea," Martha agreed. "Let's try to get completely through each of the journals we've got tonight. Then maybe we can finish the other six tomorrow."

"If we do that, we'll be in here all day tomorrow and tomorrow night too," Sebastian complained.

"Maybe we will," Doug replied. "But remember we're doing this for Lord Dinswood."

"Yeah, Sebastian," Martha said. "After all he's done for us and the school, it's the least we can do."

"I know, I know," Sebastian agreed reluctantly.

Feeling a little sorry for Sebastian, Emma said, "If we're lucky, we'll only spend one more day in the library. Then we can spend the rest of the time outside looking for sculptures."

As Emma had hoped, Sebastian's expression brightened at the thought. "That's right," he said with a grin, his good humor restored.

They stayed in the library until everyone had had a chance to finish going through their journals. Emma hadn't found anything more in hers, but she noticed that Sebastian and Doug had each marked at least one page in their respective journals. She was dying of curiosity, but it was getting late. A glance at her watch confirmed that it was ten o'clock. They'd been in the library two hours. Deciding it would be better to wait until they'd gone through all of Rebecca's writings to share what they'd discovered with each other, she closed her journal and yawned.

Seeing that the others were finally finished, Sebastian jumped up with an energy that Emma envied. After an afternoon of swimming and an evening spent playing badminton, Emma was exhausted. Sebastian acted as if he'd just awakened from a good night's sleep.

Doug stood up and stretched. He'd been sitting for far too long and was more than ready to call it a day. The others quickly followed suit. Once the journals were safely put away, they turned off the table lamps and Sebastian, Martha, and Emma went downstairs. Doug stayed upstairs just long enough to turn off the overhead lights. As no one had thought to turn on any of the lights downstairs, Doug's action plunged the library into almost total darkness. Martha let out a little shriek of surprise.

"Hey, guys, somebody's gonna have to turn a light on down there so I can find the stairs," Doug called from above them.

Remembering that there was a light switch just to the right of the library door, Martha began feeling her way like a blind person. Heading in what she thought was the correct direction, Martha promptly bumped into Sebastian who was attempting to do the same thing. A few sharp words were exchanged, followed by a good deal of jostling.

For her part, Emma was frozen to the spot. She was experiencing that same eerie feeling she'd had a while ago—the feeling that someone was watching them. In rising panic, Emma looked around as her eyes began to adjust to the dark, all the while telling herself that she was just being foolish. Suddenly, she detected movement off to her right. Turning quickly, she saw a dark shape coming toward her from the area underneath the second story loft. The shadowy figure, which was outlined by the meager light coming in through the west windows, seemed to be gliding along soundlessly on a cushion of air. Convinced that she was seeing a ghost, Emma was just opening her mouth to scream when the lights came on. Emma blinked in surprise, and when she opened her eyes again, she saw that her ghost was actually Dean Harwood.

Both Martha and Sebastian jumped in surprise when they turned away from the light switch to see Dean Harwood standing there.

"I didn't mean to scare you," Dean Harwood said. When no one spoke, Dean Harwood hastened to explain why he hadn't made his presence known sooner. "I came to see how you were getting along. I was just starting up the stairs when I felt a draft. It was then that I noticed that one of the windows was open. I went over to shut it and was just on my way back when the lights went out. I'm afraid I scared the daylights out of Emma."

Emma wondered how he knew that, but if she could have looked in a mirror at that moment, she would have understood. She was as white as any ghost she could have imagined. Dean Harwood was smiling at her kindly. Embarrassed now at being so foolish as to believe in ghosts, Emma looked away.

Doug, who'd been trying to find the upstairs light switch again, came to the top of the stairs and looked down to see what all the commotion was about. Seeing his father, he said, "Hi, Dad."

"Hello, son. I just came to see how you all were getting along on your research," Dean Harwood repeated.

"We're making a list of all of the places where Darius might have hidden the sculptures. We've got a few more of the journals to go through, but I think we'll be finished by tomorrow. Then we can start looking."

"Good. Just let me know when you need to go somewhere, and I'll make the necessary arrangements. Remember now, I promised your parents that I'd accompany you on all of your searches, so don't get impatient and go off on your own." Dean Harwood looked at them all in turn, obviously waiting for their promises of compliance.

"We won't, Dad," Doug said for the group.

Dean Harwood nodded and turned to leave, but when he got to the door, he stopped. Turning back, he asked, "Did any of you open that window?"

They all shook their heads in the negative. With a frown, Dean Harwood said good night and left. It was obvious from his expression that he thought it was odd that one of the windows was open. Emma began to wonder about it herself. The castle was air conditioned, so why would someone open a window? Figuring there must be a logical explanation, Emma decided she'd let Dean Harwood solve the mystery of the open window.

After Dean Harwood left, Doug quickly descended the spiral staircase, and together they all left the library. After a murmured good night, they went to their respective dorm rooms to get ready for bed. If this had been a school night, they would have gotten in trouble for being out after curfew. During school, curfew was nine o'clock, and lights out was at ten o'clock. School was not in session, however, so the regular rules did not apply.

As she walked with Martha to the suite they shared, Emma thought about the task Lord Dinswood had assigned them. Tomorrow would be Wednesday, so they only had the remainder of this week and then two more weeks to complete the job. Once school began again, they wouldn't have much time for searching. However, the time factor wasn't Emma's only concern. She had begun to worry that they wouldn't be able to find the other sculptures at all. She could only imagine how disappointed Lord Dinswood would be if that were the case. He had looked so ill the other night; Emma didn't think he could take any bad news. After all Lord Dinswood had done for the school, Emma was determined not to let him down. With a firm resolve to spend all day and all night in the library tomorrow if necessary, Emma prepared for bed.

CHAPTER SEVEN
AN UNEXPECTED TWIST

The next morning, Emma awakened to the patter of rain on the window above her bed. It was a gentle steady rain, the kind that could last for hours. Emma got out of bed and looked out the window. The sky was a dull gray for as far as the eye could see. It was going to be a dreary rainy day—a perfect day for doing research in the library. Even Sebastian couldn't object to spending time in the library on a day like this. Emma was sort of glad that it was raining. At least now they wouldn't have to listen to Sebastian whining about wanting to go outside.

Quickly, Emma got ready for breakfast, and by the time she'd finished brushing her teeth, Martha was awake and getting dressed. Emma and Martha were the first ones to enter the dining hall, but it wasn't long until Doug and Sebastian made an appearance. Breakfast was completed with little conversation. Even though it was raining outside and there was nothing else better to do, Sebastian still seemed to be pouting about having to spend the day in the library. Emma just hoped he'd keep his feelings to himself.

By dinnertime, they had each managed to get through another journal, and they had begun a list of places where the remaining sculptures might be hidden. As the day had worn on, it had eventually stopped raining, and the clouds had begun to break up with the sun peeking through every now and then. There were still two journals to go through, but Emma didn't have the heart to make Sebastian stay in the library all evening. He had been very good all day long. He had kept his fidgeting to a minimum and hadn't said a word of complaint about having to stay inside. She felt that he had earned an evening of freedom, and she said as much to Martha. Martha agreed with her completely and suggested that just the two girls stay in the library after dinner to look through the remaining two journals. When they shared their plan with the boys, Sebastian was elated, but Doug hesitated. He didn't feel right about the girls having to do extra work.

When Sebastian left to empty his dinner tray, Martha said to Doug, "You'd be doing us a favor by keeping Sebastian out of our hair. He's been sitting all day long, and I don't think we should press our luck."

"Yeah, Doug, if you don't go with him, he won't have anything to do, and then he'll be back in here driving us crazy," Emma added, and then another thought occurred to her. "You could make arrangements with your dad to check out the first location on the list. We're running out of time, and we need to start looking as soon as possible."

Realizing that the girls were right, Doug finally agreed, and soon after dinner was completed, he and Sebastian left to go talk to Doug's dad and then spend some time outside. The two girls returned to the library. Emma really didn't mind staying inside. She had gotten caught up in Rebecca's writings. Rebecca and Darius had certainly had an interesting life together, and even though Emma knew the story didn't have a happy ending, she was eager to read what Rebecca had had to say when she'd learned that she was finally going to have a child. It was for this reason that Emma asked Martha if it was okay if she took the last of Rebecca's ten journals. Martha didn't mind in the least. She had not been eager to read Rebecca's last entries. She hated books and movies that ended tragically. If she knew ahead of time that they were going to end badly, she refused to read or watch them. Generally, Emma felt the same way, but she found herself drawn to Rebecca's story in a way she couldn't explain.

After retrieving the last two journals from the shelf, the girls sat at the same study table they'd been using all day and began to read. They read in silence for what seemed like minutes, but when Emma finally looked up, she realized that it was starting to get dark outside. Without a word to Martha, who was engrossed in the entry she was reading, Emma reached up and switched on one of the table lamps. A half hour later, Martha closed the journal she'd been reading.

"Did you find any places to add to our list?" Emma asked. The list they'd compiled before supper already contained ten locations to be checked out. It seemed like an awful lot of territory to cover in the amount of time they had. Emma was secretly hoping that Martha hadn't found any others, so she was relieved when Martha shook her head in the negative. So far, Emma hadn't found any in her journal either. Of course, Rebecca had been pregnant during the time frame Emma's journal covered. It had been a difficult pregnancy, and Rebecca hadn't been going out much.

"How about you?" Martha asked in return.

"No, and I don't think I will. I've only got a few entries left to read. Rebecca's getting ready to have her baby, so the doctor has confined her to bed rest."

"You sure you want to read the rest? We've already found out what we need to know." Martha looked at Emma with concern. Knowing that Rebecca was going to die shortly after the birth of her baby was going to make those last few entries hard to read. Martha knew how much Emma still missed her own mother and was worried that Rebecca's story would bring those feelings to the surface again. She didn't want to put Emma through that unnecessarily.

Emma understood Martha's concern, but she was determined to finish. She'd just as soon be alone when she did though. "Yeah, I'm going to finish just in case Rebecca might mention some fond memory from the past. You don't have to stay though. Why don't you go ahead and call your mom like you mentioned earlier? I'll finish up here and then meet you in our room."

Martha did have some things she needed to do, but still she hesitated. "You sure you don't mind?" She looked at Emma and realized that, in a nice way, she was trying to get rid of her. Understanding Emma's desire to be alone, Martha agreed.

Emma waited until Martha had gone before she turned her attention back to her journal. The truth was she only had one entry left to read. It was the last thing Rebecca would ever write, and it was a letter to her unborn child.

My dearest child, the doctor tells me that you could arrive any time now. I can't tell you how excited I am. Your father and I have been waiting for you for so long. I can't wait to hold you in my arms and see your sweet little face for the very first time. What a wonderful life we will all have together. There are so many things I want to show you and teach you—so many places I want you to see. I don't know if you are a boy or a girl, but one thing I do know is that I love you more than words can say. I've loved you from the moment I learned that you were on the way. I've always heard that there's nothing as strong or as powerful as a mother's love, and now that you're almost here, I understand. I want to defend you and protect you from all hurts that may come your way. I know that's not very realistic. I won't be able to stop you from scratching your knee when you climb a tree or stop you from crying when someone hurts your feelings, but I promise to do everything in my power to see that you grow up healthy and happy. I love you, my little darling, and I'll see you soon.

When Emma finished reading, she realized that she was crying. It was sad and so unfair. Rebecca would have been such a wonderful mother. Emma consoled herself with the fact that at least Rebecca had gotten to hold her little boy before she'd died. As Emma reached up to wipe the tears off her cheeks, she thought about her own mother. Emma had only been five when she'd died, and she didn't remember a lot about her. Her memories of her mother were vague and indistinct, but she knew one thing for certain, her mother had loved her as much as Rebecca had described in her letter. Emma's tears began to flow anew at the thought.

She was just closing the journal, determined to put a stop to her depressing thoughts, when she heard it—a creak of the floorboards from somewhere off to her right. Hastily, Emma stood up, her chair loudly scraping the floor as it was suddenly pushed backward. She began looking around, but darkness had fallen while she'd been reading, and it was difficult to see beyond the little circle of light cast by the table lamp. Emma waited with her heart pounding wildly in her chest to see if the sound would come again. She was just beginning to think she had imagined it, when it came again. This time it was closer.

"Who's there?" Emma called out in panic. "Sebastian, if that's you, this isn't funny!"

As Emma feared, there was no response. Even Sebastian knew better than to tease her like this. A moment later, Emma felt the hair rise on the back of her neck as another frightening sound began to issue forth from one of the aisles directly behind her. At first, it sounded like the panting of a dog, and then Emma recognized what it was—an eerie whispered laughter. Emma wanted to run, but her legs didn't seem to be getting the message. She was literally frozen in terror. Icy fingers of fear began to snake their way down her spine. Then Emma felt something brush her arm. She screamed and whirled around. A cloaked and hooded figure stood a few feet away from her. The hood was pulled over the figure's head in such a way that it appeared faceless. Reminded of the grim reaper, Emma screamed again and threw her chair at it in an effort to buy her enough time to escape. She didn't wait to see if the chair hit its intended target. Instead she bolted for the stairs, leaving the journal lying on the table. With only the faint light from the table lamp and the soft moonlight coming in through the large north windows, Emma flew blindly down the spiral staircase, heedless of her own safety. Thankfully, she arrived at the bottom unharmed. Without pausing, Emma rushed to the exit, yanked the door open, and barreled right into Doug who'd just been going into the library to talk to her and Martha. Doug grabbed hold of both of her arms to steady her. Emma screamed at the sudden and unexpected contact and immediately began trying to break free, her only thought to get as far away as possible.

Doug tightened his grip to prevent her escape and asked, "Emma, what on earth is going on? Where's Martha?"

Emma stopped struggling and began trying to speak, but she was having trouble getting her breath after her mad dash. "Th-th-there's someone in the library," she finally managed to stammer. "H-h-he was laughing, and it was dark, and I couldn't see who it was."

Doug continued to hold Emma by the arms as he tried to make sense of what she was saying. She was clearly terrified. He could feel her shaking and her eyes were wide and wild looking. "Emma, try to calm down and tell me what happened. Were you in the library alone?" Doug couldn't imagine Emma running off and leaving Martha, especially if she were in danger.

Emma managed to nod as shivers of fear continued to course through her body. Then, to Doug's dismay, she began to cry. Not knowing what else to do, he pulled her close and put his arms around her. "It's okay, Emma," he whispered. "You're safe now."

By the time he finished speaking, she had put her arms around him too and was nearly squeezing the breath out of him. He'd only seen her like this one other time. He found himself getting angry with Martha. Where was she, and why had she left Emma in the library alone? In the next instant, he realized that Martha couldn't have known what was going to happen. *Why would anyone want to scare Emma?* he wondered. He began to get a sinking sensation in the pit of his stomach. Things were beginning to happen like last year when they'd been searching for the treasure. Apparently, what they had thought would be a simple search for the remaining sculptures wasn't going to be so simple after all.

Gradually, Emma's tremors subsided, but she continued to hold onto Doug as if he were a lifeline. "Can you tell me what happened now?" Doug asked quietly. Doug knew how truly courageous Emma could be. He had witnessed her courage firsthand last spring, but that was when they were facing a known enemy. It was the unknown that was so frightening to Emma.

With one last hiccup, Emma finally let go of Doug and backed away. She began to talk softly, her voice quavering despite her best efforts to control it. "Martha finished her journal before I did, so I told her she didn't need to wait for me. I was almost finished myself, and I knew Martha had promised to call her mom." Emma took another deep breath and then continued. "After Martha left, I was sitting there, and I heard the floorboards creaking like someone was walking on them. Then I heard another sound, a weird laughing sound. Someone was right behind me. He was wearing a black cloak and hood, and I couldn't see his face." Emma shivered again at the memory. "I ran for it, and that's when I bumped into you."

"If someone was in the library a few minutes ago, they should still be in there. We're standing in front of the only way into and out of the library," Doug reasoned.

"You're not thinking of going in there, are you?" Emma couldn't believe it. Some lunatic was running amok in the library, and Doug wanted to go in and look for him. That was the last thing Emma wanted to do after her near escape.

"That's exactly what I'm going to do. We need to find out why someone would want to scare you and what they're really up to."

Doug stepped around Emma and reached out to push the library door open, but Emma grabbed his arm. With a big indrawn breath, Emma said, "I think you're crazy, but if you insist on going in there, then I'm going with you."

Now there was the courageous Emma that Doug remembered. He smiled down at her. "You don't have to come with me, you know." He knew even as he said it that it was pointless. He could see the determination in her eyes.

Emma responded with a weak smile of her own and said hastily, "But this time, let's turn on all of the lights."

With Doug in the lead, they entered the library and switched on the lights by the door. The six large chandeliers chased the darkness away from every part of the first floor except for the area under the loft. They would have to turn on another bank of lights to illuminate that area. If Doug had been with Sebastian, he would have suggested that Sebastian check that area while he went upstairs to search the second floor, but he didn't want to leave Emma by herself. He noticed that she was sticking to him like glue. It made him feel good that she trusted him to protect her.

Together they searched the area under the loft. Leaving all of the first-floor lights illuminated, they then climbed the stairs to the second floor. Emma immediately turned on the three banks of lights upstairs. They looked down each and every aisle and even checked the gated area housing Lord Dinswood's private collection. Except for the sounds of their own shoes on the wood floor, the library was silent. Everything was just as it should be. The lamp on the study table where Emma had been sitting was still glowing. Emma's gaze traveled to the journal she'd left lying on the table and her breath caught in her throat.

At the sound of Emma's indrawn breath, Doug turned around. "Emma, what is it?"

"There's an envelope on the journal. It wasn't there when I left."

Emma felt that now familiar shudder of fear. What was going on?

Cautiously, Doug approached the table and picked up the envelope. It hadn't been sealed, so Doug quickly opened the flap and drew out the paper inside. He read for a moment and then handed the note to Emma.

Emma experienced a feeling of dread at Doug's grim expression. She looked down at the handwritten page and began to read.

I know about the Mortals and that you have been engaged by Lord Dinswood to find them. You will still find the sculptures, Douglas, but instead of working for Lord Dinswood, you will now be working for me. Regrettably, the first of the Mortals is already in the hands of Lord Dinswood, but the other six are not. You have two weeks to find the second Mortal. When you have found it, Douglas, you will hang one of the academy's school banners in your dorm window. I will then instruct you where to take the sculpture. If you tell anyone of our arrangement or fail to meet the first deadline, the lives of your father and Lord Dinswood will be in jeopardy. To prove that my threats are genuine, you will find a chess piece on the mantel in your father's suite—a bishop to be precise. Good luck, Douglas. Remember, lives depend on your success.

Emma looked at Doug in disbelief. This couldn't be happening. "What are we going to do?" she asked in a whisper.

Doug was already heading for the stairs. "I'm going to check on Dad. Get Martha and Sebastian together. We'll meet in the lounge." With that, he was gone. Emma was left standing there holding the terrible letter. A second later, she recalled her earlier experience in the library. Not wanting to be left in the library alone again, she followed Doug out and went in search of Martha and Sebastian.

CHAPTER EIGHT
A TANGLED WEB

W hen Doug entered his dad's suite, he immediately went over to the fireplace. He heaved a huge sigh of relief after a quick scan of the mantel revealed no chess piece. He could hear his father rummaging around in his room, so he called out, "Dad, are you there?"

Upon hearing his son, Dean Harwood came out of his room. In his hands, he was carrying a couple of dive masks. "I didn't expect to see you again so soon," he said, eyeing Doug curiously. "What brings you back up here?" he asked.

After a brief hesitation, Doug replied, "I just thought of something we should take with us tomorrow when we go to the arch."

The arch was the first location on their list. In one of her journals, Rebecca had mentioned visiting a natural arch. Doug had since learned that a natural arch or natural bridge, as it is sometimes called, is a rock formation that is sometimes formed by the eroding effects of moving water. He and his father had asked Lord Dinswood about it, and as natural arches aren't all that common, he had known precisely the location to which Rebecca had been referring. According to Lord Dinswood, there was a natural arch about five miles east of the castle.

As they had no way of knowing if Darius had buried the sculpture in the ground or hidden it somewhere in the creek itself, they were going to have to prepare for either possibility. This explained the diving masks Dean Harwood was holding.

Doug realized his dad was waiting for him to elaborate on his last statement. Looking at the masks gave him an idea. "Maybe we should take an oxygen tank too," he said quickly.

Dean Harwood shook his head. "I don't think that will be necessary, son. Remember, Darius wouldn't have had anything like that, so it's unlikely we'll need one."

"I guess you're right," Doug replied. His dad probably thought he was losing it, but at least he'd found out that there was no chess piece on the mantel and that his dad was okay. "I'll see you in the morning then," he said, turning to leave.

Doug was just opening the door when his father said, "Oh, I forgot to ask you. Did you lose one of your chess pieces? I found one on the mantel a little while ago."

Doug froze with his hand on the door knob. A chill swept through his body that had nothing to do with the temperature. Hoping his father hadn't noticed his strange reaction, Doug turned back around in time to see his dad pull a small wooden chess piece out of his pants pocket. Just as the note had said, it was a bishop. Doug stared at the object in his dad's hand as if it was a tarantula instead of a harmless chess piece. Then Doug realized his dad was holding it out so that he could take it. Hoping his expression didn't betray the shock he was feeling, he reluctantly took the bishop and put it in his own pants pocket.

If Dean Harwood noticed anything unusual about Doug's behavior, he didn't let on. Doug murmured a quick thanks and made his escape before his father could question him further about the chess piece. Then his thoughts turned to Lord Dinswood. He had been threatened in the note as well. Doug ran down the hall and halted abruptly in front of the dark cherry wood door that led to Lord Dinswood's suite. He rapped loudly on the door so that Lord Dinswood would be sure to hear him. Doug put his ear to the door and listened, greatly relieved when he heard Lord Dinswood call out permission for him to enter.

He found Lord Dinswood sitting in his favorite chair. Upon seeing Doug, Lord Dinswood folded the newspaper he'd been reading and laid it on the table next to him. After eyeing Doug speculatively for a moment in that special way of his, he asked, "Is everything all right, son? You look a little shell shocked."

Doug started in surprise. Lord Dinswood was too observant by far. Doug was going to have to do a better job of hiding his emotions. The lives of two of the people he loved most in the world depended on it. Doug took a deep breath and tried to calm the wild hammering of his heart. Lord Dinswood continued to look at him calmly, and Doug realized he was still waiting for an answer to his question.

"I'm okay, sir," Doug answered. "I just wanted to stop by and tell you we're going to the arch tomorrow to look for the second sculpture." This last statement wasn't strictly true, but Doug could hardly tell Lord Dinswood the real reason for his visit.

Lord Dinswood cocked his head and watched Doug closely a moment longer. Doug grew uncomfortable under Lord Dinswood's close scrutiny and realized that he hadn't fooled the old man. Lord Dinswood had the uncanny ability to detect a lie, no matter how small.

Deciding that Doug wasn't going to say any more, Lord Dinswood sighed and said, "I know. I spoke with your father earlier. The arch is a lovely spot. I've been there many times myself. Of course, that was in my younger days. I'd like nothing better than to go with you tomorrow, but I'm afraid the mile hike along the creek would be a little strenuous for me now."

"I wish you could go too, sir." This time Doug was speaking the absolute truth. He would like nothing better than to see Lord Dinswood feeling well again—to see him restored to the vigorous man he'd been when they'd first met him last year.

Lord Dinswood smiled, and Doug could see the light of love shining from his tired blue eyes. With another sigh, he said, "Well, there's no sense in wishing for what can't be, so I'll just wish you good luck and tell you to be careful. I'd hate to see any of you kids come to harm trying to do a favor for an old man."

"We're happy to do it, sir."

"I know you are, son. That's why I picked you."

Doug turned to leave then, but Lord Dinswood stopped him.

"Just a second. I've got something I want to give you. It was something I had as a boy and it always brought me good luck. Maybe it'll work for you too."

With that, Lord Dinswood rose slowly from his chair and shuffled off down the short hallway to his bedroom. He was back a moment later with a faded black ball cap in his hands. Above the bill of the cap was an emblem that Doug didn't recognize. It was a red shield with a wide green band at the top. On the red portion of the shield was a gold lion. The green part of the shield contained two crossed swords in silver. Lord Dinswood pointed to the emblem and explained, "This is the Dinswood family crest. The lion represents fierce courage, and the red background stands for a great warrior. I'd like you to have it."

Doug just stood there for a moment, temporarily at a loss for words. He felt truly honored that Lord Dinswood would give him something he cherished from his own childhood. The fact that it also displayed the Dinswood family crest made it even more special.

"Thank you, sir," he finally managed to say. He put the cap on his head. It fit perfectly.

"It suits you," Lord Dinswood said, smiling. Doug would have been humbled to know what Lord Dinswood was thinking at that moment; the cap fit Doug in more ways than one. Doug was the living embodiment of what the Dinswood crest symbolized—strength and courage.

Doug smiled back. Swallowing the lump that had suddenly formed in his throat, he said, "Well, I'd better get going."

As he closed the door behind him, he heard Lord Dinswood call out, "Good luck tomorrow."

By the time Doug returned from checking on his dad and Lord Dinswood, Emma had managed to track down Martha and Sebastian, and they were all waiting for him in the lounge. Emma had let them both read the note, and their reactions had been similar to hers and Doug's—shock and disbelief.

"Is your dad okay?" Emma asked anxiously as soon as Doug entered the lounge.

"He's okay," Doug replied, his expression as grim as Emma had ever seen it.

"Was the chess piece on the mantel?" Sebastian couldn't help asking even though it was apparent from Doug's face that everything had been just as the author of the note had said it would be.

Doug didn't reply; he simply nodded. It made him angry that someone could gain access to his dad's private rooms so easily. He knew for a fact that his dad always kept the door locked when he was out. That left only two possibilities: either someone had a duplicate key, or there was another way, maybe a secret passage, into the suite. It didn't really matter how the intruder had gotten in. What mattered was that his dad was in danger, and Doug was powerless to do anything about it.

"What about Lord Dinswood?" Martha asked, breaking into his thoughts.

"I checked on him too," Doug answered. "He's okay. He wished us good luck tomorrow and gave me this cap—said it always brought him luck when he was a boy." Doug was silent for a moment as he tried to gain control of his emotions. In the short time he'd known Lord Dinswood, he had become like a grandfather to him. Doug knew that Lord Dinswood was very fond of him as well. It made him physically ill to think that from this moment forward they were going to have to lie to him. Assuming they were successful in locating the other six Mortals, they wouldn't be able to tell Lord Dinswood. The thought of what would happen if they were unsuccessful was too awful to contemplate.

They sat in silence for several long minutes, each one thinking about how hard it was going to be to lie not only to Doug's dad, but to Lord Dinswood as well. Every time Emma thought about the excited look on Lord Dinswood's face as he had told them the story of the Mortals, she wanted to cry. Lord Dinswood was counting on them, and they were going to be letting him down in a big way. But disappointing Lord Dinswood wasn't the only thing that had Emma on the verge of tears. Lord Dinswood was obviously ill. She had been hoping that finding the other Mortals would cheer him up and put him on the road to recovery. How was their apparent failure at the task he had assigned them going to affect his health?

"What are we going to do?" Martha asked, finally breaking the silence.

"We're going to do exactly what this lunatic wants," Doug replied angrily. "We're going to find the sculptures and give them to him."

"How are we going to do that?" Sebastian asked. "We've already made arrangements with your dad. He's coming with us tomorrow to look for the second sculpture."

"We'll have to make sure we don't find it, at least not when Dad's with us." Doug had been giving it a lot of thought. They would have to pretend to look tomorrow and then sneak back later without his dad to complete a more thorough search. It was going to be tricky though. Doug's dad was not going to be easy to fool. They would have to be very convincing.

"That might work for tomorrow, but what about all the other places we listed on our sheet? He'll expect to come with us when we search those too. He's going to get mighty suspicious if we come up empty every time," Sebastian countered.

"Not necessarily. Remember, we have no actual proof that the other sculptures are still out there somewhere. Lord Dinswood is only hoping that they are."

Sebastian was beginning to see where Doug was going with this line of reasoning. "I get it," he said, nodding. "Your dad knows about the arch, but have you actually shown him the list?" When Doug shook his head no, Sebastian continued. "After tomorrow, we'll take your dad to random places. You know—ones that aren't actually on our list. Of course, we won't find anything. When we keep coming up short, your dad will become convinced that the other sculptures aren't around anymore, and he'll tell Lord Dinswood." All of this was said without Sebastian's usual enthusiasm. It was apparent from his tone that Sebastian would take no pleasure from deceiving Doug's dad.

"It'll break Lord Dinswood's heart," Emma said quietly.

"It's the only way to keep him and Dad safe," Doug said with a sigh. He hated the whole plan, but there didn't seem to be any other way. Whoever had written that note meant business.

Doug found himself praying that the other six sculptures were still around and that the four of them would be able to find them. Although he wasn't aware of it, the others were doing the same.

CHAPTER NINE
THE FIRST LIKELY SPOT

The next morning Emma, Martha, Sebastian, and Doug waited on the front steps of the castle. Each of them carried a backpack loaded with a canteen of water and sandwiches for lunch. The sun was shining brightly in a cloudless sky. The temperature was supposed to climb into the nineties by midafternoon, but even at this early hour, it was already stifling. Emma noticed that Doug was wearing the cap Lord Dinswood had given him. Dean Harwood had gone to get his Ford Explorer out of the academy's combination bus barn and garage. The bus barn was located southeast of the boy's dormitory and directly south of the chapel. Like the chapel, it sat back in the woods a little way so that in the summer, when the trees were all leafed out, it wasn't visible from the school. A short gravel road led to the barn that housed not only the school's six buses, but also the cars owned by the faculty.

While they waited, Doug took the opportunity to remind them of their plan. "Remember, we're supposed to act like we're really searching. Make it convincing. If you should happen to find something, you can't let on, and you can't tell the rest of us until we're back at the castle and Dad's not around. Got it?"

"Got it," the others said in unison.

No one spoke after that. They were each contemplating the difficult day ahead. Doug had made it sound so simple, but they all knew that Dean Harwood wasn't going to be that easy to fool. Emma just hoped they'd be able to pull it off. As Doug had said last night, lives were at stake.

Just as Dean Harwood pulled up in the Explorer, Miss Jennings came outside. Like the others, she was carrying a backpack. Thinking that, as one of the school's science teachers, Miss Jennings would be interested in seeing a natural arch, Dean Harwood had invited her to come along. The kids had only learned that Miss Jennings would be accompanying them this morning at breakfast.

Emma couldn't help wondering if Dean Harwood had had another reason for inviting Miss Jennings along. After all, he was an unmarried man, and Miss Jennings was an attractive single woman. Emma had always thought Miss Jennings was pretty. She had bright green eyes and shoulder-length chestnut-colored hair. Along with her pretty face, she had a nice petite figure and was, as near as Emma could tell, about five feet three inches tall. In addition to her physical attributes, Miss Jennings had the type of personality that made her a pleasure to be around. She smiled often and had a kind and compassionate nature. Emma could see why Dean Harwood would be attracted to her. She could also see why Miss Jennings would be attracted to him. With dark hair that was starting to gray at the temples and deep-brown eyes, he was an older version of Doug. He had a lean well-muscled build and, like Doug, was a couple of inches over six feet.

As soon as the SUV came to a stop, they all piled in. Miss Jennings sat up front with Dean Harwood. Martha and Emma sat behind them, and Doug and Sebastian climbed into the seat in the very back. Dean Harwood and Miss Jennings conversed casually as they drove along. Emma noticed that Miss Jennings called Doug's dad Jake, and he called her Louisa. Their lack of formality surprised Emma until she realized it would be silly for the two of them to spend the entire day calling each other Dean Harwood and Miss Jennings. After all, they weren't on a school outing. Today's mission had nothing to do with school. It occurred to Emma that perhaps Dean Harwood and Miss Jennings were more than just boss and employee. They certainly seemed comfortable with each other. Emma turned around to observe Doug's reaction, but he was busy looking out the window at the passing scenery. She considered asking him about it later but, in the next instant, decided against it. It really wasn't any of her business, and she didn't want Doug to think she was being nosy.

Emma looked out her own window and, putting thoughts of a possible romance between Dean Harwood and Miss Jennings aside, drank in the view before her. Tree-covered rolling hills led up to mountains in the distance. Due to the unusual amount of rain the region had experienced this summer, the trees and low-lying vegetation that flanked both sides of the highway were still a lush and vibrant green. Wild flowers in yellow, orange, and purple grew in profusion in the cleared areas and along the road. Emma never failed to appreciate the natural beauty surrounding the academy.

In no time, they were turning off the main highway onto the gravel road that led to Crawford Creek. When they came to the low-water bridge Lord Dinswood had described, Dean Harwood pulled the SUV off on the shoulder and parked. They would have to walk from here.

Everyone got out of the SUV and began adjusting their backpacks for the mile-long trek upstream. Doug noticed that his father was taking something out of the back end of the vehicle. When he saw what it was, his heart dropped into his stomach. Things had just gotten a lot more complicated. He began mentally kicking himself for not realizing that his father, who was an extremely intelligent man, would have the good sense to bring a metal detector along. The first sculpture had been found in a metal box, so it made sense that the others, if they still existed, would be as well. Assuming the second Mortal was buried somewhere around the arch, the metal detector would make its discovery almost a sure thing. Doug racked his brain as he tried to figure out what to do. One thing was certain. He could not allow his dad to find the sculpture. Maybe he could volunteer to carry the metal detector and then purposely drop it. Immediately, he rejected that idea. They might need the detector to find the other sculptures.

He looked over at Emma to see if she had noticed what his father was carrying. She was looking at him with an expression that bordered on panic. Not only had she seen the instrument but had correctly surmised the problem it posed.

"What are we going to do?" she whispered to Doug as soon as his dad was out of earshot.

"I haven't got a clue. I was hoping you had an idea."

"All I know to do is pray that either there's no sculpture at the arch or that it's in the water."

"I guess that's all we can do," Doug said, taking off the cap Lord Dinswood had given him and running his hand through his hair in a gesture that was uniquely his.

"We could give the metal detector to Sebastian. He's bound to mess it up some way or another," Martha commented dryly after overhearing the exchange between Doug and Emma.

"Hey, I heard that," Sebastian said. He had come up behind Martha as she was speaking. Whether she had known he was there or not was anyone's guess. Sebastian didn't seem to be angry though. His attention was riveted on the instrument Dean Harwood was carrying. "That's one of the most powerful pulse induction metal detectors made."

"In other words, we're in major trouble," Martha stated matter-of-factly, seemingly unsurprised at Sebastian's apparent knowledge of metal detectors. Last spring, Sebastian had proven himself very knowledgeable where ships and sailing were concerned. Martha had since learned that Sebastian was actually very intelligent but didn't bother to apply himself unless the subject was something he was interested in.

It was Doug who asked the obvious question. "How do you know so much about metal detectors, Sebastian?"

"My dad has a friend who's an amateur archeologist. He goes relic hunting as a hobby and has a metal detector similar to the one your dad's holding. Most metal detectors only work to a depth of a foot or less, but the one your dad's got will detect a good-sized metal object to a depth of eleven or twelve feet."

"That's just great," Martha said sarcastically.

Ignoring Martha's comment, Sebastian said, "I wonder where your dad got it. That's a pretty expensive piece of equipment."

"I'd say Lord Dinswood got it for us to use," Doug guessed.

"He sure does want us to find those sculptures," Sebastian said with a shake of his head.

The others were silent for a moment as they considered the magnitude of the task before them. They were going to have to somehow avoid finding anything today and then find a way to return tomorrow on their own, all the while lying to Doug's dad and Lord Dinswood.

Dean Harwood and Miss Jennings, who had already started walking upstream, turned back and noticed the four youngsters huddled together in a group as if they were planning a prison break.

"Hey, you kids coming?" Dean Harwood called cheerfully.

Doug answered his dad with a wave and then turned back to the others. "Well, we better get going," he said with a sigh. "It's going to be a long day." He let the others go first on the pretense of needing to adjust the straps of his backpack. He let them get a little way ahead before he took Emma's advice and said a silent prayer.

They trudged along in silence for a while, carefully picking their way over the gravel bar that paralleled the creek on the north side. A bluff that rose nearly one hundred feet bordered the south side. Under normal circumstances, Emma would have enjoyed the day and the scenery, but in addition to their current worries, it was so oppressively hot that she was soaked through with perspiration before they'd gone very far. Her clothes began sticking to her, and she started looking longingly at the deeper parts of the creek they passed. A mile hadn't seemed that long when they were discussing it, but because of the gravel they were forced to walk on, it was taking much longer than Emma had anticipated. It was the better part of an hour before they reached the arch.

Dean Harwood and Miss Jennings didn't seem to notice the heat. They continued to converse amiably the entire trek to the arch. Every now and then, Miss Jennings would laugh at something Dean Harwood said, and her laughter would drift back to the youngsters who were following several feet behind. Each time, Emma would look over at Doug, but he didn't seem to notice. Emma guessed he was too worried about what they would find at the arch to care about anything else.

Finally, they were standing before the arch. It was a beautiful sight to behold—a natural rock bridge carved over eons of time by the passage of water. It was covered with grass and climbing vines and was tall enough that even Doug could walk under it without ducking. The Crawford Creek Arch, as it was called, was truly a wonder of nature. Miss Jennings had brought her camera along and immediately began taking pictures of the arch. She also took one of all of the youngsters standing beneath the arch and then one that included Doug's dad. Not wanting Miss Jennings to be left out, Doug's dad took one of her with the group. Miss Jennings was just starting to put her camera away when Doug did something that surprised Emma. He offered to take a picture of just his dad and Miss

Jennings. They readily agreed, and as they posed beneath the arch, Dean Harwood put his arm around Miss Jennings's back. Emma looked over at Martha to gauge her reaction. Martha raised her eyebrows and grinned slyly. Emma's gaze then shifted to Doug. He was watching his dad and Miss Jennings with an unreadable expression.

Emma's thoughts were interrupted when Dean Harwood announced that it was time to get down to work. With a sinking feeling, Emma watched him lift the metal detector and turn it on.

"I'll search the area around the arch with this for a bit," Dean Harwood said to the group. Then seeing how hot they were, he suggested, "Why don't you guys cool off in the water for a while? Then you can get the dive masks we brought and start looking in the water."

"Sounds like a good idea, Dad," Doug agreed.

"When did you want to eat lunch, Jake?" Miss Jennings asked.

Doug had never told Emma his father's given name, but she knew that Jake was short for Jacob. Of course, it was possible that Jacob was Dean Harwood's middle name. Sometimes people went by their middle names, especially if their first name was something awful. Emma made a mental note to ask Doug about it later.

"I thought we could search for a while and work up an appetite," Dean Harwood answered with a smile. "Everyone's probably too hot to eat now anyway."

Miss Jennings nodded and then said to the group in general, "We all need to make sure we stay hydrated. There's plenty of water in your canteens, so don't hesitate to take a drink every now and then. Don't wait until you're thirsty either. Sometimes by the time our bodies get the signal we're thirsty, it's too late to prevent heatstroke."

"Good advice," Dean Harwood said.

The morning went quickly even though the youngsters lived in constant fear that the metal detector would go off. Dean Harwood searched every square inch of the ground around the arch, but the detector remained blessedly silent. By lunchtime, Dean Harwood had concluded that if the sculpture was near the arch, it wasn't buried.

They stopped briefly to eat the lunches they'd brought. Lunch consisted of peanut butter and jelly sandwiches, chips, and apples. It wasn't exactly fine dining, but it was nutritious and satisfying. Once lunch was concluded and all of the trash had been packed away in their backpacks, the kids and Miss Jennings continued their search of the water. This time Dean Harwood joined them. They spent the entire afternoon searching every swimming hole within shooting distance of the arch, but to no avail. There was no hint of a metal box anywhere.

Doug didn't know how to feel about their lack of success. He hadn't wanted his dad or Miss Jennings to find the sculpture, but he had hoped that one of the four of them would. It looked like they were wrong about the arch. They still had nine other locations to check, but time was running out. They'd better find something before the two weeks stipulated in the note, or... Doug consciously stopped that train of thought—it didn't bear thinking about. He couldn't, however, stop the niggling doubt that kept creeping into his brain. *What if we're wrong about all of the locations? What if there aren't any sculptures to find?* Doug took a deep breath in an effort to suppress the fear that threatened to overwhelm him. They would find the other sculptures, he tried to reassure himself. They had to.

Dean Harwood looked at his watch. It was nearing time for supper, so he instructed the group to get dried off as best they could with the towels they'd brought in their backpacks and prepare for the mile trek back to the car. Sebastian was trying to cram one of the dive masks into his already stuffed pack when it happened. The mask fell out and, after rolling down the slight embankment upon which Sebastian was standing, dropped into one of the deeper pools by the arch. It landed in the water with a loud plop and immediately began to sink.

Giving the rest of the group a sheepish look, Sebastian said, "Sorry about that. Don't worry. I'll get it."

The pool in which the mask had landed was next to the bluff and almost eight feet deep. Sebastian would need the other dive mask to locate the one he'd dropped. Realizing this, Doug, who had the other mask, wordlessly dug it out of his own pack and absently handed it to Sebastian. He was still worrying about what their next move should be and, in his preoccupation, barely glanced at Sebastian as he handed him the mask.

Mistaking Doug's behavior for irritation, Sebastian apologized again. This snapped Doug from his worrisome thoughts and seeing the hurt look on Sebastian's face, he hastened to reassure him. "It's no big deal. I was just thinking about something else." He said the last two words with special emphasis.

Sebastian gave a little nod, indicating he understood what that something else was. They had all been convinced that Darius had hidden one of the sculptures at the arch. The fact that they hadn't found anything cast serious doubt on all of the other locations they'd put on their list. Sebastian knew Doug was deeply worried about what that could mean for his dad and Lord Dinswood. With a sigh, he put the dive mask on and adjusted it. As soon as he was finished, he dove cleanly into the clear water of the creek. The clarity of the creek's water was due to its gravel bed, and it was so exceptionally clear that even though this particular spot was almost eight feet deep, it was possible to see the bottom from where they were standing.

While the others watched, Sebastian entered the pool and felt the refreshing water rush over his body. He effortlessly kicked to the bottom and was just reaching for the sunken dive mask when he happened to look toward the bluff only a couple of feet away. He blew out a stream of bubbles in his surprise. There was a hollow space in the side of the bluff that extended back approximately four feet.

The small cave was about three feet wide, and its roof rose little more than a foot above the creek bed.

Sebastian immediately realized why they hadn't noticed it before. The overhanging rock made it impossible to detect from above. It could only be seen by someone who was almost lying on the bottom in this particular spot.

It wasn't the discovery of the little cave alone that had Sebastian almost drowning in his excitement. It was the metal box wedged in the very back of it. The box was exactly like the one Lord Dinswood had shown them that first night in his apartment—the one in which the sculpture of Ruth had been found. Quickly, Sebastian grabbed the dive mask lying on the bottom and began to kick toward the surface, eager to tell the others about his discovery. Just before his head broke the surface, he realized that he couldn't say anything—at least not with Doug's dad and Miss Jennings around. He'd have to behave as if nothing had happened, and it was going to require the greatest acting performance of his life.

Sebastian surfaced and waved the dive mask with a flourish. "Got it," he exclaimed as if the successful retrieval of the mask was the sole reason for his cheerfulness.

"Good job, Sebastian," Dean Harwood commended. "Dry off and then we'd better get going."

Sebastian did as instructed, and soon they were ready to go once more.

The walk to the car and ride back to the castle were accomplished in silence on the part of the youngsters. Dean Harwood and Miss Jennings chatted casually the entire time, attributing the behavior of the kids to tiredness. Martha, Emma, and Doug were all worrying over the frightening threats in the note they'd found. Trying not to give anything away, Sebastian managed to appear as sullen as the others. If the others had known what he was holding back, they would have immediately nominated him for an Oscar in the best actor category.

As soon as Dean Harwood pulled the Explorer to a stop in front of the castle's main entrance, Miss Jennings and the four youngsters got out. Sebastian waited until Miss Jennings had gone into the castle and Dean Harwood had driven around to park the car before he exploded with the news of his discovery.

"I found it!" he shouted.

"What are you talking about?" Martha asked tiredly.

"I found the sculpture!"

"You what?" Martha responded, her tiredness suddenly vanishing.

Doug stood looking at Sebastian with an incredulous expression. *Could it be true?* He studied his friend's face and slowly realized that Sebastian wouldn't tease about something as important as this. Blessed waves of relief washed over Doug. Sebastian's discovery confirmed two things. First, it was now almost certain that all of the pieces Marnatti had sculpted for Darius still existed, and second, as they had thought, Darius had hidden them in places special to him and Rebecca.

Even though Sebastian had discovered the metal box entirely by accident, Doug felt a welling of gratitude for his friend. Thanks to Sebastian, his dad and Lord Dinswood were safe, at least for another two weeks. Not knowing how else to express what he was feeling, Doug simply looked at his friend and said solemnly, "Thanks, Sebastian. I owe you."

"No problem," Sebastian replied with equal seriousness.

Emma and Martha watched the exchange between the two boys with amusement. *Boys really are the strangest creatures*, Emma couldn't help thinking. It was obvious from Martha's wry expression that she was thinking something similar.

The next moment everyone began talking at once. It was as if a great burden had been lifted from their shoulders. Doug would have been gratified to know that his friends were just as relieved as he was at this new discovery.

They stood on the steps of the castle a few minutes longer as Sebastian explained how and where he had found the metal box. Finally, when all of their questions had been answered, they entered the castle and went to their rooms to get washed up for supper. Later that evening, they sat in the lounge and made plans to return to the arch at Crawford Creek.

CHAPTER TEN
SEEKING SARAH

S itting in cushioned chairs upholstered in a floral pattern and arranged in a circle around one of the lounge's coffee tables, Sebastian began the conversation with a question. "How are we
going to get back to the creek tomorrow? I mean I guess we could
walk, but its five miles just to the creek and then another mile to
the arch."

"Well, one thing's for sure. We can't ask Doug's dad to take us,"
Martha answered, stating the obvious.

Doug nodded and said, "Dad's already told me he's got a meeting with the board tomorrow, so he can't go with us to check out any
of the other locations. At least that leaves us free tomorrow. I've already asked him if we could go swimming like we did the other day,
and he said it was okay."

"That gives us until suppertime to get to the creek and back,"
Emma said, entering the conversation. *That should be plenty of time*,
she thought, *as long as we don't have any problems*. Time wasn't the
only factor that needed consideration however. They were going to
have to figure out how they were going to get the metal box back to
the school. Emma shared this last concern with the others.

"I've thought about that," Doug said, nodding again. "We don't really need the box. We just need the sculpture. If we took a blanket, we could wrap the sculpture up in it and stick it in one of our backpacks."

"Good idea!" Martha praised. "I've got a little lap blanket I keep on the foot of my bed that should do the trick."

Suddenly, Doug's eyes lit up as another idea occurred to him. "I just remembered something!" he cried excitedly. "I can't believe I didn't think of it before."

"What?" the others asked in unison.

"Come with me, and I'll show you." Without another word, Doug got up and headed for the lounge's double doors. Not wanting to be left behind, the others quickly followed.

A few minutes later, they were standing in the school's bus garage looking at a wide assortment of mountain bikes. "I forgot we had these. I found them when I was exploring a couple of summer's ago."

"Where'd they come from?" Sebastian asked.

"I asked Dad that same question when I first discovered them. He told me that the school had a teacher a few years back that started a mountain biking club. After he left, no one wanted to take over sponsorship of the club, so the bikes have just been sitting here."

"Just waiting for us," Sebastian said with a smile. He, for one, was very glad they weren't going to have to walk twelve miles in ninety-degree heat tomorrow.

Emma counted the bikes. There were twenty in all, and they all had red or green frames—the colors of Dinswood Academy. "Do you think the tires are still good?" Emma asked.

"First let's each pick one that looks like it's in pretty good shape," Doug suggested. "There's a tire pump on the bench over there, so we can air up the tires if we need to."

Needing no further prompting, they each set about choosing a bike. Once they'd made their selections, Doug and Sebastian checked all the tires and aired the ones that needed it. In no time, they had four bikes ready to go for the next day.

With nothing else to do, they returned to the castle. They were just about to go inside when Sebastian suggested a game of badminton. As it was still fairly early, the others readily agreed, and soon they were swatting at birdies under the shade of a large oak. When it got too dark to see the birdie, they decided it was time to go in. After agreeing to meet in the dining hall at eight the next morning, they went to their dorm rooms to prepare for bed. They were going to need a good night's sleep for the long day ahead.

Emma awakened the next morning at seven o'clock. She yawned sleepily and sat up. A glance out the window confirmed that it was going to be another hot and sunny day. Emma was thankful that Doug had remembered the bikes. Walking in this kind of heat would have been nearly unbearable. Of course pedaling a bike wasn't going to be any picnic either, but at least it would get them to the creek faster. With that thought, she went in the bathroom to get ready for breakfast, and when she came out, she saw that Martha was already dressed for the day.

Emma dressed while Martha took her turn in the bathroom. Then they left for the dining hall. When they got there, the boys were waiting for them.

"We'd better eat up this morning," Sebastian commented as they filled their trays with an assortment that included scrambled eggs, bacon, and toast. "We'll need all the energy we can get today."

"Don't eat too much, Sebastian," Martha cautioned. "If you do, you'll get sick in this heat."

"Yeah, I hadn't thought of that," Sebastian agreed.

After making their selections from the breakfast buffet, they returned to their table and ate in relative silence. When everyone was finished, Doug stood up to empty his tray and said, "We'd better get going. Why don't you girls go get your backpacks, and we'll meet back here to get some sandwiches for lunch. We need to make sure we fill our canteens too." He was just turning away when he remembered something else. Turning back around, he said to Martha, "Don't forget your lap blanket. We'll need it to wrap the sculpture in."

Martha nodded her understanding. She had a little first aid kit she intended to bring along as well. Martha wasn't expecting to need it, but one never knew when an accident might occur. She thought back to last spring when they were searching for the treasure. There were a couple of times her first aid kit would have come in handy.

"I've still got the dive masks, so I'll bring those," Sebastian said as they parted ways outside the dining hall.

Moments later, they were back in the dining hall filling their backpacks with the sandwiches, chips, and fruit the cooks had prepared for them. They also filled their canteens. After checking to be sure they had everything they needed, they headed outside and made their way around the east side of the castle to the bus barn where their transports waited. Before leaving the bus barn, Doug walked over to one of the workbenches along the south wall and picked up a small crowbar, explaining that they would need it to open the metal box. After stuffing the crowbar into his backpack, he put on the cap Lord Dinswood had given him and got on his bike.

Doug had been wearing that cap everywhere he went ever since Lord Dinswood had given it to him. Emma had to admit he looked good in it. She also knew it would please Lord Dinswood to know how much Doug appreciated his gift.

With a wave that signaled the others should follow, Doug rode out of the bus barn. As they pedaled to the driveway in front of the castle, Emma couldn't help smiling. It had been a long time since she had ridden a bike. Her father had taught her as a little girl. It had been the summer after her mother had died, and she had just turned six. For her birthday she had gotten her first bicycle, complete with training wheels. As with most little girls, at that time her favorite color had been pink. Knowing this, her father had purchased a small bicycle with a pink frame and bright pink streamers hanging from the rubber grips of the handlebars. Emma had been ecstatic. It had been the first time she'd been truly happy since her mother's death.

Emma's dad had firmly resolved that by the end of the summer Emma would no longer need the training wheels. He had been a kind and patient teacher, and it was one of Emma's fondest memories of her father. Of course, things had changed after he had married Vera. Her smile faltering, Emma brushed that thought away. Determined to enjoy the day, she lifted her face to take full advantage of the cool morning air rushing past it.

They were now on the school's driveway and were coasting down the hill at a fairly rapid rate. She and Martha were riding side by side behind Doug and Sebastian. Sebastian let out a whoop and lifted his hands from the handlebars of his bike. "Look, Mom. No hands," he joked.

"You'd better hold on before you kill yourself," Martha admonished from behind him. "We don't have time to stop and bandage you up."

Sebastian turned around to make a face at Martha and nearly wrecked. Quickly, he turned back around just barely managing to get his bike under control once again.

"See what I mean?" Martha couldn't help shouting.

In answer, Sebastian suddenly put on his brakes, causing Martha to do the same in order to keep from plowing into him.

"You idiot!" she screamed. "Are you trying to kill me?"

"No, just shut you up," Sebastian said with a grin. Wanting to see Martha's reaction, he had turned around in his seat so that he could look at her as he delivered his reply. She didn't disappoint him.

Martha was so surprised by Sebastian's answer that, for the moment, she didn't know what to say. This was the first time he had stood up to her.

Hearing the exchange behind him and knowing that it would only be a matter of time before Martha responded with something that was sure to anger Sebastian, Doug brought his own bike to a stop and turned to look at them both with a solemn expression. "Look, guys. No horsing around. All of our focus needs to be on getting what's in that metal box Sebastian found. Remember what's at stake."

Realizing that Doug was right, Martha frowned at Sebastian but said nothing. Sebastian smiled sweetly at Martha and turned back around. A battle had been averted, but Emma could tell from Martha's expression that the war had just begun.

At the bottom of the hill, Doug slowed and turned onto the main highway. In silence, they began the four-mile trek to the gravel road that led to the creek. The terrain along this particular portion of the highway was relatively flat, so they were able to make good time. On the way, they encountered very little traffic. As it was now after nine o'clock, those traveling to work had long since arrived at their destinations. Occasionally, a car would pass them going in the opposite direction, most likely heading into town. Emma paced herself by pedaling vigorously and then coasting for a while. Next to her, Martha was doing the same thing. The boys were doing less coasting and were soon several yards ahead of the girls. Emma wasn't concerned. She knew they would catch up to the boys when they got to the gravel road.

As she and Martha rode along, Emma took the opportunity to enjoy the scenery. Both sides of the road were heavily forested, but every now and then, Emma caught a glimpse of a house nestled back among the trees. They passed several dirt roads, which Emma assumed led to more houses. Emma began to wonder about the cottage that Darius and Rebecca had lived in while the castle was being built. Lord Dinswood had said that it was still standing. It was very possible that it was somewhere close by, and it seemed like a logical place for Darius to have hidden one of the sculptures. Emma planned to ask Doug about it as soon as they got to the creek. They may not have time to look for the cottage today, but they might be able to ask Lord Dinswood about it when they got back to the castle.

A few minutes later, Emma could see the turn off that led to Crawford Creek. The boys had stopped their bikes on the side of the road and were waiting for the girls to catch up with them. As soon as the girls drew even with them, the boys started off down the gravel road. Fortunately, there were grooves in the road where the gravel had been beaten down into the dirt. These ruts provided a smoother surface and thus a less bumpy ride than they would have had otherwise. Everyone made an effort to stay in these tire-worn areas, but even so, they encountered some rather rough patches causing them to slow their pace. As a result, the one-mile trip down the gravel road took twice as long as the four-mile ride down the highway. Emma held tightly to the handlebars of her bike, her arms becoming numb at the constant jarring. All of her concentration was on staying upright on her bicycle. She didn't dare look over to see how Martha was fairing for fear of wrecking. When they finally reached the creek, Emma gave a huge sigh of relief. Quickly, she got off her bike and began rubbing her arms in an effort to restore some feeling. Emma noticed the others were just as glad that the bike portion of their journey was over for the time being.

Doug suggested that they hide their bikes back in amongst the trees before heading to the arch. He wasn't worried that someone would steal them; he just didn't want anyone to see their bikes and follow them down to the arch. When they had finished hiding their bikes, they adjusted their backpacks and set off along the creek.

It was now midmorning and the temperature had already risen into the mid-eighties. The limbs of the trees along the creek bank were limp and lifeless without even the hint of a breeze to reanimate them. It wasn't long before Emma began to feel like the tree limbs.

The morning's exertions combined with the heat were beginning to sap her strength. She had just begun to think longingly of the cool water in her canteen when Doug suddenly stopped up ahead and suggested a rest.

Soon they were all sitting on the bank in the shade of one of the trees lining the north side of the creek, opposite the bluff. They sipped from their canteens and savored the cool water as they attempted to cool off. After about a fifteen-minute rest, they set off for the arch once again. As they walked, Emma began to notice the appearance of puffy white clouds in the sky. When they had set out that morning, the sky had been perfectly clear. She also noticed a slight breeze, which seemed to coincide with the arrival of the clouds. This change in the weather prompted her to ask, "Is it supposed to rain today?"

"I don't think so," Doug replied, scanning the sky. "I didn't really listen to the weather report though."

Emma said no more. They would have had to come anyway regardless of the weather. It was unlikely they would get another opportunity to get the sculpture without Doug's dad coming along—at least not in the two weeks the note had given them. Besides, a few clouds didn't necessarily mean that it was going to rain, and even if it did, a little rain never hurt anyone.

Finally, they arrived at the arch. Doug and Sebastian wasted no time. They immediately began preparing to pull the metal box from its resting place under the rock shelf. Sebastian dug the dive masks out of his pack, and Doug withdrew a long length of coiled rope with a large hook tied on the end from his. Then both boys stripped off their shirts, leaving their jean shorts to serve as swimming trunks.

"I know exactly where it is, so I'll hook the rope to the hasp on the box," Sebastian volunteered.

Doug had been prepared to do it, but Sebastian had brought up a good point. He was the only one of them that had actually seen the box in its underwater home. "Okay," he agreed reluctantly. Sebastian had previously described the box's location in some detail, and Doug knew that it was going to be tricky getting in and out of such a small space.

Sebastian adjusted one of the dive masks on his face and was just preparing to dive into the deep water next to the bluff when Doug stopped him. "Wait, Sebastian. You'd better take one of the glow sticks I brought. If the opening to the cave is as small as you said, when you go in, you'll block off all the light with your body, and you won't be able to see."

"I hadn't thought of that," Sebastian said.

Doug rummaged in his backpack for a moment until he located one of the sticks. After breaking it to make it glow, he handed it to Sebastian. With the glow stick in one hand and the hook end of the rope in the other, Sebastian dove cleanly into the water. He felt the pressure on his eardrums as he descended to the bottom of the eight-foot pool. Quickly locating the opening in the rock wall, he swam through it before he had time to change his mind. Getting the hook through the hasp on the box took longer than he'd anticipated. The hook was almost too big, so he had to really work to get it through securely. By the time he finished fastening the rope to the box, he was beginning to feel the need for air. Realizing that there was no room for him to turn around, he used his hands to push off the bottom, intending to back out of the opening. But nothing happened. Thinking that he may not have pushed hard enough the first time, he tried again but with more force. Still he remained in the same spot. He pushed two more times before he realized that the reason he wasn't making any progress was that his jean shorts were caught on something. Trying to remain calm, Sebastian reached back in an attempt to unhook himself from whatever he was hung on, but he couldn't reach back far enough. Frantic now, he began pushing off the bottom over and over again and wriggling his body, thinking that if he squirmed enough he'd be able to tear himself free. By this time, his need for air was desperate. His attempts to free himself had used up the last of his reserves. His last thought before he passed out was that this was a stupid way to die.

Doug had been watching Sebastian's progress from above. From his position, he could see Sebastian's feet and the lower part of his legs sticking out of the opening. It seemed to be taking Sebastian an awfully long time. He looked over at the girls, worry evident in his expression. When he looked back down into the water, he could see Sebastian's feet flailing violently and realized his friend was in trouble. Without bothering with a dive mask, he dove into the water and kicked hard for the bottom. Bracing his feet on either side of the opening, Doug tried to grab hold of Sebastian's wildly kicking legs but with no success. Suddenly, Sebastian went limp. At last able to get a good grip on Sebastian's legs and with adrenaline pumping furiously through his veins, Doug pulled with all he had. After a brief resistance, Sebastian came free. As soon as Sebastian's head cleared the opening, Doug grabbed his friend under his arms and swam for the surface.

The two girls were already standing on the creek bank waiting to help pull Sebastian from the water. Soon they had him laid out on the same flat rock the girls had been sitting on just moments ago. Doug felt for a pulse and checked to see if Sebastian was breathing. Martha began crying softly and saying his name over and over again in a kind of chanting prayer. Emma looked on helplessly and said a silent prayer of her own.

Doug was relieved to find a pulse, but Sebastian was not breathing. Grateful that his father had insisted on his taking a course in CPR, he began mouth-to-mouth resuscitation. He'd only given Sebastian a few breaths when he began to cough and spit up water. Doug quickly rolled him over on his side until he was finished. Slowly, Sebastian sat up and looked at the worried faces of his friends.

What happened next was totally unexpected. Martha knelt down next to Sebastian, threw her arms around him, and began crying hysterically. Her only thought was that Sebastian had almost died thinking she was mad at him. "I'm sorry, Sebastian," she sobbed into his shoulder.

For his part, Sebastian appeared to be a little dazed and unsure of what was going on. He didn't even seem to be aware that Martha was blubbering all over him. Thinking that Sebastian could probably use a little breathing room, Emma knelt down behind Sebastian so that she was facing Martha. "Sebastian's going to be okay now, Martha," Emma said quietly in an effort to calm her friend. When this did not have the desired effect, Emma tried another tack. "Martha, Sebastian could probably use some air." This last statement seemed to get through to Martha. With one last hiccup, Martha finally let go of Sebastian and stood up.

Emma looked over at Doug. He was seated on the gravel bar a few feet away with his head bowed. Emma couldn't be certain if he was praying or not, but it reminded her to send up her own prayer of praise and thanksgiving for a life spared.

When Doug had attempted to rise after reviving Sebastian, he'd found that his legs wouldn't support him. He'd managed to stagger a few feet away on wobbly legs, and then he'd had to sit down again as the reality of what had just happened began to settle in on him. After the rush of adrenaline that he'd experienced during the rescue, it seemed Doug was suffering from a mild form of shock. Although his body wasn't responding, his mind was perfectly clear. Grateful that Sebastian was still alive, he bowed his head to give thanks.

Emma's attention was drawn back to Sebastian when Martha shouted, "Sebastian, you're bleeding."

Emma was standing behind Sebastian at the time, and at Martha's exclamation, she began looking for signs of injury on Sebastian's back. Seeing that his back was clear of any wounds, she quickly ran around to where Martha was standing. Sure enough, Sebastian was bleeding from a jagged looking cut on his abdomen. The cut appeared to be about two inches long, but it was hard to tell how deep it was because of the blood. By this time, Doug was kneeling beside Sebastian, examining the wound. "Martha, get me that first aid kit you brought. I don't think it's too deep, but we probably ought to clean it and bandage it."

Thankful that she'd had the foresight to bring the kit and mentally kicking herself for not thinking of it first, Martha hurried to get her backpack. In no time, she was kneeling beside Doug with the kit in hand. Doug reached out to take the kit from Martha, but she pushed his hand away. "I'll do it," she said, surprising Doug. Seeing Martha's look of determination, Doug stood up and backed away so that Martha could scoot closer to Sebastian.

Doug looked at Sebastian with raised eyebrows. Sebastian, who was now sufficiently recovered from his brush with death to enjoy all of this attention from Martha, was smiling over the top of her bent head. Martha was busy getting antiseptic and cotton balls from the kit and thankfully didn't see his grin. With Sebastian looking on, Martha gently swabbed the wound with cotton balls soaked in antiseptic. Although it had to have stung like the dickens, Sebastian never made a sound, submitting stoically to her gentle ministrations. Martha was relieved to see that, just as Doug had suspected, the wound wasn't very deep. When Martha was finished cleaning the cut, she applied some antibiotic ointment. There were no bandages in the kit large enough to cover the wound, so she taped some gauze over it.

"That ought to do it," Martha said as she put on the last piece of tape.

"Thanks, Martha," Sebastian said.

Martha looked up at him then and saw that for once he was being totally serious. A little embarrassed by what else she saw in his expression, she busied herself packing the items she'd used back into the little white box.

"I'm sorry, Sebastian," Doug said, breaking the silence that had fallen. "I guess you scraped your stomach on the rocks when I pulled you out of the cave."

"It's okay, Doug. You saved my life. Now I owe you one," Sebastian said with a smile.

"Let's just call it even," Doug answered with a smile of his own.

"I hate to break up this meeting of the mutual admiration society, but we still need to get the sculpture out of the water," Martha said, sounding more like her usual self. While Doug and Sebastian had been talking, she had noticed the end of the rope that Sebastian had successfully hooked to the metal box. It had reminded her of their purpose in coming.

At Martha's words, Sebastian started to get up. "Don't worry, Martha. Doug and I will have that thing up here in a jiffy."

"I don't think you should get that bandage wet," Martha said.

"Doug can't do it by himself. I'll have to help him," Sebastian argued.

"I can help him," Emma said quickly. Seeing that both Doug and Sebastian were about to object, she continued. "Sebastian has already done the hard part. Now all we have to do is drag the box out of the cave, and then everyone can help pull it to the surface."

Sebastian was opening his mouth to disagree when Doug forestalled him. "She's right, Sebastian. You did the hard part. Emma and I can handle the rest." Then he looked over at Emma. "We can take turns dragging the box till we get it free of the cave. Just grab the rope and brace your feet on the cliff. Pull until you need air, and then we can switch places."

Emma nodded her understanding. Saying that he would go first, Doug dove into the water. The others watched from above as he strained on the rope. At first it seemed that nothing was happening.

Emma began to worry that the box was hung on some rocks. Suddenly, Doug's upper body fell back a bit as the box began to move. Reaching further up the rope, Doug gave another mighty pull, and then he was kicking for the surface and some needed air.

Emma dove into the water before Doug's head cleared the surface. After grabbing hold of the rope, Emma braced her feet on the bluff as Doug had done and pulled with all she had. She was gratified to feel the box moving. She was able to drag it to the outer edge of the little cave before she too had to get some air. As she swam toward the surface, Doug dove past her on his way back down. In no time, Doug had the box completely clear of the bluff. He appeared a moment later with the end of the rope in his hands.

"Doug and I can take it from here," Sebastian said. He had anticipated Doug's return and was already standing at the edge of the water, ready to grab hold of the rope.

Emma, who was still trying to catch her breath, didn't argue.

"Why don't we let Doug and Emma rest for a minute? You and I can handle this part," Martha interjected as she came up to stand beside Sebastian.

Working together and with the buoyancy provided by the water, the two had the box up in no time. Quickly, they pulled it to the edge of the creek and into shallow water. Doug helped Sebastian drag it onto the gravel bar as Emma went to get the crowbar out of Doug's backpack.

The others held their breaths as Doug applied the crowbar to the rusted hasp of the padlock. On the third try, it broke free with a dull clunking sound. Doug lifted the lid of the metal box. It was filled with straw just like the one in which the sculpture of Ruth had been found. With shaking hands, Doug swept some of the straw away to reveal an object wrapped in linen cloth. No one uttered a sound as Doug gently lifted the object and began to free it from its blanket of linen. Soon, he had exposed the treasure within—a polished white marble figure of a woman.

"Which one is it?" Martha asked quietly.

"I don't know," Doug answered. Carefully, he examined the sculpture to see if Marnatti had left any clues as to the identity of his creation.

"Look around the base," Martha suggested.

"Maybe it says who it is on the bottom," Sebastian said when the base failed to produce anything useful.

Carefully, Doug turned the sculpture upside down so he could look on the bottom. Emma and Martha let out of little gasp of surprise when Doug's action revealed a sweeping *S* carved in the center.

"It's Sarah," Sebastian said.

Having verified the identity of the woman Marnatti had sculpted, Doug turned the figure back over so that they could examine it more closely. It was similar to the sculpture of Ruth they'd seen in Lord Dinswood's suite a few nights back, but there were a few differences. Where Ruth's head had been covered with a scarf, Sarah's flowing tresses were free of any encumbrance. Sarah was dressed differently too. She was wearing a sleeveless floor-length gown cinched at the waist with a belt that resembled a length of fine chain. The dress hugged her frame and emphasized her lovely figure. The greatest difference between the two sculptures, however, was in the face. Marnatti had given Ruth angelic features, but he had given Sarah an exquisite beauty—the kind of beauty that made fools of men. This wife of Abraham had indeed been described as very beautiful in the Bible. In fact, her beauty had sometimes caused problems for Abraham as they traveled from place to place. All of these thoughts ran through Emma's mind in quick succession as she gazed at the marble figure in Doug's hands. She glanced over at Martha to see that she was equally enthralled.

"We'd better get it wrapped up," Doug said, breaking the spell.

Martha pulled the little blanket from her backpack. A moment later, they had the sculpture wrapped and safely stowed in Doug's pack. The top of the sculpture stuck out a bit, but because it was wrapped in a blanket, no one passing by would be able to tell what it was. They'd had to remove Doug's lunch from his pack before putting the sculpture in it, and this had reminded them all that they hadn't eaten since breakfast.

"Why don't we take a break and eat lunch before we head back to our bikes?" Doug suggested.

"Sounds good to me," Sebastian readily agreed. It had been quite an eventful morning, and they still had the ride back to the castle to look forward to.

As they sat by the creek and ate their sandwiches, Emma noticed that the sun had disappeared altogether. The puffy white clouds she had observed earlier had given way to a solid mass of white. The temperature had dropped a bit as well. At least the trek back to their waiting bicycles wouldn't be as miserably hot as the walk to the arch had been. Emma just hoped there wasn't any rain on the way. They had to get back to the castle with the sculpture before Doug's dad began to worry about them. *Why do things always have to be so difficult?* Emma wondered as she took another bite of her sandwich. A moment later, Emma had to admit that despite the scare they'd had with Sebastian, one good thing had come of the morning. They had managed to rescue the sculpture of Sarah from its watery resting place, and now Doug's dad and Lord Dinswood would be safe for a while longer.

CHAPTER ELEVEN
UNFORESEEN DEVELOPMENTS

Emma decided not to mention her concern about the weather to Doug. If it decided to rain, there was nothing he could do about it anyway. He had enough on his mind without her adding to his worries. Getting the sculpture had just been the first step. Next Doug would have to signal the Reaper by hanging the school banner in his dorm window. They had all begun calling their unknown adversary the Reaper after Emma had described her impression of the hooded figure she'd seen in the library.

The note had said that after Doug gave the signal, he would be told what to do next. That was the part that worried Emma. What would the Reaper make Doug do, and would he have to do it alone? With a sigh, Emma ended her musings and began packing up the remainders of her lunch. While Sebastian and Martha did likewise, Doug loaded the now empty metal box with rocks and pushed it into the deep part of the creek next to the bluff. It was unlikely that it would be found any time soon, and it really didn't matter if it was. They had the precious cargo it had contained.

As they prepared to leave, Doug and Sebastian donned their shirts once again, and Doug put his cap on. Emma was glad not to have to look at the bandage on Sebastian's stomach anymore. It was a reminder that they had almost lost him. It would be a very long time before she would forget the way he'd looked when Doug had pulled him from the water.

Without a word to the others, Doug set off along the creek bank back the way they had come. Emma, Martha, and Sebastian dutifully followed. They were almost to the gravel road when it began to sprinkle. Although they all noticed, no one made a comment, perhaps superstitiously thinking that if they didn't mention it, it would soon stop. This was not to be the case, however. They had gotten on their bikes and were traveling on the gravel road back to the highway when it began to come down a little faster.

"Great! This is all we need," Sebastian complained.

"I'm sorry, guys," Doug said. "I guess I should have listened to the weather report."

"It's not your fault. We'd have had to come anyway," Martha said, putting voice to what Emma had been thinking earlier.

Nothing more was said for a while as everyone struggled to remain upright on their bikes. The rain was beginning to soften the dirt under their tires. Emma just hoped they could make it to the highway before it got too muddy to ride. She wasn't looking forward to having to walk her bike the rest of the distance to the main road. As it turned out, they were able to make it to the paved road. Cautiously, they turned onto the highway. The pavement was wet and slippery, but fortunately, there was no traffic. Doug slowed his pace to compensate for the poor road conditions, and they continued to ride in the steady downpour. After what seemed an eternity to Emma, the spires of the castle came into view, and Emma knew they were about a mile from the drive leading up to the academy. By this time, they were soaked through, but Emma consoled herself with the fact that they were almost there. She'd no sooner had the thought than the sky was lit with a jagged streak of lightening. A loud crash of thunder followed seconds later. All of a sudden, what had previously been a steady rain turned into a deluge. The rain began coming down so hard and fast that Emma could no longer see where she was going. The rain beat at her as she continued to pedal, stinging her face and the exposed skin of her arms and legs.

Up ahead, she could hear Doug shouting, but the combination of wind and rain made it impossible to tell what he was saying. A few seconds later, she almost rode past him. He and Sebastian had pulled off onto the shoulder of the road. Quickly, she applied her brakes and felt her bike sliding out from under her. She hit the pavement hard and skidded along with her bike for a few feet before coming to rest on the shoulder of the road just slightly ahead of where Doug had been waiting. Doug was there in an instant to help her up.

"Emma, are you okay?" he asked, as rain dripped steadily from the brim of his cap.

For a moment, Emma was too busy examining her injuries to reply. She had some nasty- looking scrapes on her right forearm, right thigh, and lower right leg. Thankfully nothing appeared to be broken. Her scrapes were raw and bleeding slightly. The unrelenting rain was making them sting even more. Determined to put on a brave face, Emma sucked in her breath. The pain was bearable, and there was nothing she could do about it now anyway.

"I'm really sorry, Emma. I didn't mean to make you wreck. I was just going to tell everyone that I think we should get off the highway. With it raining so hard, cars might not be able to see us, and the lightning makes it too dangerous for us to be out in the open."

"It's okay, Doug," Emma said loudly in an effort to be heard over the sounds of the storm. "I'm all right." Her concern now shifted to Martha. She hadn't seen her waiting with Doug and Sebastian when she had ridden past them on the side of the road.

"Where's Martha?" she shouted.

"I'm here," Martha answered. She had been riding behind Emma. Although Martha had also had to brake quickly, she'd managed to keep her bike upright. She'd come along just in time to see Emma wreck. "Are you sure you're okay?"

"I'm fine," Emma said a second time. "I just hope my bike isn't messed up."

Doug knew that Emma's injuries, although not serious, had to be painful. But she was determined not to cry. Once again admiring her courage and satisfied that she was essentially all right, Doug picked up her bike and began looking it over. Other than some scratches on the frame and right-side handlebar, it was in good condition. Relieved that it was still in working order, Doug looked over at Martha and repeated what he'd just told Emma.

"What are we going to do?" Martha asked when Doug had finished.

"I think we should turn down this side road here."

For the first time, the others noticed that Doug had stopped at the turn off to one of the many side roads they'd passed on their way to the arch earlier that morning.

"What's down this way?" Sebastian asked.

"I don't know, but at least we'll be off the main highway. Maybe we'll find a barn or something we can take shelter in."

As the others had no better suggestions, they got back on their bikes just as another flash of lightning brightened the sky overhead. The sharp crack of thunder that followed had them pedaling furiously down the side road. The road was muddy and slowed their progress more than Emma would have liked. At least the rain had let up a little, so they could see where they were going. As they struggled along, they looked among the trees on either side of the road for anything they could use as shelter. In a few minutes, they passed a sign that stated that the road on which they were traveling was a dead end. *Could things get any worse!* Emma wondered angrily. Sebastian must have been thinking the same thing. But never being one to keep his thoughts to himself, he didn't hesitate to voice his complaint.

"This day just keeps getting better!" Sebastian shouted with an angry snort loud enough to be heard over the rain.

Ignoring Sebastian, Doug continued to lead them down the road until they encountered a gate that ran the width of the road. A sign on the gate warned, "Private Property—no trespassing."

While the others were wondering what to do next, Doug said, "I was hoping this was the road." Then he turned to Sebastian, Martha, and Emma. "Just leave your bikes and follow me."

"You want to tell us what's going on?" Martha asked as she laid her bike down.

"Let's get out of this rain first, and then I'll tell you," Doug answered.

Emma had questions of her own, but she trusted Doug. Without a word, she put her bike down next to Martha's and stood ready to follow Doug. When he saw that everyone was ready, he climbed over the gate and began walking along a narrow dirt road that led uphill. Trees on either side of the little lane prevented them from seeing what was at the top of the hill, but Doug seemed to know where he was going. Suddenly, they reached the end of the lane and found themselves standing in a clearing. In the center of that clearing stood a two-story stone cottage with a slate roof and latticed windows. The windows on the first floor had been boarded up, and some of those on the second floor were broken, but the lattices remained. The cottage was obviously vacant and in a horrible state of disrepair.

Boldly, Doug led them up the front steps to a wooden door badly in need of a good sanding and some paint. The door was locked when Doug tried the handle, but that didn't deter him. After shrugging out of his backpack and handing it to Sebastian, he began trying to bust the door open by repeatedly ramming it with his shoulder.

"Doug, what are you doing?" Martha asked. "This is private property. We could get arrested for breaking and entering."

Doug said nothing for a moment as he continued to ram the door with all he had. His efforts were rewarded with a creaking sound and on the next shoulder thrust the door burst open. For some reason, Emma's first thought was that they shouldn't go into someone's house with muddy shoes. Looking down at her feet, she saw that they'd been standing on the porch long enough for the rain to wash away most of the mud. Ridiculous as it sounded, even to her own ears, Emma heard herself asking, "Shouldn't we take off our shoes before we go in?"

Doug, who had already gone inside, looked back at Emma and smiled. "It's okay, Emma. I don't think we're going to ruin anything in here."

"What is this place?" Emma asked as she stepped into the dim interior. With the windows all boarded up, it was hard to tell what the inside of the cottage looked like. As if reading her thoughts, Doug began removing some of the wooden planks that had been nailed across the windows. The boards looked as old as the rest of the cottage and the nails holding them in place were almost rusted through, so Doug wasn't having any trouble pulling them off. Once the windows were free of their ugly coverings, Emma could see that they were standing in a small entryway. To her left was a fairly large room with a fireplace on the far wall. On her right was a smaller room that also contained a fireplace. An old wood-burning stove sat in the corner. This room had undoubtedly served as a kitchen many long years ago. Directly ahead was a badly deteriorated staircase. Although Emma would have loved to look around the second floor, she knew she would be risking life and limb if she tried to climb that set of rickety stairs. She'd just have to content herself with poking around the first floor. A short hallway to the right of the stairs led to a small room that had probably been a bedroom. On the other side of the hall was a room that looked about the right size for a washing room. Even in its current dilapidated condition, Emma found the cottage charming. She couldn't help thinking how sad it was that the owner had let it fall into such ruin.

While Emma had been conducting her tour, the others had been doing some looking around of their own. When they'd satisfied their curiosity and were once again all assembled in the entryway, Emma asked her question again. "Doug, what is this place? Do you know who owns it?"

"Yes, I do," he answered with a smile. He continued to look at her in a way that suggested she should know where they were too. Emma furrowed her brow for a moment, and then suddenly her eyes widened.

"You don't mean..." she began. Doug was already nodding his agreement before she could finish her sentence.

"You guys want to let us in on what you're talking about?" Sebastian asked, looking from one to the other and then over at Martha.

Martha, however, had hit upon the answer almost at the same instant as Emma. Sebastian seemed to be the only one still in the dark. Martha couldn't help asking, "You're kidding, right? Don't tell me you still haven't figured it out?" When Sebastian continued to look at her with a blank expression, Martha gave an exaggerated sigh and, with barely concealed impatience, said, "We're standing in Darius and Rebecca's cottage. You know—the one they lived in while the castle was being built."

"How do you know that?"

"Doug just told us."

"No, he didn't," Sebastian argued.

Doug interrupted before Martha could reply. "I didn't realize we were on the right gravel road until we got to the dead end and the private property sign. Lord Dinswood told me about the cottage a few days before you guys arrived at the school. He said he was planning to have it restored and modernized. I think he wants to live in it when it's done. I asked him where it was, and he described its location as about a mile from the castle down a gravel road on the north side of the highway. He said the road comes to a dead end and an unpaved driveway leads to the cottage at the top of the hill."

The others were silent as they digested what Doug had told them. It occurred to Emma that one of the other five sculptures might well be somewhere near or in the cottage. They ought to look for it while they had the chance. There was no telling when they would get another opportunity to come to the cottage without a chaperone.

Similar thoughts must have been running through Doug's mind because a moment later, he said, "You know this was one of the places on our list. We might as well look for the third sculpture while we're here. If we can find another one today, we'll be ahead of the game when the Reaper sets the next deadline."

"I'm game," Sebastian said. He was in no hurry to go back outside in the rain.

"Do you have any idea where we should look?" Martha asked.

"Not really," Doug replied with a shake of his head. "But I don't think Darius would have made it easy to find."

"No offense, Doug, but that's not very helpful," Martha remarked with a frown.

"Actually, it is," Emma said slowly. "If what Doug said is true, that pretty well eliminates anywhere inside the cottage." When the others continued to look at her skeptically, Emma explained. "Well, if you think about it, wouldn't Darius have realized that the cottage could be torn down sometime in the future? He wouldn't want to risk the sculpture being discovered or destroyed in the process. I agree with Doug. Darius hid the sculptures intending that they would remain hidden forever as a tribute to Rebecca."

THE MISSING MORTALS | 115

"If that's true, he didn't do a very good job of it," Sebastian said with a smirk. "We've already found two."

"Where do you suggest we look?" Martha asked at almost the same time. Then hearing Sebastian's comment, she raised her eyebrows and couldn't help correcting him. "Technically, we've only discovered one. The first one was found by the construction crew."

"Good grief, Martha, I just meant that two of the sculptures have been found."

"Well, I'd say Darius did a pretty good job of hiding the sculptures. Especially when you consider the fact that it took almost three hundred years to find the first one."

"So what's your point?"

"My point is that we shouldn't get too cocky and think that it's just going to be a breeze finding the other sculptures."

"I never said it was going to be easy," Sebastian countered, beginning to get angry.

Martha took a deep calming breath. For what seemed the hundredth time that afternoon, she pictured Sebastian as he lay unconscious on the rock by the creek. Determined not to fight with him anymore, she said slowly, "I know, Sebastian. I just don't want any of us to get hurt. You almost drowned getting the last one, and I don't want to go through anything like that ever again."

Surprised by Martha's words, Sebastian's anger drained quickly away. She was right after all. When he told her so, it was her turn to be surprised. No one said anything for a moment. It seemed that his near-death experience had changed him, and they were all trying to adjust to this new Sebastian.

Martha finally broke the silence by repeating her earlier question. "Well, where should we start?"

"Well, if not in the cottage, how about under it?" Emma suggested.

"You mean like buried beneath the floor or in the basement? Does this place even have a basement?" Martha asked in quick succession. She didn't remember finding a door to a basement during her brief tour of the cottage.

"I don't think so," Doug answered. "But I think it has a root cellar. I saw the entrance to one behind the cottage when we first got here."

"What's a root cellar?" Sebastian asked.

"It's a dirt room where they used to store fruits and vegetables in the old days. It kept them from freezing in the winter and spoiling in the summer. They were usually dug into the side of a hill like the one Doug's talking about," Martha answered for him. She had also noticed the root cellar upon arrival.

"Well, I don't think it's very likely Darius would have put a sculpture in there. It would be too easy to find."

"He could have buried it in there," Martha pointed out when Sebastian had finished his objections.

Sebastian wrinkled his nose in distaste. Digging around in an old musty dirt room was not his idea of a good time. Maybe they would find the sculpture before they had to resort to looking in the root cellar.

Doug suggested they split up and begin exploring the grounds around the cottage. Not having any better ideas, the others agreed. The rain had stopped, and the sun was trying to peek out as they wandered around in the wet grass for several minutes. Doug and Sebastian took a quick look inside the root cellar, but other than a few old gardening tools, it appeared to be empty. Finally, Martha broke the silence. "This is impossible. We'll never find it like this."

Doug sighed. "You're right. If it's buried, we'll need the metal detector to find it. I'm afraid we're wasting our time."

"I'm sorry, Doug," Emma said. She knew how worried he was about his dad and Lord Dinswood.

"We can come back tomorrow and find it with the metal detector," Sebastian suggested. Even as he said it, he knew there was no way they could get the detector without Dean Harwood's knowledge. Then Dean Harwood would insist upon coming along with them.

"Let's just get back to the castle," Doug said, running a hand through his hair. It had been a long tiring day, and right now, he just wanted to get back to the school.

As they went back inside the cottage to get the backpacks they'd left on the floor, Doug consoled himself with the fact that at least they had found one sculpture and would be able to make the first deadline. There would be plenty of time to worry about the next deadline later.

They were leaving the cottage when it happened. Martha was trying to get her backpack on her shoulders when her first aid kit fell out. The kit came open when it hit the ground, and an untimely gust of wind began blowing its contents in every direction. With a cry of dismay, Martha dropped her pack on the ground and began trying to round up the scattered items. The others came quickly to her aid, chasing down and grabbing what they could. The wind, however, refused to cooperate, blowing packets of gauze as far as the stand of trees behind the cottage. Determined not to let them get away, Sebastian followed. He had just reached the trees when suddenly, with a loud cry, he disappeared from view.

"Sebastian!" Martha cried as she, Emma, and Doug raced to see what had happened to him.

They found him lying on his stomach in the tall grass. When he rolled over to get up, Emma saw what he had tripped over. Lying at his feet was a flat concrete slab that Emma immediately recognized as a grave marker. Emma frowned as she tried to figure out who could possibly be buried here. Darius and Rebecca didn't have any children when they lived in the cottage, and it couldn't be either of them. Emma bent down to get a closer look at the marker. Maybe it would have a name. By this time, the others had noticed it too and were kneeling over it.

"It's got a blackbird and a rose carved on it," Sebastian remarked.

"That's not a blackbird," Emma responded as a tingle of excitement began to spread through her body. She looked at Martha knowing she would understand what she was about to say. "It's a raven."

Martha nodded knowingly, while Doug and Sebastian continued to look on in confusion. "Do you think one of the sculptures could be buried here?" Martha asked Emma.

"Why else would there be a marker?"

Doug's eyes widened as he began to understand what the girls were saying. A second later, he was kicking himself for not realizing it sooner. The pirate ship Darius had sailed was named the Raven, and in one of Rebecca's journals, she had mentioned that Darius liked to call her his Irish Rose. Energized by the discovery, Doug raced to the root cellar with Sebastian following closely on his heels. He remembered seeing a shovel among the gardening tools. As he ran, he explained the significance of the symbols on the stone to Sebastian.

In moments, he was back at the marker with shovel in hand. Sebastian managed to lift the stone clear, and Doug immediately began digging where the stone had been. The recent rain had made the ground soft, so Doug was able to make quick progress. He had dug to a depth of four feet when the next shovel thrust resulted in a clanging sound. They had found another metal box. With all four of them working together, they were able to pull the box from its resting place. It looked exactly like the two others they'd seen. The rusty padlock broke easily after a few hard raps with the shovel, and soon Doug was holding up another of Marnatti's magnificent sculptures. He held it up triumphantly, feeling as if a great weight had suddenly been lifted from his shoulders. An engraving on the bottom identified the sculpture as Martha. The figure was dressed in a long robe and was holding a bowl in one hand and a spoon in the other. On her head was a long flowing scarf. Emma remembered that Jesus had often eaten with Martha, Mary, and Lazarus when he was in their hometown, Bethany. This would explain the bowl and spoon Martha was holding. It seemed as if Marnatti had captured her in the middle of preparing a meal.

Sebastian stood by quietly, while the others talked excitedly. Finally, Martha noticed him and couldn't help asking, "Sebastian, why aren't you saying anything?"

"I don't understand why there was a marker for this sculpture and not for any of the others."

It was a valid question, and the others were silent for a moment as they tried to figure out the answer. It was Doug who finally hit upon a plausible explanation.

"You know, there may have been a marker for the one behind the school, but it would have been out in the open—not protected by trees like this one. Exposed to the elements for three hundred years, the symbols would have faded away. It would have looked like any other flat stone."

What Doug said sounded reasonable. The entire area around the academy was set on bedrock composed of limestone. This explained why there were so many caves and also why rocks were present in abundance. Doug had heard the school's gardener complain more than once that the things that seemed to grow best in the flowerbeds were rocks. No matter how many he removed from the garden each day, the next day there were always more in their place. The construction crew wouldn't have noticed anything out of the ordinary when they were digging the foundation for the gymnasium. If what Doug had said was true, the marker would have been worn smooth and would not have looked any different from any other flat rock.

Although he agreed with Doug's hypothesis, Sebastian continued to look confused. "But what about the sculpture at the arch? There wasn't a marker for it."

It was Martha who answered this time. "Darius wouldn't have needed one. The arch itself was the marker. From there, he'd know exactly where he'd hidden the sculpture of Sarah."

"I get it," Sebastian said with a nod. "Now, I only have one other question."

"What's that?" the others asked in unison.

"Why leave markers at all? I thought Darius didn't want the sculptures to ever be found."

"We'll probably never know for sure, but I have a theory," Doug replied after a moment's thought. "Lord Dinswood said that the night Rebecca died Darius went crazy with grief, but maybe even in his grief, he realized that someday he might wish he had the sculptures back again."

Believing she understood what Doug was trying to say, Emma said, "You mean, years later when his grief wasn't so fresh and painful, he might want the sculptures to remember Rebecca by?"

Doug simply nodded, and as he did so, Emma was once again struck by his maturity. It was amazing how Doug seemed to be able to connect so easily with the thoughts and feelings of someone who had lived so long ago—someone he'd never known. If she didn't know better, it was almost as if Doug himself was a descendant of Darius. Following closely on the heels of that thought was the realization that she was letting her overactive imagination have too much free reign. Smiling at her own foolishness, Emma followed the others who were already heading back to the cottage with their newest find.

A short time later, with the second sculpture of the day wrapped in Doug's shirt and stowed safely in Sebastian's backpack, they walked down the hill to their waiting bikes and headed back to the castle. It had been a tiring but successful day.

CHAPTER TWELVE
THE FIRST DELIVERY

When they got back to the school, Doug and Sebastian took both sculptures to their room. They would be safe there, at least until Phil and Tom returned at the start of school. Phil and Tom had been Doug and Sebastian's roommates last year and were going to be again this year. Doug decided not to signal the Reaper until just before the deadline. If they signaled their success too early, the Reaper might not give them as much time to find the next sculpture. Of course, they already had the next sculpture, but the Reaper didn't know that.

The remainder of the time before the start of school was spent taking Dean Harwood to various fake locations. More often than not, Miss Jennings accompanied them. It was becoming increasingly clear, at least to Emma and Martha, that the two of them had feelings for each other. If Doug realized it, he never commented on it, and Emma still hadn't gotten up the nerve to ask him about it. She didn't want to stick her nose in where it wasn't wanted, so she bided her time. Someday Doug would open up and talk to her about it.

Emma's injuries continued to be painful for the next couple of days. The one on her thigh was a particular problem because her shorts rubbed against it. Each day after showering, Emma put anti-biotic ointment on it. Then Martha would help her tape gauze over it to ease the discomfort. Fortunately, it healed quickly and seemed to go unnoticed by Dean Harwood and Miss Jennings when they were all together on a search.

As they had hoped when they had first hatched their plan, after visiting the fifth site with no success, Dean Harwood became convinced that the other sculptures were no longer in existence. On the evening of their last outing, Dean Harwood visited Lord Dinswood to deliver the bad news. As far as Doug's dad was concerned, the search for the missing Mortals was over. Doug hated disappointing Lord Dinswood, but under the circumstances, there was nothing else that could be done. Lord Dinswood's safety and that of his father had to come first. Even so, Doug's heart ached for the old man he'd come to love.

The day before the Reaper's deadline, Doug hung the Dinswood Academy banner in his window. The next morning when he checked his mailbox, he found a sealed envelope. Without opening it, he went in search of Sebastian, Emma, and Martha. When they were all assembled in the lounge, Doug showed them the envelope.

"Where did you find it?" Martha asked.

"In my mailbox."

Just inside the double doors in both the boys' and girls' dorms were a bank of small rectangular mailboxes—one for each student. It was how the academy's students received their mail. The boxes had the names of their owners on them and were basically just open cubbyholes. Anyone with access to the dorms would also have access to any of the mailboxes.

"What does it say?" Sebastian asked impatiently once Martha's question had been answered.

Without a word, Doug opened the envelope and drew out the note inside. He quickly read it and then handed it to the others so they could read it for themselves. The note was brief and to the point. It instructed Doug to take the sculpture to the storage room beneath the kitchen and place it in an old wooden barrel that could be found at the very back of the room. Never having been in the storage room, Emma had no idea what the note was talking about. "Do you know where this barrel is?" she asked Doug.

"No, I've never been down there," Doug answered with a shake of his head.

"I have," Sebastian said proudly. "But I don't know about any barrel."

"Well, that's just great!" Martha exclaimed sarcastically. "Why don't you tell us what you do know?"

Ignoring Martha's tone, Sebastian answered with a smile, "I know it's never locked."

That got Martha's attention. Last year, Sebastian had chosen cooking as his hobby class. His dream was to someday become a great chef. As part of his cooking class, he had gotten to spend quite of bit of time in the school's kitchen. Although she'd never thought about it before, it made sense that Sebastian would have also become familiar with the area where all the food was stored. Maybe he didn't know about the barrel because he'd never had occasion to go to the very back of the large room. Martha just hoped that they would be able to find it. The trick was going to be finding a time when the cooks weren't around. That would probably mean getting into the storage room in the evening after the cooks had finished for the day.

"I guess I'd better deliver the sculpture of Sarah tonight after the cooks have gone," Doug said. "I shouldn't have any trouble finding the barrel."

"I'm going with you," Sebastian immediately insisted.

"We're going too," Emma quickly added, feeling she could safely speak for Martha. She looked over at Martha for confirmation and saw her nodding her agreement.

"Look, guys, I really appreciate it, but the note says for me to deliver the sculpture." Doug was grateful for their offers of help, but he didn't want to risk angering the Reaper and thereby endangering his dad or Lord Dinswood.

"The note doesn't specifically say you have to deliver it alone," Emma pointed out. This was exactly what she had feared, that Doug would think he had to do this by himself.

"The Reaper must know we're all working together to find the sculptures. Surely, he would expect us to do this part together too," Martha added in an attempt to persuade Doug to let them help.

"Look, Doug, we're not going to let you do this alone," Sebastian said in a no-nonsense tone that the others had never heard him use before. "If the Reaper doesn't want us along, then he'd better say so in the next note. This time we're coming."

Doug looked at the determined faces of his friends as he tried to decide what to do. What they had said made sense. The note didn't actually state that he had to deliver the sculpture alone. As long as the Reaper received the goods, why would he care who brought it to the drop site? Doug wasn't afraid to carry out the task by himself, but he would rather have the company of his friends. After another moment, Doug relented. "Okay, you guys win. We'll go together."

Emma let out the breath she'd been holding, her shoulders sagging in relief. She had been certain that Doug would not agree to let them go with him. She could tell from their expressions that Sebastian and Martha were equally relieved.

Sebastian clapped Doug on the back with a smile and said, "Okay, let's plan our strategy."

Compared to some of the things they'd had to plan last year when they were hunting for the treasure, this was going to be a piece of cake. After a brief discussion, it was agreed that they would all make their way to the kitchen just after dark. The halls would be clear of any traffic at that time as most of the staff would have retired to their rooms, and at the moment, there were no other students to worry about. Although the school employed three security guards, they didn't begin their rounds until after ten o'clock. Emma realized that once school started, it was going to be a bit more difficult to get the sculptures to the storage room, especially since Bobby Wilcox had promised at the end of school last year that he would be watching their every move. Oh well, they'd just have to worry about that when the time came. Right now, they needed to focus on delivering the first sculpture to the Reaper.

The rest of the day passed quickly. Sebastian suggested that they go swimming one last time. It was a sunny day, and the weatherman on the radio had promised a temperature in the upper eighties, so the others readily agreed. It was their last full day alone together before the start of school, so they made the most of it. The next day would be Friday, and the new seventh graders would be arriving for orientation. The rest of the student body would begin arriving on Saturday and Sunday. School would officially begin on Monday.

There was a part of Emma that was eager for the new school year to begin, but there was also a part that hated to see the summer end. She was going to miss the freedom they had enjoyed the last couple of weeks. When school started, their wanderings would once again be confined to the school grounds. Sneaking off to look for the remaining sculptures would mean breaking a long-standing school rule and facing possible expulsion from the academy. Although they'd broken school rules in the past, it was never something that Emma enjoyed. This time, however, they really had no choice. Two lives hung in the balance.

Later that evening, just after dark, Emma and Martha crept from their room to the double doors that marked the entrance to the girls' dorms in Brimley Hall. Martha pushed one of the doors open just enough for her to take a quick peek down the main hall. Seeing that it was clear, she pushed the door open the rest of the way and motioned for Emma to follow. Their sneakers were nearly sound-less on the polished floor as they quickly made their way past the library and lounge to the kitchen on the southeast side of the cas-tle's ground floor. Even so, Emma didn't relax until they were safely inside the kitchen. The boys had not arrived yet, so the girls waited quietly. Fortunately, there was still enough light coming in through the kitchen's south-facing windows to allow Emma to get an idea of the room's general layout. There were several industrial-sized ovens in a row in the center of the room. On either side of the ovens were rows of stainless-steel countertops. Numerous pots and pans hung from hooks above the counters. Several large sinks ran along the west wall of the kitchen. Industrial-sized stainless-steel refrigerators and freezers ran along the east wall. During mealtimes, a portion of the north side of the kitchen opened into the dining hall and con-sisted of a long buffet table containing warmers from which the food could be served. A partition of glass separated the students from the food much like a salad bar in a restaurant. A large metal roll-down door that reminded Emma of a garage door closed this area off when not in use. The appliances gleamed in the meager light coming in through the windows, and everything looked clean and spotless. She was just beginning to wonder where the door to the storage room was when the boys arrived. Doug entered first with the sculpture wrapped in a sheet. Sebastian followed closely behind.

"Where's the storage room?" Emma asked Sebastian immedi-ately upon seeing the boys.

"It's to the left of the last refrigerator. Just follow me," Sebastian replied, enjoying his role as leader. As they were now standing in the opposite corner of the kitchen, Emma immediately understood why she couldn't see the door to the storage room. The ovens were block-ing her view.

No one spoke as they all followed Sebastian to the far wall lined with refrigerators and freezers. Just as Sebastian had said, there was a door next to the last refrigerator. Without hesitation, Sebastian grabbed the doorknob. Emma held her breath. Sebastian had told them that this door was never locked, but he had been wrong before. She needn't have worried though. The knob turned easily in his hand, and in seconds he was pulling the door open. Before heading down the stairs, Sebastian flipped a switch just to the right of the door, and a light came on. He then led them down a wooden staircase and flipped another light switch at the bottom of the stairs. Two banks of lights came on, and they found themselves in a huge windowless underground room. The room contained row upon row of shelves all filled with canned goods, sugar, flour, and an assortment of other food items for the upcoming school year. Along the walls were more refrigerators and freezers, which were no doubt also well stocked. Emma was amazed at the amount of food stored down here. It looked like enough food to feed the academy's students and staff for an entire year. Considering the school's location in the mountains and the harsh winters it experienced, it made sense that the school wouldn't be able to rely on weekly deliveries of groceries and would have to keep a rather substantial supply of food on hand.

"Where's the barrel, Sebastian?" Martha asked, interrupting Emma's musings. Emma had been so busy looking around that, for a moment, she'd forgotten their reason for being there. Feeling a little guilty, she headed to the back of the room in search of the barrel the Reaper had described in his note.

Doug, however, had gotten there ahead of her and was shaking his head in disbelief.

"What's the matter, Doug?" Emma asked with a sinking feeling.

"See for yourself. There's no barrel."

"What?" Sebastian asked in disbelief. He had come up behind Emma just in time to hear Doug's statement. "There's got to be a barrel here somewhere."

"Well, there's not," Doug said angrily, running a hand through his hair in frustration.

"I don't get it. Why would the Reaper tell us to put the sculpture in a barrel that doesn't exist?" Sebastian asked, beginning to get angry himself. Why couldn't things ever be easy? Why did they always have to be so difficult?

"Hold on here," Martha said in a calming tone. "Before we get too excited, let's think. Exactly what did the note say?"

"It said to put the sculpture in the old wooden barrel in the back of the storage room beneath the kitchen," Doug said, pulling the note from his pocket. "See for yourself."

Martha took the note from Doug and read it for the second time. In a moment, she looked up and said, "That's what it says all right, so what are we missing?"

"We aren't missing anything!" Doug shouted, causing Martha to flinch in surprise.

Emma had never seen Doug so angry. He was normally even-tempered and easygoing. No one said anything for a long moment. It was so unlike Doug to behave this way. They were all too shocked to speak.

Doug, who had been standing with his head bowed, sighed loudly and seemed to be making an effort to pull himself together. Finally, he raised his head and said quietly, "I'm sorry, Martha. I shouldn't have yelled at you. You were only trying to help." Emma was certain she could see unshed tears glistening in his eyes. He was under more stress than any of them had realized.

"It's okay, Doug," Martha replied.

"No, it's not. It's never okay to talk to your friends like that." Doug would have liked to have said more but didn't trust himself to continue.

Relieved that the old Doug was back, Sebastian put a hand on his shoulder and said, "We'll figure this out, Doug. We always do."

"Yeah, Doug, we won't quit until we find that stupid barrel," Martha agreed, putting a comforting hand on Doug's other shoulder.

Without a word, Emma came up behind Doug and put a hand on his back until they were all standing around Doug in a manner that reminded her of laying hands on the sick. Doug bowed his head again and struggled to get a grip on his emotions. He didn't deserve friends like these, but even so, he sent up a prayer of thanks for them. It was in that moment that an idea came to him. He raised his head suddenly, startling those around him. "Could there be another room besides this one?"

"I don't know," Sebastian answered. "This is the only one I've ever been in."

"Look for another door," Doug said. "It could be behind something. If it's got stuff like an old wooden barrel in it, it's probably not been used in a long time."

Emma found herself getting caught up in Doug's reasoning. What he said made sense. Everything in the room they were currently in was relatively new. Why would anyone keep an old barrel in it? There must be a door to another room somewhere. The note had said that the barrel was at the back of the room, so if there was another room, the door leading to it should be along the back wall. Emma began searching along the back wall, peering behind the shelves and other objects that lined it. The others were doing likewise.

A moment later, Sebastian shouted, "I found it!"

Quickly, the others rushed to his side. Sebastian had found an old wooden door behind one of the room's many refrigerators. The refrigerator was plugged into an outlet just to the left of the door and was tall enough that it hid the door from view.

"I owe you another one, Sebastian," Doug said.

"Let's just hope the barrel's in here," Martha said, crossing her fingers.

"It's gotta be," Sebastian exclaimed.

Together, he and Doug rolled the refrigerator forward so they could open the door. It swung open on rusty hinges with a loud creak. It was apparent from the door's condition that it hadn't been used for some time. The room inside was dark and had an earthy smell. A shaft of light from the storage room revealed a single bare bulb hanging from a beam in the center of the room. Without a word, Doug walked over to the bulb and pulled the string. The light from the bulb showed old wooden shelves lining the walls on either side. Along the back wall, standing next to another door, was an old oak barrel.

Emma could have cried in relief, and she was certain Doug was feeling the same way.

"There it is!" Sebastian couldn't help exclaiming loudly.

Doug had set the sculpture down in the storage room in order to help Sebastian move the refrigerator. He went to get it now. He was back in seconds and walked quickly over to the barrel as if he were afraid it would disappear if he didn't act immediately. Sebastian lifted the lid and watched silently as Doug laid the wrapped sculpture gently on the barrel's floor. Then Sebastian replaced the lid and dusted his hands on his pants.

"Let's get out of here. This place smells," Sebastian said with a sniff.

"It sure does," Martha agreed.

Martha, Emma, and Sebastian headed to the storage room door. Doug, however, remained by the barrel, looking curiously at the closed door beside it.

"Come on, Doug," Sebastian prompted.

"I wonder where this door goes," Doug said as if he hadn't heard Sebastian. Without waiting for a reply, he walked over to the mystery door and tried the handle. It was locked. Doug did not seem to be surprised.

Emma wanted to know what that was all about but decided she could ask him later. Right now, all she wanted to do was get out of the basement and into some fresh air. Sebastian was right; the room they'd just discovered smelled, and for some reason it was giving her the creeps.

"Come on, Doug," Sebastian urged again. This time Doug followed. After moving the refrigerator back into position, they turned off the lights and headed upstairs.

They didn't encounter anyone on their way back to their dorm rooms. Although it seemed as if they'd been in the storage room for an eternity, only fifteen minutes had elapsed.

Later that night, Doug lay in bed unable to sleep. He felt badly about the way he'd behaved earlier. He'd have to do a better job of holding himself together, or he'd never make it to the end of this terrible nightmare. There were still four more sculptures to find and deliver. Before falling asleep, he prayed for strength in the days to come.

CHAPTER THIRTEEN
WELCOME BACK

The next morning, Emma awoke with a feeling of excitement. The seventh graders would be arriving in just a few hours, and already the castle had a different feel to it, almost as if it were coming alive after a winter's sleep. Emma looked over at Martha and saw that she was beginning to stir. They might as well get up and have some breakfast before the new students arrived. It was going to be nice being eighth graders this year. No longer would they be the youngest class. Emma remembered back to that day last year when she had first arrived at the academy. She had fallen in love with the castle and its grounds at first sight, and in no time, Dinswood had begun to feel like home. Emma hoped the new arrivals would feel the same way. With a happy sigh, Emma hopped out of bed and went into the bathroom to get ready.

Doug and Sebastian were already in the dining hall by the time Emma and Martha arrived. Most of the school's teachers were also present. Emma noticed that Mr. Criderman appeared to be the only new member of the faculty. Once again, she was struck by his handsomeness and how unlike a librarian he looked. Remembering what had happened the last time the subject of Mr. Criderman had come up, Emma wisely kept her thoughts to herself.

"And so it begins," Sebastian stated as Emma and Martha took their seats on the opposite bench. "In a few short hours, we'll be overrun with seventh graders."

"We were seventh graders once," Martha couldn't help pointing out.

"Yes, but we've matured so much since then," Sebastian said in a deep voice meant to mimic Mr. Godfrey, the school's math teacher. Instead, his tone reminded Emma more of Miss Grimstock. When she told Sebastian what she was thinking, Sebastian raised his eyebrows and shuddered. "Don't remind me of Grim. It's taken me all summer to forget her."

"Well, you'd better get a grip, because we'll probably have her for history again this year," Martha stated without sympathy.

Sebastian didn't reply but merely shuddered again. Emma and Martha laughed at Sebastian's exaggerated response. Doug smiled and slapped him on the back. "It's okay, buddy. She's really not that bad."

"That's easy for you to say. She doesn't glare at you with those beady eyes of hers like she does me. I'm telling you that woman doesn't like me."

"Well, I can see her point," Martha replied and then laughed at Sebastian's shocked expression. "I'm just kidding, Sebastian."

They continued their light-hearted conversation throughout breakfast. As they were putting their trays up, Doug said, "Oh, I almost forgot. Dad wondered if we wouldn't mind showing the new students around today. I mean, they'll get the usual tour by Miss Grimstock, but they might need help finding their dorm rooms and stuff like that. Dad suggested we show them around the grounds too."

"Sounds good to me," Emma said as Sebastian and Martha nodded their agreement.

The rest of the day passed quickly as the buses began to arrive from the airport. Miss Grimstock and Dean Harwood greeted each new group. Then Doug, Sebastian, Emma, and Martha would take over. Some of the seniors were also on hand to act as guides and go over the rules with the "new recruits" as Sebastian called them.

Emma fell into bed that night tired but happy. Tomorrow was Saturday, and some of the older students would begin arriving. Clarice had called Martha earlier in the week to say that she and Susie weren't coming until Sunday. Emma and Martha would have the suite to themselves one more day. Although Clarice could be a bit of a snob, Emma was still looking forward to her return. She kept things lively with some of her outrageous statements. Susie did her best to emulate Clarice but possessed too sweet a nature to succeed fully.

Saturday dawned bright and clear. It was going to be another beautiful day. At breakfast, Doug informed them that his dad had offered to take the four of them to Windland so they could purchase their school supplies. Once again Emma was reminded of what a thoughtful man Doug's dad was. Emma had been so caught up in the search for the sculptures that she had completely forgotten about getting supplies for the upcoming school year. She could tell from their looks of surprise that Martha and Sebastian hadn't thought of it either.

Shortly after breakfast, they found themselves on the front steps of the castle waiting for Doug's dad to pull around in his silver Ford Explorer. Emma wondered if Miss Jennings would be coming along, but when Doug's dad brought the car to a stop, Emma could see that he was alone. Maybe Dean Harwood didn't think it would be appropriate for him to be dating one of the teachers while there were students in residence. Whatever the reason, the trip to Windland was made without the cheerful presence of Miss Jennings.

Windland was a small town approximately thirty miles southwest of the academy. Every weekend during the school year, weather permitting, a group of students from the academy was taken to Windland. The trips were taken by class and were designed to give students an opportunity to purchase any personal items they might need. Although it was a small town, it boasted a lodge-style motel and several businesses, including a bank and an insurance office. Lining the main street of the town was a restaurant, a candy store, a general store, and the bookstore Lord Dinswood owned.

When they arrived in Windland, Doug's dad parked the car in front of the general store. Last year, Emma had learned that the Windland General Store was a miracle of sorts. Although it occupied little space, it gave new meaning to the term "variety store." The diversity of items it contained was enough to boggle the mind. They should have no trouble finding everything they'd need for school in there.

As they got out of the car, Dean Harwood said, "Take as much time as you need. I'll wait for you in the restaurant across the street. I could use a good cup of coffee and a chance to catch up on town news." Then with a smile and a wave of his hand, he left them to do their shopping.

When they entered the store, by mutual consent, the two girls separated from the boys. "I don't want to waste time looking at fishing poles and sports gear," Martha told Emma.

"Me neither. I'd much rather waste time looking at clothes and makeup," Emma said with a laugh.

Knowing that Dean Harwood was waiting, however, kept the two girls from wasting too much time. Instead they concentrated on getting school-related items. Along with the usual paper and pencils, Emma found a backpack in the academy's colors of red, green, and black. Although the store did stock a small assortment of clothes, the girls really didn't need to shop for any as they would be wearing the school uniform most of the time. The Dinswood Academy girls' uniform consisted of a black pleated skirt, a white blouse, and a green and red plaid vest. The boys' uniform was similar except they wore black pants, and the plaid vest along with a white shirt and black tie.

When the girls had made all of their selections, they went up to the cash register to pay. Before splitting up, the boys had told them they would meet them later in the restaurant along with Doug's dad. Assuming that the boys had already finished, the girls didn't wait around in the store but left immediately after making their purchases. When they entered the restaurant, they saw that the boys had indeed finished before them. The boys wisely made no comment on the fact that the girls had taken longer and scored even more points by saying that they hadn't been waiting long. Dean Harwood just looked on with a smile. The boys were quickly getting the hang of dealing with girls.

The trip back to the school was spent showing each other what they had bought. The boys at least managed to feign interest in all of the girls' purchases, which had Dean Harwood smiling again. The boys were finally coerced into getting out the things they had selected, although neither Doug nor Sebastian could understand all the fuss over folders and pencils. By the time they arrived back at the school, Doug's patience was wearing a little thin. Using the excuse that he wanted to spend a little time with Lord Dinswood, Doug left the others saying he'd see them all at supper. Sebastian was eager to see if Phil and Tom had arrived yet, so he left the girls as well. Emma and Martha barely noticed that the boys had gone. They were eager to open all of their packages and get everything organized for school.

THE ARRIVAL OF Clarice and Susie the following afternoon was preceded by the appearance of an impressive amount of luggage. It had been the same last year. Emma had entered the suite for the first time to find her one tattered suitcase sitting forlornly on her bed, while a mound of luggage had awaited her suitemates. It

looked like Clarice had once again packed enough clothing to out-
fit Dinswood's entire student body for the whole year. Considering
the fact that they would be wearing their uniforms most of the time,
Emma didn't understand why Clarice felt compelled to bring her entire wardrobe to school. There was no use asking her about it though,
because she would undoubtedly give some caustic reply. Clarice was
from one of the richest families in the country and wanted to be sure
everyone knew it. Her father, Samuel Danvers, was the founder and
owner of Danvers Communications, a company involved in everything from computers to cell phones.

Susie Penniman's family wasn't as rich as Clarice's, but that
didn't stop Susie from imitating Clarice in everything she did.
Emma didn't hold it against her though. Susie was so sweet that it
was easy to overlook this one flaw. It was Susie who got the conversation going. "How was everyone's summer?" she asked brightly as
she opened her first suitcase.

Martha looked over at Emma before answering. They had
agreed at breakfast just that morning that it would be wise not to
mention anything about returning to school early or the task Lord
Dinswood had given them.

Realizing that Susie was still waiting for an answer, Martha answered just as brightly, "Mine was great. Dad took the whole family
to Paris, and we spent a couple of weeks in Hawaii."

"Oh, I've always wanted to go to Paris," Susie said with a sad
sigh. Then brightening once again, she added, "I've been to Hawaii
though. We spent a couple of weeks touring the islands last summer.
This summer, we spent a month in Greece. I absolutely loved it! The
water is so blue, and all of those old buildings are just fascinating.
Have you ever been there?"

Emma had to stifle a laugh at Susie's mention of old buildings.
Emma assumed she was referring to ancient Greek temples such as
the Parthenon. She looked over at Martha and saw that she was

struggling to keep from smiling. It took her a moment to compose herself enough to respond.

"No, I've never been to Greece, but I've always wanted to go."

"We're planning on going next summer," Clarice said, finally joining the conversation. "This summer, we went to Rome and then toured some of southern Italy."

Emma was definitely beginning to feel out of place. She hadn't been anywhere of note this summer except to the water park a couple of times. Her family couldn't afford elaborate vacations like those of her suitemates. Dinswood Academy was the farthest she'd ever been from home, and last year she'd taken her very first plane ride. Martha came to her rescue by changing the subject.

"Wait until you see the new librarian. You're not going to believe it."

"Yeah," Emma agreed with a grateful look at Martha. "He's young and handsome—about as far from Mr. Hodges as you can get."

The conversation centered on Mr. Criderman for the next several minutes and then switched to boys in general. Both Clarice and Susie had met cute boys on their vacations and were more than happy to fill Emma and Martha in. By the time Clarice and Susie had shared all the glorious details, they had finished unpacking and it was time for supper. As the girls entered the dining room, Clarice said, "Oh, I forgot to tell you that my cousin Preston Danvers is going to school here this year. He's a freshman. I'll introduce you to him as soon as he comes in."

The girls found seats near the door so Clarice could watch for Preston. Emma was picturing someone like Reggie, short with black-rimmed spectacles and dark curly hair, so she was totally unprepared when Clarice said, "That's him."

Emma looked at the boy Clarice was pointing to in disbelief. Preston Danvers in no way resembled Reggie. He was as tall as Doug and just as handsome, only where Doug was dark, Preston was fair.

He had a lean muscular build, blond hair, and brilliant blue eyes—the kind you'd notice from across the room. Emma heard Martha's indrawn breath of surprise and wondered briefly if she'd involuntarily made that same sound at her first sight of Preston. He appeared totally at ease as he walked into the room. It was the kind of confidence often seen in the rich and that Emma had always envied. He looked around the room and spotted Clarice. She waved for him to come over. Emma couldn't help the little shiver of excitement that coursed through her as he approached. He really was a sight to behold.

"Preston, I'd like you to meet my suitemates," Clarice began cheerfully and then introduced them each in turn. Preston smiled and politely acknowledged each introduction, but when Clarice was finished, his gaze returned to Emma. He was just opening his mouth to speak when he was forestalled by the arrival of Reggie.

"Clarice, there you are. I've been looking all over for you," Reggie exclaimed in a rush. It was almost as if he was afraid Clarice would be mad at him for not seeking her out sooner. Last year, Reggie had had quite a crush on Clarice, and if his current behavior was anything to go by, his feelings toward Clarice hadn't changed. Reggie, although short in stature and nerdish in appearance, was the sole heir to a vast fortune. His father, Jonathon Reginald Wentworth, owned a very successful chain of high-priced department stores. Clarice had always seemed to tolerate Reggie's presence better than anyone else's. At first Emma had thought it was because Reggie's family was nearly as rich as hers, but even if that had been true in the beginning, Emma was now convinced that Clarice was genuinely fond of Reggie. Although he could be a pain at times, he was also capable of being very sweet and considerate. In addition to these attributes, Reggie was extremely intelligent. Last year, he had unwittingly made the breakthrough that had enabled them to find the treasure.

"As you can see, I'm here," Clarice responded with a roll of her eyes and then went on to introduce Reggie to her cousin.

"Nice to meet you," Reggie said, vigorously shaking Preston's hand. "What brings you to Dinswood Academy?"

"After everything Clarice told me over the summer, I wanted to see the place for myself," Preston replied amicably as he tried to free his hand from Reggie's enthusiastic grip.

"Exactly what did she tell you?" Martha asked, trying to hide her concern. At the end of last term, Lord Dinswood had instructed all of those involved in the treasure hunt not to tell anyone about the secret passages located beneath the castle. He'd made them all promise upon threat of expulsion. It was a matter of safety, he'd said. Of course, rumors of the treasure had soon spread throughout the student body, but that's all they were, unsubstantiated rumors. Martha had kept her promise, and she knew that Emma, Sebastian, and Doug had too. Clarice, Susie, and Reggie were the only other students who knew what had really happened. Lord Dinswood would be extremely angry if any of them had broken their promises. Preston's next words made her realize she needn't have worried.

"She told me how great it is here! She said the teachers are top notch and the castle and grounds are beautiful. I wasn't entirely sold on the idea of coming here until she mentioned that the academy is in the process of building a first-rate sports complex."

"Oh, what sport do you play?" Sebastian asked from somewhere behind Preston. He must have arrived just in time to hear Preston's last comment. Sebastian's presence meant Doug was probably somewhere close by. Emma wondered what Doug would think of Preston Danvers.

Preston turned around to find the person who had asked the question, and as he did, Emma could see that Doug was standing next to Sebastian. Preston gave Doug a quick assessing glance before answering. "I play several sports, but my favorite is basketball," he replied after a moment.

"Did you hear that, Doug? We're going to have a great team next year when the gym is finished."

Before Doug could reply, Clarice was once again making introductions. "Sebastian, Doug, I'd like you to meet my cousin Preston Danvers. Preston, this is Sebastian Conners and Doug Harwood. Doug's father is the dean." As she spoke, her pride in her cousin was unmistakable.

Ignoring Sebastian, Preston focused his attention on Doug. "So you're the dean's son," Preston said in a way that suggested he'd heard about Doug before coming to Dinswood.

Doug merely nodded. Because she knew him so well, it was obvious to Emma that Doug did not like Preston, although she had no idea why. Thankfully, Preston didn't seem to notice Doug's unfriendliness. "I hear you're pretty good at basketball yourself."

"I do okay," Doug replied quietly. "Who told you I could play?"

"Clarice, of course," Preston replied with a smile. "She's told me so much about all of you that I feel like I already know you." His gaze took in the entire group before coming to settle on Emma once again.

Emma probably would have been embarrassed if she had noticed, but she was too busy watching Clarice and trying to make sense out of what Preston was saying. She couldn't imagine Clarice talking about Dinswood Academy in such a positive light. Clarice had spent the majority of last year complaining to anyone who would listen about anything and everything associated with the academy. She hadn't been that friendly with Emma and Martha either. The only people she'd really spent time with were Susie and Reggie. It seemed very unlikely that she would waste any of her valuable time telling Preston all about her suitemates. Last year it had seemed that Clarice loathed Dinswood Academy, and now here was her cousin going on about how much she loved it here. Something was definitely fishy, but Emma couldn't quite put her finger on it.

Emma looked over at Doug and found that he was watching her with a curious expression. She was in the process of trying to figure out the meaning of that look when a loud voice called out to Preston.

"Preston, come sit with us."

A chill went through Emma as she recognized the owner of that voice. It was Bobby Wilcox. Another chill struck her at Preston's next words. "Well, it was nice to meet all of you. I guess I'll go sit with some of the other freshman. I just met Bobby this morning. I'm in the same dorm room with him, Dave, and Brandon. I'll see you all later." Preston gave Emma another appreciative glance before turning to leave.

Flattered in spite of herself, Emma risked a look at Doug to see his reaction. As before, his expression was hard to decipher, but one thing was coming through loud and clear. Doug had absolutely no use for Preston Danvers. The fact that Preston was rooming with Bobby didn't help matters. They would all have to be very careful whenever Preston was around.

Emma assumed that after Preston's departure, Doug and Sebastian would sit with them, but instead they went over to where Phil and Tom were sitting. Emma tried not to read too much into Doug's hasty departure. After all, he hadn't seen Phil and Tom for three months, and the boys probably had some catching up to do. Clarice, Susie, and Reggie kept the conversation going during the meal. Emma was content to sit and listen as they told stories about their summer travels. Emma noticed that Martha was unusually quiet, and once or twice when she happened to look at Martha, it seemed almost as if Martha was mad at her. Emma figured she must be imagining it because she could think of no earthly reason why Martha would be upset with her.

After supper, all the students were supposed to meet with their dorm advisors to go over the school rules again and also to get their schedules. This year their dorm advisor was an energetic girl named

Penny Parnell. As Penny bounced enthusiastically into their suite shortly after supper, Emma was immediately reminded of a cheerleader. Penny stood a little over five feet and had the athletic build of a gymnast. Her light brown hair was pulled back in a ponytail. It was a shame that Dinswood Academy didn't have a basketball team, because Emma had no doubt that Penny would have been selected captain of the cheerleading squad. Emma would have shared what she was thinking with Martha, but Martha was still behaving strangely. After Penny left, Emma asked Martha about her class schedule. Last year, their schedules had matched up exactly, and Emma was hoping that would be the case again this year. Martha handed her schedule over wordlessly when Emma asked to see it, and Emma was left in no doubt that there was something seriously wrong. She would have asked Martha about it then and there, but she didn't want Clarice and Susie to overhear their conversation. As the time for bed drew near, Emma realized she'd have to wait until tomorrow to find out what was bothering Martha. At least one good thing had come of the evening. Martha's schedule was the same as hers. As Emma climbed into bed, she wondered whether Doug or Sebastian would be in any of her classes.

Emma didn't sleep well that night. She was a little nervous about the start of school, and she spent most of the night trying to figure out what she had done to make Martha mad. She finally fell asleep around three o'clock only to dream that she had missed a whole semester of classes and now had to take all of her final exams.

CHAPTER FOURTEEN
FIRST DAY

Emma awakened the next morning determined to find out what was bothering Martha. She decided she'd wait until Clarice and Susie left for breakfast so she could talk to Martha in private. However, as the four girls got ready for school, Martha appeared to have returned to her usual self. She talked with everyone, including Emma, as if last night had never happened. Emma was glad to see that Martha was back to normal and thought it best to leave well enough alone. Obviously, whatever had upset Martha last night was no longer an issue. Maybe Martha just hadn't been feeling well, Emma reasoned.

Later, when they entered the dining hall, they found that Doug and Sebastian were already seated and eating their breakfast. After hurriedly filling their trays with pancakes and bacon, Emma and Martha took the vacant seats opposite the boys. Emma was eager to see the boys' schedules. Both girls were disappointed to learn that neither of the boys had any classes with them. Last year, Sebastian had had the same schedule as the girls. Emma was going to miss Sebastian's shocked expressions and funny comments whenever the teachers assigned homework. It seemed that this year Sebastian's schedule lined up exactly with Doug's. Emma was glad that at least the two boys would be together.

It didn't really matter whether or not they had the same schedules, because they would all have the same subjects with the same teachers, only at different times. The benefit was that they would still be able to study together. Because the teachers they'd had last year taught both the seventh and eighth grades, they would be having Mr. Godfrey for math, Mrs. Perkins for English, Miss Grimstock for history, and Miss Jennings for science again this year. Emma didn't mind because at least with the same teachers, she knew what to expect.

"Hey, I just had a thought," Sebastian said suddenly as he finished his last bite of toast. "This is the last year we'll have to have PE in the ballroom."

It was then that Emma noticed the sounds of construction coming from somewhere behind the castle. Emma had grown so accustomed to the noise that she didn't register it until it was brought to her attention as Sebastian had just done.

"Won't that be nice," Martha agreed.

"Dad says everything is going according to schedule," Doug said. "The sports complex should be done by the end of next summer. Once the walls are up, they're going to start bringing up everything they need to finish the inside, so when winter gets here, they won't have to worry about trying to transport stuff up the mountain roads."

"That's a good idea," Martha replied.

Emma was only half listening to the conversation, because just as Doug had begun to talk, Preston Danvers had entered the dining hall. Emma's eyes had been drawn to him like a magnet. She watched as he walked over to where Bobby was sitting. Before taking his seat, he looked around the room and waved when he spotted Emma. Self-consciously, Emma waved back.

Wondering whom Emma was waving to, Doug turned around in his seat to take a look. Upon seeing Preston, his expression turned grim. A moment later, he was gathering up his tray to leave. "Come on, Sebastian. We'd better get going."

"Sure, okay," Sebastian replied, a little surprised by Doug's sudden desire to leave. With an apologetic look at the girls, he added, "I guess we'll see you guys later."

Martha watched Doug and Sebastian's departure without comment, but once they were gone, she turned to Emma. "What do you think you're doing?" There was no mistaking the anger in her voice.

"What do you mean?" Emma had the feeling she was about to find out what Martha had been upset about last night.

"Two words—Preston Danvers."

"What about him?" Emma still had no idea what Martha was talking about.

"First of all, Preston is Clarice's cousin. That alone ought to be enough to make you think twice about having anything to do with him. Second, he's rooming with Bobby Wilcox. Bobby hates Doug, and for all we know, he could have Preston spying on us for him. Third, have you forgotten we have a mission to complete? Doug is counting on us to help him find the rest of the sculptures. We can't have Preston following us around like a lost puppy all year long because he's infatuated with you." This last statement was said with particular emphasis on the last two words.

Emma sat for a moment in stunned silence, so shocked by Martha's tirade that for a minute she didn't know how to respond. Then she began to get angry. She barely knew Preston Danvers. All she'd done was return his greeting, and here was Martha accusing her of being disloyal to Doug. She was just opening her mouth to defend herself when Martha held up a hand to stop her.

"Don't bother denying it. I see the way you look at him, and I'm telling you right now I won't stand for it."

With that Martha got up and, after emptying her tray, left the dining room. Emma remained where she was for several long moments trying to sort out what had just happened. One thing was certain—Preston Danvers must be related to Clarice because he'd only been at the school for one day, and already he was causing problems. *He was too handsome for his own good*, Emma thought with a sigh. It was probably all a moot point anyway. Preston was a freshman, and it was unlikely that he would have anything to do with Emma. Besides, just because she thought he was cute didn't mean she wanted to go out with him. Emma liked Doug and had no intention of letting him down. Martha had been out of line. The more Emma thought about it, the madder she got. She was still sitting there fuming when the first bell rang. Emma now had only five minutes to get her books and get to class. With another long drawn out sigh, Emma hurriedly left the dining room.

Emma and Martha didn't speak to each other all morning long. This was made easier by the fact that every teacher insisted on seating their students alphabetically, and as it happened, there were several students whose names fit between Higsby and Merriweather. Emma would have liked to see Martha's reaction when Mr. Godfrey gave them their very first math assignment. This year all the eighth graders were required to take algebra. In most other schools, algebra was a freshman course, but Dinswood Academy set higher standards for its students. Martha had always struggled with math, and therefore, it wasn't one of her favorite subjects. Emma was on the verge of mouthing words of encouragement to Martha, who was seated a few seats back on her left, when she remembered that she wasn't speaking to her.

When it was time for lunch, Emma was the first to enter the dining hall. She didn't waste any time but quickly filled her tray and found a seat where she could see the door. *Now it's up to Martha*, Emma thought, curious to see if Martha would sit with her or not.

When she saw Martha come through the door, she hastily averted her eyes and pretended to be totally engrossed in her lunch. In truth, Emma was hardly aware of the chicken nuggets and mashed potatoes she was cramming into her mouth like a starving prisoner. She was so absorbed in her thoughts that the clack of a tray being set on the table right next to her startled her. After giving a little jump, she looked up to see that it was Martha. Martha took a moment to get settled and then turned sideways so she could look at Emma.

"Look, Emma, I'm sorry about this morning, but it seemed like Doug was hurt, and he's going through so much now I just couldn't bear it—especially not over the likes of Preston Danvers." There was a lot more she would have liked to say, but knowing that it would serve no useful purpose, she kept her tongue. Last year, Martha had been the first to notice how cute Doug was. For a time, she had liked him, but when it became obvious that he liked Emma, Martha had accepted it and not acted out of jealousy, as most girls her age would have done. She still cared about Doug as a good friend and didn't want to see him get hurt. "He needs his friends now more than ever," Martha continued when Emma didn't immediately respond. When Emma still didn't say anything, Martha added quietly, "Emma, he needs to know you're still behind him."

The reason Emma hadn't responded was because of the lump that had suddenly formed in her throat. At Martha's last words, tears welled up in her eyes. Emma swallowed hard and finally managed to say just as quietly, "I am."

It was a simple statement, but Martha could hear the sincerity in it. Satisfied, Martha turned around and began to eat her lunch. Emma wiped away the tears that had spilled onto her cheeks and put her fork down. She wasn't hungry anymore. A moment later, Clarice, Susie, and Reggie joined them. Emma was glad to see them. Maybe they could help lighten the somber mood that had fallen.

Clarice spent most of the meal complaining about all of the homework they'd already been given and about the teachers responsible. She seemed to be particularly upset with Mr. Godfrey. "It's our first day back for heaven's sake. I don't understand why we need algebra anyway. I mean, when are we ever going to use it?"

Although Clarice had intended it to be a rhetorical question, Reggie was ready with an answer. "Actually, Clarice, it depends on what you want to do when you graduate." He would have said more, but the look on Clarice's face stopped him.

"Why can't you ever just agree with me, Reggie? Honestly, sometimes I think you're trying to make me mad."

With that, she picked up her tray and left the dining hall with Susie in tow. Reggie was left sitting opposite Emma and Martha with an expression that was a comical mixture of surprise and confusion. Emma and Martha smiled at each other. One day, Reggie would learn when to keep his mouth shut, but unfortunately for him, today wasn't that day.

THE REST OF the week passed quickly with little time for worrying about Preston Danvers or anyone else for that matter. Sometimes, Emma would see Preston as he passed her in the hall. Usually, he would say a quick hello, but he made no effort to seek her out after classes were over for the day. *It was just as well*, Emma thought. His attention would only cause friction between her and Martha, and she didn't want to hurt Doug.

Each evening after supper, Emma and Martha could be found working on their homework, either in the lounge or library. Doug and Sebastian usually joined the girls for these study sessions. Emma was glad that things at least appeared to be back to normal. She couldn't help noticing how tired Doug looked. Martha had noticed Doug's haggard appearance as well and had commented on it to

Emma. Both girls wished there was something they could do. If things didn't change soon, Doug's grades would begin to suffer, and then he could lose his scholarship.

Doug was checking his mailbox every morning and evening for a note from the Reaper that would tell them when the next sculpture was due. He hoped they would be given more than two weeks this time. In the meantime, Doug had wrapped the sculpture they'd found at the cottage in a blanket and hidden it in a suitcase he kept in his closet. When the note came, they would be ready. Doug's main worry now was finding the other four sculptures. If they were going to stay a step ahead of the Reaper, they needed to be looking for the fourth sculpture now. The problem was going to be getting to the rest of the locations on their list. Only one was within walking distance of the castle. The others were along the river and would require a boat. How they were going to get their hands on a boat, assuming they could even get to the river, was what was keeping Doug awake at night.

Saturday morning, Doug found a small white envelope in his mailbox. He held it in his hands for a few seconds without opening it, afraid of what it might say. With shaking hands, Doug took a deep breath and tore the envelope open. Quickly, he scanned the brief note inside.

Thank you for the lovely sculpture of Sarah, Douglas. I knew I could count on you. I've decided that since school has started and it will undoubtedly be more difficult for you to "get away," I will give you until the end of the month to deliver the next Mortal. When you have it, hang the school banner in your window as before. The next evening, put the sculpture in the same wooden barrel. I will not send another note unless you fail to do your part. Remember what's at stake, Douglas. Happy hunting!

Doug put the note back in the envelope and hurried to the dining hall in search of Sebastian, Emma, and Martha. He had been so tired that he had slept later than usual that morning. He had awakened to find that his roommates had already gone to breakfast. Knowing how little rest he'd been getting lately, Sebastian had probably decided to let him sleep. Doug had to admit the extra sleep had done him good. He was feeling much better.

He found Sebastian in the dining hall, but it seemed that the girls had already eaten and gone outside to enjoy the fresh air and sunshine. Sebastian waited while Doug had his breakfast, and then the two boys left the castle in search of Emma and Martha. They found the girls sitting on a swing under the oak tree nearest the castle's main entrance. On the way over to the girls, Doug noticed that several of the academy's other students were also taking advantage of the fine day. He couldn't blame them. The temperature was in the low eighties, and there was a nice breeze. Although it was still early September, the air had a different feel to it. Fall was on its way. Even after receiving the latest note from the Reaper, Doug found it hard to be gloomy on a day like this.

Emma looked up and smiled when she saw Doug approaching. She was relieved to see him smile back. He looked a lot better this morning. The dark circles under his eyes were gone, and he appeared to be in good spirits. At breakfast, Sebastian had told the girls that Doug was sleeping in. Emma was glad to see that it had helped him. He looked well rested and ready for whatever the day would bring.

The boys got a bench from under a neighboring tree and positioned it so they could sit across from the girls. Once they were settled, Doug showed everyone the note he'd found in his mailbox. He hadn't told Sebastian about it at breakfast because he'd wanted to tell them all at once.

"Well, we'd better start looking for another sculpture," Sebastian said after reading the note.

"Yeah," Martha agreed with a shake of her head. "Which spot on our list should we search next?"

"There's only one within walking distance of the castle," Doug replied. "I guess we should try it first."

"When do you want to go?" Emma said.

Doug didn't answer for a moment. He was thinking about the other locations on their list and how hard it was going to be to get to them. He'd been worrying about it ever since they'd gotten the first note from the Reaper. With a sigh, he decided it was time he shared his concerns with his friends. Maybe they'd have some ideas that he hadn't considered.

"What's wrong, Doug?" Emma asked when Doug didn't respond.

"Well, it's just what I said earlier. We've only got one spot on our list that we can get to without help. The rest of them are along the river. How are we supposed to get to them?"

Even though she knew the answer, Emma asked, "That's what you've been so worried about, isn't it?"

Doug looked into Emma's beautiful green eyes and nodded. He could see concern etched in her lovely face. He saw similar expressions on the faces of Martha and Sebastian, and he was reminded of something he'd forgotten: he was not alone. Now that he'd shared his worries with his friends, he felt as if some of the burden had been lifted from his shoulders. He began to wish that he'd talked with them about it sooner. If he had, he might have saved himself a lot of sleepless nights.

"I think I have an idea," Sebastian said to everyone's surprise.

"By all means, enlighten us," Martha replied with a lift of her right eyebrow.

Sebastian would have liked to let the suspense build a bit before satisfying Martha's curiosity, but he couldn't do that to Doug, so he answered without hesitation. "I was thinking that we could ask Mr. Munsen to help us."

The group was silent for a moment as each weighed the pros and cons of Sebastian's idea. Mr. Munsen had helped them last year when they'd needed a ride to Cal Thrabek's cabin. The cabin, located a few miles outside of Windland, had been too far away for them to get to on foot. Mr. Munsen had taken an instant liking to Doug and had given Doug and Sebastian a ride out to the cabin without asking a lot of questions. As it turned out, he'd ended up saving the boys' lives. Mr. Munsen was a big bear of a man with a mustache and a full beard. He had reminded Emma of a mountain man when she'd first seen him. His wife, Alice, and daughter, Becky, ran the bookstore in Windland for Cal. Emma felt they could trust Mr. Munsen.

Martha had been thinking along the same lines as Emma. As much as she hated to admit it, she thought Sebastian's suggestion was a good one. Ultimately, however, it would be up to Doug whether or not to enlist the aid of Mr. Munsen. After all, it was his father whose life was on the line. Martha looked over at Doug and tried to gauge his reaction to Sebastian's idea. It was difficult to tell what he was thinking from his expression. She looked over at Emma and Sebastian and saw that they too were watching Doug intently.

Finally, Doug spoke. "Sebastian, I think you've found the answer. I'm pretty sure that if I explain everything to Mr. Munsen, he'll help us." Doug liked and respected Mr. Munsen, and more importantly, he trusted him. They would have to find a way to talk to him the next time they were in Windland. Thinking of Windland reminded him of Emma's earlier question.

"Next Saturday, it'll be the ninth graders' turn to go to Windland. I think we should look for the fourth sculpture while Bobby Wilcox is out of the way. I'm convinced he's got some of his goons watching my every move." Doug looked over at Emma. What he didn't say was that he thought Preston Danvers was one of the ones Bobby had enlisted to help him keep an eye on Doug. Bobby was hoping to catch Doug breaking a school rule so he could have his dad and the rest of the school board expel him from the academy. Doug was just as determined to keep that from happening, but constantly being watched certainly did complicate things.

They spent the next several minutes making plans for the following Saturday. The location they would be searching was an artesian well located a couple of miles down the mountain on the castle's north side. Doug's dad had shown him the spot the first summer he was at the academy. Rebecca had mentioned the well in her journal, explaining that she and Darius had been out walking when they'd come across it. The water erupting from the ground had amazed them both. A couple of years later, Darius had ordered the construction of a fountain around it. At Rebecca's request, he had also placed some stone benches nearby. It had become one of Rebecca's favorite spots. According to her journal entries, she would often go there to read and enjoy the natural beauty of the area.

"What exactly is an artesian well?" Martha asked Doug when they'd finished talking about what they were going to do the following Saturday.

"Well, according to Dad, it's what happens when water from a higher elevation runs down and gets trapped between two layers of rock or clay that are impermeable to water. The water has nowhere to go and pressure forces it to defy gravity and erupt from the ground."

"Sounds cool," Sebastian said.

"I bet the fountain is beautiful," Emma said, looking at Martha. It sounded like the sort of thing that would appeal to Martha's artistic nature. Emma felt certain that Darius had gone all out to create something wonderful for his wife to enjoy. She had to admit that she was looking forward to seeing the fountain herself.

"I just hope we can find one of the sculptures there," Doug said. "I don't remember seeing any carvings of ravens or roses when I was there with Dad."

"Yeah, Doug, but you weren't really looking either," Martha pointed out. "It'd be easy to miss something like that unless you were really looking."

"I guess so," Doug replied with a frown.

Suddenly, Sebastian stood up and stretched. "I'm tired of sitting around here. Let's do something. It's too nice a day to waste it sitting under a tree."

The others agreed, and at Sebastian's suggestion, they decided to play croquet until it was time for lunch. After lunch, they teamed up with some of their classmates and spent the afternoon playing volleyball. The combination of fresh air and exercise had them all famished by suppertime.

Later that evening, the foursome sat around one of the tables in the lounge and played board games. By unspoken agreement, they had decided to put off their homework until the following afternoon. There would be plenty of time to work on it tomorrow.

Emma fell into bed that night tired but happy. It had been a wonderful day. It was a relief to see Doug behaving more like his usual self. Just before falling asleep, Emma prayed that things would go well for them next Saturday.

CHAPTER FIFTEEN

SUMMER IN SEPTEMBER

The warm weather returned during the week, and by the time Saturday arrived, the temperature was forecasted to rise to near ninety degrees by the afternoon. It seemed that the dragon of summer had decided to unleash one final blast of its fiery breath before bedding down for the winter. Although the temperature wasn't going to be ideal, Emma was at least thankful that it wasn't supposed to rain.

At breakfast that morning, the foursome decided that it would be best to leave for their little excursion after lunch. The buses wouldn't be departing for Windland until ten o'clock, and then they would only have two hours until lunch. Doug wasn't sure if two hours would be enough time to locate the sculpture, and it certainly would look suspicious if four students didn't turn up for lunch. If they left immediately after the noontime meal, they would have almost six hours until supper. That should be ample time, assuming that one of Marnatti's masterpieces was indeed hidden somewhere near the well.

At ten o'clock, Doug and Sebastian watched from the ballroom windows as the buses pulled up to take the freshmen to town. They wanted to be sure that Bobby and all of his goons got on the buses. This was one day they couldn't afford to have anyone spying on them. Doug was relieved to see that almost the entire freshman class had decided to take the trip to town—including Bobby and his crew. After the departure of the buses, the time until lunch seemed to drag by. They played a half-hearted game of badminton and then walked around to the back of the castle to see how work on the sports complex was coming. As they turned the corner around Bingham Hall, the boys' dorm, they saw that the construction site had been cordoned off for safety purposes. Even so, they could see that the walls of the gym were up and the trusses for the roof had been set. Soon the exterior would be finished, and work could begin on the inside. It looked like things were moving along nicely. By the time they'd finished satisfying their curiosity about the construction crew's progress and returned to the front of the castle, it was time for lunch.

They ate quickly so they would be the first to get back outside and hopefully be able to slip away unseen. As they exited the castle by way of the main entrance, they took a quick look around to make sure they were alone. Satisfied that they were not being observed, they once again headed around the east side of the castle. Only this time, their destination was the bus barn. All of the tools that had once been stored in the old shed behind the school had been moved to the bus barn. The shed had recently been torn down to make way for all of the new construction. Doug felt reasonably sure that they would at least need a shovel and a crowbar. He wished they'd been able to bring their backpacks along, but then it would have been obvious that they were up to something.

"There's a path that leads down to the fountain just behind the bus barn," Doug told the others once they had what they needed in the way of tools. Without any further comment, Doug led them around the south side of the barn. The bus barn was set back far enough in the woods that it was unlikely that anyone from the school would see them even if they were outside. They found the dirt path without any difficulty. The path took them right through the heart of the woods and was so narrow that they were forced to walk single file. Doug took the lead with the shovel slung casually over his shoulder. Emma went next, followed by Martha. As had become his custom, Sebastian brought up the rear. Emma smiled to herself when she saw that Sebastian was carrying the crowbar in a manner similar to Doug.

The air was hot and muggy as they trudged down the steeply sloping path. Although the dirt had been packed down, the path was still rocky and uneven. A layer of dead leaves added an extra element of slipperiness, and at times, it was difficult to keep their footing. There was little conversation as everyone was busy concentrating on staying upright. Before reaching the bottom of the hill, they'd each had moments where they'd almost ended up on their backsides. No one complained though, not even Sebastian.

"At least we're in the shade," Sebastian commented after almost falling on his bottom a second time.

"Don't you dare fall, Sebastian," Martha warned after seeing him slip yet again. "If you do, you're likely to take us all down with you. Honestly, knowing how clumsy you are, you probably should have gone first."

Instead of getting angry at Martha's comments, Sebastian replied calmly. "Well, since I don't know where we're going, it would be pretty stupid for me to lead the way, wouldn't it?"

"He's got you there, Martha," Doug said without turning around. Emma couldn't see his face, but she was pretty sure he was smiling. Smiling herself, Emma turned around to see if Martha was upset by the fact that Doug had taken Sebastian's side.

At the same time, Sebastian said, "I'm not doing it on purpose, but now that I think about it, it would get us to the bottom of the hill a lot faster."

Martha turned to glare at him, but when she saw his expression, she started laughing instead. He was grinning from ear to ear, and it was obvious that he was just trying to get a rise out of her. "I think I'd rather walk if it's all the same to you."

"Your wish is my command," Sebastian replied with a bow.

Martha turned back around with a shake of her head. "Just don't knock me down. That's all I ask."

A few minutes later, the path began to level out and lead in a more easterly direction. Now that they were on level ground, it was easier to walk, and they made better time. Suddenly, they stepped into a small clearing. In the center of the clearing was the fountain Darius had built for Rebecca. The circular base was constructed of layers of natural rock and was about eight feet in diameter. In the center was a stone pedestal in the shape of a hexagon. Sitting atop the pedestal and carved in the same stone was a birdbath with a raven perched on its rim. Emma smiled when she saw that the raven held the stem of a rose in its beak. The raven and the rose seemed to be the theme of Darius and Rebecca's marriage. Apparently, Darius had wanted to be sure that Rebecca would think of him every time she visited her favorite spot.

The fountain was designed so that water from the artesian well came up through the stem of the birdbath and filled the bowl at the top. As the bowl filled with water, it overflowed into the base of the fountain below. Emma walked around the fountain and saw that a hole had been cut in the circular base so that water would begin to drain out when it neared the top. A channel had been dug so that the excess water was directed to a small creek several yards away.

"Well, where do you suppose Darius hid the sculpture?" Sebastian asked as he circled the fountain. "Is it somewhere in the fountain, or around it?"

It was Martha who answered. "First of all, Sebastian, we're not even sure if Darius hid a sculpture here. Second, how are we supposed to know? We don't have any more information than you do."

Once again, Doug came to Sebastian's rescue. "I'd be willing to bet money that Darius hid a sculpture here. After all, it was one of Rebecca's favorite spots, so it would have been special to Darius too." Doug had been looking at Martha while he spoke, but now he turned to Sebastian. "I think we should look around the fountain first, and then if we don't find anything, we can check out the fountain itself."

"Sounds like a plan," Sebastian replied as he leaned the crowbar against the fountain's rock base.

No more was said for a while as they spread out and began searching for clues. A stone bench sat a few yards away in the shade of an ancient oak tree. Impulsively, Emma walked over to it and sat down. The seat was surprisingly smooth and had a glossy finish that reminded Emma of highly polished marble. The bench felt wonderfully cool in the afternoon heat, and it provided a perfect view of the raven atop the birdbath. It was incredible to think that Rebecca had often admired the fountain from this very spot. With a sigh, Emma stood and started searching the grass around the fountain for any sign of a raven or a rose.

After a search of the ground in the immediate vicinity revealed nothing out of the ordinary, they widened their sweep to include the surrounding trees. "I hope we're all looking for the same thing," Martha said after they'd been searching for a little over a half hour.

"What do you mean?" Sebastian asked.

Martha rolled her eyes and looked skyward as if praying for patience. "I mean we should all be looking for anything that has a raven and a rose carved on it."

"Oh, yeah. I have been," Sebastian said with a nod. "But if it's hidden inside the fountain, Darius probably wouldn't have made a marker. Remember, we didn't find a marker at the arch."

"We didn't find one because at the time we didn't know to look for one," Martha answered.

"Or maybe, there wasn't one to begin with."

It seemed Sebastian was not going to let Martha have the last word. He looked at Martha with raised eyebrows and waited for her rebuttal, but she merely shrugged and said, "I guess we'll never know for sure unless we go back and give the spot a good going over."

Amazed by her easy capitulation, Sebastian smiled. "You're right, Martha. Maybe someday when this whole mess with the Reaper is over, we'll get a chance to go back and look."

While Sebastian was speaking, Martha was remembering their last visit to the arch. They'd nearly lost Sebastian for good that day. "Frankly, I wouldn't care if I never saw the place again."

Sebastian was surprised by the vehemence in her tone, but he immediately understood the reason for it.

"I think I'm with Martha on that one," Doug said, to everyone's surprise.

"Me too," Emma was quick to agree.

Sebastian realized the hidden meaning behind the words of his friends. They all cared about him and were not eager to be reminded of what had happened that day. Swallowing the lump that had suddenly formed in his throat, he set to work examining every rock forming the base of the fountain.

A few minutes later, they had to admit defeat. Either the sculpture wasn't in the base of the fountain, or it was as Sebastian had suggested: Darius hadn't felt the need to mark its location. They had been searching for more than an hour, and the temperature had risen steadily as the afternoon had worn on. Emma began to look longingly at the cool spring water filling the fountain. For a moment, she was tempted to jump in clothes and all. Sebastian must have been thinking along the same lines.

"Why don't we cool off in the fountain for a minute? I'm about to die of heatstroke," Sebastian exclaimed as he used the bottom of his T-shirt to wipe the sweat off his face.

"It's very tempting," Martha agreed. "But how would we explain our soaking wet clothes when we get back to school?"

"We'd be mostly dry by then. We don't have to be back until suppertime."

It was Doug who spoke next. "Actually, we need to be back before the buses return from Windland. If Bobby Wilcox catches us coming out of the woods, he'll know we've been off school grounds, and he'll rat on us."

"You're right. I hadn't thought of that," Sebastian replied with a shake of his head.

Emma hadn't thought of that either. It looked like they'd have to forego a swim in the fountain. At least, she could splash a little water on her face. She was on her way to do just that when Sebastian made another suggestion.

"We could at least take off our shoes and get our legs and feet wet. Besides, we still need to check the pedestal in the center. It's big enough to hold one of those metal boxes."

"Yeah, I guess it is," Doug agreed. Without another word, he began taking off his shoes. "Are you girls going to get in?"

"Might as well," Martha answered.

Sebastian let out a whoop and, after removing his shoes in record time, jumped into the fountain and began splashing around.

"Stop it!" Martha shouted. "We can't get in while you're throwing water around like that. Remember, the idea is to cool off without getting totally drenched."

"I know," Sebastian said with a grin. "I just had to get it out of my system."

"Well, now that you have, maybe we can get a closer look at the pedestal." As she spoke, Martha stepped into the fountain and sucked in her breath as her feet sank into the icy water. "Oh, that's cold," she said with a shudder.

"Yeah, isn't it great?"

Obviously feeling that Sebastian's question was purely rhetorical, Martha didn't bother to reply. Doug got in next and was quickly followed by Emma. They waded around for a couple of minutes until they were sufficiently cooled off, and then they set to work examining the six-sided stone that served as the platform for the birdbath. The stone appeared to be seamless and bore no symbols of any kind.

"I just don't understand it," Doug said, shaking his head. "I was positive Darius had hidden one of the sculptures here."

Emma looked at Doug and saw that his brow was once again furrowed in worry. Worry had been his constant companion since this whole thing with the Reaper had begun. Emma had hoped that finding one of the Mortals today would give him a brief respite from his cares, but it appeared Doug was right. For reasons known only to a dead man, none of the sculptures were hidden here. "We all thought we'd find something here, but we still have some other places to check," Emma said, trying to sound positive.

Doug ran a hand through his hair and nodded. It was obvious he was trying to hide his concern. Emma's heart went out to him, and a feeling of helplessness swept over her as she realized there was nothing she could do to change things. She just hoped that someday the Reaper would be caught and get what he deserved for putting a boy Doug's age through such anguish. The more she thought about the Reaper, the angrier she got. She was positively fuming by the time she stepped out of the fountain. Grabbing her shoes, she all but stomped over to the bench so she could sit down and put them on. She was just tying her second shoe when it hit her. Within seconds, she was on her knees examining the underside of the bench, and there it was just as she'd hoped—two small but very visible carvings, one of a raven and one of a rose. She jumped up, nearly hitting her head on the seat of the bench, and shouted, "I've found it!"

"Found what?" Sebastian asked. He was sitting on the edge of the fountain, putting his shoes on. Now he got up and walked over to where Emma was standing.

"What do you mean, found what?" Martha cried in exasperation as she too made her way over to the bench. "She means she's found the sculpture."

"Have you?" Doug asked. He didn't want to get his hopes up only to have them dashed again.

"Come and see for yourself," Emma answered, barely able to contain her excitement.

Sebastian and Martha stood back to let Doug through. Hesitantly, he got down on his knees so he could look at the portion of the bench that Emma had indicated. When he sat up, he was grinning from ear to ear. "Emma, you're a genius. I don't know why we didn't think of it before. This is where Rebecca sat, so this is where Darius hid the sculpture."

Doug stood up then and let Sebastian and Martha take a look. Once everyone had had a chance to see the carvings, Sebastian asked the obvious question. "Okay, now how do we get the sculpture out of a stone bench?"

"The base must be hollow. I bet the seat just slides right off," Doug answered.

"That makes sense," Sebastian said with a nod.

"It looks awfully heavy," Martha commented. "Do you think we'll be able to move it?"

Emma had been thinking the same thing. She had sat on the bench, and although the base may be hollow, the stone from which the seat had been fashioned most definitely was not.

"All we can do is try" was Doug's reply. While he was speaking, Doug positioned himself on one end of the bench and put his hands under the edge of the seat. "Sebastian, you get a hold of the other end, and we'll try to slide it off."

Sebastian quickly moved to the side of the bench opposite Doug and grabbed hold of the seat with both hands. "Okay, I'm ready."

"On the count of three, we'll try to slide it to the right," Doug instructed. "One, two, three, go!"

There was a lot of groaning and grunting as both boys strained to break the inertia of a stone seat that hadn't been moved in centuries. Emma began to worry that they'd hurt themselves when suddenly there was a scraping sound. At first, the seat's movement was almost imperceptible, but it wasn't long until the boys had moved it forward far enough that gravity began to help. Then it was all Doug and Sebastian could do to keep from dropping the seat. Despite their best effort, they ended up letting it fall the last foot or so. Fortunately, the area in front of the bench was grassy so the seat landed intact with a dull thud.

Emma peered over Doug's right shoulder to see what the seat's removal had revealed and saw a metal box tucked safely in the center of the bench's rectangular base. The box looked like all of the others they'd found, but the only way to be sure it contained one of Marnatti's Mortals was to open it. Sebastian had already gone to get the crowbar that he'd left leaning against the fountain. By the time he returned, Doug had lifted the box from its three-hundred-year resting place and set it on the ground. Sebastian used the crowbar to break the padlock open, and Doug lifted the lid. Then to Emma's surprise, he stepped back and said, "Emma, you were the one who figured out where it was hidden, so I think you should be the one to take it out of the box."

Emma hesitated for a moment, but Doug smiled at her encouragingly, so she knelt down and began pulling out the straw that Darius had used as packing material. In no time, she was lifting what had to be the most beautiful sculpture yet from the box.

Martha's gasp of delight seemed to indicate that she was in agreement with Emma.

"Oh, Emma, it's gorgeous!"

The woman Marnatti had sculpted was wearing a small crown over bountiful tresses that seemed to flow down her back. A floor-length royal robe was draped over her delicate shoulders and tied in front with braided cords. The gown she wore underneath fell to the tops of her sandaled feet and was loosely belted around a narrow waist. The woman's features were delicate and exquisite—her neck slender and swanlike. She wore an expression of confidence, and Marnatti had even managed to convey something noble in her bearing. Emma remembered that Esther was a Jewess and had risked her life to save her fellow countrymen from a death edict issued by King Xerxes. In the time of King Xerxes, it was against the law to approach the king in his inner court without being summoned. Knowing this, Esther had still sought an audience with him. Fortunately, he had extended his golden scepter to her, an action that indicated he wished to spare her life.

"Who is it?" Sebastian couldn't help asking.

"I think it's Esther," Emma answered.

"How do you know?"

Martha sighed in exasperation. "Honestly, Sebastian. Don't you ever read your Bible? If you did, you'd know that Esther was a queen. Surely even you can see the crown on the woman's head."

"Yes, I can see the crown," Sebastian answered with deceptive calm. It was clear from his face that Martha had finally succeeded in making him angry. "However, if you'd ever read your Bible, you would know that Esther is not the only queen mentioned in Scripture."

"That's true," Martha conceded. "But Esther was the only queen that Marnatti sculpted for Darius."

"All right, you win that one, but just for the record, I'm not stupid." Sebastian turned away from her then and said to Doug, "We should probably put the seat back on the bench."

"Yeah, but I'm afraid it's not going to be as easy as it was to take it off. This time we're going to have to lift it."

"We can help," Emma said, referring to herself and Martha.

"Yeah, we'll help," Martha agreed. She glanced over at Sebastian, but he refused to look at her. It was obvious that he was still mad at her. She had regretted what she'd said to him the minute it had left her lips, but words spoken could not be taken back. That day at the arch when Sebastian had nearly drowned, she'd made a vow to be nicer to him. Why did she find it so hard to keep her vow? With a sigh, Martha moved to help lift the seat.

Doug hadn't been kidding. The seat was a lot heavier than it looked. It took some doing, but they were finally able to get it into its original position. By the time they were finished, they were all hot and sweaty again, but there was no time to refresh themselves in the fountain. The buses would be coming back from town soon, and they needed to be back at school before then. Because they hadn't brought anything to wrap the sculpture in, Doug thought it would be best to put it back in the metal box. Hopefully, the hay would keep the sculpture of Esther from being damaged as it was transported back up the hill. By unspoken agreement, Doug carried the box while Sebastian carried the shovel and crowbar they'd brought. The girls had offered to carry something, but Sebastian had angrily grunted that he didn't need any help.

Martha looked at Emma and shrugged her shoulders. Emma would have liked to tell Martha that she should apologize to Sebastian, but she was afraid Sebastian would hear her, so she said nothing.

The trek up the hill was accomplished in silence. Doug was busy concentrating on keeping the metal box securely on his shoulder, and Sebastian was too mad to make small talk. Martha was feeling guilty and didn't feel much like talking either, so Emma was left to her own thoughts. She had just begun to wonder how they were going to get the box into the school without anyone noticing when Doug spoke, "I think we'd better hide the box in the bus barn. I can find a way to smuggle it into the school later."

"Do you think that's safe?" Emma asked. "What if somebody notices the box?"

"Nobody goes into the bus barn much except on the weekends, and I know some places I can stash it where no one will find it. Besides it'll only be for a day or two, just until I can figure out how to get it into the school."

"Well, if you're sure," Emma said uncertainly. She still didn't think it was a good idea, but they didn't seem to have any other options open to them.

Doug turned around to look at her then and smiled. "It'll be okay, Emma. I promise."

The look he gave her was a mixture of gratitude and something else that had her blushing a bit. She didn't have time to ponder the meaning of the look though because in the next moment they reached the bus barn. They moved along the south side of the building in single file. Then one at a time, they slipped around the corner and entered through the barn's smaller door. The south side of the barn served as storage for a wide assortment of tools and what looked to Emma to be a bunch of junk. It was here that they had found the bikes they'd used on their last adventure. The buses entered through a huge automatic garage door on the building's north side. The enormous area where the buses parked reminded Emma of an airplane hangar.

Once inside, Doug didn't hesitate but strode quickly to the very back of the storage area. They watched quietly as he began maneuvering his way between boxes and broken pieces of machinery until he disappeared from view completely. A minute later, they heard some clanking noises, and then the barn was silent again. They waited patiently while Doug extricated himself from the mass of discarded objects and made his way back to them.

"That should do it," he said as he wiped the dust from his hands. "Nobody will…"

"Quiet!" Martha shouted, interrupting Doug in midsentence.

Everyone looked at Martha, surprised at her rudeness. Then they heard it too. The buses were returning from Windland.

"The buses must be early!" Sebastian exclaimed.

Emma looked at her watch in disbelief. It was five o'clock! "No, we're late," she informed the others, panic evident in her tone. The return trip must have taken them longer than they'd anticipated. Of course, they'd had to travel uphill, and Doug had been going more slowly because of the sculpture. It seemed that despite all of their planning, events were unfolding exactly as they had feared. In minutes, the buses would be pulling up in front of the school to disgorge their load of students. Their next stop would be the bus barn.

CHAPTER SIXTEEN
AN ENEMY AROUND EVERY CORNER

"What are we going to do?" Sebastian asked. "There's no way we can make it to the main driveway before the buses get here."

Although there was no school rule prohibiting students from visiting the bus barn, it was not something that was generally done. Thus, it would look awfully suspicious for the four of them to be seen coming from that area. The lane to the bus barn wasn't visible from the front of the castle, but it was in full view of the boys' dorm.

"We can't afford to be seen around here," Doug answered Sebastian. "With the sculpture hidden in here, we can't risk drawing attention to this place."

"We could hide in here until the bus drivers park their buses and leave," Martha suggested.

"Too risky," Doug said, shaking his head. "We've got to get out now before the buses start down the lane."

Without further comment, Doug led them out the small door they'd entered only minutes before and ran toward the barn's south side. Rounding the corner, he stopped for a moment to let the others catch up and then filled them in on his plan. "We'll hide behind the barn till the drivers have gone. Then we'll run down to the chapel using the woods as cover. We can walk to the school from the chapel. It'll just look like we've been visiting with Reverend Palmer."

"Since we don't ever visit Reverend Palmer, won't that look a little suspicious?" Sebastian asked, pointing out the flaw in Doug's plan.

"Yeah, but at least no one will know where we've really been and that's the important thing."

Doug had a good point, and since no one else had a better plan, they waited behind the barn as Doug had suggested. When they were certain that the bus drivers had had enough time to return to the castle, they headed deeper into the woods and carefully picked their way down to the back of the chapel. Standing behind the chapel, Doug was reminded of the two times last year when he'd seen a man with a red hat walking into the woods from this very spot. Emma had stopped him from following the man the first time, but she hadn't been around to stop him the second time. Doug had not hesitated to track the man that time and had nearly lost his life. Doug shook his head at the memory and tried to focus once again on the task at hand.

"Okay, so far so good. Now comes the tricky part. We need to walk slowly to the front of the chapel. If we run, it'll look like we've been up to something."

"What if we're seen coming around the chapel? Won't that seem odd?" Martha couldn't help asking. Although the chapel did have a side entrance, it was seldom used by anyone, so Martha's point was a valid one.

"We're just going to have to risk it. Besides, everyone should be inside the castle getting ready for supper."

They were standing on the chapel's north side, which was the side farthest from the castle. No one inside the castle could see them in their current position, and there didn't seem to be any students out on the front lawn. At least for the time being, things seemed to be working in their favor. Doug led them to the chapel's northwest corner and peeked around it. "It looks clear. Let's go," he said with a wave of his hand.

They had to fight their natural inclination to run and will themselves to stroll nonchalantly to the sidewalk leading from the chapel's main entrance. Once they were all on the sidewalk, Emma let out a small sigh of relief. As far as Emma could tell, they had not been seen coming around the chapel. The front lawn was completely devoid of students, and the castle's front windows looked dark and empty. They were walking up the front lawn when Emma found out how wrong she had been. She couldn't stop the small scream of surprise that escaped her lips when Bobby Wilcox suddenly appeared from behind one of the big oak trees directly in front of them. He didn't say anything for a moment but eyed them speculatively as he leaned casually against the tree.

"Where have you all been? Sneaking off school grounds again?"

Caught completely off guard, no one spoke for several moments as their minds scrambled to come up with a plausible explanation. Bobby waited patiently with a smirk on his face. Then as the silence continued, he raised his right eyebrow and crossed his arms in front of his chest. Doug was the first one to find his voice.

"It's none of your business what we've been up to, Wilcox. You don't run things around here."

"Maybe I don't, but my dad does," Bobby sneered.

"Sorry to break it to you, but we've been through this before. Your dad is just one of seven on the school board. That hardly makes him the boss."

"Oh, you haven't heard then. The rest of the board is starting to see the light. They realize that giving out those scholarships may have been a mistake, and due to recent events, they're beginning to question their decision to hire your dad as dean."

Sebastian could tell from Doug's expression that Bobby's last statement had had its intended effect. In an attempt to diffuse the situation, Sebastian said, "You don't know anything, Wilcox. It's all just wishful thinking on your part. Besides, your dad's a liar like you."

"Sebastian!" Martha exclaimed. "You're not helping things."

"I'm tired of this guy accusing us of things and watching our every move. We haven't done anything wrong," Sebastian exclaimed. Then he looked at Bobby and ground out angrily, "Last time I checked, the chapel is considered school grounds."

"But what were you doing behind the chapel? That's the real question, isn't it?" Bobby asked. Bobby looked at Doug and then at Sebastian once again. Both boys looked ready to jump him. If he hadn't been alone, he might have welcomed the battle, but he didn't think he could take them both by himself. "I'll let the liar remark slide for now, Conners," he said with deceptive calm. "We both know what the truth really is."

Bobby started to leave, then stopped suddenly as if he'd just thought of something. Turning back to them, he warned, "Remember, you're being watched and not just by me. With any luck, we'll have you all expelled by Christmas." Chortling softly, he walked toward the castle.

They all watched him go without comment. Each of them had different thoughts swirling through their minds. Doug was relieved that Bobby hadn't seen them coming from the bus barn. Sebastian was thinking how much he'd like to punch Bobby in the nose. Martha was worrying about what Bobby would do next. His statement about getting them all expelled from Dinswood Academy by Christmas had had an ominous ring to it. Emma was worrying too, but for a different reason. Bobby had said the school board was rethinking their decision to award scholarships to qualifying students. Without a scholarship, there was no way Emma could continue to attend Dinswood.

When Bobby had finally disappeared inside the castle, Sebastian broke the silence. "That guy is starting to be a major pain in the neck. We've got to do something about him and all of his flunkies."

Sebastian's words brought a quick response from Doug. "That's just exactly what he wants. We're too clever to let him catch us breaking school rules, so his next best option is to goad us into a fight. I got a break last year when Bobby and I mixed it up, but the board isn't likely to let me get by with it a second time."

"What about me?" Sebastian asked. "I haven't been in a fight before. I'd be glad to give Bobby what he deserves."

"You'd still be risking expulsion. Besides, it's me Bobby wants to get rid of."

"I've never really understood why he hates you so much," Martha said. "There's got to be more to it than just the fact that you're not from a rich family."

"It doesn't really matter why he hates me. We just need to remember that he does and make sure that we don't let him trick us into doing something stupid."

The others nodded their agreement. It wouldn't be easy, but they couldn't let Bobby get to them, or they'd be playing right into his hands.

"I don't know about anyone else, but I'm hungry," Doug said. "I say we forget about Bobby for a while and go get some supper."

As if on cue, Sebastian's stomach growled. "I'm with you," Sebastian said, patting his stomach.

Emma let the others get ahead of her as they walked up the lawn to the castle's main entrance. She was still worrying about what Bobby had said. Doug noticed that something was bothering Emma, so when he got to the castle door, he let Sebastian and Martha go on inside and waited for her to catch up. He was pretty sure he knew what the problem was.

"Emma, don't let what Bobby said worry you. There's no way the board can decide to take away the scholarships now. Bobby doesn't know what he's talking about."

"But what about next year? What if there are no scholarships next year?" Emma asked.

"You're forgetting one important thing."

"What's that?"

"After all you've done for the school, there's no way Lord Dinswood would let the board take your scholarship away. He may have signed the castle over to the state, but he didn't give up control of what goes on here. The board may make the day-to-day decisions, but Lord Dinswood has the final say on things." Doug looked at Emma closely. The look of concern he'd first seen in her face had been replaced by one of sadness.

"What if something happens to Lord Dinswood?" Emma asked quietly. Knowing how much he cared about him, she hated to remind Doug of Lord Dinswood's declining health. Doug grew quiet for a moment. It was evident from his expression that he didn't want to consider the possibility that Lord Dinswood might die.

"Nothing is going to happen to Lord Dinswood," he said, trying to convince himself as much as Emma. "We're going to get the guy who's stealing the sculptures and give them back to Lord Dinswood. Then everything will be all right."

Emma could see the pain in Doug's eyes. Even though she couldn't bring herself to fully share his optimism, she found herself saying, "You're right, Doug. When Lord Dinswood sees the sculptures, he'll perk right up and start getting better."

Doug wasn't fooled. He knew that Emma was agreeing with him because she had a kind heart and didn't want to see him hurt. Impulsively, he put his arms around her and drew her close. "Thanks, Emma," he whispered into her hair.

Tears welled up in Emma's eyes and a lump began to form in her throat. Unable to speak, she pursued the only other option available to her; she hugged him back.

CHAPTER SEVENTEEN
REPRIEVE

They stood like that for another moment, and then Emma felt Doug loosen his hold and pull back slightly. Emma looked up to see that he was staring at her intently. Slowly, he began to lower his face toward hers. Emma felt a shiver of excitement as she realized that he was going to kiss her. Never having been kissed before, she was unsure of what to do, but she'd seen enough kissing on television to know that she should close her eyes. It seemed a natural thing to lift her chin and wait for him to close the distance between them. He was close enough that she could feel his breath on her face, when suddenly the castle's front door flew open with a bang and a loud voice boomed.

"Are you guys coming?"

The voice belonged to Sebastian, and at the sound of it, Doug let go of Emma and quickly backed away. Emma's eyes flew open, and she staggered a bit at the sudden loss of support. After regaining her balance, she turned to see Sebastian and Martha standing in the doorway. That they had been witnesses to the near kiss was evident from their expressions. Sebastian was grinning from ear to ear and kept looking back and forth between Doug and Emma. Martha's right eyebrow was raised and the knowing look she gave Emma had her blushing in embarrassment. Doug, on the other hand, appeared more upset by Sebastian's ill-timed interruption than embarrassed.

"Don't bother answering that question. I think I can figure it out myself," Sebastian joked after a brief silence.

Doug muttered something to Sebastian about his terrible timing as he brushed past him and went inside. After giving Emma one last sly grin and a wink, Sebastian followed. Emma felt her blush deepen and began to mentally berate herself for being embarrassed about something that hadn't actually happened. A second later, Emma experienced a keen pang of disappointment. In a couple of months, she would be turning fourteen, and she had yet to be kissed by a boy. *What was the normal age for a first kiss?* she wondered. It was then that she noticed that Martha was still standing in the doorway—no doubt waiting for Emma to fill her in on all the details.

"I apologized to Sebastian," Martha said quietly, taking Emma completely by surprise. At Emma's look of total incomprehension, Martha explained, "You know, for making it sound like he was stupid over the Esther thing."

Emma had been so convinced Martha would ask her about the scene she had just witnessed that it took her a moment to shift her focus and get a handle on what Martha was telling her. She should have known that Martha would not pry. She would do what she always did, let Emma confide in her if and when she decided to. It was clear that Martha had been feeling guilty about her treatment of Sebastian, and that making things right with him had been uppermost in her mind.

"I'm glad," Emma said, smiling. "I take it from his mood just now that he accepted your apology."

"He did. He's nicer to me than I deserve." Martha looked so forlorn that Emma was prompted to give her a hug.

"Trust me, Martha. You're the nicest person I know, and you deserve every good thing that comes your way."

When Emma let go of Martha, she was surprised to see tears glistening in her eyes. "If I'm so nice then how come I'm so mean to Sebastian?"

"Only you know the answer to that. I'm sure if you think hard enough it will come to you." Emma pulled gently on Martha's arm and, in a lighter tone, said, "Now let's go get something to eat. I'm starving."

As they made their way to the dining room after washing up, Emma pondered the answer to Martha's earlier question. Sebastian had been standing up for himself a lot more lately. It seemed the boy was finally on his way to becoming a man. Maybe Martha was having a hard time adjusting to the new Sebastian. With a sigh, Emma realized it was something Martha would have to work out for herself.

After dinner, Emma and Martha had a moment alone in their dorm room. Clarice and Susie had gone to the lounge to hang out with Preston and some of his friends. Clarice was enjoying the fact that she had an older cousin at school to introduce her to the freshman boys. Emma was surprised to discover that the past couple of weeks she hadn't even thought about Preston. Doug had been occupying her thoughts lately. After what had almost happened tonight, she felt certain that that particular trend would continue.

"We didn't actually kiss, you know," Emma told Martha after filling her in on the events leading up to the scene she'd witnessed.

"I guess Sebastian and I are to blame for that. Sorry," Martha replied with a wry grin. "Would that have been your first kiss?"

Emma nodded, disappointment evident in her expression. Then she asked the question she'd been dying to ask since supper. "Martha, have you ever been kissed by a boy?"

"Once when I was twelve," Martha answered with a smile. "I don't know if you could really call it a kiss. We touched lips is a better description of what happened. His name was Tim, and he was walking me home after a friend's birthday party. One minute we were standing on my front porch together. A second or two later, he'd kissed me and was gone."

"Did he ever kiss you again?"

"No. The birthday party took place right after school got out for summer break. I didn't see him anymore over the summer, and I didn't go back to my old school last year. I started here at Dinswood."

"I wonder what would have happened if Tim had come to Dinswood Academy too," Emma conjectured with a grin.

"I'm glad he didn't," Martha answered. "I like things just the way they are."

"Me too," Emma agreed wholeheartedly. If Tim had come to Dinswood maybe Martha wouldn't have become friends with her, Sebastian, and Doug. Emma couldn't bear to think about that, so she turned her thoughts to what Martha had told her about her first kiss. It made her wonder what Doug's kiss would have been like. That thought prompted her to ask, "Do you think Doug will ever try to kiss me again?"

"No doubt about it," Martha replied without hesitation.

Emma was comforted by the certainty in Martha's voice, but she realized it might be quite some time before another opportunity presented itself. At least she had the hope of a kiss, and that was enough to provide her with pleasant dreams that night.

The next morning at breakfast, Doug told the others his plan for delivering the next sculpture to the Reaper.

"I hung the school banner in my window last night, so I'll have to put one of the sculptures in the barrel tonight. I'm going to give him the one we found at the fountain. It'll be easier for me to get it into the kitchen without arousing suspicion, and it'll be easier if I do it alone."

Knowing that the others would want to argue that last point, Doug continued on without giving them a chance to interrupt. "Earlier this summer, Dad and I were in the bus garage with the state transportation inspector. All the school buses have to be inspected each year. You know, to make sure they're safe. Anyway, while we were waiting for this guy to do his thing, Dad and I began rummaging through all the junk in there. I ran across a box filled with some really nice pieces of lumber—some cherry wood, some oak, and stuff like that. Later, we asked Lord Dinswood about it, and he said it was some of the wood left over from when he built his boat and the furniture we saw in his cabin. I asked him if I could use what was in the box to build some things for my hobby class. He said it would be okay, but after that, I kind of forgot about it. Yesterday when we were in there, I saw the box and thought it would be the perfect way to get the sculpture of Esther into the school."

"Good idea, Doug," Martha said, understanding what Doug was planning. "You can just put the sculpture in the box along with the lumber and trot right up to the school with it. If anyone asks about it, you have a perfectly good explanation that both your dad and Lord Dinswood can verify."

"Even though I have a good reason for going to the bus barn, I'd still appreciate it if you guys would keep an eye on Bobby for me. I thought I'd wait until everyone's working on homework after supper tonight. If we play it right, I can slip out, deliver the sculpture, and be back before Bobby even notices I've been gone. He might even think that I've just gone up to spend some time with Dad."

Emma didn't like the idea of Doug making the delivery alone, but she could see the logic in his plan. If they all disappeared after supper, Bobby would be alerted that something was going on. She didn't say anything for a moment as she played Doug's plan out in her mind, looking for any flaws that he might have missed. Finally, she was forced to conclude the plan was sound, and barring any unforeseen difficulties, it should work. The cooks would leave after cleaning up the kitchen for the evening, so Doug should be able to bring the box into the castle through the back door. This door, seldom used by anyone but staff, opened into a short hallway. The entrance to the kitchen would be the first door on the right. It should be a simple matter for Doug to slip into the kitchen unseen, deliver the sculpture, and then proceed to the main hall with the box of lumber.

"You sure you don't want me to go with you?" Sebastian asked.

"Thanks, but I really think it will work better if I go alone."

No more was said for a while as they finished eating. Emma glanced up at the dining hall's large clock and realized that the Sunday morning chapel service would be starting in fifteen minutes.

"We'd better get going, or we'll be late for chapel," she told the others.

Without comment, they emptied their trays and headed to the chapel. As they approached the rectangular building with its stained-glass windows and steeple, complete with a bell tower, Emma was reminded of the night before when they'd been hiding behind it. She looked at the others but couldn't tell from their expressions whether or not they were having similar thoughts. Thinking about last night soon had her thinking about the near kiss, as she'd begun to think of it. Emma risked a quick glance at Doug. His expression was solemn. It was clear that his mind was on far weightier matters. Emma sighed and wondered for the hundredth time if he would ever try to kiss her again.

As was often the case lately, it seemed like Reverend Palmer had prepared his sermon with the four of them in mind. He spoke about relying on God and trusting Him when trials come our way.

Reverend Palmer told them, "God's promise isn't that we won't have trials but that when we do, He'll be with us through them."

Emma left the service feeling comforted, and she hoped that Reverend Palmer's words had been a comfort to Doug as well. After all, it was Doug who was really in the heat of battle. The rest of them were merely trying to help as best they could from the sidelines.

The day passed quickly. They spent some time enjoying the fine weather outside. It was supposed to be the last warm day of the week, so they wanted to take full advantage of it.

After supper, they found Bobby and his buddies in the lounge. As luck would have it, they were sitting in the corner farthest from the door. Doug led them to a spot near the door where they could see Bobby and he could see them. Being next to the door would make it easier for Doug to slip out without Bobby noticing right away. They couldn't have asked for a better seating arrangement. Emma was reminded of what Reverend Palmer had said just that morning. God was certainly helping them through this particular trial.

As planned, Doug sat with them for a while and attempted to concentrate on his homework. It was clear, however, from the number of times he ran his hands through his hair that his mind wasn't on the book sitting in front of him. Emma couldn't help feeling sorry for him.

Finally, Doug gave up the pretense of studying all together and, after a quick glance to see that Bobby wasn't looking their way, slipped out of the room. Emma fretted the whole time he was gone, her mind imagining all kinds of scenarios where Doug got caught with the sculpture. After a while, she realized that she'd been staring at the same page for the last fifteen minutes. With a sigh, she closed her book and looked over at Martha.

"I can't study either," Martha said.

"Me neither," Sebastian said. "I wish he'd get back."

As it turned out, it would be another forty-five minutes until Doug would return. During that time, the three of them pretended to study, occasionally talking quietly. Emma was facing Bobby, so it was up to her to keep an eye on him without alerting him to her interest. Every couple of minutes, Emma would glance his way. Bobby was usually busy talking and didn't notice her surreptitious looks. The next time Emma risked a peek at the far corner of the room, she was disconcerted to see Preston Danvers watching her. After a few more minutes, it became clear to Emma that Preston thought she was looking at him.

"Uh-oh," Emma said softly.

"What?" Martha asked quickly.

"Well, I've been trying to keep an eye on Bobby, but every time I look over there, Preston is staring at me. I'm afraid he thinks I'm flirting with him or something."

"That's all we need," Martha said with a roll of her eyes.

"Well, at least Bobby doesn't know we're watching him," Sebastian pointed out.

"Yeah, but we don't want Preston to get the idea that Emma likes him. We can't have him tagging along after us because he's in love with Emma. We've still got three more sculptures to find."

"Well, then why don't I trade places with Emma? That way I can do the spying, and Emma will have her back to Blondie," Sebastian suggested.

"Won't that look a little suspicious?" Emma asked.

The others agreed that it probably would seem a little odd for them to suddenly trade places. They were quiet for a moment as they each tried to come up with a solution. They were saved from their current dilemma by the timely return of Doug.

"What took you so long?" they asked in unison.

"Sorry," Doug said as he took the empty seat next to Emma. "I had to get the key to the bus barn from Dad first. Thankfully, he was still working in his office."

"Did you have any trouble getting into the room with the barrel?"

"No, everything went like clockwork. It just took a little longer than I'd thought. After I put the sculpture in the barrel, I had to take the key back to Dad, and he wanted to talk a while. I didn't mean to worry you guys."

"It's okay, Doug. We should have remembered you'd need the key," Sebastian said.

"Did Bobby notice that I was gone?"

"I don't think so." This time it was Martha who answered. She wasn't sure whether she should tell him about the problem with Preston or not. Knowing how much Doug disliked Preston, she decided against it. She would leave it up to the others whether or not to say anything. Sebastian and Emma must also have decided against mentioning it, because nothing was said. It was just as well. Doug already had enough to deal with. It was then that Martha noticed the worried look on Doug's face. "What's wrong, Doug?" she asked quickly.

"Well, it's just that I delivered the sculpture a couple of weeks ahead of schedule. I was afraid that if I left it in the bus barn someone might find it, and I didn't want to risk trying to get it to my room. Besides, I don't have any more places in my room to hide things."

"So what's the problem?" Sebastian asked, obviously not understanding what Doug was worried about.

"He's afraid that since we delivered the sculpture so quickly, the Reaper won't give us as much time to find the next one," Emma answered, looking at Doug for confirmation of her hypothesis.

"That's it exactly," Doug answered, nodding.

"I never thought of that," Sebastian said with a frown. "I sure am glad we already have another one hidden away."

"Me too," Doug said, running a hand through his hair. "But I was kind of hoping we could stay one ahead."

"Next Saturday, it's our turn to go to Windland. We'll talk to Mr. Munsen and see if he'll help us check the places on our list that are along the river. It's possible we can still stay one step ahead of the Reaper," Martha said in an encouraging tone.

Doug didn't say anything for a moment. It was clear from his expression that he didn't share Martha's optimism. Finally, he sighed and said, "Well, it's too late to change things now. We'll just have to take things as they come. Martha's right about one thing though. We need to make sure we talk to Mr. Munsen Saturday."

Doug didn't know what they'd do if Mr. Munsen didn't agree to help them. His stomach clenched tightly at the thought. Something of his inner turmoil must have shown on his face, because when he looked up, the others were watching him closely with obvious concern. Inexplicably, his thoughts returned to what Reverend Palmer had said just that morning. God would be with him in the trials ahead. As Doug thought about that and looked at his friends, his stomach muscles gradually relaxed, and he was comforted.

Doug checked his mailbox every day for the next week, fully expecting another letter of instruction from the Reaper, but none came. Saturday morning, Doug hurriedly got ready and, as had become his habit, headed to his mailbox. Today was the eighth-graders' turn to go to Windland, and he wanted to check it before he left. Once again, the box was empty. Doug didn't know whether he should be relieved or worried. As he made his way to the front entrance, he decided he was relieved. No news was good news. Doug met up with Sebastian on the castle's front steps. He shook his head in answer to Sebastian's questioning glance. When Emma and Martha appeared, he once again shook his head in the negative.

"No word?" Martha asked.

"Not a thing," Doug replied. It seemed that, for whatever reason, they had been given a reprieve.

CHAPTER EIGHTEEN
RETURN TO WINDLAND

They waited on the steps a few more minutes before they saw the buses pulling into the main driveway from the direction of the bus barn. The sun was shining, and there wasn't a cloud in the sky. The temperature was in the low seventies. It was a perfect day for a trip to Windland. Last year, a torrential downpour had marred their first trip to the little town. In fact, it had rained so much that flooding had kept them from returning to the castle until the following morning. The entire group of seventh graders had been forced to spend the night in the town's only motel. Emma hadn't minded. She liked the Windland Inn, which was designed in a manner similar to a lodge, with a high ceiling and a large central fireplace. That fateful day a year ago had marked the beginning of the treasure hunt.

With a sigh, Emma looked at the sky again. It didn't look like the weather was going to be a problem this year. Emma was glad. They already had enough to worry about. She just hoped that Doug would get a chance to talk to Mr. Munsen and that he would agree to help them.

Emma's thoughts were brought to a halt when she was jostled from behind by the crowd of eighth graders surging toward the waiting buses. She boarded the second bus in the line with Martha right behind her. Doug and Sebastian, however, were nowhere in sight. With all of the pushing, they must have gotten separated. Emma took the first available seat and scooted over so that Martha could sit next to her. The bus was filling up fast, and there were only a few seats left. Emma waited anxiously to see if Doug and Sebastian would board. A moment later, the doors closed with a hiss, and Emma realized the boys must have ended up on one of the other buses. It didn't really matter. They would meet up once they reached Windland.

Emma listened to the racket made by the other students as they conversed excitedly and smiled at Martha.

"You'd think we were on our way to an amusement park," Emma remarked loudly so that Martha could hear her.

"I know. It's hard to believe that anyone could get so worked up about a day in Windland," Martha agreed.

"I bet it's nothing compared to Paris," Emma said with a laugh.

"Not even close."

The two girls gave up trying to converse after that and instead sat in companionable silence, content to watch the passing scenery.

Doug and Sebastian were doing the same thing in the bus directly behind them. Doug was too worried about what he was going to say to Mr. Munsen to take part in casual conversation. Sebastian must have understood what Doug was going through, because for once he was silent.

All too soon the buses were pulling into the Windland Inn's large parking lot where they would remain until it was time to transport the students back to the school. The school's buses always used the inn's parking lot because it was the only one in town big enough to accommodate them without impeding the parking of other customers.

Emma and Martha stepped down onto the pavement and watched as the bus carrying the boys maneuvered into a spot. In no time, the boys had joined them, and by mutual consent, they headed to the bookstore to talk to Alice. Alice was Mr. Munsen's wife and ran the bookstore for Lord Dinswood. She would know how to get ahold of her husband.

As they walked briskly down the sidewalk leading to the bookstore, Emma noticed that Mr. Munsen's truck was parked in front of it. What a lucky break for them! Mr. Munsen was probably in the store at this very moment talking to his wife. It looked like Doug would get his chance to talk to him. As they got closer, Emma could see that Mr. Munsen's truck was towing a boat and trailer. He was probably planning to do a little fishing that afternoon. If that were the case, maybe he wouldn't mind taking them to at least one of the places on their list. Emma looked over at Doug to see if he had seen the boat. The smile he gave her when he noticed her gaze was all the answer she needed.

When they entered the store, Mr. Munsen was at the counter talking to his wife just as they'd anticipated. The first time Emma had ever seen Mr. Munsen he had reminded her of a great big bear. He did again today, even without the winter coat and fur hat he'd been wearing upon their first acquaintance. As it had last winter, a mustache and full beard covered his face. He was tall with a sturdy build—a large man with a loud booming voice to match. Although his appearance was rather intimidating, they had learned last year that he was a good man with a kind heart. Suddenly, Emma felt certain that he would agree to help them.

Doug didn't waste any time. He went up to Mr. Munsen and waited patiently for him to finish speaking to his wife. When Mr. Munsen turned to leave, Doug spoke up quickly. "Mr. Munsen, could I talk to you a minute?"

"Why, howdy there, Doug. I didn't notice ya standin' there. It's good to see ya again."

"It's good to see you again too, sir."

Something in Doug's tone must have alerted Mr. Munsen because he looked at Doug more closely. The boy was a little thinner than when he'd last seen him, and the worry in his expression was hard to miss. Mr. Munsen's bushy eyebrows came together in a frown, and he said in a softer tone, "What can I do for ya, son?"

Doug hesitated for a moment and then said quietly so that only Mr. Munsen could hear him, "Sir, could we please talk in private?"

Mr. Munsen nodded. "Follow me."

Mr. Munsen led Doug around behind the counter and up to the door leading into the storage room. Emma watched as they both disappeared inside and felt her nervousness return. Mr. Munsen was their only hope. If he didn't agree to help them, she didn't know what they'd do. Emma felt, rather than saw, Martha come up to stand beside her. Sebastian soon joined them. The three of them stared anxiously at the storage room door as if it could tell them what was going on inside. Mrs. Munsen was helping a customer at the time and didn't appear to have noticed her husband's strange behavior. However, as soon as Alice Munsen had finished with the student at the register, Emma found out how wrong her assumption had been.

Alice looked over at the three of them standing rooted to the spot like a trio of statues, and it was obvious that her curiosity had been aroused. She came around the counter and stopped when she was directly in front of them. "What's going on in there?" she asked, inclining her head in the direction of the storage room.

Not knowing how to respond, the three of them stared at Alice in silence for several long uncomfortable seconds. Emma racked her brain for a plausible explanation, while Alice continued to look at them with raised eyebrows. Emma looked over at Martha and Sebastian and received a shrug from both of them. Realizing that Alice wasn't going to go away until she'd gotten an answer, Emma decided to tell the truth or at least a small part of the truth. "Doug needed to talk to your husband for a minute."

"About what?" was Alice's quick response.

Emma hesitated for just a moment and, giving Martha and Sebastian a sidelong glance, replied, "I really couldn't say."

Martha tried not to smile at the genius of Emma's answer. She had in essence told the truth. All Emma had said was that she wasn't free to tell Mrs. Munsen what Doug wanted to talk to her husband about. However, her reply could be easily misinterpreted, and that was precisely what Emma was hoping for.

It was hard to tell whether Alice Munsen had been fooled by Emma's vague response or not. She continued to stare the three of them down in what appeared to be an effort to intimidate them into giving more information. Fortunately, a moment later, another student stepped up to the counter to pay for some books, and Mrs. Munsen was forced to return to her position behind the counter. Emma wished Doug would hurry up. Mrs. Munsen had only been temporarily sidetracked. Emma didn't know what she'd say if Mrs. Munsen decided to press the issue.

All three of them breathed a huge sigh of relief when Doug and Mr. Munsen emerged from the storage room. Emma couldn't tell a thing from Doug's expression. Mr. Munsen promptly left the store and could be seen getting into his truck through the store's big front window. Emma was about to conclude that Doug had failed in his efforts to enlist Mr. Munsen's help when Doug motioned for the three of them to follow him back into the storage room. What in the world was going on?

Sebastian and Martha looked just as confused as Emma but followed along nonetheless, bypassing Alice as they skirted around her on their way to the storage room. Alice gave them a strange look but was too busy checking out another customer to stop them or question them further. Emma had no doubt that she would interrogate her husband thoroughly at the first opportunity.

Once they were all in the storage room and the door had been closed, Doug filled them in.

"I told Mr. Munsen the whole story, and he said he'd help us. He's going to take us to the two locations on our list that are on the river today."

"If he's going to help us, why did he leave just now?" Martha asked.

This time, it was Sebastian who answered, "He's going to pull off on a side road to pick us up. That way we won't be seen leaving town by any of our classmates. Last year when Mr. Munsen helped us, we went out the store's back door and ran down the alley to meet him. I'm guessing we're supposed to do the same thing now." As this last was said, Sebastian looked over at Doug for confirmation.

Doug nodded. "That's exactly right. You two girls are supposed to ride in the truck with Mr. Munsen. Sebastian, he wants the two of us to climb into the bed of the pickup since there's not room for all four of us in the truck. We'll need to make sure we stay out of sight until we get out of town."

Emma was dying to know all that had transpired between Doug and Mr. Munsen, but now was not the time to ask. If they were going to visit both locations today, there was no time to waste. Besides, if they stayed in the storage room any longer, Alice Munsen might come in and start questioning them once more. This last thought prompted Emma to say in urgent tones, "We need to get going before Mrs. Munsen comes in here and asks what we're doing."

"Yeah," Sebastian and Martha agreed in unison.

Doug needed no further prompting. He was anxious to get started too, so without further comment, he went over to the door leading into the alley and opened it. After a quick peek to make sure the coast was clear, he stepped out into the alleyway and beckoned for the others to follow. As they headed to the east end of the alley, they saw Mr. Munsen pull up in his pickup truck. When they got to the truck, the girls quickly opened the passenger-side door, climbed inside, and crouched down. The boys jumped into the bed of the truck and ducked down so they couldn't be seen.

As soon as the kids were all loaded and hidden, Mr. Munsen put the truck in gear and headed out of town toward the river access road. As he drove, he mulled over everything Doug had told him. At first, he'd had a hard time believing that someone would threaten Lord Dinswood and Doug's dad, but if the sculptures the kids had found were really the Mortals, they would be worth a fortune in today's market. People had been killed for a lot less.

Mr. Munsen liked Doug a lot. It was clear the boy was carrying an awful burden—a burden no one should have to carry, especially a fourteen-year-old boy. When Doug had asked for his help, he couldn't refuse. In fact, he'd felt honored that Doug trusted him enough to ask for his help. His first impulse had been to inform the police, but when Doug had explained that the lives of his dad and Lord Dinswood were at risk, he'd had to rethink things. For now, he'd take the kids to the places along the river. Then later, he'd have time to figure out a way to nail the monster who was using kids to do his dirty work. There had to be a way to catch this guy, and he wouldn't rest until he found it.

As soon as they were out of town, Emma and Martha got up from their crouched positions and sat on the truck's bench seat. Curious to see how the boys were faring, they turned and looked out the back window. Doug and Sebastian were sitting comfortably in the bed of the truck, enjoying the breeze as the truck sped along the paved road they were currently on. Soon they turned off onto a gravel road and traveled a mile or so before turning left onto an intersecting road. This road paralleled the river.

The water was so clear that in most places you could see the rocky bottom. It reminded Emma of glass, and when she mentioned this, Mr. Munsen explained that that was how the river had gotten its name. *Hyaline* means transparent as glass. Where the water was deep, it appeared to be an emerald green. Emma could see a bridge up ahead that would take them to the river access ramp on the opposite side. The Hyaline River wasn't large as rivers go, only approximately one hundred and fifty feet across at its widest point, but it was large enough to offer all the diversions people were fond of such as fishing and boating.

Mr. Munsen instructed them to get out of the truck before backing the boat and trailer down the boat ramp. Emma watched as Mr. Munsen carefully maneuvered the trailer into the water until the motor was in water deep enough that he could start it. Then he got out of the truck and climbed into the boat, starting the motor with one pull. Carefully, Mr. Munsen backed the boat off the trailer and brought it alongside the dock so that Doug could grab the rope he offered. Doug kept the boat from floating away while Mr. Munsen parked the truck and trailer in one of the spots in the parking lot provided for that purpose.

When Mr. Munsen returned, he was carrying two large flashlights. "You'll need 'em for the cave. I keep 'em in the truck in case of emergencies," he said by way of explanation.

After stowing the flashlights in the bow of the boat and climbing into the back so he could operate the motor and steer the boat, he told the boys to get in and sit on the seat toward the bow. The girls were told to sit on the seat in the middle. Mr. Munsen's fishing boat had a flat bottom with square ends. Emma learned later from Doug that it was a johnboat. All she cared about at the time was that the boat was plenty big enough for the five of them to ride comfortably.

With apparent ease, Mr. Munsen pulled the boat away from the ramp, and in no time, they were cruising down the river at a good clip. They only had to slow down in places where the water was relatively shallow. Mr. Munsen wanted to make sure the motor's propellers didn't hit the rocky bottom.

Emma noticed that the water flowed faster in the shallow spots and seemed to move at a lazy pace in the deep areas. Mr. Munsen told them that the deep areas were called eddies and the shallow areas were called shoals. He also explained that normally they would have had to drag the boat over the shoals, but due to recent rains, the water level was high enough that the shoals could be motored through if one was careful.

Emma sat back and enjoyed the ride. The air felt good as it hit her face, and the scenery was amazing. Trees lined the riverbank on their right, and bluffs towered above them on the left. Every now and then Emma could see openings in the rocky bluffs and wondered briefly what mysteries those caves might possess. The caves looked impossible to get to, and Emma found herself hoping that the cave they would be searching would be easier to access.

"I'll take you to Sylar Springs first," Mr. Munsen shouted over the sound of the motor.

Sylar Springs was one of the places on their list. Doug had found out that it was a natural spring along the river. The water from the spring flowed into the river from an opening in the bluff just below the water line. The water was said to be clear and extremely cold. Swimmers were warned to stay out of it because the sudden drop in temperature as one went from the relatively warm river water into the water of the spring could cause muscles to cramp and eventually hypothermia. Emma was hoping that if one of the sculptures was hidden there, it would be somewhere around the spring and not in the water itself.

Suddenly, Mr. Munsen cut the motor and guided them to a spot close to the bluff.

"Here we are," he said as he dropped the boat's anchor into the water. "Stick your hands in the water and see how cold it is."

Mr. Munsen chuckled at their gasps of surprise as they complied. The water was downright icy. Emma couldn't imagine anyone swimming in water that cold.

"Doug, you said the other sculptures were marked by some kind of symbols, right?" Mr. Munsen asked.

"Yes, sir. We should look for carvings of a raven and a rose." Then Doug went on to explain the significance of the symbols.

"Well, I've never noticed any carvings before, but I wasn't really looking for any," Mr. Munsen replied with a shrug.

The next several minutes were spent carefully examining the rocky surface of the bluff for any symbols. Climbing vines covered the rock in places so when the visible sections revealed nothing, Mr. Munsen used an oar to bring the boat closer to the bluff so that Doug and Sebastian could pull the vines aside. This wasn't as easy as it sounded, and several times both Doug and Sebastian almost ended up in the water. While the boys worked on removing the vines, the girls examined the portions of the bluff just beneath the waterline. After nearly an hour of looking, they were forced to conclude that Darius had not chosen Sylar Springs as a resting site for one of Marnatti's sculptures.

Seeing the look of disappointment on Doug's face, Mr. Munsen said, "Don't worry, Doug. I've got a feelin' in my bones that you'll find something in the cave."

Without waiting for a reply, Mr. Munsen pulled up the anchor and, after starting the motor, headed further down river. A few minutes later, Mr. Munsen began to slow the boat again. He let the motor idle for a moment. "There's a lot of caves along this river, but from your description, Cathedral Cave is the one ya want. It's called Cathedral Cave because it has a rock formation that looks like a giant pipe organ. Ya know, the kind of thing you'd see in a big cathedral.

There's a larger cave further downstream that you can pull a boat into, but I'm pretty sure this is the one ya want. If ya don't find anything here, we can try the other one if there's time."

That was the problem. They were running out of time. They'd already used up an hour at Sylar Springs, and it had taken them at least a half hour to get to the river and get the boat in. They had to be back in Windland to board the buses by four o'clock. This cave would probably be the only other spot they'd have time to search today. Emma prayed that this time they'd find something.

Mr. Munsen motored the boat over to the bank and onto a gravel bar a little downstream of the cave. The entrance to the cave was just a short uphill climb from their current position.

"The cave goes back quite a ways. You'll come to a real narrow passage before ya get to the big room the cave is named for," Mr. Munsen informed them. "There are branches off the main passage every now and then, but they don't go very far, and they all come to a dead end. Ya shouldn't have any trouble finding the cathedral, as folks round here call it."

"Have a lot of people explored the cave?" Doug asked as he climbed out of the boat. He was having a hard time imagining how one of the Mortals could have remained hidden in a cave all these years, especially if that cave had seen a lot of foot traffic.

"Couldn't really say. We used to go in it some when we was kids, but not too many young folks are into spelunking these days. All most kids wanna do nowadays is play video games—present company excepted of course," Mr. Munsen added with a look at the four youngsters.

"They don't let us play video games at the academy," Sebastian pointed out with a note of pride.

Mr. Munsen looked at Sebastian through narrowed eyes for a moment. "That's a good thing," he said after a moment and then, on a sigh, added, "Well, I think I'll do a little fishin' while you guys search the cave. Just give me a whistle when you're ready to go." Before pulling the boat away, Mr. Munsen handed Doug and Sebastian the flashlights he'd had the foresight to bring along. They wouldn't have been able to get very far in the cave without light.

"Thanks, Mr. Munsen," Doug said as he accepted one of the flashlights. "We really appreciate your help."

Frank Munsen heard the sincerity in Doug's voice and felt a swift tide of rising emotion. Anger was among the many emotions he was experiencing. Once again, he vowed to find a way to catch the maniac that was blackmailing Doug. Doug had told him they called the guy the "Reaper." Mr. Munsen felt that that was too grand a name for a man who was a criminal and a coward. In an effort to regain his composure, he cleared his throat and said quickly, "Remember, just whistle."

Then he started the motor, and Doug and Sebastian pushed the boat off the gravel bar. They watched as Mr. Munsen headed the boat a little way up river before stopping and dropping anchor. He would remain there fishing until they needed him. Emma found the knowledge that Mr. Munsen was close by very comforting.

"Well, we'd better get going," Doug said, breaking the sudden silence that had fallen. Without waiting for a reply, he set off briskly toward the cave entrance.

With a last look at Mr. Munsen, the others followed.

CHAPTER NINETEEN
CATHEDRAL CAVE

t was clear from Doug's expression that he didn't expect to find anything in the cave. Emma would have liked to reassure him, but she didn't hold out much hope either. Too many people had been in the cave since the time of Darius and Rebecca. Anything Darius might have hidden in the cave would surely have been found a long time ago. Nevertheless, the cave was one of the places Rebecca had mentioned more than once in her journals, and it needed to be searched on the off chance that Darius had somehow managed to find a perfect hiding place for one of the sculptures. At least then they could mark it off their list.

The entrance to the cave was a large open area, but it quickly narrowed to a passage that required them to go single file. The rocky walls of the cave were uneven and pitted. Doug led the way with his flashlight, followed by Emma, then Martha, and lastly Sebastian. The cave had the smell of damp earth and was several degrees cooler than the air outside. At times, the passage opened up a bit. Emma used these sections to breathe deeply and attempt to get over the closed-in feeling she was experiencing. She knew they would soon come to a much narrower passage, and she wasn't looking forward to it. At least they didn't have to worry about getting lost. If they made a wrong turn, it would quickly come to a dead end, and they could just retrace their steps back to the main passage.

The cave was quiet except for the sounds of their shoes on the rocky floor. Other than the four of them, there didn't appear to be another living thing in the cave. Emma knew that there were probably spiders, lizards, bats, and other undesirable critters in the cave hiding just outside the beam of light cast by Doug's flashlight. She was glad she couldn't see them because then she could pretend they weren't scurrying about in the darkness as the four of them passed by.

"Do you think there are any bats in here?" Martha whispered.

"Probably," Sebastian replied before Emma could say anything to reassure Martha.

"Sebastian!" Emma scolded.

"What? I'm not gonna lie to her."

"Feel free to lie to me from now on," Martha said as she worriedly scanned the ceiling of the cave, "but only about bats."

Although the passage they were currently in was narrow, the ceiling was at least thirty feet above their heads. Martha could only see blackness as she looked up. Doug was keeping the beam of his flashlight trained on the cave floor in front of him so that he could see where he was going. Up until now, Sebastian had been doing the same. At Martha's comment, he turned his flashlight upward. Much to Martha's dismay, it revealed hundreds of bats hanging from the roof of the cave. Fortunately, Sebastian's brief illumination hadn't disturbed the bats.

His illumination of the ceiling had been brief, because with a speed approaching that of light, Martha had turned around and punched him. He had instinctively lifted both of his arms in self-defense and had nearly dropped his flashlight.

"Ouch!" Sebastian said, rubbing his arm.

"Are you crazy? What do you think you're doing? Are you trying to get them all stirred up?"

"Don't get all excited. They're nocturnal, remember?"

"I swear if a single bat starts flapping around, I'm out of here, and I'll spend the next eight months plotting how to get even. You got it?"

"Calm down, Martha. I promise I won't let them get you," Sebastian said, laughing.

"And just how do you plan to stop them?"

"If a bat comes your way, I'll knock you down and cover you with my body."

"That is the stupidest thing I've ever heard, and you'd better not knock me down for any reason."

"You're awfully hard to please," Sebastian said, and although Emma couldn't see it, she was certain he was grinning from ear to ear.

Martha didn't have time to reply because Doug had come to a fork in the passage, which prompted him to ask, "Well, which way? Right or left?"

"The left passage looks bigger," Sebastian pointed out.

"Left it is then."

This turned out to be the correct choice because it did not immediately come to a dead end. Emma was glad. She didn't want to have to spend any more time in the cave than necessary. They continued on until they came to another fork, but this time they took the wrong tunnel and had to retrace their steps.

"Does this passage ever end?" Martha complained when they came to yet another fork.

"We're bound to be close," Emma said more to convince herself than Martha.

Her words turned out to be prophetic because, a few seconds later, the passage opened up into a huge room. Doug swept his flashlight around the room, as did Sebastian. The girls simply looked on in awe. Emma had never seen anything like it.

The stalagmites on the right side of the room stood in a pool of water that shimmered each time the beam of one of the flashlights swept over it. Above each stalagmite was the icicle-shaped stalactite that had produced it. Emma knew that both types of formations were made by dripping water, and that the different colors were due to the presence of different minerals. The white ones were composed primarily of calcite; the red ones were mostly iron. The formations that Emma thought the most beautiful were a combination of both. The ceiling on the right side of the room was quite a bit lower than that on the left side, and in some places, the stalactites and stalagmites had grown together to produce columns and pillars. Most of the formations, particularly the ones made of calcite, reminded Emma of foam insulation because of their wavy appearance. However, when Emma reached out to touch one of them, there was no doubt that it was rock.

"There it is," Doug said suddenly, his voice echoing in the cavernous room.

There was no need to ask what Doug was referring to. He had his flashlight trained on the far wall, illuminating what appeared to be a pipe organ constructed of closely packed white cylinders that tapered to a point at the bottom. All that was missing was the keyboard.

"You can sure see why they call this Cathedral Cave," Sebastian commented. "It really does look like something from the Phantom of the Opera."

"That is the neatest thing I've ever seen," Martha said with a sigh. "I just wish I had my camera."

"Maybe sometime we can come back," Sebastian offered.

"You'd have to get rid of the bats first" was Martha's quick response. It really was a shame that she hadn't thought to bring her camera because, as wondrous as Cathedral Cave was, she knew that she would never set foot in it again.

With one last look at the calcite pipe organ, Doug said, "We'd better start looking for any markings Darius might have left."

Emma had been so enraptured by the rock formations that for a moment she'd forgotten why they had come. Sebastian's murmured "Oh yeah" let Emma know she hadn't been the only one.

They split up into pairs so that they could make a quicker survey of the room. Sebastian and Martha began checking the cave wall on the left side, and Doug and Emma began examining the walls to the right and left of the opening through which they had entered. The area with the standing water was going to be more of a problem, so they left it for the time being.

"We didn't find anything," Sebastian told Doug after a few minutes.

"We didn't either," Doug replied with a sigh. He had been hoping they wouldn't have to check the area with the water. Now they had no choice.

"How deep do you think the water is?" Sebastian asked as if he had read Doug's mind.

Doug shined his flashlight into the water, which was clear enough that you could see the muddy bottom. It didn't appear to be more than a foot deep. Just to make sure, Doug put his arm in the water and was relieved when his hand hit the bottom, the water coming up a little past his elbow. Without another word he took off his shoes and socks and rolled his jeans up to his knees.

"Wait, I'll help," Sebastian said. He gave Martha his flashlight while he quickly removed his own socks and shoes and rolled his pants up like Doug had done. He sucked in his breath as he joined Doug in the frigid water. Taking his flashlight from Martha, he directed its beam into the water and began carefully making his way around the stalactites and stalagmites. Both he and Doug had to move about in a crouched position because the ceiling was so low. Emma and Martha watched and waited in the semidarkness, hoping against hope that the boys would find something. Emma tried not to think about the mud that must be squishing between their toes, and Martha tried not to think about the critters that might be in the water. Soon the boys were stepping back onto dry ground.

"Well, there's nothing in the water," Doug informed them. "It's just like I thought. This was a big waste of time."

"Yeah, we got our feet frozen off for nothing," Sebastian agreed. Then both boys began putting their shoes and socks back on while the girls held their flashlights.

Martha watched them in silence for a moment and had the strange feeling that they shouldn't give up just yet. "I think we should look around some more. We probably won't get a chance to come back here again, so we'd better make sure we haven't missed anything." After she finished speaking, Martha could have kicked herself for suggesting that they spend even more time in the cave. After all, the longer they stayed in the cave, the greater the chance they'd be bitten by a rabid bat. Martha consoled herself with the knowledge that at least there didn't appear to be any bats in this particular part of the cave.

"Martha's right," Sebastian quickly chimed in.

Although Doug didn't think it would make any difference, he agreed to look around one more time. They spent another fifteen minutes carefully examining the cave walls for carvings of a raven and a rose but had no luck.

"I guess Darius didn't hide anything in here," Sebastian finally conceded.

Emma could hear real disappointment in his tone. Apparently, Sebastian had been the only one of the four of them to actually believe that Darius had hidden one of the sculptures in the cave.

"Let's get out of here. We've wasted enough of our time." Even though he hadn't really expected to find anything in the cave, Doug still felt frustrated. They'd had two places to check today, and they hadn't found anything at either one. Their list of likely hiding spots was getting shorter, and they still had three sculptures to find. His stomach knotted with worry as he thought about what could happen to his dad and Lord Dinswood if they failed to recover the rest of the Mortals.

Doug took a deep breath in an attempt to clear his head of all its worrisome thoughts, then turned and led the way out of the cathedral room. Eager to return to sunlight, Emma and Martha followed. It was then that it happened. Later Emma would come to look upon it as a genuine miracle. Sebastian started to follow them out of the room and then suddenly decided to take one last look at the pipe organ formation on the far wall. When he whipped back around, his feet got tangled up, and he lost his balance. As he fell, his flashlight went flying through the air finally landing in a depression several feet from where he lay. Amazingly, it hadn't broken but continued to send out its powerful beam at an upward angle.

"Sebastian, are you all right?" Martha asked as she hurried to his side.

"Yeah, I'm okay."

With a shake of his head, Sebastian rolled over and sat up, gratefully taking the helping hand that Martha offered. While Martha strained to get Sebastian back on his feet, Doug began picking his way over to where Sebastian's flashlight had come to rest. Emma was the only one left to see what its beam had revealed.

"Doug, don't touch that flashlight!" Emma shouted.

"What?" Curious, Doug's eyes followed the shaft of light cast by Sebastian's flashlight. It was shining on a portion of the cave wall near the ceiling and to the right of the entrance. From this angle, carvings of a raven and a rose could be seen clearly. Suddenly feeling ashamed that he'd been so quick to give up, Doug sent up a silent prayer of thanks.

Sebastian was the first to find his voice. "Well, what do you know about that. Why didn't we see them before?"

Emma had been wondering the same thing. The walls of the cave were uneven with a multitude of rocky outcroppings, especially near the ceiling. One such outcropping obstructed the view of the carvings unless you were looking at that section from exactly the right angle. Miraculously, Sebastian's flashlight had managed to land in the one spot from which the carvings could be seen.

"You've got to be looking at them from the right angle," Doug finally answered, having reached the same conclusion as Emma. Everything made sense now. It explained why none of the people who had previously explored the cave had found the carvings. If it hadn't been for Sebastian's "accident," they wouldn't have found them either.

"We've found the carvings, but where is the sculpture?" Sebastian asked.

"There must be a ledge or some kind of opening up there," Doug replied.

"How did Darius get up there? It looks like it's at least twenty feet or more." Martha pointed out. She was afraid of heights, or more precisely, she was afraid of falling from them.

"He must have climbed," Emma responded.

Doug swept the beam of his flashlight over the portion of the cave wall beneath the carvings. There were plenty of hand and footholds. A man like Darius, who had spent most of his life on a ship, would have had no difficulty climbing such a wall.

"Darius probably climbed the wall and then pulled the sculpture up with a rope," Doug concluded. "Emma, hold my flashlight. You and Sebastian keep your lights trained on the wall, while I go see if there's anything up there."

"Doug, I don't think you should try it. What if you fall? You could really get hurt." Martha was nearly beside herself with worry. She couldn't imagine climbing the wall herself, and it scared her to think that someone else would try it. Besides if something happened to Doug, it would be a long time before they could get him any help.

"I don't really have a choice. Like you said a minute ago, we might never get another chance to come back here. I promise I'll be really careful. If you'll take Sebastian's flashlight, he can spot me."

"Good idea," Sebastian said, quickly giving Martha his flashlight.

Martha still didn't like it, but it appeared Doug's mind was made up. She looked over at Emma and saw an expression of worry that must have mirrored her own. Keeping her light focused on the wall so that Doug could find the best places to put his hands and feet, Martha began to silently pray for his safety. Standing beside her, Emma was doing exactly the same thing.

As Doug began to climb, Sebastian took a position next to the wall directly below him. If Doug fell, at least he'd land on something a little softer than rock. True to his word, Doug climbed slowly, carefully choosing where he put his hands and feet and testing each new foot placement before putting his full weight on it. In no time, he was peering over the top of the ledge.

"I think I see something, but I'm going to need one of the flashlights," Doug informed them. "I'm going to go ahead and climb onto the ledge. Sebastian, can you throw one of the flashlights up to me?"

"No problem. Just tell me when you're ready."

Silently, Martha handed Sebastian the flashlight as Doug disappeared from view. Soon his head reappeared. He was lying on his stomach with his head and arms hanging over the ledge so he could catch the flashlight. Emma kept her light trained on the cave wall just beneath Doug. She didn't want to shine it directly in his face and blind him. If he missed the flashlight, it would most likely break, and they'd be down to one source of light. Emma held her breath as Sebastian called out, "Here it comes."

Thankfully, the toss was perfect. Doug caught the flashlight effortlessly and disappeared from view once again. Emma let out a huge sigh of relief and waited expectantly while Doug looked around his rocky perch. In a moment, they heard him exclaim, "I found it!"

"Is it in a metal box like the others?" Martha asked. If it was, she wondered how they were going to get it down. Although she hadn't asked the question out loud, it was answered by Doug's next words.

"Yeah, and there's a rope around it. Darius must have pulled the box up just like I thought. I can use the same rope to lower the box down to you guys."

"That rope's more than three hundred years old. Are you sure it isn't rotten?" This time it was Emma who asked the question. She could just see the rope breaking as they tried to lower the box. Even packed in straw, the impact would probably break the sculpture inside.

"It seems to be in pretty good shape. Anyway, it's all we've got." Doug spent another few minutes examining the rope and tugging on it in various spots to make sure it would hold. *The box couldn't be all that heavy*, he reasoned. After making sure that the rope was tied securely around the box, he began pushing it over the ledge with his feet while he held onto the rope with his hands. The flashlight sat on the ledge to his right so that he could see what he was doing. Once the box went over the edge, he braced his feet on the uneven ledge floor and began to slowly lower it. As he could no longer see the box himself, he had to rely on instructions from Sebastian. All was going well until the box was about ten feet from the ground. Suddenly, the rope broke and the box began bouncing along the sloping cave wall. With a cry of surprise, Sebastian rushed to catch it but the box seemed to have a will of its own, changing course as it encountered the different contours of the uneven rocky surface. Sebastian dashed back and forth and was finally able to stop the box's rapid descent when it was only a few feet from the ground. Emma just hoped all the jarring hadn't damaged the treasure inside.

Doug who had somehow managed to get to the edge in time to see Sebastian's save said, "Good job, Sebastian. That was really close. I just hope the sculpture's okay."

"Me too," Sebastian agreed. Although the air in the cave was only about sixty degrees, beads of sweat glistened on his forehead as he gently lowered the box the rest of the way to the ground. "Whew! Let's not do that again," he exclaimed, wiping his forehead with the back of his hand.

Although Emma was eager to see what the box contained, she knew it was only right for them to wait for Doug. When she looked up, she saw that Doug was already on his way down to them. Before beginning his descent, he had tossed his flashlight back down to Sebastian.

"Be careful!" Emma and Martha called in unison. It would be terrible if, after finally locating the sculpture, Doug were to fall now. Just then, Doug's foot slipped, and he began to slide down the wall just as the box had done. He didn't slide far though before finding a secure foothold. Emma let out the breath she'd been holding. Doug continued on without any further mishaps and soon was standing on solid ground next to the box he'd discovered. It was padlocked just like all the others they'd found.

"We'll have to wait to open it. Mr. Munsen probably has something we can use," Doug said as he bent down to grab one end of the box. Wordlessly, Sebastian handed his flashlight back to Martha and picked up the other end of the box. Emma led the way out of the cave this time. The boys followed, carrying the box, and Martha lit the way from behind. In no time, they were back out in the sunlight. After taking a moment to let their eyes adjust to the bright light, they picked their way down to the riverbank where Doug whistled a signal to Mr. Munsen. True to his word, he was fishing exactly where they'd left him over an hour ago.

They watched in silence as Mr. Munsen reeled in his line and pulled up the anchor. The sound of the motor starting echoed off the bluffs, disturbing the tranquility of the scene. Expertly, he motored the boat over to where they were waiting. Doug and Sebastian set the box down for a moment so that they could pull the bow of the boat up onto the bank.

Seeing the box, Mr. Munsen said, "I see ya found somethin'. Is it one of the Mortals?" He'd first heard the story of the Mortals when he was a little boy. The legend of Marnatti's sculptures was widely circulated in the small towns surrounding the academy, along with the belief that they no longer existed. He had been incredulous when Doug had told him that not only did the sculptures still exist but that four of them had already been found. If there really was one of Marnatti's sculptures in the box the kids had found, he was about to see something that very few people had seen.

"We don't know for sure," Doug answered in response to Mr. Munsen's question. "We need something to break the padlock so we can see what's inside."

"I've got somethin' we can use in the truck. Climb aboard, and we'll get going. Just set the box on the floor by your feet."

Eager to see the contents of the box, Mr. Munsen revved the motor and headed the boat up river back toward the boat ramp. As they skimmed along the surface of the water, Emma checked her watch. It was now a few minutes before three o'clock. That gave them only an hour before they had to be back on the bus.

"We only have an hour left," Emma shouted over the sound of the motor.

"No problem," Mr. Munsen said. "It won't take me long to get the boat back on the trailer. While I'm doin' that, you kids can work on gettin' the box open."

When they got to the ramp, Mr. Munsen had the boys remain in the boat while he backed his truck and trailer down. Once he was back in the boat, he said to the boys, "I can take it from here. Look in the truck behind the driver's seat. There should be a crowbar you can use to pop that padlock off."

While Doug searched Mr. Munsen's truck, Sebastian carried the box up the ramp and set it down in the parking lot. Soon Doug appeared with the crowbar. Using it as a lever, he quickly broke the padlock and lifted the lid. As with all of the other boxes, this one was packed full of straw. Doug began sifting through the straw until his hands encountered a wrapped bundle. Gently, he separated it from the clinging straw and lifted it out. Unlike the other sculptures they'd found, this one was wrapped several times with a thick piece of cloth and was only half as tall. Emma began to worry that it wasn't one of the sculptures after all.

"It doesn't look like all the others," Sebastian commented.

"We won't know what it is until Doug unwraps it," Martha said with a frown. She had been thinking the same thing but didn't like hearing her own doubt stated out loud.

Carefully, Doug unwound the cloth, and everyone let out a collective sigh of relief when the object inside was finally revealed. It was a sculpture of a woman kneeling. The woman's head was tilted back slightly as if she were looking at someone above her. Her features were delicate and beautiful and held an expression of rapt attention. Her hands were folded in her lap—the fingers long and slender and the wrists small and fragile. The simple gown she was wearing was belted at the waist with what looked like a rope. Emma immediately identified the woman as Mary, the sister of Martha and Lazarus. She looked as if she was sitting at the feet of Jesus, drinking in His every word. Emma couldn't get over the look on her face. The slight smile on her lips conveyed both love and adoration.

"It's beautiful." Martha breathed in awe. "I think this is the best one so far."

Emma was nodding her agreement when Mr. Munsen joined the group. "Well, what do ya know 'bout that?" he exclaimed upon seeing the object Doug was holding. "I wouldn't have believed it if I hadn't seen it with my own eyes."

Unlikely as it seemed, these four youngsters had actually recovered one of the missing Mortals. This one piece alone was probably worth millions. Along with that realization came the full understanding of what grave danger the kids were in.

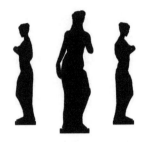

CHAPTER TWENTY
WORDS TO LIVE BY

While everyone was standing around admiring the new find, an important question came to Emma's mind. "How are we going to get it back to the school?"

"I guess we didn't think about that," Sebastian said, earning a frown from Martha.

"That's easy," Mr. Munsen said, after recovering from his amazement. "I'll give you a book bag from the store. You can wrap the sculpture back up and put it in the bag. It'll just look like you've bought some books."

"I think Martha should carry the bag. It'll look less suspicious when we get back to the school," Doug said after a moment. What he didn't say was that he didn't want Bobby Wilcox to get suspicious. It would be out of character for Doug, or Sebastian for that matter, to return from a trip to Windland with a bag full of books. Martha buying a bunch of books was more believable.

"What'll we do with the box?" Sebastian asked.

"I think I'll keep it," Mr. Munsen replied. He was already working on a plan to trap the Reaper, and the box would make a good decoy. As he hadn't thought everything through yet, he didn't want to say anything to the kids. He didn't want to get their hopes up.

Doug lifted his arm to consult his watch, and it was then that Emma noticed that both of his forearms were scratched and bleeding slightly. It must have happened when his foot had slipped as he was climbing down from the ledge.

"Doug, your arms are bleeding," Emma exclaimed.

Mr. Munsen had also noticed Doug's wounds. "They don't look too bad. We'll stop by my house on the way back to town so you can wash those scratches and put some antibiotic ointment on them."

"I'm okay, Mr. Munsen. There's no need to make a special stop," Doug said as he examined his cuts.

"No arguments, son. I was plannin' on stoppin' by the house anyway. I've been thinkin' it's probably best if I don't ask Alice for a store bag. She'll ask questions, and I'll wager she's already curious about what you kids wanted. I can give ya one of the bags we've got at the house. Then when we get to town, you'll be all set to go."

On the ride to Mr. Munsen's house, Doug began to feel bad for ruining Mr. Munsen's fishing trip. Instead of enjoying his Saturday, he'd ended up hauling a bunch of kids around. Doug vowed right then that someday he would repay Mr. Munsen for his help.

At Mr. Munsen's house, Doug took care of his arms while Mr. Munsen got a bag for the sculpture. They needed to hurry. The buses would be headed back to the academy in less than fifteen minutes. When they got to town, Mr. Munsen let them out on a side road. While the others waited on the sidewalk, Doug went over to talk to Mr. Munsen who was still sitting in the truck.

"I can't thank you enough for helping us today, Mr. Munsen. You don't know how much I appreciate it."

"I think I do, son. Before ya go, let me give ya my phone number. I want ya to call me if ya need help again, and I want ya to promise me two things."

"I at least owe you that much," Doug said solemnly.

"First, promise me that you and your friends won't do anything foolish. What I mean is don't put your lives at risk."

Doug hesitated for only a moment. "I promise, sir."

"I know that was hard for ya, son. The next thing won't be as hard. It's critical that ya let me know before ya deliver the last sculpture. I didn't want to say anything to the others, but I'm hoping I can find a way to catch the guy who's blackmailing you. I need to do some investigating first though. I can't call ya at school without arousing suspicion, so you'll have to keep in touch with me. Can ya do that, son?"

"I can and I will. I promise."

After writing his phone number down on a scrap of paper he had rummaged from his glove box, he handed it to Doug and said, "Better get going now, or you'll be late."

Doug walked away from the truck feeling lighter than he had since this whole mess had begun. No longer were the four of them in this alone. Mr. Munsen was going to help them. Not only that, but Doug had a hope in his heart that he hadn't had before. Mr. Munsen had implied that there might be a way to get the sculptures back and return them to their rightful owner. Doug found himself imagining the look of joy that would transform Lord Dinswood's ailing features upon seeing the Mortals.

"Come on, Doug," Sebastian urged. Lost in his thoughts, Doug had begun to lag behind the others.

Another look at their watches had them running the rest of the way to the Windland Inn. They boarded their respective buses out of breath and with less than a minute to spare.

As Mr. Munsen watched the kids walk away, he began to rehash everything Doug had told him earlier that day in the bookstore's storage room. It was an incredible story, but knowing Doug's character, he never once doubted that Doug was telling him the truth. Doug had begun the story by describing the discovery of the first sculpture and explaining the mission that Lord Dinswood had given them. Then he'd related the events leading up to the discovery of the first note from the Reaper and the instructions the Reaper had given him for delivering the sculptures. Putting together everything that Doug had told him, Mr. Munsen had come to the conclusion that the person responsible had to be a member of the school's staff. Because of the location of the barrel, it made sense that the guilty party was one of the cooks. But when he'd said as much to Doug, he had quickly nixed the idea saying that with the exception of the head cook, who was a widowed woman in her mid-forties, all of the other cooks were grandmotherly types. Not only that, but Emma had been pretty sure that the masked figure she'd seen in the library was a man. It occurred to Mr. Munsen that there could be more than one person involved. After all, even grandmothers had been known to commit crimes with the right incentive.

Mr. Munsen sighed and scratched his head. There was only one way to find out who the Reaper was. They'd have to catch him in the act, and to do that they'd have to have the answers to two important questions. How was the Reaper getting the sculptures out of the castle, and where was he storing them? Mr. Munsen was fairly certain that the Reaper would try to sell the sculptures as a set, excluding, of course, the piece already in Lord Dinswood's possession. It would be far too risky to try to fence each piece individually—that would involve too many buyers. On the other hand, locating one buyer wealthy enough to buy the set would take some time and effort. That was probably why the deadlines the creep was giving the kids were so generous. The Reaper was stalling until he could find a buyer.

With another sigh, Mr. Munsen started his truck. He had a pretty good idea how to begin finding the answer to at least one of the questions.

When they got back to the academy, Doug was glad he'd let Martha carry the book bag because Bobby was standing in the lobby as the eighth graders came in. Doug found it odd that none of his buddies were with him.

"Have a good time in Windland, Dougie?" Bobby asked with a sneer as Doug walked past him.

Doug glared at him but didn't answer. Sebastian, who was right behind Doug, would have liked nothing better than to punch the sneer right off Bobby's face. Only the knowledge that that's exactly what Bobby wanted kept him from it. Still he couldn't resist saying something.

"We had a great time, Booby," Sebastian said with an exaggerated grin, purposely mispronouncing Bobby's name. As Sebastian brushed past Bobby, he saw that his words had had the desired effect. Bobby's face was red, and his hands were clenched into tight fists. He was nearly choking with the effort to contain his anger. Satisfied that he'd at least managed to make Bobby mad, Sebastian wisely said no more.

By the time Emma and Martha entered the castle, Doug and Sebastian had already gone to their room to get ready for supper, but Bobby was still standing there. Seeing his red face, they could only wonder what had occurred to make him so mad. He glared at the two girls when he noticed them. They hurried past, blissfully unaware that as Bobby stood there silently fuming, he was plotting a terrible revenge.

On the way to their room, Emma asked, "Why was Bobby standing in the lobby? Do you think he was spying on us?" Somehow that didn't seem likely to Emma. What could Bobby possibly hope to catch them at? Besides it was very unusual to see Bobby without all of his buddies around.

Martha shook her head in the negative. "He was probably waiting for his girlfriend. He's going out with one of the girls in our class.

I've been seeing him with her. Her name is Natalie, I think." Of course, the term "going out" simply meant that Bobby and Natalie were boyfriend and girlfriend.

Emma nodded her understanding. That would explain why Bobby was waiting in the lobby and why he was alone. However, it did not explain why he was so mad. Emma hoped it wasn't something Doug or Sebastian did. Bobby hated them enough already.

At supper that evening, Emma, Martha, and Sebastian were already seated in the dining room when Doug came in carrying an envelope. Emma felt a shiver work its way up her spine as she recognized the handwriting on the outside. It was addressed to Douglas. Nobody called Doug Douglas except the Reaper.

"I just stopped by my mailbox and found this," Doug said as he took a seat next to Sebastian. He didn't appear to be as upset as he usually was after receiving one of the Reaper's notes. Emma hoped that Doug's calm demeanor meant that it was good news for once.

Knowing that the others were curious to see what the note said, Doug wordlessly handed it to Emma. He had already read it through several times. With trembling fingers, Emma slid the note from the envelope and unfolded the paper inside. Sebastian and Martha crowded around so they could see as well. Silently, they all began to read.

Congratulations, Douglas. You've already delivered two of the Mortals. The last one was even ahead of schedule. In light of your outstanding performance thus far, I've decided to make it a little easier for both of us. From now on when you find one of the Mortals, signal as before and leave the sculpture in the prescribed location. I must have the sixth and final piece in my possession by the last day of school. If you fail, Douglas, there will be a "death in the family" so to speak. Heed my warning well. For your father and Lord Dinswood, these are truly words to live by.

"This is good news. Don't you think so, Doug?" Sebastian asked when he had finished reading. "I mean we've only got two sculptures left to find. Surely, we can find the other two before school ends in June. It's only the end of September now."

Doug nodded his agreement. They hadn't had too much difficulty finding the sculptures so far, and now they had Mr. Munsen helping them. Doug was also fully aware that they'd had some divine help along the way; and if God was with them, as He certainly appeared to be, how could they fail?

CHAPTER TWENTY-ONE
THE ALPHA-O'S

With the Reaper's last note, Doug began to breathe a little easier. For the first time since the school year had begun, he felt like he could concentrate on his studies, and with midterms approaching at the end of October, he needed to buckle down. He had a month to get his grades up to where they should be. He had a talk with the others, and they agreed that they shouldn't deliver the next sculpture until sometime in November. After that they could decide when to make the next delivery. Doug had told the others what Mr. Munsen had said, so they planned to notify him before they were ready to deliver the last sculpture. Everything hinged on them being able to locate the last two Mortals. Although things had gone well so far, there was no guarantee that their luck would continue. All they could do was hope and pray and continue to search whenever the opportunity presented itself.

By mutual consent, they'd decided to take a little break from the hunt and spend some quality time each evening studying in the library. Emma found that Mr. Criderman, the handsome new librarian, was a lot easier to be around than Mr. Hodges had been. At least she didn't have the feeling that he was watching them all the time. Emma thought he was cute at first, but after a couple of weeks, her opinion of him changed. Oh, he was still good looking. The problem was that he knew it. He seemed to enjoy flirting with the girls in the upper grades. Emma thought it was gross for a man his age to flirt with high school girls. Emma wondered what Dean Harwood would think if he knew how his new librarian was behaving. Mr. Criderman never crossed the line, but Emma still found his antics revolting.

The next few weeks passed quickly and then in mid-October, Doug, Emma, and Martha received an invitation to join the academy's honor society. The society was called the Alpha-Omegas, but the students called it the Alpha-O's for short. The invitation was based on the grade point averages they had earned last year as seventh graders. This accounted for the fact that Sebastian did not receive one. He hadn't exactly strained himself academically last year. Emma felt a little sorry for him, but it was his own fault. If he did well this year, it was possible he would be invited to join next year. Martha couldn't resist giving him a hard time when she learned that he hadn't gotten an invitation.

"We tried to get you to study more last year," Martha stated with a note of reproach. "Now you can't get in until next year."

"Big deal," Sebastian replied with a roll of his eyes. "All it means is, I won't get to be a part of the nerd herd."

"That's not all you'll be missing," Martha retorted angrily. "The Alpha-O's get to do some fun things."

"Like what?"

Martha took her letter out so that she could consult it. "Well, first it says that if we accept the invitation to join, we'll be inducted at a formal ceremony in the ballroom next Thursday evening. We'll get a gold pin, a membership card, and a certificate. They're going to have refreshments after the ceremony."

"It sounds terribly exciting so far," Sebastian said sarcastically.

"I'm not finished yet," Martha said, getting angrier by the second.

Emma understood her frustration. Whatever the society had planned wasn't going to be as much fun without Sebastian around. Even though he didn't seem to care about not receiving a letter, Emma suspected that it was just an act. Still, some good could come of it. It might motivate Sebastian to work harder, so he could get in next year.

"For your information, the society is hosting a hayride and hot dog roast the Friday before the Octoberfest," Martha continued. "I've never been on a hayride, and it sounds like a lot of fun to me."

"Whoopie," Sebastian said, twirling a finger in the air. "I'll be sorry to miss that. You'll probably sit around the campfire holding hands and singing Kumbaya."

"Well, guess whose hand I won't be holding!"

With a huff, Martha left the table that they'd all been sitting around in the lounge. Sebastian watched her as she stalked out of the room. It was clear from his expression that he hadn't thought of that. With a sigh, Emma looked at the clock and saw that it was nearly nine o'clock. Curfew was at nine, so with a murmured goodnight, she gathered up her books and followed Martha. She gave Sebastian a sympathetic smile as she passed by him.

Sebastian sat there scowling after the two girls had left. An image of Martha cozying up to another guy in front of a campfire played across his mind. Gradually he became aware that Doug was laughing at him.

"If you could only see your face," Doug said.

Sebastian's scowl was replaced by a smile as he realized he was letting his imagination get the best of him. "Sorry 'bout that," he said ruefully.

"I'll make sure no one moves in on your girl," Doug promised with a smile.

"She's not really my girl though. I mean I like her, but I don't know if she likes me."

"There's only one way to find out."

"I'm not ready for that yet. I don't think I could take the rejection if she said she didn't like me."

Doug nodded in understanding. He'd never actually told Emma he liked her either, but she seemed to already know. Things were going good, and he and Emma were getting along fine, so he'd decided to leave well enough alone. Maybe it would be better if Sebastian just let things go along like they were.

"Still, Martha's got a point," Doug said after a moment. "You need to make sure you get into the Alpha-O's next year."

"I've already got it covered," Sebastian quickly replied. "Ever since school started, I've been working hard to get my GPA up. Dad wasn't very happy with my grades last year. He promised me that if I could earn an A average this year, he'd take me on a two-week sailing trip. I don't know if I told you this, but Dad bought that new schooner he was looking at last year. He's keeping it in storage until next summer. Then, if my grades are good, he and I will take it out on its maiden voyage. It's going to be great!"

"It sounds like it," Doug agreed. "And now you've got another reason to do well in your classes."

"Yeah," Sebastian replied, his expression turning solemn once again. "I sure do." Martha would have been humbled and flattered to know that Sebastian viewed this second reason as more important than the first.

Emma and Martha found out that Clarice had also received a letter when they got back to their room. Clarice told them that Reggie had gotten one too. This was no surprise to Emma. As far as she was concerned, he was the smartest student at the academy. Without a doubt, he was the brightest eighth grader. Clarice proudly showed them her letter and then went on to explain that Preston hadn't been invited to join the society this year because he hadn't been a student at the academy long enough. Students had to have attended the academy one full year and maintained an A average during that year to qualify for admittance into the society. As Preston had just come to the academy this year, he didn't meet the requirements. Clarice informed them in her haughtiest tone that he would most certainly receive an invitation next year. Emma felt a twinge of disappointment at hearing that Preston wouldn't be a part of the group's activities. She immediately felt guilty for caring one way or the other and, knowing that Martha wouldn't be pleased, wisely kept her thoughts to herself.

Almost a week later, the night of the ceremony arrived. Emma, Martha, and Doug were sitting in the general audience with the other inductees, waiting for the ceremony to begin. Emma looked around to see who some of the other inductees were. Most of the inductees were eighth graders, but there were some upperclassmen as well. Clarice and Reggie were sitting in the row behind them along with Doug's roommates, Phil and Tom.

At seven o'clock on the dot, the society's president mounted the steps to the stage and went to stand behind the podium. The current president of the Alpha-O's was a senior boy named Nathan Boyd. Nathan had a narrow face with a long, pointed nose upon which rested a pair of wire-rimmed glasses. Emma noticed that he seemed to prefer looking over the top of his glasses rather than through them. Emma had seen him around but didn't know him personally.

After explaining the tenants of the society to those assembled before him, he began calling the names of the inductees in alphabetical order. When Nathan had finished calling names and all the inductees were in position with a lit candle, he led them in repeating the society's pledge. Mindlessly, Emma echoed the president's words. Later, she vaguely remembered vowing to uphold the principles of the society. She had no idea what those principles were but felt certain that they would be explained fully to the new members at some later date.

"You may now blow out your candles and be seated," Nathan told them after they had finished reciting the pledge. Dutifully, the new recruits obeyed.

Then the speaker for the event was introduced. Emma was surprised to hear that the speaker was going to be Mr. Criderman. She learned later that Mr. Criderman was the society's new sponsor. Last year's sponsor, Miss Culpepper, had retired.

Emma listened as Mr. Criderman congratulated them on being inducted into the Alpha-Omegas, but she didn't hear anything he said after that. Her attention was thereafter focused on Bobby Wilcox. Bobby was sitting out in the audience in the second row. As the inductees were seated on the stage, the audience was now comprised solely of members of the faculty and students who were already members of the society. Current members of the society always attended the induction ceremony to help welcome the new members. At first Emma was surprised that Bobby was an Alpha-O, but when she thought about it, it made perfect sense. Bobby's dad was a member of the school board. How would it look if a school board member's son didn't get selected to be a member of the school's only honor society? Bobby may be mean, but he wasn't stupid. However, it wasn't her shock at learning that Bobby was an Alpha-O that kept her glancing back at him from time to time. It was the look of sheer hatred that he was shooting at Doug.

Emma looked over at Doug to see if he had noticed. Doug appeared to be totally oblivious, but Emma suspected it was just an act. A second later, Doug turned to her and inclined his head ever so slightly in Bobby's direction. Emma nodded to indicate she'd seen him too. After that, she did her best to ignore the boy in the second row, and so did Doug. She spent the rest of Mr. Criderman's speech worrying about what the looks Bobby was giving Doug might mean. What was Bobby up to now?

As soon as Mr. Criderman's speech was over, Nathan once again went to the podium and invited everyone to partake of the refreshments. The new inductees needed no further encouragement but promptly stood and began filing off the stage. Emma and Doug went to stand in the line that had already formed by the cake table. Martha soon joined them. As they got closer to the table, Emma could see that the cake had been decorated in the light blue and gold colors of the society. The writing on the cake said simply "Congratulations New Alpha-O's." After they had each received a plate with a piece of the delicious-looking white cake on it, they went over to the punch table. With plate and cup in hand, they then threaded their way over to some chairs in the corner of the room.

Knowing that they would soon be joined by some of the other eighth-grade inductees, Martha used the brief time the three of them were alone to ask, "Why was Bobby Wilcox shooting daggers at Doug during Mr. Criderman's speech?"

"So you noticed it too," Emma responded quickly in surprise.

"It was kind of hard to miss," Martha replied wryly. Then she gave an exaggerated shudder. "After a while, it started to give me the creeps."

"He's probably just trying to freak us out—you know, make us think he's up to something," Doug said in a tone that suggested he wasn't at all concerned.

"Well, it's working," Martha muttered.

Emma was inclined to agree with Martha, but she could see that Clarice, Reggie, Phil, and Tom were on their way over to sit with them, so she didn't say any more on the topic. Emma looked over at Doug. He had made it sound like he wasn't at all worried about what Bobby may or may not be up to, but she wasn't totally convinced. While he talked with Phil and Tom, she watched him closely. He appeared to be totally relaxed. With a sigh, Emma realized she'd never understand boys.

From time to time throughout the evening, current members of the society would come by to congratulate them. Bobby, however, stayed far away. Emma was relieved. She had been half afraid that he would come over and make a scene. She should have known that Bobby would know better than to start trouble with so many witnesses. He was much too clever for that.

Thirty minutes later, the party began to break up. Emma and Martha were ready to leave, but Doug was still talking with Phil and Tom. It was almost nine o'clock anyway, so the girls said a quick goodnight to the boys and made their way to the entrance.

As they were leaving, Martha whispered in Emma's ear, "My feelings are hurt. Bobby didn't come by to congratulate us."

Emma looked at Martha and saw from the broad smile on her face that she was kidding.

"What are you two talking about?" Sebastian asked startling the two girls as they came out of the ballroom. He'd been waiting in the hallway for the party to get over.

"None of your business, Mr. Nosy Noserson," Martha answered.

"Well, how was the party? From what I could see, it looked like a real exciting evening."

Sebastian's sarcasm was not lost on Martha. "The excitement comes later when we're on the hayride. You'll be sorry you didn't get in then."

"It won't be as much fun without me," Sebastian pointed out confidently.

Martha felt exactly the same way, but she wasn't about to tell Sebastian that. His self-confidence made her angry, and she couldn't resist the urge to goad him a bit. "I'll just have to find someone else to have a good time with."

Martha was sorry the minute the words were out of her mouth, and she would have taken them back if she could. Sebastian looked as if he'd just taken a knife to the heart. Without a word, he turned and walked away. Shocked at her own behavior, Martha stood where she was, looking miserable. Emma, who had witnessed the whole exchange, was momentarily at a loss for words. Her heart went out to Sebastian. He'd looked so hurt. She was about to tell Martha that this time she'd gone too far when Doug appeared.

"Martha, what's wrong?" he asked when he saw the look on her face.

Martha didn't answer but instead burst into tears and started running down the hall in the direction of the girls' dorm. With an apologetic look at Doug, Emma hurried after Martha.

"I'll tell you all about it later," she called back over her shoulder as she ran.

With a shrug and a sigh, Doug headed in the opposite direction. As he walked, he wondered what in the world could have happened in the few short minutes he hadn't been with the girls. He may not be able to ask Emma, but he was pretty sure Sebastian would know.

When Emma got to the room, Martha was lying on her bed on her stomach with her face buried in her pillow. Despite the muffling effect of the pillow, every now and then a sob could be heard. Emma took a quick look around the room and saw that, for now at least, she and Martha were alone. Susie was probably waiting for Clarice and Reggie in the lounge, but it wouldn't be long before the two girls showed up. That didn't give Emma much time to get Martha calmed down. With that thought in mind, Emma went over and sat down on the end of Martha's bed. Martha rolled over and looked at Emma.

"You don't h-have to s-say it!" Martha struggled to get out between sobs. "I know I sh-shouldn't have s-said that to S-Sebastian.

It's just that he m-makes me so m-mad sometimes, I just lose control." Martha began crying again in earnest, stopping only long enough to add, "I'm a horrible p-person."

"No, you're not," Emma said, placing a hand on Martha's shoulder. "If you were such a terrible person, you wouldn't be feeling so badly now. Tomorrow, you'll tell Sebastian you're sorry, and things will be all right again."

"What if h-he won't forgive me this t-time? This will be the s-second time I've h-had to ask."

"Sebastian is a good person. He'll forgive you as many times as you ask. Just like God forgives us." Emma was remembering the sermon Reverend Palmer had given just last Sunday. It had been a real eye opener for her. Reverend Palmer had told them that the Bible was very clear on the subject. We are to forgive others if we wish to receive God's forgiveness. Martha must have remembered it as well because she began to calm down, her sobs reduced to intermittent hiccups. At Emma's prompting, she got up and went into the bathroom to splash cold water on her face. Not long after that, Clarice and Susie came in, so no more was said on the subject of Sebastian. As she got ready for bed, Emma prayed that she was right about Sebastian.

CHAPTER TWENTY-TWO
THE HAYRIDE

M artha had intended to apologize to Sebastian at the first opportunity, but it soon became clear that Sebastian was avoiding them. He didn't sit with them at breakfast, lunch, or supper;
and after the evening meal, he and Doug were nowhere to be found.

"Sebastian must really be mad at me," Martha said as she
glanced at the lounge entrance for the tenth time since she and
Emma had come in. She was hoping that Sebastian would eventually make an appearance, but with only fifteen minutes until curfew, it
seemed less and less likely.

The two girls had been sitting in the lounge playing Parcheesi
for the last hour, but it had been obvious from the start that Martha's
mind was not on the game. She had needed a reminder from Emma
to take another turn the last two times she had rolled doubles. When
it happened a third time, Emma gave up with a sigh and began putting the game away.

"What are you doing?" Martha asked when she finally noticed.
"The game isn't over yet."

"Oh yes, it is," Emma replied kindly but firmly. "We are going to find Sebastian, so you can apologize and straighten this whole mess out."

Martha nodded wordlessly. Nothing would suit her better. As soon as Emma had returned the game to the shelf where she'd gotten it, the two girls left the lounge and headed to the library. A quick look around the nearly empty room confirmed the boys weren't in there. Next they went to the dining hall. Sometimes, students used the tables as desks to do their school work on, and although it wasn't likely on a Friday night, maybe the boys were in there. When they opened the doors to the dining hall, however, they saw that it was completely empty.

"They could be in their room or outside," Emma suggested. "We could ask someone to check their room for us."

"Okay," Martha agreed dismally. They were running out of time, and even if they did find the boys, there was no guarantee that Sebastian would be willing to talk to her.

Emma led the way back to the lounge where earlier she had seen Phil and Tom sitting at a table in the northwest corner of the room. Maybe they would know where Doug and Sebastian were. When they got to the lounge, Emma was relieved to see that Phil and Tom were still there. Quickly, she threaded her way over to them, while Martha remained by the door. Martha watched as Emma talked to Phil. A moment later, Emma was on her way back.

"Phil says the boys have gone up to see Doug's dad and they're planning on spending the night."

"Well, that's that then," Martha said on the verge of tears. She had been hoping that by the end of the day things between her and Sebastian would be back to normal, but it was not meant to be.

Emma could see how distressed her friend was. In an attempt to console her, she put her arm around Martha's shoulders and gave a little squeeze. "There's always tomorrow," she said gently. Then with a teasing smile, she added, "Sebastian can't hide from us forever."

Martha wasn't so sure about that, but she said nothing as she let Emma lead her to their room. When the two girls arrived, they found Clarice and Susie sitting on their beds talking. They had entered just in time to catch the tail end of the conversation.

"I can't believe you're not going! It sounds like a lot of fun," Susie was saying.

"What sounds like fun?" Emma couldn't help asking.

"Clarice isn't going on the Alpha-O hayride Friday night," Susie exclaimed in an incredulous tone. If she had been a member of the society, she would have gone in a heartbeat. Thanks to Clarice's cousin Preston, Susie had gotten to know several of the freshman boys, and she particularly liked Daniel Jacobs. Susie sighed dreamily as she pictured herself sitting next to him around a campfire.

"Why not?" Martha asked, forgetting her own misery for the moment and snapping Susie back to the present.

"Sitting in a filthy wagon on a scratchy bale of hay is not my idea of a good time," Clarice responded defensively. "Reggie totally agrees with me."

Emma was once again amazed at Clarice's selfishness. Reggie probably would have enjoyed the hayride very much, but because of Clarice, he wasn't going to go. Emma knew she would never be able to convince Clarice of that, so she said nothing. Besides, she couldn't really feel too sorry for Reggie. He was going to miss out on a good time, but it was his own fault for not standing up to Clarice.

As Emma lay in bed that night, she found herself looking forward to the hayride and the school's annual Octoberfest. She imagined sitting close beside Doug on a hay bale gazing at the stars as the wagon rolled slowly along. He might even try to kiss her again. Then her thoughts turned to the dance that would take place the next evening. Last year, she hadn't gotten to dance with Doug a single time, but she was determined that this year was going to be different. If he didn't ask her to dance, she would ask him. Emma fell asleep secure in the knowledge that nothing was going to keep her from dancing with Doug this Saturday.

The next morning, Emma and Martha decided that they'd better start studying for their midterm exams. The exams were slated to begin Monday and run through Friday. Because Emma and Martha had the same class schedule, they also had the same exam schedule, so they could study together.

Except for mealtimes, they didn't see the boys. Emma just assumed they had decided to spend the entire weekend with Doug's dad, staying in his suite on the third floor. Emma hated to admit it, but they probably wouldn't have gotten as much studying done if Sebastian had been around. Martha must have felt the same way because she hadn't once complained about the boys' absence.

The girls' exams went off without a hitch—even the art exam with Mr. Dubois hadn't been too difficult. By the time Friday rolled around, Emma had to admit that she had been wrong about two things. First, Martha still hadn't gotten the chance to apologize to Sebastian. All week long, the boys hadn't come to sit with them at mealtimes, and they had mysteriously disappeared after supper each evening. By Friday, Martha was nearly at the end of her rope. As distressing as it was for Emma to see her friend so unhappy, the worst blow came Friday morning. Emma learned from Phil that Doug had been taken to the school nurse with a headache, sore throat, and high fever. It turned out that he had strep throat, and because his illness was so contagious, the nurse insisted that he stay isolated in the infirmary at least through Saturday. He would miss both the hayride and the Octoberfest dance. Emma was crushed. In one fell swoop all of her hopes and dreams for the weekend were dashed.

Emma dressed for the hayride that evening with little enthusiasm. She noticed that Martha was feeling down as well. *What a pair we are. We're going to be a lot of fun to be around tonight*, Emma thought as she grabbed her jacket.

It had been a nice day, but this time of year, the evenings could be on the cool side, so in addition to her jacket, Martha was bringing a blanket to put over their legs. Susie sat on her bed and watched as the two girls got ready. She couldn't help wishing once again that she could go too. Daniel Jacobs would be going on the hayride, and there was supposed to be a full moon that night. With a sigh, she told Emma and Martha to have fun.

"I wish you were coming," Emma said and meant it. Susie really was a sweet girl. In spite of her own disappointment, Susie was hoping Emma and Martha had a good time.

"Me too," Susie agreed wistfully. As the two girls started to leave, Susie stopped them. "Could you guys do me a favor?"

"Sure," Emma answered. "What do you want us to do?"

Susie hesitated for a moment as if embarrassed. "Well, could you guys kind of keep an eye on Daniel Jacobs for me? You know, like who he sits with and stuff like that."

"You mean if he sits with a girl?" Martha asked with a knowing look.

"Yeah." Susie nodded.

By this time, Susie's cheeks were two bright red spots. It was obvious that she had a major crush on Daniel. Emma wondered if Daniel knew that Susie liked him and, more importantly, if Daniel liked Susie in return. Emma hoped so for Susie's sake.

"We'll do our best," Emma promised on her way out.

As the two girls passed the lounge, Martha noticed that Sebastian was sitting alone at a table close to the door. There were a handful of other students in the lounge, but they were sitting in the back corner of the room—out of earshot. She might not get a better chance to talk with him. Hurriedly, she told Emma that she would meet her outside in a few minutes. Then she entered the lounge and walked nervously toward Sebastian. He stood up when he saw her coming. For a moment, she was afraid that he was going to leave, but his next words relieved her on that point.

"I've been waiting for you," he said with a smile.

"You have?" Martha asked surprised. She had been so sure that he was still mad at her.

"Yeah," Sebastian answered.

An awkward silence followed, and then both of them started talking at once.

"I'm so sorry for what I said last Thursday. I didn't mean it," Martha blurted out.

"I wanted to show you something," Sebastian said at the same time.

Martha had been so intent on her apology that it took a moment for Sebastian's words to register. Things weren't going exactly as she had planned, but one thing was clear: Sebastian was no longer angry with her. Confused but grateful, Martha found herself asking, "What?"

Sebastian grinned broadly and held up a piece of paper. On closer inspection, it turned out to be a printout of all of Sebastian's midterm exam scores. He had gotten above a 90 percent on every test.

"Sebastian, that's amazing! Great job!"

If possible, Sebastian's grin widened all the more, and if he'd been wearing a button-up shirt, Martha was convinced he would have burst every button in pride at his accomplishment.

"I bet I get into the Alpha-O's next year," he boasted.

"I bet you do too," Martha agreed with a smile of her own. She was beginning to get an inkling of why the two boys hadn't been around all week. Sebastian's next words confirmed her suspicions.

"Doug and I have been going up to his dad's suite every night after supper to study, and we stayed with him over the weekend too.

I figured I would do a better job of studying if I didn't have so many distractions around."

Martha could have cried in relief. Sebastian hadn't been avoiding her as she had thought. He'd merely been trying to ensure that he got good grades on all of his tests so that next year he'd be invited to join the Alpha-O's. As happy as the news made Martha, she knew it didn't excuse her behavior last Thursday. She still owed Sebastian a big apology. Not knowing if he had heard her earlier, she began again. Knowing he wasn't angry with her any longer made it a little easier.

"Sebastian, I've been wanting to tell you since last Thursday how sorry I am for what I said. I didn't mean a word of it, and I hope you'll forgive me."

Sebastian's expression grew serious. "It's okay, Martha. Anyhow, I figured I kind of asked for it."

Martha could have hugged him right then and there, but they weren't completely alone, so she refrained. Sebastian really was a great guy. All of a sudden, she felt like crying again—this time in happiness.

Sensing her emotional struggle, Sebastian said brightly, "So you're off on the hayride, right?"

All Martha could do was nod.

"Well, have a good time."

As Martha turned to leave, she called back over her shoulder, "It won't be any fun without you." Embarrassed by the boldness of her statement, Martha rushed out the door. If she had looked back, her heart would have been lifted by the joyous expression on the face of one Sebastian Conners.

Emma was waiting on the terrace with the other Alpha-O's when Martha appeared. The happy smile on Martha's face said it all. Martha's conversation with Sebastian had gone well. While the other students began climbing aboard the two hay wagons parked in front of the castle, Martha quickly filled Emma in on the details.

"I told you things would work out okay," Emma said when Martha had finished her narrative. "Sebastian is a good guy, and you gave him all the motivation he needed to do well on his midterms."

"I don't know about that," Martha replied with a shake of her head. "I'm just glad he's not mad at me anymore."

"It doesn't sound like he ever was."

"Maybe not, but he had every right to be."

"Well, it's all history now, so let's see if we can't have some fun on this hayride."

By the time the two girls finished their conversation, one of the wagons was full. They quickly climbed aboard the second wagon and found a hay bale to sit on. Once they were settled, Emma looked around to see who else would be riding with them and was dismayed to see the smirking face of Bobby Wilcox. Too late, she realized their mistake. With the exception of herself and Martha, all of the riders on their wagon were older students. A quick look at the other wagon confirmed that the rest of the eighth-grade Alpha-O's were seated on it.

"Oh no," she whispered softly.

"What's wrong?" Martha asked. She had been watching Mr. Dorfman, the boys' PE teacher, start up the tractor that would be pulling their wagon and hadn't noticed Bobby yet. Mr. Criderman was driving the tractor that was pulling the other wagon.

"Look who's on the wagon with us."

Martha looked around then, and Emma heard her sharply indrawn breath as she realized they'd be spending the next hour or so in Bobby's company.

"It'll be okay," Martha whispered back. "What can he do to us here?"

"I don't know, but I'm sure he'll think of something." Emma surveyed the group again. It wasn't just Bobby she was worried about. He had all of his buddies with him and some of the freshman girls that thought Bobby was the greatest thing going.

They didn't have long to wait to discover Bobby's line of attack. The moment the wagon began to move, he started in. He was fully aware that the sound of the tractor's motor would prevent Mr. Dorfman from hearing anything that was said.

"You'd think it was December instead of October," Bobby sneered, pointing at the blanket that Martha was holding.

Embarrassed, Martha looked around. None of the others on the wagon had brought blankets. Martha couldn't prevent the blush that crept into her cheeks.

Seeing her blush, Bobby laughed out loud. "They shouldn't let eighth graders into the Alpha-O's. They're so immature."

Barb and Daphne, the two freshman girls sitting on the hay bale next to Bobby, smirked at Emma and Martha as they nodded their agreement.

"Just ignore him," Emma said under her breath. Maybe Bobby would leave them alone if they didn't respond to his taunts.

The rest of the hayride was nothing short of torture for Emma and Martha. Although Bobby didn't address them directly, he kept whispering things to Barb and Daphne, who would then look at the two girls and laugh hysterically. It couldn't have been more obvious that he was making fun of them. Emma and Martha tried to tune them out by talking quietly to each other, but they weren't completely successful. By the time the wagon pulled into the campsite where they would roast hot dogs and make s'mores, Emma was nearly in tears. She wanted nothing more than to return to the castle.

As they got down off the wagon, Emma's frustration turned to anger. *I don't care if Martha and I have to walk back to the castle. We're not riding on that wagon again*, Emma thought. She would ask Mr.

Dorfman if the two girls could switch wagons at the first opportunity. She didn't tell Martha her plan in case it didn't pan out. She didn't want to get Martha's hopes up.

The other wagon pulled up just then, and grabbing Martha by the arm, Emma hurried them both over to it. At least they would be able to spend the next hour or so in the company of their classmates. Some fun might yet be salvaged from the evening.

While the two girls waited for their friends to join them, Emma took the opportunity to look around. The campsite was set in a heavily wooded area on the side of the mountain. There were picnic tables scattered around, and a sign to the right of the picnic area indicated that there were restrooms available down a dirt path. Beyond the picnic tables were wooden benches with a circle of stones at its center where a campfire could be safely built. Several walking trails took off in various directions from the picnic area. A sign on one indicated that it led down to the river. Another trail advertised that it led to an overlook of Boulder Falls.

While the teachers and some of the senior members of the Alpha-O's set about building a campfire and making preparations for the hot dog roast, the rest of the members were free to do a bit of exploring. Their only instructions were to stay in groups of at least three and to be back at the campsite before dark. Emma and Martha made it a point to stick with the other eighth graders. They weren't going to give Bobby any more opportunities to make fun of them. Emma decided to wait until Mr. Dorfman was alone before trying to speak to him about changing wagons. She didn't want any of Bobby's bunch to overhear her request. She refused to give him that satisfaction. In the meantime, she and Martha could hang out with Phil and Tom.

Phil and Tom gladly welcomed Emma and Martha into their little group. Cindy and Kim, who were also in the eighth grade, joined them as well. Emma had been on the point of suggesting that they take the trail leading to the view of the falls when she saw Bobby's group heading in that direction. Much to her relief, Phil and Tom chose the trail leading down to the river instead. They had probably noticed Bobby starting up the other path too. Emma knew that Phil and Tom didn't like Bobby either, and it may have been their own dislike of the troublemaker that prompted their decision to take the river path. Whatever their reasons, Emma was just glad to be headed in a direction opposite to that of one Bobby Wilcox.

Together they made a happy group as they walked along. The path, bordered by trees on both sides, was wide enough for two people to walk side by side. It was clear from the start that Phil and Kim liked each other. They held hands as they led the way down the dirt path together. Emma could see why Phil liked Kim. She was tall and slim with long blonde hair and bright blue eyes. In addition to being pretty, Kim had a quick wit that kept them laughing all the way to the river. Although she was rich and beautiful, she didn't have the superior attitude that Clarice often displayed. Tom and Cindy followed directly behind Phil and Kim, and although they didn't hold hands, Emma suspected that Tom liked Cindy. Tom probably would have liked to hold Cindy's hand, but he was shy by nature and lacked the degree of self-confidence his friend Phil possessed. Cindy was just the opposite of Kim as far as looks went. She was short—barely over five feet tall—with dark brown eyes and short dark hair that just brushed the tops of her shoulders. Emma thought she was just as pretty as Kim and she seemed just as nice.

Emma and Martha were content to bring up the rear as they made their way down the hill. Normally, Emma would have felt like a fifth wheel, but she was so relieved to be away from Bobby that tonight she didn't care. She just hoped she'd get a chance to talk to Mr. Dorfman about switching wagons for the ride home.

When they got to the gravel bar at the river's edge, the boys began searching out some flat rocks to skip. Phil was the first to send his rock skipping along the surface of the water. Tom went next with equal success. Emma was amazed at their skill. This was obviously something they'd done many times before. The girls tried, but their poor attempts were met with laughter from the boys.

"Instead of making fun of us, why don't you show us what we're doing wrong," Kim said with a laugh, when instead of skipping along the surface, her third attempt landed in the water with a loud plop and promptly sank to the bottom.

"Yeah," Cindy chimed in.

The boys were more than happy to oblige.

"Well, first you have to find the right rock. It's got to be pretty flat," Phil instructed as he searched the gravel bar for the perfect specimen. "Hold it horizontally, like this," Phil said, demonstrating as he spoke. "Then flick your wrist as you toss it."

Once again Phil's rock went skipping effortlessly over the water.

"You make it look so easy," Kim said with a sigh.

"Here, I'll help you," Phil said. After searching out another flat rock, he handed it to Kim and then stood behind her so that he could take hold of her right arm to assist her in her throw. To Emma, it looked like a good excuse for Phil to put his arms around his girlfriend. Phil was definitely enjoying himself, and Kim didn't seem to mind either. The others watched as Phil helped Kim toss her rock and clapped and cheered when it went skipping along the surface just like it was supposed to.

"See," Phil said, grinning. "I told you it's all in the wrist."

Encouraged by Phil's teaching success, Tom found a rock and proceeded to help Cindy by holding her arm just as Phil had done with Kim. Emma had to hide her smile when Cindy's rock sank to the bottom like all of her previous attempts.

"Don't give up," Tom said quickly as his face grew red in embarrassment. "We'll try again."

"I think we'd better head back up to the campsite," Phil said then. "It's starting to get dark."

Emma wasn't sure if Phil had mentioned the need to leave in order to save his friend from further embarrassment or if he really thought they should get going. In any case, Tom seemed relieved and quickly agreed.

Like the others, Emma had been so engrossed in their game that she hadn't noticed the sun sinking behind the mountains. Twilight was already upon them by the time they were halfway up the trail. Thankfully, solar lights had been positioned at regular intervals along the path, so they could see where they were going.

By the time they reached the campsite, some of the students had begun roasting hot dogs over the campfire. Phil and Tom gallantly offered to roast hot dogs for everyone, so the girls got plates and prepared the buns. Mustard, ketchup, and an assortment of chips had been set out on one of the picnic tables along with the makings for s'mores. Coolers containing canned soda sat on the ground at the end of the table. Once everyone had had their fill of hot dogs, they began roasting marshmallows to make s'mores.

Everything tasted delicious, and Emma found herself enjoying the evening even though it had started so horribly. Emma had been glancing at Mr. Dorfman from time to time, hoping for an opportunity to speak to him out of earshot of everyone, but every time she looked over at him, he was surrounded by students. Knowing the group wouldn't be leaving the campsite until the traditional sharing of scary stories had taken place, Emma decided to relax, certain that she would get a chance to speak with Mr. Dorfman alone before the ride home.

When everyone had finished eating and all of the food and coolers had been packed away, the Alpha-O's sat around the campfire and listened with rapt attention as President Nathan Boyd began the tale of the "Wailing Widow." Although it didn't seem to match his appearance, Nathan had the perfect voice for storytelling—deep and clear. As Emma listened, her gaze was drawn to the fire. It continually popped and crackled, sending up little sparks that left glowing trails as they spiraled upward. At times, the trails seemed to twist and spin in a sort of primitive dance. Emma followed them upward until they disappeared, their glow extinguished as if by some unseen hand. It was then that she noticed a full moon had risen above the mountain. Chiding herself for her too fanciful imagination, Emma turned her attention back to Nathan and his story.

"The tragic tale of the 'Wailing Widow' is well known in these parts," Nathan told them. "It began many years ago when a newly married pioneer couple built a home here in the mountains. One day, the husband went down to the river to do some fishing and was never seen or heard from again. Some of the folks that lived in these parts at the time believed that a bear or some other wild animal had attacked and killed him. Some thought he had drowned but, as his body was never found, there was no way to be sure of what had happened. The fact that they never found his body eventually drove the man's poor widow mad. Every night after her husband's disappearance, she would walk down to the river and spend hours calling his name. She would call and call until she could call no more. One night, she waded into the river and drowned. No one knows for sure what exactly drew her into the water, but some say she saw the face of her dead husband reflected on the surface. They say her ghost still walks the path down to the river every night, and when the wind blows up the hollow, you can hear her calling his name."

As if on cue, the wind suddenly picked up and began rustling the few leaves that still clung to the trees. Emma shivered in spite of herself and looked over at Martha whose eyes were still fixed on Nathan.

"What was his name?" someone finally asked.

"Nobody knows for sure, but if you listen carefully, you can hear it in the wind," Nathan replied.

For the next several seconds, everyone sat quietly as they tried to discern a name in the wind.

"I hear it," Bobby said in a tone heavy with sarcasm. "It's whispering the name Frank."

"No, it's Garth," a friend of Bobby's chimed in with a laugh.

It was clear that Bobby and his buddies were making fun of the story, but what had started as mockery quickly became a hilarious game as other Alpha-O's began to throw out names—each one more ridiculous than the last. Some of the names offered for consideration had Emma laughing so hard her side hurt.

Nathan waited with a slight smile on his face. His whole demeanor reminded Emma of an indulgent father waiting patiently for his rowdy children to settle down before attempting to tell them a bedtime story. When the game finally wound down, Nathan let his gaze roam slowly over the group before asking, "Now, would you like to hear the other version of the story, the one most people believe is what actually happened?"

Nathan's question was quickly answered with a resounding yes from those assembled.

When everyone was sitting quietly once more, Nathan began again. "Most people believe that the man's wife was completely insane, a fact she managed to hide from her husband until after the marriage. One day in a fit of madness, she killed her husband and hid his body so that it would never be found. Not long after that, in a search for revenge, the husband's angry spirit appeared to the woman during the night and led her down to the river. Repeatedly calling her name, he lured her into the water knowing full well that she couldn't swim. By the time she realized her plight, it was too late. She screamed and struggled in vain. No one was around to hear her cries for help as the swiftly moving icy water of the river overwhelmed her and pulled her down into its depths."

Nathan paused for effect and then continued with his narration. "With his need for revenge satisfied, the husband's spirit departed this world, but the woman's spirit remains to this day. Every night she walks the path along the river calling the names of any who will listen. It is said that if you ever hear her calling your name, your own death is near at hand."

Now that's a scary story, Emma thought when Nathan had finished. Around the campfire, it was absolutely quiet. Only the howling of the wind, as it swept up and over the bluffs, could be heard. Then, as if afraid they would hear their names being whispered, everyone began talking at once. Nathan remained where he was with a satisfied look on his face. The story had had the desired effect.

After that, some of the other senior Alpha-O's took turns telling scary stories. There was the usual story about the maniacal killer with a hook for a hand and the killer who always wore a hockey mask. The other stories were good, but none of them had the same effect on the group as Nathan's.

When the stories were over, Mr. Dorfman and Mr. Criderman instructed the group to pick up any trash around the campsite and to use the restroom if they needed to. Martha got up to look around for trash, and Emma was just getting ready to follow her when she noticed Mr. Dorfman over by one of the wagons. At the moment, he was alone. Realizing that this was her chance, she quickly went over to him.

"Mr. Dorfman," Emma began quickly before she could lose her nerve, "would it be okay if Martha and I rode back on the other wagon?"

"I guess that would be all right," Mr. Dorfman responded after a moment. "Just make sure you tell Mr. Criderman that you'll be riding back with him."

"I will," Emma quickly agreed. She headed back to the campfire intending to tell Mr. Criderman right away that she and Martha would be riding back on his wagon, but she couldn't find him. Reasoning that he'd probably gone to use the restroom himself before the trip back to the castle, Emma decided to tell Martha the good news instead. There was only one problem with Emma's plan: Martha was nowhere in sight either. Emma began moving around the campsite asking some of the other Alpha-O's if they'd seen where Martha had gone. No one seemed to know. Emma was just beginning to get concerned when finally someone said they had seen her.

"She was looking for you," an older girl Emma didn't know informed her. "Someone told her you'd gone up the trail to the falls."

Why would anyone tell her that? Emma wondered with a frown. Then it hit her. It would be just like Bobby or one of his friends to send Martha off on a wild goose chase.

Thanking the girl for the information, Emma hurriedly set off on the path that led up to the falls. She needed to find Martha in a hurry. The group would be leaving soon to go back to the castle. As Emma walked, she called Martha's name. Like the path leading down to the river, this one had solar lights set along it at regular intervals. These, in addition to the light from the full moon, provided sufficient illumination for Emma to safely pick her way along the path. Emma hurried as fast as she could, expecting to meet Martha coming back down at any time. Soon the path left the trees and began to follow along the edge of the bluff. Too late, Emma realized that she too had been sent on a wild goose chase. Martha was afraid of heights and would never have come up the trail this far. Emma was about to turn back when she heard it—the sound of the waterfall. She must be very close to the lookout. As if drawn by an irresistible force, Emma continued up the path. This might be her only chance to see the waterfall firsthand. She would take one quick look and then head back down to the campsite. Martha was probably there waiting for her right now.

Emma climbed quickly, all the while telling herself that she should be headed in the other direction. However, desire won out over reason, and she kept moving upward. The viewing spot turned out to be farther away than she'd thought. The sound of the falls had been amplified by the surrounding bluffs, making it seem closer than it really was. Finally, Emma reached the lookout and had to admit that the climb had been worth the effort. She could see immediately why it was called Boulder Falls. It appeared as if an enormous chunk of rock had broken off and come crashing down the mountainside, finally coming to rest in one of the mountain's many runoff streams. The water was diverted by the huge boulder in such a way that, instead of following its natural course down the side of the mountain, it was forced over the edge of the bluff. It was a magnificent sight especially with the light of the full moon reflecting off the water as it leapt over the edge and fell hundreds of feet to the river below.

Emma lingered only long enough to memorize how the falls looked in the moonlight. Then she turned and headed back down the trail, all the while regretting her foolish impulse. She was probably going to get in trouble for making everyone wait. When Emma finally reached the campsite, she stopped abruptly, shocked at the sight that greeted her eyes. Everyone was gone along with both of the wagons. Emma hurried to the gravel road they'd come in on earlier that evening, hoping that she could still catch the wagons, but they were nowhere in sight. Apparently, they'd left some time ago. *What am I going to do?* Emma thought, beginning to panic. *And where is Martha?* Surely, Martha wouldn't have let them leave without her.

She was still standing there in indecision when she heard a rustling noise coming from the river path. Convinced that it was the ghost of the mad woman coming to get her, she was in the process of looking for a place to hide when Martha appeared. Emma could have cried in relief at the sight of her friend. As she rushed over to her, Martha exclaimed angrily, "Where have you been? I've been looking all over for you. Someone told me you'd gone back down to the river to look for one of your gloves."

"They told me you'd gone up the path to the falls," Emma replied. She wasn't offended at Martha's anger. She could hear the worry behind Martha's words.

"Well, I guess we've been tricked," Martha fumed. "And I bet I know who's behind it all."

"Bobby!" both girls cried in unison.

Martha looked around the now vacant campsite. "How could they just go off and leave us like that? Mr. Dorfman must have seen that we didn't get on his wagon."

"I'm afraid that's my fault," Emma said with a grim expression. "I asked Mr. Dorfman if we could ride back to the castle on the other wagon. He said it was okay but that I needed to make sure I told Mr. Criderman right away. Mr. Criderman wasn't around just then, so I decided I'd tell you the good news first, but I couldn't find you either. Then some girl told me you'd gone up the path to the falls looking for me." Emma paused for a moment and looked sheepishly at Martha. "I should have known you'd never go up that way."

"Well, the question is what do we do now?"

"I guess, we'll have to walk back to the castle," Emma replied. The problem was she had no idea which direction to go. She hadn't been paying any attention to the route the wagons had taken on the way to the campsite. Bobby and his mean friends were to blame for that too.

"Surely when the wagons get back to the castle, someone will notice that we're missing," Martha reasoned. "Phil and Tom, or even Kim or Cindy, will surely see that we aren't with the group."

"Maybe," Emma replied. "But I don't think we should count on it. The wagons may not get back to the castle at the same time. All of the eighth graders could be in their rooms and in bed before Mr. Dorfman's wagon arrives or vice versa."

Martha frowned. She hadn't thought of that. Emma was right. They needed to at least try to get back to the castle on their own. She didn't relish the idea of staying at the campsite any more than Emma did. All of the scary stories they'd just heard had given her the creeps.

"Do you know the way back?" Martha asked after a moment.

"No, I was hoping you did."

"Well, that's just great! I guess we're just supposed to wander around in the dark until some guy with a hook attacks us," Martha railed.

Despite the seriousness of their current situation, Emma found herself laughing at Martha's reference. Martha frowned at Emma for a split second before she started laughing too. With their laughter, some of girls' anxiety drained away. No matter what the next couple of hours might bring, at least they had each other.

CHAPTER TWENTY-THREE
A WALK IN THE MOONLIGHT

"I wish Doug and Sebastian were with us," Emma said wistfully as the two girls set off down the gravel road.

"Well, they're not, so we're just going to have to do the best we can without them," Martha responded. Although she agreed with Emma wholeheartedly, she knew it wasn't going to do them any good to dwell on circumstances they couldn't change. They needed to focus all of their efforts on getting back to the castle.

For the next several minutes, the girls walked along in silence. Thankfully, the full moon provided enough light for them to avoid stepping in the road's numerous potholes. All went well, until a few minutes later, they came to the first fork in the road. Both girls came to a stop in the middle of the crossroad and looked intently in each direction.

"Which way do you think we should go?" Martha asked.

"I don't know," Emma said with a shake of her head. "They both look the same to me."

"Well, we can't just stand here all night. We're going to have to make a choice."

Emma looked down at the road thinking that the tractors might have left some tracks they could follow, but the hard-packed earth revealed nothing. Then she noticed a clump of hay lying on the road on her left.

"Look!" Emma cried, excitedly pointing to her discovery.

"Good eyes," Martha said. "I guess we go left."

After that, the girls kept an eye out for more hay. Additional clumps of hay spaced along the road at irregular intervals convinced the girls that they were going the right way. It seemed to Emma as if someone was intentionally leaving them a trail to follow. Maybe on the trip back to the school, Bobby had begun to regret tricking the girls and had decided to help them. Almost as soon as she had the thought, Emma rejected it. It wasn't like Bobby to be sorry about anything he did. Perhaps one of the others involved in the plot was dropping the hay. With a sigh, Emma realized it really didn't matter who, if anyone, was helping them. As long as they had a trail of hay to follow, they would be okay.

Emma's thoughts grew fanciful as she walked along next to Martha. She began to imagine that she and Martha were following the trail of breadcrumbs left by Hansel and Gretel. She just hoped it didn't lead to a witch's house where they'd find the two children locked in an oven.

Emma shivered as a fresh gust of wind hit her. The temperature was beginning to drop, and the wind seemed to have more force behind it. She began to think longingly of a warm oven.

"Oooh! That wind is awful," Martha exclaimed with a shiver as she pulled up the collar on her jacket.

"I know," Emma agreed. "It's getting colder too."

"That's all we need. The wind may blow our trail away."

Emma hadn't thought of that. Just as she began to worry that they might lose their trail, a cloud passed over the moon. The sudden loss of light caused her to stumble.

"I never realized how dark it could get out in the middle of nowhere," Martha commented beside her. "I can't see where I'm going."

"Me neither," Emma said. She looked up to see high wispy clouds scudding across the sky. Thankfully, the cloud currently covering the moon wasn't very large. In moments, the moon would be reappearing. "We'll be able to see again in a minute. The cloud's almost past."

"Oh!" Martha cried out in the next instant. "I think I just sprained my ankle. Stupid potholes!"

"Are you okay? Can you walk on it?" Emma hurried over to where Martha stood, massaging her right ankle.

"It's not too bad. I think I'll be able to walk on it." Martha put her right foot down and gradually began shifting her weight onto it. She sighed in relief as it held her weight with only a slight twinge of pain.

"It's just a little sore," she informed Emma. "I'm not ready to run a marathon by any means, but I can make it back to the castle."

Emma let out the breath she'd been holding and sent up a small prayer of thanks. She had no idea what she would have done if Martha hadn't been able to continue. In all the time they'd been walking, they hadn't passed any houses where she could have gotten any help.

"Put your arm over my shoulder, and I can help you walk," Emma offered.

"I'm okay for now. If the pain gets any worse, I'll let you know."

"Okay. We'll just take it slow, and if you need to stop to rest your ankle, just say the word."

"You've got yourself a deal," Martha said.

The moon had reappeared, so the girls set off down the road once again but, this time, at a slower pace. The wind continued to blow, its breath getting frostier by the minute. The shivering girls huddled close together as Martha limped along without complaint. Miserable and cold, Emma lost track of time. It seemed like they'd been walking for hours, and still the castle was nowhere in sight. Was it possible they had taken a wrong turn somewhere? Emma was just about to share her doubts with Martha when a car's headlights appeared in the distance.

Startled, the two girls looked at each other. Every instinct told Emma to hide. After the stories they'd heard earlier that evening, Emma envisioned the driver of the car as a serial killer cruising along lonely back roads looking for likely victims. She and Martha were the perfect prey for such a maniacal predator. Without hesitation, Emma pulled Martha off the road and into the woods. Martha must have been thinking along the same lines as Emma because she went along without argument. Once they were far enough away from the road, the girls crouched down behind a couple of large trees and waited for the car to pass.

For the first time since this whole ordeal had begun, Emma was genuinely afraid. Would they ever make it back to the castle? Emma began to calculate how long it would be until someone at the school finally noticed the girls were missing. Clarice and Susie, their roommates, would probably get up in the morning thinking the girls had already made their beds and left for breakfast. Clarice and Susie liked to sleep in on the weekends, while Emma and Martha got up at their usual early time. Doug was still in the infirmary, so that left only Sebastian. Surely, Sebastian would notice the girls were gone and tell someone. At any rate, if the girls didn't make it back to the castle tonight, it would be a long time before anyone came looking for them.

All of these thoughts ran through her head as they waited for the car to pass their hiding spots. It seemed to be taking an unusually long time to get to where they were. When the car finally reached them, Emma knew why. Whoever was driving was just barely creeping along. Emma had plenty of time to get a good look at the car, but from her position and in the reduced light, all she could tell was that it was a dark-colored sedan. She couldn't see inside the car at all.

"Why is that car going so slow?" Martha whispered beside her.

"I don't know," Emma whispered back. *Maybe the driver's just very old*, Emma thought. Nothing more was said as they waited until the car was no longer in sight. When they were sure it was safe, they left the woods and began walking along the gravel road once again. After what seemed an eternity, they came to another fork in the road. Emma scanned both directions for any clumps of hay, but the moon had begun its descent in the west, and it was getting harder to see. Sending up a silent prayer, Emma took a deep breath.

"I say we go left again," she told Martha.

"That's what I was thinking," Martha said with a nod.

With Martha's confirmation, Emma didn't hesitate but immediately set out on the road they'd chosen. She wanted to get back to the castle before any other cars came along.

Emma noticed that Martha's limp was growing more pronounced, and every now and then, a little moan would escape her lips. It was obvious her ankle was beginning to cause her more pain. Without asking this time, Emma took Martha's right arm and put it over her shoulder.

"Lean on me and use me as a crutch," she instructed Martha.

Emma knew Martha was really suffering when she didn't argue. It was even slower going now, and Emma felt like crying. They were cold and tired, and Martha was hurting. In an effort to keep back the tears that threatened, Emma thought of how much she'd like to get her hands around Bobby Wilcox's neck. He was the cause of this whole nightmare. The problem was she had no proof. Once the two girls got back to the castle, Emma would probably be blamed for the whole thing because she hadn't followed instructions and informed Mr. Criderman right away that they would be riding back with him. The more she thought about it, the more convinced she became that she was going to be in serious trouble when, and if, they ever got back to the castle. As she contemplated what her punishment might be, Emma felt tears welling up again. Only this time she wasn't able to hold them back.

She turned her head away from Martha so she wouldn't see the tears streaming down her cheeks, but Martha wasn't so easily fooled. In truth, she felt like crying herself. Still she tried to comfort her friend.

"It's okay, Emma. I'm sure we're getting close to the castle now."

"It's not that," Emma said with a sniff. Then she told Martha what she'd been thinking.

"That's ridiculous! How could any of this be your fault? We were lied to."

"But we don't have any proof. The girl who told me you'd gone up to Boulder Falls can always claim she really thought you had. And there's absolutely no way we can prove Bobby put her up to it."

"I guess you're right," Martha said with a frown. "I wonder if it was the same girl that put me up to going down the river path to look for you."

"Probably, but it could have been any one of Bobby's groupies," Emma said with disgust. Then with a sigh of resignation, she added, "It doesn't really matter. We still can't prove a thing. I'm gonna take the fall for this."

"No, you won't!" Martha cried. "It was Mr. Criderman's and Mr. Dorfman's responsibility to see that everyone was on the two wagons before they left the campsite. Mr. Dorfman should have checked to be sure we were on the other wagon."

Martha had a good point, but Dean Harwood might not see it that way. At least Martha had given Emma some hope. With a sigh, Emma tried to put it out of her mind. They needed to worry about getting back to the castle first. Then they could worry about who was going to get in trouble and for what.

Emma was so focused on her conversation with Martha that for a moment she failed to notice the appearance of the castle's spires over the tops of the trees on her right. Even when she looked up, it took a moment to register on her consciousness. When it did, she began jumping up and down joyously.

"Look, Martha! Look! The castle!"

"Thank goodness! I don't think I could have gone much farther on this ankle."

Their spirits lifted by the sight of the castle's spires, the girls' energy returned, and they managed to move along at a quicker pace, even with Martha's sprained ankle. When they came to the next fork in the road, they knew exactly which way to go.

Soon they were headed up the driveway leading to the castle's front entrance. When they rounded the last curve, they could see the castle in its entirety, and a most curious phenomenon greeted their eyes. The full moon had begun its descent in the western sky and was shining directly in the windows of the west tower, but that isn't what had the girls stopping and staring in wonderment. Bright rays of light were streaming out of the tower's turret windows as if a star had been placed inside it. The light coming from the turret was so bright it reminded Emma of the powerful beams cast by a lighthouse.

"What in the world is that?" Martha asked in a tone of reverence.

"I have no idea, but it's the coolest thing I've ever seen."

"Do you think it shines like that every night?"

"I don't know. I've never been outside the castle this late at night before," Emma answered.

"Maybe Doug will know what's causing it," Martha suggested. Because Doug was in the infirmary, it would be Sunday before they would be able to ask him. Martha wondered if she could wait that long to have her curiosity satisfied. Then another idea occurred to her. "We need to get inside that tower and have a look for ourselves."

"We can't," Emma replied.

"Why not?"

"I asked Doug about the towers one time, and he told me that the entrances to both the east and west towers were sealed a long time ago. Apparently, the stairs had become unsafe."

"Why didn't they just fix the stairs?" Martha asked, pointing out the logical solution.

"I don't know. It didn't make any sense to me either, so I asked Doug that same question. He just shrugged and said that's what Lord Dinswood told him."

"Where is the entrance to the west tower? I've never noticed it before."

"The entrances to both towers were bricked over. Now there's a wall where the doors used to be," Emma explained.

"So there's absolutely no way to get in there?" Martha wasn't ready to give up hope just yet. There had to be a way.

Emma shook her head and answered regretfully, "None that I know of."

"Well, there is definitely something in there, and it had to get in there somehow," Martha pointed out.

"It could have been in there before the entrances were bricked over," Emma countered.

"Maybe there's something extremely valuable in there, and that's the reason the towers were sealed. It probably had nothing to do with unsafe stairs."

"I guess it's possible, but we'll never know."

"How can you give up so easily? I still say there has to be a way into the towers. We need to talk to Lord Dinswood and get him to open them up again."

"Doug says Lord Dinswood hasn't been feeling well. Doug's really worried about him. Anyway, I don't think it's a good time to bother Lord Dinswood about this. Maybe Doug knows something about what's up there. We can talk to him Sunday once he gets out of the infirmary."

"I guess that's all we can do," Martha said with regret. "What do you think it is? What could possibly reflect the moonlight like that?"

"I don't know," Emma said for the second time. As Emma walked and Martha limped up the stairs to the front entrance, Martha continued to conjecture on what could be up in the west tower. Emma didn't feel the need to reply. It was obvious that Martha was totally engrossed in her guessing game. The closer they got to the door, the more Emma began to worry about the trouble she could be in. Of course, it was entirely possible that no one was aware that the two girls were missing, and everyone had already gone to bed. If that were the case, they could slip quietly into the school, sneak to their room, and no one would be the wiser. All hopes for this scenario were dashed the moment they opened the enormous oak doors.

The lobby was all lit up and was literally a beehive of activity. Dean Harwood was in the process of instructing several of the faculty to take their cars in various directions to search for her and Martha. When he spied the two girls, he stopped in midsentence. In seconds, all heads turned in their direction, and everything came to a sudden halt. Emma immediately began to feel uncomfortable under the stares of all those assembled.

Dean Harwood's first words were "Thank the good Lord! Are you girls all right?"

He was looking at them with such concern that Emma began to consider how bedraggled they must look after their ordeal. No doubt their hair was in wild disarray from the wind, and the frosty blasts had probably given their cheeks a healthy red blush. Then there was the fact that Martha was limping and still had Emma's arm around her for support.

"We're okay," Emma replied finally, "but Martha has sprained her ankle." Emma's stomach started churning, and she began to feel sick. She had the sinking feeling that she was in serious trouble.

"I'll send for the nurse immediately," Dean Harwood said quickly. "While we wait, I'd like to hear what happened."

After sending for the nurse, Dean Harwood thanked the teachers involved in the search and told them they could return to their rooms. Then he led the girls into his office. When they were all seated, he looked pointedly at Emma and said, "Now let's hear your side of the story."

Emma held nothing back. She told Dean Harwood how Bobby had made their trip to the campsite so miserable that she had asked to switch wagons. Then she went on to explain how the two girls had been tricked into going in opposite directions, resulting in their being left behind.

Dean Harwood listened to Emma's tale quietly. When she finished her story, he began to ask questions. "Why didn't you tell Mr. Criderman immediately that you would be riding on his wagon?"

"He wasn't around at the time, so I decided to tell Martha the good news first. That's when I was sent up the wrong trail."

"And you think this misdirection was intentional?"

"I'm sure it was, but I can't prove it," Emma answered truthfully.

"Martha, do you feel you were also purposely misled?"

"Yes," Martha answered quickly, speaking for the first time since they'd entered the castle.

"Well, lucky for you two that you returned when you did. I was about to call your families to tell them you were missing. I'm glad we were able to spare them that worry. How were you able to find your way back?"

"We followed the trail of hay," Martha blurted out.

Dean Harwood smiled then. "I see, sort of like Hansel and Gretel and the trail of breadcrumbs."

Emma started in surprise. "That's exactly what I thought!"

Dean Harwood seemed to be more relieved than angry, and for the first time since getting back to the castle, Emma began to have some hope that she wouldn't be blamed for what had happened.

"I sent people out to look for you. I'm surprised you didn't see any of the cars I sent."

Emma and Martha looked at each other sheepishly.

Seeing the exchange, Dean Harwood asked, "You did see a car, didn't you? I guess my next question is, why didn't the driver see you?"

Emma hesitated for a moment, embarrassed by the explanation for their behavior. Still, she wasn't going to lie to Dean Harwood.

"It's stupid really. We were telling scary stories around the campfire earlier. One of the stories was about a serial killer with a hook for a hand. Anyway, when we saw the car, we were kind of spooked, so we hid till it passed by."

Dean Harwood said nothing for several seconds, and it seemed to Emma that he was trying very hard not to laugh. Of course, she could have been mistaken.

Then Dean Harwood's expression sobered once again, and he cleared his throat. Emma knew that he was about to pronounce sentence, and her palms began to sweat.

"There's no denying, Emma, that you failed to follow Mr. Dorfman's instructions. You should have waited for Mr. Criderman and then informed him of the switch. For failure to follow the directive of a teacher, beginning Monday, you will serve two weeks of after-school detention with Miss Jennings."

Emma could have cried in relief. She was going to be punished, but detention with Miss Jennings didn't sound too terribly awful. Miss Jennings was a lot nicer than Miss Grimstock who usually had detention duty. It seemed like Dean Harwood was trying not to be too harsh with Emma's punishment.

Martha looked over at Emma and gave her that I-told-you-so look. Emma raised an eyebrow in response to Martha's silent gloating as Dean Harwood continued.

"I'll be having a little chat with Bobby Wilcox tomorrow morning to let him know that bullying will not be tolerated at Dinswood Academy. Since you have no proof, I'm afraid my hands are tied on the other matter. However, I will instruct the faculty to keep a closer eye on Bobby."

Bobby will hate us even more than he already does, Emma thought as Dean Harwood finished speaking. Before Dean Harwood could say anything else, Emma hurried to ask a question of her own.

"Sir, I was wondering how you knew that Martha and I hadn't returned with the group? We started walking because we thought it would be morning before anyone noticed that we were missing."

"It was Martha's blanket," Dean Harwood replied. Seeing the blank look on the two girls' faces, he continued his explanation. "Mr. Dorfman found Martha's blanket on his wagon. As his wagon had returned to the school first, he decided to wait for Mr. Criderman's wagon so he could give it to Martha. When you two weren't on Mr. Criderman's wagon, Mr. Dorfman immediately reported your absence to me."

Emma had forgotten all about Martha's blanket. It was apparent from the look on Martha's face that she had too. How ironic that the blanket that had caused Martha such embarrassment earlier that evening would be the very object that would alert school officials that the two girls were missing.

A knock on the dean's office door interrupted Emma's thoughts. Dean Harwood called out permission to enter; and the school's head nurse, Mrs. Godfrey, entered. She was wearing a plush ruby-colored robe over her flannel pajamas and had slippers of the same ruby color on her feet. Emma was reminded of the magical ruby slippers in the well-known movie *The Wizard of Oz*, but she kept the observation to herself.

"I'm sorry to disturb you, Mrs. Godfrey, but Martha has injured her ankle," Dean Harwood explained.

"Well, we'd better have a look then," Mrs. Godfrey said. She didn't seem to be the least put out by having to come down to the dean's office in the middle of the night. Emma reasoned that as the head nurse, she was probably used to students getting sick or injured at all hours of the day or night.

Mrs. Godfrey knelt before Martha and began examining her ankle. Martha winced in pain as the nurse gently turned it. After a moment, having completed her examination, Mrs. Godfrey rose. "Well, the good news is it's not broken, and the sprain is a mild one. I think with some medication for pain and inflammation, Martha will be as right as rain in no time," she reported to Dean Harwood. Then looking at Martha, she said, "Stay off that ankle as much as possible for the next couple of days, and when you're sitting down, keep it elevated."

Martha nodded her understanding as Mrs. Godfrey added, "I'll get the pills you'll need from the infirmary and bring them by your room. You're to take one every four to six hours. If the pain worsens, send Emma to let me know."

"Thank you, Mrs. Godfrey," Dean Harwood said as the nurse departed.

Thinking that the meeting was now over, Emma started to get up.

"Just so you know," Dean Harwood said, stopping Emma in midrise, "I'll also be taking disciplinary action against Mr. Dorfman. Ultimately, it was his responsibility to make sure that you two girls got on the other wagon."

Emma didn't look at Martha who was probably, at this very moment, giving her another I-told-you-so look. Instead, she said goodnight to Dean Harwood and left his office with Martha trailing behind her. A soft moan reminded her that Martha could probably still use her help. Wordlessly, she took Martha's arm and put it over her shoulder. *Now Mr. Dorfman's going to be mad at me too*, Emma worried as she helped Martha hobble down the hall toward the girls' dorm.

Before they reached the double doors leading into Brimley Hall, Martha asked, "Where do you suppose the entrance to the west tower used to be?"

Emma realized then why Martha hadn't said anything in the last few minutes. She had been busy examining the hallway's brick walls for any area that looked like it may have been bricked over. In all the excitement of their return and her subsequent punishment, Emma had forgotten all about the strange light emanating from the west tower.

"You don't give up, do you?" Emma said with a sigh as she pushed open one of the double doors.

Martha's only reply was a shake of her head.

CHAPTER TWENTY-FOUR
A DAY TO REMEMBER

The next morning, Emma awakened to the patter of rain on the window. It seemed the cold front that had caused the drop in temperature last night had also brought rain. It didn't look like they would be playing any carnival games on the front lawn this year. Emma wondered what the faculty would do instead. The children's hospital in Benton counted on the money brought in by the school's annual Octoberfest. The event was too important to simply dismiss because of bad weather. Emma felt certain that the school would have some sort of backup plan.

Emma got up and looked out the window. The sky was leaden. It didn't look like the rain would be ending any time soon. That meant that the relay races scheduled for the afternoon would also have to be canceled. Emma's spirits sank as she contemplated the day ahead. It was bad enough that Doug couldn't be with them, but now they would be stuck indoors the entire day with nothing to do.

Martha, Clarice, and Susie were just beginning to stir when someone knocked on the door to their suite. Emma called out for whomever it was to come in as Clarice grumbled something about being disturbed so early in the morning. Hearing Clarice's comment, Emma looked over at her alarm clock. It was already nine o'clock. She and Martha had slept later than usual—probably due to the events of the night before. At any rate, Clarice's idea of early wasn't the same as Emma's.

Emma smiled to herself as the door opened, and in bounced Penny Parnell, their dorm advisor. Penny hadn't visited the girls since school had begun in September. It was apparent from the excited expression on her face that she had important news to impart.

"It's raining outside," Penny said, pointing out the obvious.

"We noticed," Clarice responded dryly before Penny could continue. "Is that all you came to tell us?"

"No," Penny answered with a wide-eyed expression. She had completely missed the sarcasm in Clarice's tone. "I'm here to tell you that the carnival games will be played in the classrooms this morning instead of on the front lawn because of the rain. Also, there will be a trivia game in the dining hall after lunch. The seniors who want to participate will be the team captains. They are supposed to choose students from each grade level to be on their team. Each person will pay a small fee to play, and the money will be donated to the children's hospital along with all the money brought in by the carnival games. It should be a lot of fun. Hopefully, one of the teams will choose some of you guys to play in the trivia event. Well, anyway, that's all I needed to tell you. See you later." Penny started to leave and then suddenly stopped and turned back around.

"Oh, I almost forgot. The dance will take place in the ballroom after supper tonight as usual."

Then with a toss of her blonde ponytail, Penny was gone. Clarice yawned and, with a bored expression, said, "I don't intend to be on any silly trivia team."

Emma was hoping that someone would pick her and Martha. She agreed with Penny. The trivia game sounded like a lot of fun. Then Emma's thoughts turned to the dance. She had pretty much decided she wasn't going. Last year, none of the boys had asked her to dance because they had thought she was Doug's girlfriend. The problem was Doug hadn't asked her to dance either. It had been a big misunderstanding, and Emma had hoped to put things right at this year's dance. With Doug's illness, there wasn't any chance of that, so she might as well skip it this year. She was about to tell Martha her decision when Susie interrupted her.

"Did you guys have a good time on the hayride last night?"

Emma hesitated before replying. It was probably best that she didn't tell Susie about everything that had happened. However, her question reminded Emma about Susie's request that she keep an eye on Daniel Jacobs for her. So much had happened on the way to the campsite that Emma had completely forgotten about her promise to Susie. Now that she thought about it, Emma didn't remember seeing Daniel last night. Emma frowned as she tried to remember, but she didn't recall seeing him around the campfire or on either of the wagons.

"It was okay. You really didn't miss anything," Emma finally answered.

Before Emma could tell Susie about not seeing Daniel, Susie said, "Good. Now I don't feel so badly that Daniel didn't go."

"What do you mean?" Emma asked.

"Well, as it turns out, Daniel likes me," Susie replied, smiling brightly. "He told me last night that the hayride wouldn't be any fun without me along. He stayed behind so that he could spend time with me."

"Susie, that's great," Emma replied, happy for her roommate. Susie's happiness made her think longingly of Doug. She had really missed him the last couple of days, and she was going to feel his absence keenly tonight. That thought reminded her that she still needed to tell Martha she wasn't going to go to the dance.

"Nonsense," Martha replied when Emma told her about her decision. "You'll go, and you'll have a great time! If someone doesn't ask you to dance, then you do the asking."

That's just it, Emma thought. *I don't really want to dance with anyone but Doug.* Not wanting to argue with Martha, Emma decided to let the subject drop for now. Later as they left their dorm for breakfast, Emma vowed that she wouldn't let Martha coerce her into going to the dance.

As they walked down the hall, Emma noticed that Martha's ankle appeared to be a lot better. She was walking slowly, but there was no trace of a limp.

"How's your ankle today, Martha? You seem to be doing a lot better," Emma commented.

"Yeah, it's not swollen anymore, but it's still a little sore. I'm hoping if I take it easy on it today, I'll be able to dance a little bit tonight."

"Mrs. Godfrey told you to stay off it as much as possible," Emma pointed out.

"I know, but I don't want to miss all the fun. Besides, I can rest it this afternoon." Skillfully changing the subject, Martha asked, "Do you think anyone will ask us to play in the trivia game?"

"I don't know, but I hope so," Emma replied. She was glad that Martha's ankle was so much better, but she thought it was too soon for Martha to try to dance on it. It might be feeling okay now, but if she didn't stay off it, it could swell up again. Oh well, she couldn't really blame Martha. If the situations were reversed, Emma knew she wouldn't want to miss out on things either.

At breakfast, the girls met up with Sebastian and spent the next several minutes filling him in on everything that had happened the night before—including their suspicions about Bobby. When they were finished, Sebastian's face was flushed with anger.

"This time that guy has gone too far!" he began furiously. "Something terrible could have happened to the two of you."

"Please don't do anything, Sebastian," Martha pleaded. "Dean Harwood said he would take care of it. I don't want you to get into any trouble, and that's just what'll happen if you don't calm down. Besides, we don't have any real proof that Bobby was behind it."

"I don't need any proof," Sebastian ground out.

"Please, Sebastian," Martha said again. "Let's not waste the day worrying about Bobby. I want to have some fun." Martha gave Sebastian her best smile and was relieved to see his expression soften.

"Okay," he agreed after a moment, "I'll let it go for now, but believe me when I say that this isn't over."

Martha decided that was the best she could hope for as far as Sebastian was concerned. She'd meant it when she'd said she didn't want to think about it anymore. It was time to let it go and move on. She and Emma were fine, and that's all that mattered.

After breakfast, Sebastian escorted the two girls upstairs to the second floor where all of the carnival games had been set up in the classrooms. It was then that he noticed Martha's slow progress. "Hey, are you all right?" he asked Martha with a frown. Martha hadn't told him that she had sprained her ankle last night. She had hoped that he wouldn't notice. He was already mad enough at Bobby.

"I stepped in a pothole last night and sprained my ankle," Martha explained reluctantly. "It's really feeling much better now."

For a moment, it looked as if Sebastian was about to explode. His face turned beet red, and he didn't say anything for a while. It was clear that he was making a huge effort to gain control of his temper. It was probably a good thing that Bobby wasn't anywhere around just then. Finally, Sebastian took a deep breath and let it out slowly.

"Are you sure you're okay?" he finally managed to ask in a normal tone.

"I'm fine. Really," Martha added when Sebastian continued to look unconvinced.

Sebastian's nod indicated that he believed her, and for the rest of the day, he focused all of his effort on making sure that Martha took it easy on her ankle. He offered Martha his arm and helped her as they made their way slowly up the stairs to the second floor. Martha appeared to enjoy Sebastian's thoughtful assistance.

Once upstairs, they met up with Phil, Tom, Cindy, and Kim. The foursome didn't know what had happened to Emma and Martha the night before, and that's just the way the girls wanted it to remain. Martha whispered a warning to Sebastian to say nothing about the events of last evening. She quickly explained that getting everyone all riled up would only ruin the day. Frowning, Sebastian reluctantly agreed. When the others noticed that Martha was favoring her right ankle, she simply explained that she had sprained it. Thankfully, they didn't ask for details.

The group spent the morning wandering happily from game to game. They tried the ring toss, the dart game, and the shooting gallery more than once, but no prizes were won. When it was time for lunch, they made their way downstairs. Last year, lunch had been set up on the terrace picnic style, but this year the weather necessitated that lunch be moved inside. The meal was still a picnic in nature, consisting of fried chicken, sandwiches, chips, and cookies. For drinks, students could choose from lemonade, iced tea, or cherry Kool-Aid.

The dining hall was filled with the sound of light-hearted conversation and laughter as the students filled their plates. It seemed the rain had not dampened their spirits. After a week of testing, everyone needed a chance to relax and let loose a bit and they were doing just that. Emma found that she was having a good time in spite of the fact that Doug wasn't with them.

As they were eating, Nathan Boyd, the Alpha-Omega president, came by their table and invited Emma and Martha to be on his trivia team. Emma was thrilled and agreed without hesitation, as did Martha. The day was turning out better than Emma had hoped.

"I'm having a team meeting in the lounge after lunch," Nathan told them. "I want to introduce everyone and find out what everyone's strengths are."

"Okay," the girls replied in unison.

Emma hurried through her lunch. She was eager to get to the lounge to see who the other members of her team would be. Nathan would no doubt have assembled what he thought were the smartest students from each grade. For this reason, Emma was very flattered that he had asked her to be on his team.

As soon as she was finished eating, Emma stood up and went over to the garbage cans to empty her tray. Martha must have been just as excited as Emma because she got up from the table when Emma did. With a hasty goodbye to their friends, they left the dining hall.

"I wonder who else is on our team," Martha said as they walked down the main hall.

"If I know Nathan, he'll have gotten a really good team together. We should be flattered that he's asked us to join his group."

"I know," Martha said and then sighed wistfully. "I just wish Nathan had asked Sebastian to be on his team too."

"Me too," Emma agreed. Having played in a trivia event before, Emma knew that the categories weren't necessarily academic subjects. Sebastian had a lot of general knowledge and would have been a big help. Oh well, it wasn't her team, so there was little she could do about it.

When the two girls got to the lounge, the rest of Nathan's team was already assembled. Once the two girls were seated, Nathan made the introductions. The team consisted of two seniors, two juniors, one sophomore, and one freshman. Emma and Martha were the only two eighth graders on the team. Each team was allowed ten members, but there were only nine present.

As if reading Emma's mind, Nathan said, "There are twelve senior team captains, so as you can imagine, competition for team members was fierce. I wasn't able to get some of the students I had planned to ask. Still, I think the nine we have on the team are top notch."

"I know who we can ask if you'd like to have an even ten on the team," Martha piped up.

Emma knew immediately whom Martha was thinking of.

"We'd be better off to have a full team, Nathan. You can bet all of the other teams have ten members," Danielle, the senior girl, said.

Nathan must have agreed with Danielle, because he turned to Martha then and asked, "Who'd you have in mind?"

"Sebastian Conners," Martha answered and then hastened to explain before Nathan could object. "I know he's not in the Alpha-O's, but he's really smart. He just doesn't care that much about grades. He knows a lot about cooking, sailing, sports, and lots of other subjects that might come up. I think he'd really help our team."

Nathan thought for a moment and then nodded his head to signal his agreement.

"Great! I'll go get him," Martha said. With that, Martha jumped up from the couch and hurried from the room as fast as her sore ankle would allow. She wanted to get Sebastian before Nathan could change his mind.

While Martha was fetching Sebastian, Nathan asked those who remained what subjects they excelled at. When it was Emma's turn, she told the group that her best subject was science and that Martha was very knowledgeable in the field of art; Sebastian's abilities had already been discussed. By the time each team member had finished speaking, it was clear that Nathan had managed to assemble a group with a wide range of knowledge. Emma felt they had a very good chance of winning. Emma wondered if Bobby had been picked to be on a team. She fervently hoped not. Bobby didn't take kindly to losing.

A moment later, Martha entered the lounge, followed by a grinning Sebastian. It was clear from his expression that he was glad he'd been asked to be on a team. Nathan welcomed Sebastian and quickly introduced him to the other team members. The trivia game couldn't begin until lunch was over and the dining hall had been cleaned, so there was nothing to do now except wait.

Finally, an announcement over the intercom instructed all of the teams to report to the dining hall. As each team entered, they were given a number and told where to sit. At their table, they found a pad of paper, a couple of pencils, and a list of the categories for the event. Each team would get a chance to pick one of the categories.

Emma was a little nervous as her team took their places at the table. A placard on the table identified their team as team number seven. *Seven is a good number*, Emma thought. In the Bible, seven always signified completeness. To Emma, it seemed like a good omen.

"We need to make sure we don't say our answers too loud, or one of the other teams will hear us," Nathan told them once everyone was seated.

After a brief conversation with the group, it was agreed that Danielle would write down their answers for them, so she took the paper and one of the sharpened pencils.

While they waited for the game to begin, Emma took the opportunity to look around the dining hall and see who their competition would be. With eleven other ten-member teams, the dining hall was packed. A couple of tables over, she spotted Bobby Wilcox. She noticed that Daniel Jacobs and Preston Danvers were on Bobby's team. She didn't know any of the others sitting with Bobby. Emma didn't let her gaze linger there long because she didn't want

Bobby to catch her looking at him. She wondered if Dean Harwood had had a chance to talk to him yet. A little shiver went up her spine as she realized Bobby would find a way to get even with her for tattling on him.

With an effort, Emma turned her attention back to scouting out the other teams. She was glad to see Reggie sitting with a group just a table away. Seeing her look, Reggie smiled and waved.

A few minutes later, the emcee for the event, a tall brown-haired senior girl named Tracy, called for quiet. She had a microphone so everyone could hear her. After explaining the rules, Tracy drew a number from a basket.

"Team two will select the first category," Tracy announced.

Team two's captain selected a category titled On the Road Again. The category turned out to be about classic cars. Emma didn't know anything about car models, but fortunately Matthew, the team's only sophomore, did. He was able to come up with the answers to eight of the questions, and Sebastian knew the answers to the other two. After the first round was scored, only one other team had gotten ten out of ten points, team three.

As the game progressed, it became clear that the real competition was between Nathan's team and team three. After each round was scored, either team seven or team three was in the lead. It looked like it was all going to come down to the last category.

Tracy drew a number from the basket and Emma held her breath as she waited to hear which team would get to select the last category of the game. As they hadn't gotten to choose a category yet, team seven's number was still in the basket. Being able to select the last category of the game would be a great advantage for them.

"Team seven will pick the last category," Tracy announced.

Every member of team seven began clapping and cheering as if they'd just won the lottery—even Nathan, their rather reserved leader. The other teams looked on with ill-concealed displeasure. Emma happened to glance in Bobby's direction, and he looked positively livid. Emma didn't care. There would be time to deal with Bobby later. Now they needed to focus on picking a category that someone on their team knew something about.

"Okay, guys. We don't have much time, and we have to pick from the remaining categories. Which one do you think we should choose?" Nathan asked the group, all business once again.

One of the categories titled Ships Ahoy had been studiously avoided by all of the other teams. If the questions were about sailing, then Sebastian's knowledge could give them the edge they needed. The problem was that the questions could be about something else entirely. After some discussion, the team agreed to take the chance and selected the Ships Ahoy category.

The questions turned out to be about famous ships in history. Fortunately, Sebastian's interest in sailing also extended to ships in general. Thus, he was able to answer seven of the ten questions himself. Nathan and the two juniors were able to fill in the other three from their knowledge of world history. They turned their last paper in, confident that they had answered every question correctly. Now they'd just have to wait and see how team three had fared.

As the answers were read, cheers went up from each team that had answered that particular question correctly. It sounded like it was going to be very close. Emma looked around trying to figure out where team three was sitting as the scores were put on the board and totaled for the last time.

"We will now announce the winning team," Tracy said. The room quieted immediately. You could have heard a pin drop as an expectant hush fell over the crowd.

"The winning team with a score of ninety-six out of one hundred is team seven."

"We did it!" Nathan exclaimed, jumping up from his seat. The rest of the team got to its feet and began cheering and clapping.

Emma was glad that every member of the team had been able to make a contribution. It had taken all of them to win. Nathan had to be feeling good about the team he had selected.

The other teams looked on and clapped in congratulations. Emma didn't dare look over at Bobby. She was fairly certain that he would not be clapping.

CHAPTER TWENTY-FIVE
DANCE WITH THE DEVIL

At the conclusion of the trivia game, there was only an hour left before supper. The custodians hustled everyone out of the dining hall so they could get it ready for the upcoming meal. Before leaving, Emma's team voted to donate their winnings back to the children's hospital. Their first-place finish was all the reward they needed. Each of their names would go up on the bulletin board that hung in the hallway on the second floor, and there they would stay until the next trivia event was held. There was some satisfaction in knowing that Bobby Wilcox would be passing that bulletin board every weekday from now till the end of school.

A little tired from all the excitement, Emma and Martha headed to their room to relax a bit before getting washed up for supper. It had been quite an eventful day and a lot more fun than Emma had ever expected when she'd first gotten up that morning. She almost felt good enough to go to the dance—even though the chances of her getting to actually dance were slim to none. At least she could go and watch her friends enjoying themselves. Her other options were to sit in the lounge with the few other students who had no interest in the dance, or stay in her room by herself. Now, after the fun day she'd had, neither option sounded particularly good to Emma.

The problem was that just that morning she had told Martha in no uncertain terms that she would not be attending the dance. Her pride wouldn't let her admit to Martha that she had changed her mind, so later at supper she pretended to let Martha talk her into going.

Needless to say, Martha was thrilled when Emma finally gave in.

"You'll have fun. I promise," Martha exclaimed, bubbling with excitement. "Sebastian will ask you to dance, and I'm sure Phil and Tom will too. I know they're not Doug, but it beats sitting in your room by yourself."

Continuing to feign reluctance, Emma gave a half-hearted smile. She didn't tell Martha that she had reached that very same conclusion right after the trivia game. Despite Martha's assurances, Emma still held out little hope that anyone would ask her to dance, but she had decided in her own heart that she would be okay with that. She would be perfectly content to sit on the sidelines and just observe the goings on. She might even help herself to some of the goodies that were sure to be provided—if last year's dance was anything to go by.

Clarice and Susie were in the room getting ready for the dance when Emma and Martha returned from supper. As usual, both girls looked stunning. Nothing in Emma's wardrobe could match what Clarice and Susie were wearing. Emma consoled herself with the thought that she wasn't going to be dancing, so it didn't really matter what she had on. Knowing that Martha wouldn't approve, she didn't share her negative thoughts with her friend.

Susie talked nonstop, while Emma and Martha got ready for the dance. She was really excited about getting a chance to dance with Daniel. Emma remembered being just as excited before the dance last year, but things hadn't exactly worked out the way she'd hoped. She sent up a little prayer that Daniel would ask Susie to dance. If he didn't, Emma might just have to go over and thump his head. Boys could be so thick sometimes.

Soon everyone was ready, and the four girls left the room together. Emma felt a knot of nervous excitement in the pit of her stomach. The sound of music drifted toward them as they walked down the hallway. When they got inside the ballroom, they saw that several couples were already out on the dance floor. Emma took a moment to look around. The decorations all had a harvest theme and were pretty much the same as last year. The food tables, which lined the east wall, were covered with bright yellow tablecloths and decorated with twisted loops of orange streamers. Pumpkins and a large assortment of colorful gourds served as centerpieces. Clusters of red, yellow, and orange balloons were everywhere, and scarecrows wearing bib overalls and straw hats kept a watchful gaze on the proceedings from the corners of the room. Bales of hay had been stacked along the south wall and would serve as seating for those not dancing. Emma recalled spending a great deal of time on those hay bales last year and had already prepared herself for another long night of sitting on the scratchy bundles.

Daniel Jacobs must have been watching the door because as soon as the girls entered the ballroom, he came over and asked Susie to dance. She accepted with a giggle and happily followed Daniel into the crowd of dancers. Emma and Martha started over toward the hay bales to sit down, but when they looked back, Clarice was no longer behind them. Emma glanced around the room and spotted her almost immediately. A cute older boy was leading her onto the dance floor.

"Well, that didn't take long," Martha commented dryly as she watched Clarice.

"I know," Emma agreed. "Who's that boy she's with? I've seen him before but I don't know his name."

"He's a friend of her cousin. I think his name is Brandon. Of course, he's a freshman."

"That doesn't surprise me," Emma said. "Clarice and Susie have been hanging out with the freshmen more and more lately, and it's all thanks to Preston. I just feel bad for Reggie. It seems like he's getting left behind."

Martha nodded her agreement as the two girls took a seat on the lowest tier of hay. Then they spent the next few minutes watching the sometimes-comical gyrations of those out on the dance floor. Emma wasn't at all surprised to see Phil dancing with Kim, and right next to them were Tom and Cindy. Emma was glad that Tom had been able to summon up the courage to ask Cindy to dance. She couldn't help feeling a little envious of the two couples.

Just as the song was ending, Emma saw Sebastian come in. He looked quite handsome in a pair of khaki pants and a long-sleeved green polo shirt. As soon as he spotted them, he smiled and came over to where they were sitting. He didn't sit down but stood next to Martha. Emma could tell he was nervous. His face was beet red and there were beads of sweat on his forehead.

"Martha, do you want to dance? I mean if your ankle is feeling okay," Sebastian added quickly after clearing his throat.

He was trying to act casual, but Emma wasn't fooled.

"She'd love to," Emma said, quickly accepting for Martha. It would be just like Martha to say no because she didn't want to leave Emma sitting by herself. Emma was determined that Martha wasn't going to let Sebastian down on her account.

Martha looked at her quickly but didn't argue. Instead, she smiled at Sebastian and got up from her seat. Sebastian offered her his hand, and she took it, allowing him to lead her onto the dance floor. Emma watched them for a moment with a satisfied grin. Then with a little sigh, she began shifting around, trying to find a more comfortable position from which to watch the dancers. It was a moment or two before she became aware that someone was standing directly in front of her. She let her eyes travel upward and was surprised to see the very handsome face of Preston Danvers smiling down at her.

"Would you like to dance?" Preston asked before Emma could fully recover from her shock at seeing him so close. His blue eyes seemed even brighter at this range.

Emma couldn't seem to find her voice, so after a brief hesitation, she simply nodded. Just as Sebastian had done with Martha, Preston offered her a hand to help her up, and once she was up, he didn't let go. Numbly, Emma let herself be drawn onto the dance floor. Emma's heart began to pound and a wave of heat washed over her as she began to grasp the fact that Preston Danvers, of all people, had asked her to dance. Preston let go of her hand once they were in amongst the other dancers. The DJ was playing an upbeat rock tune. For a moment, Emma was at a loss as to what to do. Preston had already begun to move to the music and was looking down at her with a quizzical expression. Emma realized briefly that she'd never actually danced before. She had been so caught up in the idea of being asked to dance that she'd never seriously considered what would come next. Almost without conscious thought, Emma began to imitate the movements of those around her. After all, although she may have never danced before, she'd certainly watched enough of it to have some idea of how it was done. Her efforts must have pleased Preston because he smiled and nodded in approval. The song went on for several minutes, and as time went on, Emma began to relax and enjoy herself. The music was too loud for any conversation, so there was nothing to do but dance and look around at the other couples. Preston would always smile each time her eyes met his, and she couldn't help but smile back. He really was incredibly handsome, and that smile of his was irresistible. She liked the way his blond hair curled over the tops of his ears.

It never occurred to Emma to wonder what Doug would think of her dancing with Clarice's cousin. However, it had apparently occurred to Martha because right after the song was over she sought Emma out.

"What do you think you're doing?" Martha demanded abruptly.

"What does it look like? I'm dancing. Someone finally asked me to dance and I said yes," Emma replied defensively.

"I could see that," Martha huffed. "It's not the dancing that's the problem. It's who you're dancing with. Doug's already jealous of Preston, and he's not going to like this one bit."

"I don't think he'll mind in the least," Emma declared with a certainty she didn't really feel. In her heart, she knew that Martha was right. Doug would be upset when he found out. But it had felt so good to finally be asked to dance by someone that she'd pushed aside any thoughts of Doug and his possible reaction.

"Preston and I danced one time," Emma continued in her own defense. "He probably won't ask me again. And we were just dancing together for heaven's sake. It's not like I kissed him or anything."

Martha eyed her with obvious disapproval. "You know that's not the point."

Emma found herself getting angry. *I guess I'm not allowed to have a good time*, she thought. Aloud, she said, "Last year, I didn't get asked to dance a single time. I sat on those stupid hay bales for two hours. Not a single guy, not even Doug, my supposed boyfriend, asked me to dance. So maybe, just maybe, you could cut me some slack and be a little more understanding."

Martha's expression softened slightly. "I do understand, but why did it have to be Preston?"

"He's the only one that asked me," Emma replied in a somewhat less hostile tone.

Martha was about to reiterate that dancing with Preston was a bad idea when Sebastian came up to claim her for the next dance. With a sigh and a slight shake of her head, Martha decided that it wouldn't do any good to continue arguing with Emma. It was clear from the stubborn set of her jaw that her mind was made up. Emma was going to do as she pleased regardless of anything she might say.

Emma was on her way to the hay bales to sit down when she was hailed by Preston.

"Hey, where are you going? We've got more dancing to do."

Without waiting for a reply, Preston pulled her back out onto the dance floor. Emma knew that Martha would be mad, but for once, she didn't care. She was going to have a good time tonight. Emma was flattered that a freshman boy, especially one as good looking as Preston, had asked her to dance. The fact that all of her friends would see her dancing with him didn't hurt either.

As she danced, she silently rationalized her behavior. She and Preston were only dancing, and there was absolutely nothing for Doug to be upset about. All of these thoughts swirled through her head, but deep down inside Emma knew they were far from the truth. There was more to it than that. Emma didn't want to admit it to herself, but she had a crush on Preston, and if he knew, Doug would most certainly be upset about that!

They danced the next several dances together, and then Preston suggested they get some refreshments. Preston held her hand as they walked over to the snack tables—only letting go in order to get them each a plate and napkin. Then they walked side by side along the tables, filling their plates with whatever took their fancy. Once they were finished making their selections, Preston led them over to the hay bales so they could sit down and eat. While they ate, they watched those still on the dance floor. Emma looked for Martha but couldn't see her in the crowd of dancers.

The music was so loud that whenever Preston talked to Emma, he had to lean close to her face in order to be heard. In those moments, Emma was glad that Martha couldn't see her. She would most likely misinterpret Preston's actions.

"Was the dance this much fun last year?" Preston asked so close to her ear that she could feel his breath on her neck.

Trying to ignore the little tingle making its way down her spine, Emma struggled with how to answer. She didn't want to admit to Preston that last year's dance had been a disaster for her and that she hadn't been asked to dance a single time. Deciding that Preston didn't need to know any of that, she answered simply, "Yeah, it was great."

Preston continued to look at her as if he was waiting for her to say more on the subject, but when it became obvious that that was all the answer she was going to give, he went back to eating. When they were both finished, Preston took their plates and left Emma for a minute, while he went to dispose of them. He returned quickly and held out a hand to help her up.

"Shall we dance?" he asked with a gallant bow.

"We shall," Emma replied with a laugh. As she followed Preston onto the dance floor, she realized that the evening was turning out much better than she could have ever hoped. Thanks to Preston, she was having a wonderful time.

The minute they got back on the dance floor, the DJ began playing a slow song. Up until then, all of the songs had been fast rock tunes. Emma immediately felt awkward and unsure of what to do. Preston, however, had no such doubts. With a wry smile, he put Emma's left hand on his shoulder and took her right hand in his. Then he put his other hand on Emma's waist and leaned close to whisper, "Now, just follow me."

Emma nodded and then turned a deep red—extremely embarrassed that she hadn't known what to do and even more embarrassed that Preston had known it. As they moved together with barely an inch between them, her embarrassment faded to be replaced by other unnamed and heretofore unknown feelings. Unaccountably her thoughts turned to Doug. She began to wish that she was dancing with Doug instead of Preston. She looked around at the other couples on the floor. None of them were dancing as close as she and Preston. Emma began to feel uncomfortable. Something wasn't right. She tried to put a little more distance between herself and Preston, but the arm he had around her waist was an unyielding iron band. The more she tried to pull away, the tighter it became. Not wanting to make a scene, Emma quit struggling and prayed for the song to end. She didn't intend to dance any more dances with Preston Danvers.

As soon as the song was over, Emma broke away from Preston and excused herself, saying that she needed to visit the ladies' room.

"Hurry back," Preston called after her as she hastened from the ballroom.

Once she was out in the hall, she didn't know what to do. She couldn't just go to her room without telling Martha first, but if she returned to the ballroom, Preston would expect her to dance with him again, and he'd already demonstrated his unwillingness to take no for an answer. While Emma had never really intended to go to the restroom, she went anyway, just to give herself some time to think. While she splashed cold water on her face at the sink, a plan began to form in her mind. She would sneak back into the ballroom with a group of other girls returning from the restroom. Preston would probably be waiting near the door so if she could get past him, he'd never know that she'd already come back in. Then she could find Martha and let her know she was leaving. Emma wasn't really concerned about sneaking back out. She was sure Martha would help her figure out something once she explained the circumstances.

Emma's plan worked even better than she'd expected. Two groups of girls were going back into the ballroom just as she was leaving the restroom. Emma got in behind them and ducked down as they went through the doorway. Then she edged along the refreshment tables until she was standing next to one of the doors leading out onto the terrace. She craned her neck to see where Preston was, but if he was still waiting for her by the door, she couldn't see him. In fact, she didn't see him anywhere. Maybe he'd decided to use the restroom himself while she was gone. It didn't really matter where he'd gone. Emma was just glad that, at least for the moment, she was free of him. She'd better hurry up and find Martha before Preston returned from wherever he'd gone. Emma scanned the ballroom, but she didn't see Martha in the crowd of dancers. She made a complete circle of the room but still no Martha. Sebastian didn't appear to be in the ballroom either. They could be out on the terrace getting some fresh air, Emma reasoned. At any rate, the terrace was the only place left to look. Emma was just about to step outside through one of the French doors when a voice she recognized stopped her.

"I think she's onto me," Emma heard Preston say from somewhere out on the terrace. It sounded like he was close by.

Emma quickly ducked back inside and hid around the corner. Was Preston talking about her, and who was he talking to? She couldn't leave until she had the answers to her questions. Fortunately, the song that had been playing ended just then, and Emma was able to hear the rest of the conversation clearly.

"It doesn't matter now. The damage is already done. When Doug finds out that you've been dancing with his girlfriend all night, he'll come unglued. He'll probably never talk to her again. I'm sure they'll both be miserable, and that of course makes me very happy. You did a great job."

Emma recognized the other voice immediately. That horrible voice belonged to none other than Bobby Wilcox. Before Emma could fully process the fact that she'd been had, Bobby continued.

"Sorry you had to waste your whole night slumming with little miss nobody, but I'll figure out a way to make it up to you. Thanks for helping me teach that little brat an important lesson. Nobody tattles on me and gets away with it. As the saying goes, anyone who messes with me has to pay the piper."

"No problem. I kind of enjoyed myself. It was so easy. She didn't have a clue until that last dance. I think she really thought I liked her."

"As if you could like someone like her. She's not in our league and never could be."

"You said it. Did you see the way she danced?" Preston asked with a laugh.

"Yeah. I couldn't help laughing. I don't know how you were able to keep a straight face."

In a daze, Emma moved slowly away from her hiding spot. She'd heard enough. How could she have been so stupid? She should have known Preston was up to something. He hadn't paid her a bit of attention all year, and then suddenly there he was—acting like he was her boyfriend. She wanted to cry and rage at the same time. As Emma blindly made her way to the exit, she decided she wouldn't give them the satisfaction of tears. Instead, she would find a way to get even. Bobby Wilcox didn't know whom he was dealing with. She may be poor, but she wasn't stupid. Bobby needed a good set down, and she was just the one to give it to him. Emma was angrier than she'd ever been in her whole life, but the anger was good. It kept her from dwelling on what she may have just lost—her friendship with Doug.

CHAPTER TWENTY-SIX
PAYING THE PIPER

E mma was so upset that she forgot all about finding Martha to tell
her she was going back to the room. All she wanted to do at the
moment was get away. She was so mad she felt like she was going
to explode. Just as Emma made it to the exit, she bumped into Martha, who was coming back in.

"There you are," Martha began accusingly. One look at Emma's
face stopped her before she could say any more. Emma was as pale
as a ghost except for two red splotches high on her cheeks. It was
clear that something terrible had happened. Martha put both of her
hands on Emma's shoulders and asked, "Emma, what on earth has
happened? Are you all right? Did that beast Preston cross the line?"

Emma shook her head in the negative. "No, but he might as
well have. That's probably what Doug will think if Bobby has his
way."

"What's Bobby got to do with this?" Martha asked with a sinking feeling. Things had gone much worse than she'd imagined if
Bobby was involved.

"I'll tell you everything but not here," Emma said as she struggled to hold back the tears that threatened. She was afraid Martha's

sympathy would be her undoing, so she needed to get out of the ballroom as soon as possible.

"Wait here while I tell Sebastian that I found you. Then we can go to our room and talk."

"I've got to get out of here. I'll just meet you there," Emma managed over the lump rising in her throat. Without waiting for a reply from Martha, Emma hurried away.

Martha watched after her for a moment with a worried expression. What could have happened to make Emma so upset? Anxious to find out what was going on, she began looking for Sebastian so she could tell him that she had found Emma and that she was leaving. She caught up to him just as he was about to step out on the terrace.

"I found her," Martha said when she got close enough for him to hear her over the music.

"Where was she?" Sebastian asked. They had been looking for Emma ever since she and Preston had left the dance floor. Emma hadn't been aware of it, but Martha had been keeping tabs on her all night. She didn't trust Preston and had been highly suspicious of his sudden interest in Emma. Sebastian didn't trust Preston any more than Martha did, so when Martha had expressed her concern at not being able to see them anymore, Sebastian had readily agreed to help her look for them.

"I went to look for Emma in the restroom and ran into her when I was coming back into the ballroom. I don't know what's happened, but she was pretty upset. I told her I'd meet her in our room." Martha started to leave and then stopped and turned back to Sebastian. "I had a good time tonight, Sebastian. I hate to go, but I'd better find out what's going on."

"No problem. I hope Emma is okay," Sebastian replied. He hesitated for a moment before adding, "Just for the record, I had a good time tonight too."

Martha smiled and impulsively gave him a quick kiss on the cheek. Then she hurried away. With eyes opened wide in surprise, Sebastian watched her go.

Emma was pacing when Martha entered the room. Upon seeing Martha, she promptly burst into tears. "Go ahead and say it," Emma finally managed between sobs.

"Say what?" Martha asked.

"Go ahead and say I told you so. You tried to tell me that Preston was trouble, but I wouldn't listen. Now I've made a mess of everything," Emma exclaimed in a rush before finally taking a breath, which ended up being more of a sob.

"What exactly happened?" Martha questioned without her usual sympathy. She had indeed tried to tell Emma that she didn't trust Preston, but it had not been her intention to point it out just now.

Emma finally got a hold of herself, and after taking a deep breath, she began to relate the events of the evening, ending with the conversation she'd overheard between Preston and Bobby.

Martha listened quietly with a frown on her face. She had to admit Bobby's plan had been clever. She'd never liked Preston, but she'd never thought him capable of something like this. It made her wonder why Preston had really come to Dinswood Academy. Had he done something at his previous school to get thrown out? If his behavior tonight was anything to go by, it was entirely possible.

"Bobby was just using Preston to get even with me, and I walked right into his trap," Emma said when she had finished her story.

Martha was silent for a full minute. Finally, she said, "It's a good thing you figured out something was wrong when you did. There's no telling how far Preston would have gone with the act."

Emma shuddered at the thought. Martha was right. As bad as things were, they could always be worse. Preston may have been planning to kiss her as a culmination to the evening. It made her physically ill to think that someone like Preston might have been her first kiss. He and Bobby would no doubt have gotten a good laugh out of that, and Doug would probably never have forgiven her. He still might not forgive her, but at least she didn't have a kiss to regret. Looking back, she knew she would always be grateful to the little inner voice that had alerted her to the fact that something was wrong.

"I feel like such an idiot!" Emma railed. "I'm sorry, Martha. I should have listened to you."

"Yes, you should have!" Martha replied more loudly than she had intended. Then in a softer tone, she added, "But even I didn't suspect Preston of something like this. The question is what are you going to do now?"

"I don't have any idea. At first, I was so mad I just wanted to get even."

"That's exactly what started this whole mess," Martha responded quickly. "If you start plotting revenge, you'll be no better than Bobby. Just suppose you were able to get even. Bobby would try to get back at you, and then you'd have to get back at him. When would it all end? There's no way to win when you start playing by Bobby's rules."

Emma didn't want to admit it, but she knew Martha was right. Getting even was not the answer, but in her anger, it had been her first and only thought. Now that she'd had time to calm down, Emma realized that getting revenge wouldn't fix the problem. It would only make it worse. She also realized that she really had only herself to blame. Preston hadn't forced her to dance with him. She had gone willingly—just like a lamb to its slaughter.

It was inevitable that Doug would find out that she'd spent the night dancing with Preston Danvers, but there was no way of knowing how he'd react. Maybe he wouldn't get mad, and then again maybe he would. At the thought of the latter, Emma started crying all over again. Martha sat beside her quietly and let her have her cry. Although she knew Martha was upset with her, Emma was still comforted by her presence. Finally, it occurred to her that she had interrupted Martha's evening.

"I'm sorry I ruined your evening with Sebastian," Emma said miserably.

"You didn't ruin it. My ankle was starting to hurt again anyway," Martha responded with a sigh.

"Still, I'm sorry." Emma knew that, even with a sore ankle, Martha would have stayed at the dance with Sebastian if it hadn't been for her. Somehow, she would find a way to make it up to Martha.

No more was said as the two girls prepared for bed. When Martha turned out the light, Emma lay awake for a long time, worrying about what tomorrow would bring. She was awake when Susie and Clarice came in, but she pretended to be asleep. She didn't feel like talking, and she was in no mood to hear about the great time the two girls had undoubtedly had at the dance. Emma finally managed to fall asleep around three o'clock.

Emma's worst fears were confirmed the next morning at breakfast. She and Martha were already in the dining hall when Doug and Sebastian entered. Instead of coming over to sit with the girls, as was their usual habit, they went over and took seats next to Phil and Tom. Sebastian smiled when he spotted the girls, but Doug didn't even look their way. There was no doubt about it; Doug had heard the news about her and Preston, and he was angry.

Suddenly, Emma wasn't hungry anymore. She murmured a hasty "I'll see you later" to Martha and, after emptying her tray, left the dining hall. Emma paused for a moment in the hallway. She didn't want to go back to the room because Susie and Clarice were there. Since last evening she had been having a hard time even looking at Clarice without being reminded that she was Preston's cousin. It was possible that Clarice had even known about Bobby's plan. Emma didn't want to believe it, but neither could she rule it out. At any rate, she wasn't in the mood to face Clarice. She could go to the lounge or library, but both would probably be filled with students. Emma might run into Bobby or Preston, and that was something she wanted to avoid at all costs. She was still too angry and wasn't sure she could control her temper if she came face-to-face with either one of them.

Emma realized that her only other option was to go outside. Yesterday, it had been raining, but today the sun was out, and the sky was clear. Without bothering with a jacket, which would have required her going to her room, she pulled open one of the double doors and went outside. A cold wind hit her, and she immediately regretted not getting her jacket first. *Oh well, it's too late now*, she thought.

She sat down on one of the benches that circled the fountain. The bench she'd chosen was in the sun, and although the wind was cold, the sun provided enough warmth to allow her to remain outside without her jacket. Emma couldn't say how long she sat there with the previous night's events replaying in her head over and over again. She kept hearing Preston laugh as he made fun of her dancing. Had everyone been making fun of her? Even though she was alone at the moment, Emma felt herself blushing in embarrassment and humiliation at the thought.

As morning marched on toward noon, other students came and went, but Martha never came in search of her. Emma wasn't surprised. Although Martha was still talking to her, she was obviously angry with her.

By the time the bell in the chapel's steeple pealed the hour of high noon, Emma's morning of introspection had resulted in her reaching several important conclusions. First, she had finally admitted to herself that she had gotten exactly what she deserved. Doug had every right to be mad at her. If the shoe had been on the other foot, she would have been mad with jealousy. Second, the old saying that you can't judge a book by its cover was absolutely true. Preston may be gorgeous on the outside, but he was ugly on the inside. She should have taken the time to read a few of the pages before deciding to buy the book. The third and final conclusion Emma had reached was that she needed to apologize to Doug—not so much for him, but for herself. Doug might not even accept her apology, but she needed to do it just the same. He was probably too mad right now to listen to anything she had to say, so she would wait, and while she waited, she would pray that she and Doug would someday be friends again.

Tears welled up in her eyes as she realized that in the days to come, she was going to miss Doug terribly. Who was going to help him find the other two Mortals? Of course he would still have Sebastian and Martha to go along on searches, but she certainly wouldn't be included. It broke Emma's heart to think that her help would no longer be welcomed. There was no doubt about it. She'd really done it this time. She'd ruined everything, and all because she had thought Preston Danvers was the living end. Well he had been the end all right—the end of her friendship with Doug.

Hastily wiping her eyes, she got up to go in for a lunch she didn't really want. For a girl of thirteen, almost fourteen as her birthday was in less than two weeks, she'd had to learn some very painful lessons in a very short period of time. The only good thing that had come out of this whole mess was that she had finally learned to be more cautious. The gullible naïve girl she had been just last night was gone, and in her place was a young lady that would, from this day forward, carefully weigh the consequences before taking an action. At least that was the promise she made to herself. Whether she would always follow through with it remained to be seen.

Emma found Martha sitting with Sebastian in the dining hall. After filling her tray, she joined them. Martha didn't ask her where she'd been, and Emma didn't offer to tell her. Sebastian looked from one to the other as if sensing that things weren't exactly right between them. Unable to contain his curiosity, he finally asked, "What's going on with you two?"

Martha didn't answer, so it was up to Emma to explain. "Last night, Martha warned me that Doug would be upset if I danced with Preston, but I wouldn't listen, and now she's mad at me." Emma said this all in a rush, and by the time she had finished, her eyes had filled with tears again.

Sebastian didn't say anything for a moment but glanced over at Martha. Her expression confirmed what Emma had just told him. Finally, he sighed and said, "Well, you're right about one thing. Doug is furious. As soon as he got back from the infirmary, I told him everything. Of course at the time, I didn't know about Bobby's involvement. Martha told me the whole story after breakfast." Sebastian stopped then and looked at Emma. "Before you get mad at me for telling Doug, you need to understand that I was just being a good friend to Doug. I figured he ought to know what happened before someone else blindsided him with the news. Anyway, after I told him he didn't say anything. He was really quiet, and if you know Doug the way I know Doug, that's not a good sign. Right after breakfast, he went upstairs to visit his dad, and I haven't seen him since."

Emma listened with a sinking heart. All hope that Doug would eventually forgive her was gone. He didn't know that Bobby had put Preston up to asking her to dance, but she doubted it would matter even if he did. After all, Preston hadn't forced her to dance with him. She could have said no.

Knowing that she was only moments away from bursting into tears, Emma hurried from the dining hall. She didn't even take time to empty her tray. She left it sitting on the table—its contents untouched.

This time she did go to her room. Clarice, Susie, and Martha were all at lunch, so she knew she would be alone. The moment she got there, she climbed into her bed and got under the covers without bothering to undress. Then she cried until she couldn't cry anymore. By the time she was finished, her pillow was soaked. Emma turned it over to the dry side and continued to lie there—thoroughly and utterly miserable but unable to produce any more tears. Physically and emotionally exhausted, she eventually fell asleep.

CHAPTER TWENTY-SEVEN
AN UNEXPECTED ALLY

E mma awoke to a darkened room with a pounding headache and a sore throat. A burning behind her eyes indicated that she might be running a fever. Emma also felt a little sick to her stomach. Of course, this could be due to the fact that she'd had practically nothing to eat all day, but it could also mean that she was coming down with something. Remembering that strep throat was going around, Emma got up and went into the bathroom. Opening her mouth wide, she looked at the back of her throat in the mirror and saw two white spots. With a moan, Emma left the bathroom and began packing an overnight bag. She would most likely have to spend the next couple of days in the infirmary, so she might as well save someone else the trouble of gathering the things she'd need.

Emma packed her robe and slippers and a couple of nightgowns along with her toiletries. Then she grabbed the book she was reading for English class and the project she was cross-stitching. She didn't know if she'd feel like working on it, but she took it anyway, just in case. Christmas was only a couple of months away, and the picture depicting scenes of the four seasons was the present Emma planned to give her dad and Vera.

As Emma walked to the infirmary with her bags, she was actually glad that she was going to be away from everything and everyone for a couple of days. She needed time to regroup. Instead of being a bad thing, her coming down with strep throat might be just what she needed.

Mrs. Godfrey was in the infirmary tending to a few other sick students when Emma arrived. A brief exam confirmed that Emma had a case of strep throat. Mrs. Godfrey assigned her a bed and instructed her to put her pajamas on. Once Emma was settled cozily under the covers, Mrs. Godfrey brought her some water along with pills to take for her fever and an antibiotic tablet to begin dealing with the strep infection.

"Do any of your roommates know where you are?" Mrs. Godfrey asked as she took Emma's temperature.

Emma couldn't reply with the thermometer stuck under her tongue, so she simply shook her head in the negative.

"I'll send a message to your room then, and I'll also inform your teachers. Is there someone who can get your schoolwork for you?"

Emma nodded, and once Mrs. Godfrey had removed the thermometer from her mouth, she said, "Martha Merriweather can get it."

"All right then. I'll take care of it. Now you try to get some rest. Supper trays should be coming in another hour or so."

Mrs. Godfrey left her then to check on the few other students currently in the infirmary. Emma tried to sleep, but her head was hurting so badly that she couldn't, and by the time her supper tray arrived, she was too nauseated to eat.

The next day, Emma wasn't any better. Mrs. Godfrey gave her a shot of penicillin and a shot to help with the nausea. By lunchtime, although Emma's head was still pounding, she was able to eat a little of the chicken noodle soup on her tray.

"The infection has gotten an unusually strong hold on you, but that shot I gave you this morning should do the trick," Mrs. Godfrey said with a smile when she checked on Emma after lunch. "I'm glad to see you were finally able to eat something. How's your head?"

"It still hurts," Emma replied.

"That should start to let up soon. I'll give you something for fever and pain, and then I want you to try to rest."

Emma continued to feel terrible the rest of the day, but when she awoke Tuesday morning, her headache was gone. She was able to eat some scrambled egg and toast for breakfast, and when Mrs. Godfrey came to take her temperature, it was normal.

"Now, that's what I like to see," Mrs. Godfrey said. "This afternoon, if you feel like it, you can shower and put on a fresh gown. I'll let your teachers know that you'll be here at least until Friday. I want you to get your strength back before I turn you loose in these drafty halls."

The mention of her teachers prompted Emma to ask if Martha had brought her any homework.

"Yes, but I want you to rest today," Mrs. Godfrey answered. "If you're still feeling better tomorrow, you can work on it."

Emma took the nurse's advice and showered after lunch. By the time she had changed into a clean gown, she was exhausted. Gratefully, she climbed back into bed, and in no time, she was fast asleep.

On Wednesday morning, Emma was feeling much better. She spent the morning working on the homework Martha had collected for her. After lunch, she decided to take a little nap before finishing her homework. When she woke up, she was surprised and dismayed to see Clarice lying in the bed next to her.

As if sensing Emma's gaze, Clarice asked, "Are you feeling better? Nurse Godfrey said you've been pretty sick."

"Yeah, I'm a lot better than I was," Emma answered, somewhat shocked at Clarice's concern. "How about you? What's wrong?"

"What else? I've got strep throat. My head is killing me," Clarice finished with a moan.

In spite of the fact that she was Preston's cousin, Emma felt compassion for Clarice. "I know what you mean. That's exactly how I felt the first couple of days. I was so bad off Mrs. Godfrey had to give me a shot."

"Oh, I hope I won't need a shot. I'm afraid of needles."

"You probably won't," Emma replied in an effort to reassure Clarice. "Mrs. Godfrey said mine was an especially bad case. I spent Sunday morning sitting outside without my jacket, so that may be why I got so sick."

Nothing more was said for a minute, and then Clarice said, "Listen, Emma, I've been wanting to talk to you. I guess now is as good a time as any."

Although Emma was extremely curious to know what Clarice wanted to talk to her about, she heard herself saying, "Are you sure you feel like it? We can talk later when you're feeling better."

"No, I need to say this now." Clarice paused as if she was trying to figure out how to say what she needed to say. Then she sighed and said, "I just wanted to tell you how sorry I am about what Preston and Bobby did to you." At Emma's gasp of surprise, she hurried on. "I overheard them bragging at breakfast the next morning. I didn't know a thing about it until then."

"Thanks for telling me," Emma finally managed. She could tell from her tone that Clarice was being sincere. Emma felt guilty for thinking that Clarice had been in on the scheme.

"Preston and I never got along very well when we were kids. I used to dread the times he and his parents came to visit. Preston was always pulling some kind of mean prank on me. When he first came to Dinswood, I thought maybe he'd grown up, but I can see now that he hasn't. The only reason Susie and I started hanging out with him was so that we could meet some of the freshman boys. But guess what? Most of the freshman boys are just as immature as the eighth-grade boys. Reggie seems to be the only guy around here with any sense."

"I like Reggie too," Emma agreed. "He's a really nice guy, and he's smart." It did Emma's heart good to hear Clarice speak of Reggie in such positive terms.

"Well, anyway I know how close you were with Doug, and I really am sorry that my juvenile cousin messed it up. Is there a chance things can be fixed between you two?"

Emma shook her head sadly. "No. Sebastian told me that Doug is furious, and that's not likely to change any time soon."

Mrs. Godfrey came just then to tend to Clarice, so no more was said on the subject. As soon as the nurse left, Clarice settled down to try to sleep. While Clarice napped, Emma finished her homework. Every now and then, she would glance over at Clarice. It was hard to believe how much she had changed in the year Emma had known her. She began to suspect that the snobby rich girl persona was just an act. Maybe Clarice hadn't known any other way to behave. Since coming to Dinswood, she'd had some good examples to emulate. Not only had Reggie been a good influence on Clarice, but Martha had as well. Martha's family was extremely rich, but you'd never know it from Martha's behavior. Clarice's transformation had been taking place so gradually that it had been hard to detect, but today Emma had seen evidence of it. A year ago, Clarice wouldn't have apologized for her cousin, even if she'd thought what he had done was wrong.

After supper, Clarice was still feeling poorly, so Emma worked quietly on her cross-stitching. The next day passed in much the same way, but by Thursday evening, Clarice was feeling well enough to play a couple of games of cards with Emma.

On Friday morning, just after breakfast, Mrs. Godfrey came by to check on Emma and Clarice. She examined Emma first. She took Emma's temperature and then listened to her lungs with her stethoscope. When she was finished, she sat down on the end of Emma's bed.

"Everything looks and sounds good. You can return to class today, but I don't want you to overdo things. Remember to continue taking your antibiotic twice a day. You need to take it until it's all gone, or you'll end up right back in here," Mrs. Godfrey told her firmly.

Then she turned to Clarice and took her temperature. "Well, you aren't running any fever at the moment. We'll see how you are this afternoon. If you're temperature is still normal, I'll release you tomorrow," she told Clarice. Then she left to check on her other patients.

Emma got busy gathering all of her things together. Classes would be starting in fifteen minutes, and she still had to stop by her room to drop off her bags. Even though she was in a hurry, she found herself hesitating by Clarice's bed.

"I wanted to thank you again for what you said when you first got here," Emma said finally. "I was feeling pretty down about things, and you made me feel better. Martha's been kinda mad at me since it all happened, and it was nice to have someone on my side. I know what happened was really my own fault. The plan wouldn't have worked if I hadn't gone along with it."

"Emma, don't be too hard on yourself. If anyone understands how persuasive Preston can be, it's me," Clarice said with a sober expression. "He can be quite charming when he puts his mind to it."

Emma didn't say anything but merely nodded. Clarice was right about that. Up until that last dance, she'd been totally under Preston's spell. Thank goodness she finally knew the kind of person he really was. She wasn't going to waste another second mooning over Preston Danvers. Doug was ten times the person Preston was; too bad she hadn't recognized that fact sooner.

"Well, I guess I'll see you later," Emma said, picking up her bags and heading to the door.

"Bye," she heard Clarice call softly as she left the infirmary.

Emma hurried down the hall toward the girls' dorm, hoping that she wouldn't run into Preston, Bobby, or Doug. She wasn't up to a confrontation with any of them. Although she was feeling much better, she hadn't totally regained her strength. She'd lost five pounds this past week, and they were pounds she couldn't really afford to lose. Not only was she not prepared physically, but she wasn't ready emotionally either. Thankfully, she made it to her room without seeing anyone she knew. The room was empty when she entered. Martha and Susie were probably upstairs getting their books out of their lockers. Emma dropped her bags on her bed. There wasn't time to put things away now. She'd have to do it this afternoon after classes were over. A glance at her watch had her hastening from the room and up the stairs to the second floor.

She made it to her locker just as the first bell rang. Emma now had four minutes to grab her books and get to her first class. She took her seat in Mr. Godfrey's math class with a minute to spare. She looked around and spotted Martha sitting in her usual place. Seeing Emma's look, Martha smiled and waved. Relieved that Martha wasn't mad at her anymore, Emma smiled back. Then Mr. Godfrey began his lecture, and all else was forgotten as Emma tried to get her mind focused on the mysteries of linear equations.

After class, Martha caught up with her in the hall. "How are you feeling? Mrs. Godfrey told me you were pretty sick."

"I still feel a little weak, but other than that, I'm okay," Emma answered. "What's been going on while I've been away?"

"Oh, the same old thing—classes and homework and then more classes and more homework," Martha replied with a wry smile. "Speaking of homework, did you get the work I brought for you?"

"Yes. Thanks for getting it for me."

As they walked to their next class, Emma asked Martha some questions about the homework she'd been given while in the infirmary. She carefully avoided the subject of Doug. Emma was dying to know if he was still mad at her, but she was afraid to ask. She didn't know if she could handle it if Martha told her he was.

The rest of the morning went smoothly, but by lunchtime, Emma was beginning to feel a little light-headed. She'd just made it to the bottom of the stairs on her way to the lunchroom with Martha when it happened. Her vision blurred, and the lobby seemed to be spinning. Then suddenly everything went dark, and she felt herself falling.

The next thing she knew, she was lying on one of the couches in the lounge, and Doug was looking down at her with a worried expression. Thinking she was dreaming, she smiled at him. She knew for certain she was dreaming when he smiled back. Emma started to sit up, but in the dream, Doug put his hands on her shoulders and gently pushed her back down.

"You'd better just stay put," Doug told her. "Sebastian and Martha have gone to get the nurse."

Emma was confused. Doug's hands on her shoulders had felt real enough. Perhaps she wasn't dreaming after all.

"What happened?" she finally managed to ask.

"You fainted."

Emma let that information sink in for a minute. She'd never fainted before in her life. Then it occurred to her to ask, "How did I get here?" The last thing she remembered was being at the bottom of the staircase in the main hall.

"I carried you," Doug answered; and seeing Emma's incredulous expression, he explained. "Sebastian and I were a little ways behind you when it happened. I didn't think you should be left on that cold floor—especially after you've been so sick—so I picked you up and brought you in here."

Emma didn't know whether to be grateful or embarrassed, so she said nothing for a moment. Then she realized that she and Doug were alone, at least for the time being, and that this would be a perfect opportunity to tell him she was sorry for her behavior the night of the dance. Gathering up her courage, she said, "Doug, I wanted to tell you that I'm sorry for dancing with Preston the night of the Octoberfest."

"You have the right to dance with whomever you want, Emma," Doug replied. He may have been remembering a similar conversation the two of them had had after last year's dance. Those had been Emma's first words to him when he had apologized for dancing with what seemed like every girl except Emma.

Determined to say all of the things she'd been rehearsing in her mind this past week, Emma bravely continued, "Yes, but I know you've never liked Preston, and I should have trusted your judgment about him."

Doug hesitated a moment before responding. "It's no secret that I don't like the guy, and you've probably been wondering why. The reason I don't trust him is that I know why he ended up here at Dinswood. I promised Dad I wouldn't say anything, because it's privileged information, and if it got out, Dad could get in trouble. I see now that maybe I should have at least warned you about him."

It appeared that Doug was going to say something else but thought better of it. Intuitively, Emma knew that Doug had been going to add that she probably wouldn't have listened to his warning anyway. When Emma voiced her thoughts, Doug looked at her in surprise and then smiled.

"The thought had occurred to me. You can be a bit stubborn you know."

"And that's just one of my many faults," Emma replied with a little laugh.

Doug laughed too, and then his expression sobered once again. "I know what happened the night of the hayride, and I also know that Bobby was behind Preston asking you to dance. Those two are just lucky I wasn't around at the time." Doug looked furious for a moment. He was angry with Bobby and Preston, but he was also angry with himself. If he'd been with the girls on the hayride and at the dance, none of this would have happened.

Emma assumed that Sebastian had been the one to fill Doug in on all the details, so she was shocked by his reply when she asked him about it.

"Clarice told me. Apparently, there's no love lost between her and her cousin."

Doug's revelation was so unexpected that for a moment Emma didn't know what to say. It seemed she owed Clarice a debt of gratitude. Still there was something that Emma needed to set straight, and she didn't want to be lying on her back when she did it. This time when she started to sit up, Doug didn't stop her.

"Doug, as much as I hate to say this, I can't let Preston take all of the blame for what happened. I could have said no when he asked me to dance, and if I'd said no, I don't really think he would have forced the issue."

Doug didn't say anything, so Emma continued. There was more to be said, and she knew that Sebastian and Martha would be back with the nurse any second now.

"I wanted to dance so badly I really didn't care who asked me. Last year, I didn't get asked a single time."

Doug had the grace to look embarrassed. Once again, he was remembering his behavior at last year's dance. He started to offer an apology, but Emma stopped him.

"That's not the whole reason I accepted though. I was flattered that a cute older guy had asked me to dance, and I guess I sort of had a crush on Preston."

Emma looked at Doug and tried to gauge his reaction. His expression was unreadable, but Emma knew he couldn't help but be hurt by what she was telling him.

"I don't anymore though. You may not believe this, and I will certainly understand if you don't, but I realized that Preston was not the person I thought he was before I found out that he was involved in Bobby's scheme." Emma then went on to explain how she had come to overhear the conversation between the two boys. She purposely left out the part about that last horrible slow dance. Doug was angry enough at Preston without that incident adding fuel to the fire. She didn't want Doug getting into a fight on her account.

When she had finished with her narration, she took a deep breath. There was one more thing that she needed to say. "I really am sorry about everything, but I've learned an important lesson. Some people are beautiful on the outside, some are beautiful on the inside, and some are both." Emma stopped and swallowed hard, her courage almost failing her. Without looking at Doug, she added quietly, "You're both."

Emma kept her head down. She could not bring herself to look up, afraid of what she might see in Doug's face. The room was silent except for the ticking of the clock on the mantle.

Doug sat there unmoving. The truth was he didn't know what to say. Emma had certainly given him a lot to think about. Doug could appreciate how hard it had been for her to say the things she'd said. He had always admired Emma's courage, and today was no different.

He was saved from a response by the timely arrival of Nurse Godfrey. She came bustling in at that precise moment followed closely by Sebastian and a worried-looking Martha.

"How are you feeling, dear? Martha told me that you fainted," Nurse Godfrey said as she sat down next to Emma.

"I was feeling a little light-headed before, but I feel okay now," Emma replied. She carefully avoided looking at Doug as she talked with Nurse Godfrey.

After a quick check of Emma's pulse and temperature, Nurse Godfrey pronounced her diagnosis. "I think you're still a bit weak from your illness, and you probably haven't been drinking enough fluids. Am I right?"

Emma nodded in the affirmative. She'd had hardly anything to drink all week long. For the first several days, her throat had been too sore, and then she hadn't felt like eating or drinking much. Emma was completely unaware that while she had been talking with the nurse, Doug had slipped quietly from the room.

"I guess I let you out of the infirmary a little too soon," Nurse Godfrey continued. "I think it would be best if you stayed right where you are for a while. I'll have someone bring you your lunch along with a bottle of water. After you finish eating and drinking the entire bottle of water, you can go to your room and rest—no more classes for you today. I also want you to drink sixty-four ounces of water every day for the next three days. Then by Monday, you should be able to return to class."

Emma murmured her understanding, and as Nurse Godfrey got up to leave, she finally looked up. Her heart sank when she saw that Doug had gone. It seemed he had not forgiven her after all.

Martha offered to bring Emma her lunch. Mrs. Godfrey agreed and thought it would be a good idea if Martha ate her lunch in the lounge too.

"I'd feel better if someone stayed with Emma," she told Martha. "Make sure Emma gets to her room when you're through eating."

Martha said she would, and the nurse left to return to her patients in the infirmary. Sebastian left with Martha to go to the dining hall, and Emma found herself alone in the lounge. Her thoughts drifted back over her conversation with Doug. For a brief moment, it had seemed that things were back to normal between them, but when she'd looked up to find him gone, her hopes had been dashed once again. Suddenly, Emma felt like crying, but before she could indulge in another round of self-pity, Martha returned with lunch for the two of them.

Martha must have sensed that Emma was feeling pretty low because she did her best to cheer her up while they ate their lunch of salad, pizza, and mixed fruit. Emma had to admit that by the time they had finished eating, she was feeling much better—both physically and emotionally. As Martha walked with her to their dorm room, Emma was reminded again what a good friend Martha was.

Emma didn't realize how tired she was until she got to her room. Once Martha had left to return to class, Emma lay down on her bed and was asleep as soon as her head hit the pillow. Emma slept most of the afternoon. Around six o'clock, Martha delivered her supper tray with instructions from the nurse that she was to stay in her room for the rest of the evening. Martha had gotten permission to eat her supper with Emma. When they were finished eating, Martha took their empty trays back to the dining hall, promising that she'd be right back. True to her word, Martha returned in a few minutes, and the two girls spent a pleasant evening playing games. While they played, Emma told Martha about all of the things Clarice had said. Martha was just as amazed at Clarice's change in attitude as Emma had been.

Changing the subject, Martha filled Emma in on everything that had happened while she'd been in the infirmary, ending her narrative with something she'd learned just that afternoon.

"You're not going to believe what I found out last hour from Sebastian," Martha said with an expression that suggested she was doing her best not to laugh.

"What?" Emma asked quickly, her curiosity piqued.

"Preston was taken to the infirmary right after lunch." Martha paused for effect and then continued with a sly grin. "It seems he has a bad case of strep throat."

"I wonder where he could have gotten that," Emma said with an expression of innocence. Then she burst out laughing and Martha quickly joined her.

"How's that for justice?" Martha finally managed.

"The only thing that would make it better is if Bobby came down with it too. Just call me Typhoid Mary," Emma added, and the two girls went into gales of laughter again. Emma knew it was wrong to take delight in the ill health of another human being but felt that in this case she might be forgiven. Preston could have gotten the illness from anyone. After all, there were plenty of students sick with it right now, but it was more satisfying to believe that she'd given it to him.

"I bet he's regretting that slow dance right about now," Martha suggested with a giggle.

"Let's hope so," Emma agreed.

CHAPTER TWENTY-EIGHT
FORGIVEN

The next morning, Emma awakened feeling better than she had in over a week. Her strength seemed to have returned along with her appetite. Nothing sounded better at the moment than a heaping plate of bacon, eggs, and toast with a big glass of orange juice to wash it down. She looked at the clock and was surprised to see that it was still early. Emma tried to turn over and go back to sleep, but the empty gnawing feeling in her stomach wouldn't let her. With a sigh, Emma rolled out of bed and went into the bathroom. She might as well get ready and go get some breakfast. Emma decided not to bother Martha, who was still sleeping soundly in her bed.

When Emma got to the dining hall, it was practically empty. Most students at the academy liked to sleep in on Saturdays. The smell of bacon had Emma hurrying over to get a tray. A couple of minutes later, she was heading over to one of the tables with a full plate. She had just taken her first bite of eggs when Doug and Sebastian came in. Emma quickly averted her gaze as a sick feeling washed over her. She should have waited for Martha to wake up. If she had, she wouldn't be sitting here alone right now feeling awkward and conspicuous.

Emma tried to act natural and continue eating, but her appetite had vanished with the appearance of Doug. She was putting her fork down, disgusted with herself for wasting so much good food when someone set a tray down directly across from her. Startled, Emma looked up to see Doug grinning down at her.

"Glad to see your appetite's back," he said, pointing at the mound of food on her plate. "You must be feeling better."

For a moment, Emma was too surprised to respond, but she eventually managed to find her voice.

"I am, thanks. I was so hungry when I woke up this morning I didn't even wait for Martha to get up."

"I wondered where she was," Doug replied easily as he sat down.

Sebastian joined them then and took the seat next to Doug. "Where's Martha?" he asked, having missed out on what had just been said.

"I let her sleep. I was just telling Doug how hungry I was when I woke up. I tried to go back to sleep, but my stomach wouldn't let me," Emma explained again. "Why are you two up so early?"

"I woke up at my usual weekday time and couldn't go back to sleep. I guess Sebastian was having the same problem," Doug answered for both of them. "We figured we might as well get up and come have some breakfast. My stomach was feeling pretty empty too."

"Maybe it's the weather," Sebastian suggested. "It's supposed to get pretty cold this week. I guess winter's on its way."

"I can't wait until it snows," Emma exclaimed, thinking back to last winter. "The woods look so pretty covered in white."

"Yeah," Sebastian agreed. "Thanksgiving and Christmas will be here before we know it."

They continued to talk easily throughout the meal. Emma felt herself relaxing, and as she relaxed, her appetite returned. She was able to finish everything on her plate. Doug was behaving as he usually did, and more importantly, he was treating Emma the way he had before the whole Preston fiasco. Emma knew she didn't deserve it, but it seemed Doug had forgiven her. She was so happy she wanted to jump up and shout for joy, but she managed to contain herself. She couldn't wait to tell Martha that things were finally back to normal.

When they were finished eating, Doug offered to empty Emma's tray for her.

"I've got to go work on my project now. I'm making a rocking chair for Lord Dinswood for Christmas, and I've still got a lot to do," Doug explained as he prepared to leave. "I guess I'll see you guys later."

Sebastian stayed behind after Doug left. He wanted to ask Emma for Christmas ideas for Martha.

"I don't know what to get her this year, so I need you to be my spy and find out what she wants."

Emma had to laugh at his conspiratorial tone.

"I'll do my best," she promised.

Martha came in a couple of minutes later. Emma waved her over and told her that they would sit with her while she ate.

"Thanks," Martha said and then hurried away to get her tray.

Emma wanted to tell Martha the good news about Doug, but she could hardly do that with Sebastian sitting there. She decided on a less obvious approach.

"You just missed Doug," Emma told Martha when she returned to the table. "He's gone up to work on the rocking chair he's making for Lord Dinswood." Although her words were casual, they carried a wealth of meaning. Martha's raised right eyebrow indicated that she understood what Emma was trying to tell her. Doug had forgiven her, and the two of them were friends again. Martha was glad. Doug would need all of his friends to help find the last two Mortals.

The rest of the weekend went by quickly. After attending chapel Sunday morning, Emma spent the afternoon catching up on her schoolwork in the library. Doug, Sebastian, and Martha came along to do their own homework and to help Emma whenever she had questions.

Monday morning, Emma received a notice from the dean's office that her detention would begin that day right after school. With all that had happened last week, Emma had forgotten all about receiving detention. It should have started last Monday, but because of her illness, it had been delayed a week. Emma liked Miss Jennings, so she wasn't dreading it too badly. She would, however, miss spending that time with her friends. Oh well, it could be worse. She could have been assigned detention with Miss Grimstock!

The next two weeks were uneventful. Emma's birthday came and went, and the temperature outside dropped steadily. Last year, the first snow of the winter had occurred on November 12. Emma remembered the date because it was her birthday. This year, the day she turned fourteen was merely cloudy and cold. Her only present was a birthday card and some money from her dad and Vera. No one at school knew when her birthday was, and that's just the way Emma wanted it. She didn't want anyone making a fuss over her. Emma planned to use her birthday money to buy Christmas presents for Martha, Doug, and Sebastian on her next trip to Windland. The last trip to town was scheduled for the first Saturday in December—weather permitting of course. Trips to Windland wouldn't start up again until spring. Winters in the area were harsh and unpredictable. Heavy snows could come without warning, and Dean Harwood didn't want to risk having students marooned on a school bus in the middle of a blizzard.

Thinking about winter and Christmas got Emma thinking about what she was going to get each of her friends. Martha was easy; anything art related would do the trick. Sebastian was a chocolate lover, so a box of assorted chocolates would be just the thing.

Doug, however, was a different matter. She'd have to ask for Sebastian's help in figuring out what to get him.

On the Wednesday before Thanksgiving, Emma stood in the entrance hall hugging Martha goodbye. Doug had come to see Sebastian off as well. Martha and Sebastian were going home for the holiday. Emma's family couldn't afford to fly her home, so she would be staying at the school. The school was Doug's home, so, of course, he would be staying.

Emma and Doug waved goodbye as the bus to the airport pulled away with Sebastian and Martha on board. Although it would only be for a few days, Emma knew she was going to miss Martha. Susie and Clarice were going home as well, so Emma would be alone in the suite. Doug would no doubt stay in his father's suite. Last year, Doug had invited Emma to stay in one of the rooms in Dean Harwood's suite over the Thanksgiving break, but she had been in danger then. No such threat existed now, so it was unlikely that Doug would invite her again.

Her musings were proven correct when, as soon as the bus was out of sight, Doug turned to Emma with an apologetic expression.

"Emma, I'm sorry to run off, but I'm having trouble with my rocking chair. The shop teacher said he'd have some time to help me this afternoon, so I'd better take advantage of it. How about we play some chess after supper? I haven't given you a sound beating in a while." The last was said with a mischievous grin. Doug knew how competitive Emma was, and he was pretty sure she'd take that last statement as a challenge. He wasn't disappointed.

"We'll see about that, Douglas," Emma replied in a haughty tone. "I've been sharpening my skills. Prepare to be defeated."

"You're right. We'll have to see about that," Doug replied with a smile.

Emma watched him go with a smile on her lips. Then her expression sobered, and she realized she had some work of her own to do. She needed to finish the two afghans she was going to give her brothers for Christmas. She had been working on them all summer, so she was almost done with them. With that goal in mind, Emma hurried to her room and spent the afternoon crocheting. At five o'clock, she sat back with a sigh of satisfaction. Both afghans were done, and they had turned out beautifully. Her brothers were going to love them! She gently folded each of the afghans and put them in separate plastic bags. She would have to get boxes to mail them home at the post office in Windland. Now all she had to do was finish the cross-stitch picture she was working on for her parents. She had been working on it every day after school during detention. If she worked on it all day Friday, she should be able to get it done before the school's last trip to Windland. It was a shame that she wasn't going to have time to get it matted and framed like she'd originally planned. It would have to be mailed, minus a frame, along with the twins' afghans if her parents were to receive it before Christmas. Maybe she should send it with a note promising to have it framed once she returned home for the summer. Emma was still trying to decide whether or not to send a note as she headed to the dining hall for supper.

Doug was already there when she arrived, but he hadn't gotten his tray yet.

"Perfect timing," Doug said with a smile when he saw her. "I just got here myself."

Emma was still fretting over what to do about her parents' Christmas present, so she smiled absently in response.

Noticing her preoccupation, Doug asked, "Is everything okay, Emma?"

Emma was snapped back to the present by the worry in Doug's tone. "Yeah, I'm fine," she hastened to reassure him. "I'm just trying to decide what to do about Dad and Vera's Christmas present." Emma then went on to explain what her dilemma was.

"I think I have the answer," Doug said when Emma had finished. "If you can get the picture finished by Saturday morning, we can stop by the Frame Shop in Windland on our way to the skating rink in Benton."

"What are you talking about?" Emma asked in confusion.

"Dad said he'd take us ice-skating in Benton Saturday afternoon—that is if you want to. I'm sure he wouldn't mind stopping in Windland to drop off your picture. If you explain the situation, the shop can probably have it matted and framed for you so that you can mail it when we go back to Windland the following Saturday."

When Emma didn't answer immediately, Doug looked up to see that she was staring at him with a look of amazement. Suddenly unsure of himself, he said, "Would you like to go skating Saturday? I guess I should have asked you first."

"I'd love to go!" Emma replied. "I've never been ice-skating before, but I've always wanted to learn."

"I remember you mentioning something about it last year," Doug said, feeling relieved. For a moment there, he'd been afraid Emma was about to refuse his offer.

Emma was amazed yet again. Doug had not only solved her problem for her, but he had remembered a conversation they'd had over a year ago. He had remembered her wish to learn to ice-skate, and he had taken steps to make her wish come true. Suddenly, Emma felt like crying. She didn't deserve a friend like Doug.

"Emma, is everything all right?" Doug asked when he noticed her expression.

"You're wonderful!" Emma exclaimed in answer. Then on impulse, she gave him a quick hug.

Doug was so surprised he didn't know what to say, but he was smiling all the way through the supper line.

They played two games of chess in front of the fireplace in the lounge after supper. As they played, Emma was reminded how much

Lord Dinswood enjoyed chess in his younger days. She wondered if he still liked to play.

"Have you ever played chess with Lord Dinswood?" Emma asked.

Doug, who had been figuring out his next move, looked up in surprise at her question. "No, why do you ask?"

"Well, I was just remembering how much he loved to play when he was young and how he always kept a board set up on the very table we're playing on."

"You're right. I guess I never really thought about it before," Doug replied.

"Do you think he still likes to play?"

"I don't know, but next time I visit him, I'll see if he'd like to play a game. I'm probably not anywhere near his league though."

"I'm sure you'd be a worthy opponent, and I bet Lord Dinswood would really enjoy playing a game with you. You've said he hasn't been feeling well lately, and it might be just the thing to lift his spirits."

"I can't believe I didn't think of it before," Doug said, shaking his head. "I'll ask him for a game on my next visit. I was planning on spending some time with him tomorrow afternoon since it's Thanksgiving and all. Thanks for the idea, Emma."

"You're welcome," Emma answered with a smile.

The morning of Thanksgiving, Doug and Emma spent some time outside getting some fresh air. The air was cold but not unbearably so. In fact, it was above freezing for the first time in nearly a week. Emma was a little disappointed that it still hadn't snowed, but on the up side, Martha and Sebastian wouldn't have any weather delays when it came time to return to the academy.

They'd only been outside a half hour before they were joined by Dean Harwood, who offered to take them on a tour of the new gymnasium.

"It's not finished, of course, but I thought you might like to see how it's coming," Dean Harwood told them.

"I'd love to see it," Emma exclaimed.

"Me too," Doug agreed.

Dean Harwood led them to a side door and let them in using a key. Work had been suspended until after the holidays, so the three of them were alone—their voices echoing in the large open space. As Dean Harwood led them around, Emma was amazed at how much had been completed since she had first seen it in the summer.

"We'll be pushing things a bit, but we're still hoping everything will be ready for the start of school next year," Dean Harwood told them.

Work had begun on the pool, and all of the interior walls were up—some even had sheet rock. Most of the plumbing fixtures were in place, and a lot of the wiring had been completed.

"I know it looks like it's almost done, but it's the trim work that takes so much time. Then everything has to be painted, windows have to be put in, and so on," Dean Harwood explained as they exited, and he relocked the door.

"Thanks for the tour, Dean Harwood," Emma said.

"You're welcome," he replied. Then he glanced at his watch. "We'd better get back inside. It's almost time for our Thanksgiving feast. I hear the cooks have really outdone themselves this time."

"Great, I'm starving," Doug said as the two of them followed Dean Harwood back to the castle.

After the meal, Doug went upstairs to visit with Lord Dinswood. Emma hoped that Lord Dinswood would be feeling well enough to play a game of chess with Doug. It would not only be good for Lord Dinswood, but it would be good for Doug too. Emma knew how worried Doug was about the school's founder, and she knew he still felt guilty about keeping the discovery of the other Mortals from him.

When Doug had gone, Emma decided to work on her cross-stitch. She only had until Saturday to get it done. With a sense of urgency, Emma hurried to her room to get her project and then took it to the lounge. There she sat in one of the comfortable chairs facing the fireplace and set to work. After a while, the combination of the warmth from the fire and the delicious food she'd consumed at lunch had her feeling sleepy. When her eyes kept getting heavier and heavier, Emma finally gave up. Setting her cross-stitch on the table, she curled up in the chair and went to sleep.

Doug found her there later.

"Hey, Emma. Wake up," Doug said, with a gentle shake of her shoulder.

It took a moment for Emma to get her bearings. While she'd been sleeping, it had begun to get dark outside. Someone had turned on a few of the lamps scattered throughout the lounge. These along with the glow of the fire in the fireplace were the room's only light. Doug's face was in shadow, but she recognized his voice.

"How was Lord Dinswood?" she asked as she sat up. She hoped she didn't look too disheveled after her nap. Her hair could be standing straight up, and Doug wouldn't say a word.

"He seemed to be feeling a little better," Doug answered. "I asked him if he wanted to play a game of chess, and he said he'd really like that. Of course, I got schooled, but I think he really enjoyed it. Thanks again for suggesting it."

"I'm just glad he's feeling better. Maybe he's over whatever was making him ill."

"Maybe," Doug replied, but he didn't sound too optimistic. "I wish I could tell him about the Mortals."

"We will, as soon as this guy who's blackmailing you gets caught. Then we can tell Lord Dinswood everything," Emma said with a certainty she didn't really feel.

"By then it may be too late," Doug said quietly. Then he ran a hand through his hair, something he did whenever he was stressed.

Emma's heart went out to him, but she knew that there was nothing she could say right now that would comfort him. Instead, she reached out and took his hand. She felt him squeeze her hand lightly in acknowledgment of her gesture of sympathy.

"Sorry to be such a downer on Thanksgiving," Doug said with a sigh. Then he sat down in the chair across from Emma, still holding her hand. For a moment, the room was silent except for the crackling of the logs in the fire. Suddenly, the clock above the mantle began to chime the hour, startling Emma.

Doug couldn't help laughing as he felt her jump. With his somber mood broken, Doug stood and said in a lighter tone, "Let's go get some supper." Then he surprised Emma by grabbing her other hand and pulling her to her feet.

"Just what I need," Emma said with an exaggerated groan, "more food."

Glad for Doug's change in mood, Emma followed him to the dining hall where, despite her protests, she was able to eat a heaping plate of leftover turkey with all the trimmings.

Later that evening, they played games in the lounge with some of the other students who had remained at the school over the holidays. Introductions were made as each person joined the group; but Emma, who was terrible with names, knew she probably wouldn't remember them after tonight. It didn't seem to matter. Everyone was having a good time. The last game they played was charades. They divided into two teams—the girls versus the boys. Emma had never laughed so hard in her life. At the end of the evening, her face actually hurt from smiling so much. They played until curfew and then regretfully said their good nights.

As Emma headed to Brimley Hall along with the other girls, she thought back on the day with satisfaction. All in all, it had been a good day. Later that night, as she lay in bed, she said a prayer for Lord Dinswood and for Doug. She would have prayed even harder if she'd known that at that moment Doug was delivering the third sculpture to the Reaper.

CHAPTER TWENTY-NINE
AN ODD COUPLE

Saturday morning, Emma stood in the castle's lobby waiting for Doug and his dad to come down. Doug had told her they'd leave to go ice-skating around ten o'clock. When Doug had explained the situation, Dean Harwood had readily agreed to make a stop in Windland so that Emma could drop off her cross-stitch picture at the shop. Emma had spent all of the previous day working on it and had finally completed it just before supper. Doug had spent the day working on his rocking chair. When Emma had asked him about it that evening at supper, he'd explained that all he had left to do was sand it and stain it. Emma had asked if she could see it, but Doug had said he didn't want to show it to her until it was finished. Emma had been disappointed, but she had understood how he felt, so she hadn't pressed the issue.

While Emma was waiting, Mr. Dorfman passed by. He was carrying some books, so Emma assumed he was on his way to the library. Emma quickly looked away and did her best to pretend she hadn't seen him. He was probably mad at her over the hayride incident. She was hoping that he would ignore her and go on his way, but it was not to be.

"Emma, I've been meaning to talk with you for some time now, but the opportunity never presented itself," Mr. Dorfman began as he approached her. When he got closer, he noticed her flushed cheeks. He immediately understood the cause and hastened to reassure her. "You don't need to be afraid to talk to me, Emma. I'm not angry with you. I simply wanted to apologize for what happened the night of the hayride. I should have made sure you and Martha were on the other wagon before taking off."

An apology was the last thing Emma had expected. For a moment, it rendered her speechless. While she processed his words, Mr. Dorfman waited patiently with a kind expression. Realizing that she owed him an apology as well, Emma finally managed to find her voice.

"I'm sorry too, Mr. Dorfman. I should have done what you told me to instead of running off to find Martha."

"Well, it sounds like we've both learned an important lesson," Mr. Dorfman said with a smile. "Enjoy the rest of your holiday," he added as he turned to leave.

Emma watched him go—relieved that he wasn't angry with her. Now, she only had Bobby to worry about. She was certain she wouldn't be getting an apology from him. Instead, he was probably plotting some new way to make her and Doug's lives miserable. Sebastian and Martha might get caught in the crossfire, but she and Doug were Bobby's real targets.

A moment later, Doug came around the corner, followed by his dad and Miss Jennings. Emma was surprised to see that Miss Jennings was coming along. Some of her surprise must have shown on her face because Miss Jennings smiled and said, "Emma, I understand you've never been ice-skating before."

"That's right, but I've always wanted to learn," Emma answered politely, trying to cover her embarrassment. It should have occurred to her that Doug's dad would invite Miss Jennings to come. She shouldn't have been standing there with her mouth hanging open.

"You're going to love it!" Miss Jennings said enthusiastically. "It takes a little while to get used to the feel of the ice, but once you do, it's the nearest thing to flying."

They continued to chat as they made their way outside, and by the time they got to the car, which was waiting out front, Emma was over her embarrassment and feeling comfortable again.

The ride to Windland went quickly, and soon they were pulling up to the Frame Shop. Emma went inside, while the others waited in the car. After picking out a frame and the color for the matting, Emma asked the lady behind the counter if she could possibly have it done by the following Saturday.

"We're not as busy as we usually are this time of year, so it won't be a problem," the woman told her.

With a sigh of relief, Emma thanked the woman and hurried outside. She didn't want to keep everyone waiting any longer than necessary.

"Boy that was fast!" Doug exclaimed as Emma got back in the car.

"You didn't have to rush on our account," Dean Harwood told her with a smile.

"I already had a color in mind for the matting, and I figured an oak frame would go with our living room furniture," Emma explained. "The store had exactly what I wanted, so it was easy. Thanks for making the stop, Dean Harwood."

"I was glad to do it."

As Dean Harwood started the car and began to back out, Emma couldn't help thinking yet again what a nice man Doug's dad was, and it occurred to her that Doug was just like his dad.

Forty-five minutes later, they turned onto a road that would take them through the center of the city of Benton. Benton was a fairly large city with a population nearing a hundred thousand. As they traveled along, Emma saw a wide variety of department stores, restaurants, and banks, as well as a number of multistory office buildings. Dean Harwood explained that renovations on the entire downtown area had recently been completed. As a result, all of the buildings looked shiny and new. All in all, Emma was very impressed with the city of Benton.

They were stopped at a traffic light a couple of cars back from the intersection when Emma happened to notice a man and a woman on the sidewalk up ahead waiting to cross the street. Something about the couple seemed familiar. The light changed, and Emma continued to watch as Dean Harwood's car drew closer to the man and woman. As they passed, Emma got a good look at them and couldn't prevent the soft gasp of surprise that escaped her lips.

"What is it, Emma?" Doug asked when he heard her.

"Did you see that couple on the sidewalk?" Emma asked in a whisper. She wasn't sure why, but she didn't want Doug's dad and Miss Jennings to hear her. Doug shook his head no in answer to her question, so Emma continued, "It was the academy's head cook, Mrs. Bertram, and that construction guy, you know, the one that owns the company that's building our new gym."

"You mean Ray Sutton?" Doug asked.

"Yeah, that's the guy."

Doug thought for a minute. "Well, I guess that's not so strange really. Mrs. Bertram's a widow, and she and Mr. Sutton are probably about the same age. The cooks each get a day off during the holiday weekend. This must be Mrs. Bertram's day."

"They make an odd couple, don't you think?" Emma said with a frown. At the school, Mrs. Bertram seemed so prim and proper in her starched and spotless uniform. Under her management, the school's kitchen was always meticulously clean—the appliances scrubbed and polished after every use. Ray Sutton seemed to be just the opposite. His work clothes were always filthy, his work site cluttered with equipment and unused materials. Of course, the man did work in construction, but even allowing for that fact, Mr. Sutton didn't seem to be Mrs. Bertram's type at all. Thankfully, the two of them had been too busy talking to each other to notice Emma gawking at them through the car window. They had been holding hands, so there was no doubt that they were more than friends.

"Not really. They're probably just out on a date," Doug stated matter-of-factly, interrupting Emma's musings.

Emma had a strange feeling that something about the couple wasn't right, but Doug didn't seem to be concerned, so she decided to let the matter drop. Then a thought occurred to her. "I hope they're not planning on going ice-skating!"

Doug couldn't help laughing at the look of horror on Emma's face. "I don't think we have to worry about that. I can't picture either one of them wearing a pair of ice skates. Can you?"

"I'm trying not to," Emma answered with a giggle.

A few minutes later, Dean Harwood pulled into the parking lot of the skating rink. They had left the downtown area behind several minutes ago and were now a couple of miles out on the opposite side of Benton. A large metal building stood at the north end of the parking lot.

"Is that the skating rink?" Emma asked. Somehow it wasn't what she had expected.

Hearing the doubt in her tone, Doug smiled and answered, "I know it's not much to look at on the outside, but I promise it's really nice on the inside."

Emma nodded and swallowed nervously. Now that they had reached their destination, she was beginning to worry that she might embarrass herself when she tried to skate. After all, this was her first time, and she didn't want to look like an idiot in front of Doug. In an attempt to calm her nerves, Emma began to reason with herself. She'd been roller-skating many times before. Surely ice-skating couldn't be that much different.

"All right, everybody out," Dean Harwood said cheerfully after pulling into a parking spot close to the entrance.

Obediently, Emma got out of the car. She walked beside Doug, who was following behind his dad and Miss Jennings. As they got closer to the building, the butterflies in her stomach began doing somersaults.

Noticing how quiet Emma had suddenly become, Doug looked down at her. He was surprised to see how pale she was. "Emma, are you okay?"

Emma nodded. "I guess I'm just a little nervous. I don't want to make a fool of myself."

"Don't worry. You'll do just fine," Doug said.

That's easy for you to say, Emma thought. Doug had been ice-skating many times and had even been on a little league hockey team when he was younger. Doug had told her all of this the day he had first asked her to go on this outing. She hadn't thought much about it then, but now that the moment of truth was near, Emma was kicking herself for agreeing to come. It would have been a different matter if they had both been beginners, but Doug was practically an expert. She was bound to look gawky and awkward by comparison. *Oh well, it's too late to back out now*, she thought with a sigh.

When they got inside the building, Dean Harwood paid the admission fee for the four of them and then led them over to the counter where they could rent skates. A large area to the left of the counter had several wooden benches so that people could sit down to put their skates on. There were also rows of lockers for stowing shoes and other personal belongings. They each gave their shoe size to the teenage boy working behind the counter, and he provided them with the proper size skates. Doug requested a pair of hockey skates instead of figure skates. When the boy laid them on the counter, Emma noticed that the blade on the hockey skates looked even thinner than the blades on the figure skates. Emma didn't see how he was going to be able to balance on that single thin blade, but she was too nervous to question Doug's choice.

After grabbing their skates, Doug led Emma over to a bench opposite the one occupied by his dad and Miss Jennings. It was then that Emma realized that she didn't even know how to lace up her skates.

As if reading her mind, Doug said, "I'll help you lace up your skates, Emma."

"Okay," Emma quickly agreed. With shaking hands, she took off her shoes and put the skates on. Then Doug knelt down in front of her and went to work. His movements were quick and efficient. He obviously knew what he was doing.

"It's important that you get the laces good and tight," Doug explained while he worked. "These rental skates are usually too broken in to give much ankle support. You see, with ice-skating, it's all about the strength of your ankles."

While he worked, Emma began to worry that her ankles weren't strong enough.

"That should do it," Doug said when he had finished. Then he sat down next to her and quickly donned his own skates. Emma sat beside him, trying not to show how nervous she was.

Dean Harwood and Miss Jennings finished getting their skates on first. Of course, Miss Jennings had been able to perform the task herself, so they had finished in half the time it was taking Doug and Emma. Emma watched as they made their way over to the skating rink. They really were a nice-looking couple. Dean Harwood took Miss Jennings's hand as they stepped onto the ice. It was then that Emma noticed all the people, children and adults alike, whizzing past. She could see the children's heads over the low wall that circled the rink. Emma began to wonder if she was the only one in the entire place who didn't know how to ice-skate. She was seriously considering backing out when Doug rose and pulled her to her feet.

"Let's go," he said with an encouraging smile. Sensing her reluctance, he added, "You'll never learn if you don't try. Don't worry. I won't let you fall."

Emma didn't answer. She was too busy trying not to be sick.

All too soon, they were at the edge of the rink. Doug put his arm around her waist for support as together they stepped onto the ice. Immediately, Emma's roller-skating experience kicked in. She leaned slightly forward and began placing one foot in front of the other—gliding a little on each foot. Doug let her set the pace, gliding confidently along beside her, all the while keeping his arm firmly around her waist. As they circled the rink, Emma began to get a feel for the ice. The longer she went without falling, the more her confidence grew.

Doug was right about ankle strength being important. Emma found she couldn't keep her ankles straight. Instead they bowed inward slightly. She noticed several of the other skaters having the same difficulty, so she didn't feel too badly about it.

"You're doing great, Emma," Doug complimented her.

"Thanks," Emma replied. She was too busy concentrating to say much more. So far, she had managed to stay upright, but it was still early.

"Think you're ready to try it on your own?" Doug asked after they'd circled the rink a few more times. He didn't want to let her go. He was enjoying having her up close beside him, but she was doing so well she really didn't need his help any longer.

"I guess I won't know until I try," Emma answered.

"Okay then. I'll be right here if you need me." He'd been half hoping that she would say she wasn't ready to go solo, but he had to admit she was right. Reluctantly, Doug removed his arm from around her waist.

Emma immediately missed its comforting warmth and realized what an idiot she was. She had been so focused on her skating that she hadn't taken the time to appreciate the fact that Doug had had his arm around her. That thought caused her to stumble, but she quickly managed to regain her balance.

As the afternoon wore on, Emma began to notice that her skates were rubbing sore spots on her ankles. Doug must have noticed her slowing down.

"I think you've had enough for one day," he said.

"Yeah, these skates are starting to hurt my ankles."

Without further comment, Doug began steering them to the exit. Dean Harwood and Miss Jennings skated up behind them. They must have seen the two youngsters getting ready to leave the ice.

"Are you two about ready to go?" Dean Harwood asked. "Louisa and I have had enough for today."

"Us too," Doug replied with a grin.

"Well, how did you like it?" Miss Jennings asked as they took off their skates a moment later.

"I loved it!" Emma answered. "You were right. It takes a while to get used to the feel of the ice, but once you do, it's like gliding along on air. I'd love to learn how to spin and stuff, but I guess you have to take lessons for that."

"True, but there are still some tricks I could teach you next time we come," Miss Jennings responded with a smile.

Miss Jennings's statement made it sound like they might get to come ice-skating again sometime. Emma hoped so, because after her initial nervousness, she'd really enjoyed herself and Doug had been the perfect date. She wondered briefly if date was the right word for it, then decided just as quickly that it didn't really matter. The point was he'd skated patiently beside a frightened beginner all afternoon when there were probably dozens of things he would rather have done.

After they left the skating rink, they stopped at a restaurant in Benton's downtown area to have supper before heading back to the academy. During the meal, most of the conversation centered on the new recreation complex and what it could mean for the school. Dean Harwood was counting on it helping enrollment at the academy. Emma didn't mention that she'd seen Ray Sutton and Mrs. Bertram that afternoon. After all, it wasn't really any of her business what the man did when he wasn't working. Doug apparently felt the same way because he didn't mention it either.

Later, on the way back to school, Emma found herself getting sleepy. Dean Harwood and Miss Jennings were talking quietly in the front seat, while she and Doug sat in comfortable silence in the backseat. Emma yawned and laid her head against the back of her seat. That was the last thing she remembered. She awakened with a start when one of the doors was opened and the overhead light came on. It took her a moment to realize that her head was resting on Doug's shoulder. Embarrassed and hoping desperately that she hadn't drooled on him, Emma quickly sat up.

"Sorry about that. I guess I fell asleep," Emma said as she examined his shirt for any wet spots. Thankfully, there were none.

"No problem," Doug answered with a casual shrug.

"I'll let you all out here," Dean Harwood told them. He had stopped the car in front of the school's main entrance.

"Thank you for taking me today," Emma said to Doug's dad as she opened the door. "I really had a good time."

"You're welcome, Emma. I'm glad you had fun. You looked like a natural on the ice."

"Thanks." Emma knew she had a long way to go to be as good as Doug, but at least she hadn't totally embarrassed herself.

As Miss Jennings and the two youngsters climbed the front steps, Dean Harwood drove the car around the castle to park it in the bus barn.

"I don't know about you two, but I'm exhausted," Miss Jennings said once they were inside. "I think I'll go on up to bed. Good night, you two."

"Good night, Miss Jennings," Emma and Doug replied in unison.

Once Miss Jennings had disappeared down the main hall in the direction of the elevator, Doug and Emma were left standing alone in the lobby. Suddenly, Emma felt nervous. She wondered if Doug would try to kiss her again.

"Doug, thanks for asking me to go ice-skating. I had a great time," she said, breaking the silence that had fallen upon Miss Jennings's departure.

"Was it everything you'd hoped it would be?" he asked, looking at her intently with those dark eyes of his.

"Yes. I just wish I was as good as you."

"You will be in no time. Dad was right. You're a natural."

Silence fell between them again as they stood looking at each other. Doug had just taken a step toward her when suddenly a group of students came bustling out of the lounge. Their sudden appearance broke the spell, and Doug quickly backed away from her.

"I guess I'll see you tomorrow," Doug said, eyeing the noisy group with a frown.

"Yeah, see you tomorrow," Emma agreed quickly. With nothing else to say, Emma turned to go. She could almost feel him watching her as she headed to her room. As she walked down the hall, Emma thought about what had just happened. She was certain that Doug had intended to kiss her. Instead of being disappointed that it hadn't happened, she felt a thrill of excitement because she was equally certain that he would try again when the next opportunity presented itself. She went to sleep that night dreaming of when that might be.

CHAPTER THIRTY
A TRUCE IS CALLED

Martha returned to school the following afternoon. When the two girls were alone together in their room, Emma quickly filled Martha in on all that had happened the last few days. She even told Martha about seeing Mrs. Bertram and Ray Sutton together in Benton.

"Those two just don't seem like they go together," Martha said in surprise.

"That's just what I said," Emma exclaimed, "but Doug didn't seem to think it was strange at all."

"Well, there's no accounting for taste," Martha replied. Then she shrugged her shoulders and added, "Mrs. Bertram is probably lonely."

"I never thought of that. You're right, Martha. She's probably just glad to have someone to do things with."

"Now that the mystery is solved, tell me more about the ice-skating. Did you like it as much as you thought you would?"

"I loved it! I just wish I was better at it."

"It just takes practice," Martha pointed out.

"I'm not likely to get that any time soon. That was probably my one and only ice-skating experience," Emma lamented.

"Not necessarily. Doug says there's a pond not too far to the north of the castle. If it stays as cold as it's been lately, it'll freeze over, and then we'll be able to go skating."

"Sounds great. There's only one problem. I don't have any skates."

"I'm sure we can round some skates up somewhere," Martha answered with a suspicious twinkle in her eye.

Emma was just about to ask Martha where these mythical skates might be when Clarice and Susie came in. Emma was surprised to find that she was genuinely glad to see them. Things between her and Clarice had changed since their time together in the infirmary.

The rest of the afternoon was spent unpacking suitcases and sharing stories about all of the things everyone had done on their break. Emma listened with rapt attention as Susie and Clarice described in detail all the shops they'd visited. Then the two girls showed her and Martha the new clothes they'd bought. Martha's holiday had been more about spending time with her parents and siblings. Emma couldn't help feeling envious as Martha described all the fun her family had had playing games and watching movies together.

"What did you and Doug do while we were gone?" Clarice asked Emma with a knowing smile when Martha had finished her narrative.

Emma decided to let the suspense build a bit before telling Clarice and Susie about her ice-skating trip.

"Well, I finished all of my projects," Emma began with a woeful expression.

"What?" Clarice interrupted. "Do you mean to tell me that Douglas didn't spend any time with you at all? Well, that's just the meanest thing I've ever heard!"

Clarice was getting so upset on her behalf that Emma decided to put an end to her suspense building.

"Wait," Emma said, putting up a hand to halt Clarice's tirade. "That's not all I did."

Emma then went on to tell Clarice and Susie all about her day in Benton.

"Well, that's more like it!" Clarice declared with an unladylike snort.

"That Doug is so nice," Susie commented.

"Yes, he is," Emma agreed.

The talk then turned to Christmas. Wednesday would be December first. The entire student body would be invited to help decorate the castle on that day. Afterward, all of the volunteers would be treated to cookies and hot chocolate as a reward for their hard work. Emma was looking forward to the day. It had been a lot of fun last year. Much to Emma and Martha's amazement, Clarice even sounded enthusiastic at the mention of the event.

The rest of Sunday passed all too quickly. They had supper and then played games in the lounge until curfew.

Later that night, Emma lay in bed thinking about the upcoming Christmas holiday. She still didn't know what to get Doug, and she only had until Saturday to figure it out. Emma made a mental note not to forget to ask Sebastian for some ideas tomorrow. She finally drifted off to sleep and dreamed that she was skating on a frozen pond with Doug by her side.

Monday morning came all too soon, and classes resumed. Emma didn't mind the classes. It was the homework she hated. At least she wasn't alone. Homework was an integral part of the school's teaching philosophy, and all Dinswood students suffered equally under the burden. Emma had to admit she was learning more at Dinswood than she'd ever learned at her other schools. Students at the academy consistently earned the highest scores on national tests.

Emma was proud to be a Dinswood Academy student, so she applied herself diligently to her assignments with the realization that all of her hard work would pay off someday.

Wednesday finally arrived. There were no hobby classes after school so that students could spend the time decorating if they wished. Emma, Martha, Doug, and Sebastian volunteered to decorate the tree in the lounge as they had done last year. While the four of them worked on the tree in the lounge, other students worked on the trees in the library and lobby and assisted with the other decorating jobs.

When the foursome had finished with the tree in the lounge, they spent some time wandering around to check out all of the other decorations. The trees in the library and lobby were finished and the main staircase looked festive strung with garland and twinkle lights. Poinsettias had been placed in the windows and on some of the tables, and the castle's front doors were adorned with the largest wreaths Emma had ever seen.

"I think we've outdone ourselves this year," Sebastian exclaimed as he looked around.

"It's all beautiful," Emma agreed. "I just wish it would snow. The castle would really look Christmassy then."

"The snow needs to hold off until after Saturday. We don't want our trip to Windland canceled," Sebastian reminded her.

"You're right, Sebastian. I can't believe I forgot about that."

Emma had gotten a chance to talk to Sebastian about gift ideas for Doug at supper on Monday. Doug had stayed late in shop class to work on his rocking chair, so Sebastian had been alone when Martha and Emma had entered the dining hall. Sebastian had told her that Doug's dad was getting him a new pair of hockey skates for Christmas since he'd outgrown his old ones. Sebastian had then gone on to suggest that the girls go together to get him a hockey stick.

"I'm pretty sure I'm getting skates and a hockey stick too," Sebastian had said with a sly grin. "At least, that's what I asked for. If you guys get Doug one, then we can play hockey this winter on that pond Doug told us about."

The girls had agreed that Sebastian's suggestion was a good idea and were planning on getting Doug's present in Windland on Saturday. Sebastian was going to help them pick it out. Emma just hoped that the small town of Windland, with its limited shopping options, would have what they were looking for.

"I don't know about you, but I'm starving," Sebastian said with an exaggerated groan. "Let's go get something to eat."

Hearing no argument from the others, Sebastian started off in the direction of the dining hall. The others dutifully followed, and in no time, they were seated at a table—each with a cup of hot chocolate and a plate of goodies.

This year, the cooking class had produced a wider variety of sweets to choose from. In addition to an assortment of cookies, there were pecan tarts and little pastries stuffed with cream.

"These pastries are delicious!" Martha exclaimed after taking a bite. "They're so flaky, and the cream filling is yummy."

"I made the pastries," Sebastian announced proudly. "I wanted to try something a little harder than cookies."

"They're really good, Sebastian," Emma said after trying one. "You're going to be a great chef someday."

"I hope so, but I've still got a long way to go and a lot to learn," Sebastian answered with a pleased expression. "There's only so much they can teach me in my hobby class. I've been reading through the book Martha got me for Christmas last year and learning a lot about sauces and stuff. At least when I go to culinary school after graduation, I'll know a few things."

"Maybe Mrs. Bertram would let you try a few dishes over Christmas break," Martha suggested. It made her feel good that Sebastian liked the present she'd gotten him last year. She had already planned to get him the second cooking book in the series this Saturday when they were in Windland.

"Maybe," Sebastian said with a shrug in response to Martha's suggestion. His tone wasn't too hopeful. "Mrs. Bertram's pretty fussy about her kitchen, but I guess it wouldn't hurt to ask."

Hearing the head cook's name reminded Emma about seeing her with Ray Sutton in Benton. When she told Sebastian about seeing the two of them together, he raised his eyebrows in surprise.

"Wow, I never would have figured that," he said. "They don't seem like they go together."

"That's just what I said when Emma told me," Martha said.

"Come on, guys," Doug said. "It's not like they're getting married or anything."

No more was said on the subject of Mrs. Bertram and Ray Sutton, but Emma still couldn't shake the feeling that something about the pairing was wrong. Her worry about what Mrs. Bertram and Ray Sutton could possibly be up to was completely forgotten with Doug's next statement.

"I delivered the third sculpture. I did it the Friday after Thanksgiving. I figured it would be a good time to do it, you know with most of the students gone and the cooking staff on rotation."

"Why didn't you tell me you were planning to deliver one?" Emma asked in an accusing tone. "I would have gone with you."

"There wasn't any need for you to go. I didn't run into any problems, and I've gotten pretty good at moving that refrigerator out by myself. Besides, one person sneaking around is less conspicuous than two people."

Doug had some valid points, but Emma still didn't like it. "Please promise me you'll at least take Sebastian with you when you deliver the next one," she begged.

Doug didn't want to make that promise, but he could see the worry not just in Emma's face but the faces of Sebastian and Martha as well.

With a sigh and a shake of his head, he gave in. "Okay, I promise."

"I'm staying at school over Christmas break," Sebastian informed the group. "We can deliver the next sculpture over Christmas break."

"I'm staying too," Martha chimed in.

Doug shook his head at Sebastian. "I agree it would be a good time to do it, but the sculpture of Mary is the only one we've got left. What if we can't find the other two? Mr. Munsen told me to let him know before we delivered the last sculpture because he's working on some kind of trap. If we don't find the other two sculptures, we'll need the one of Mary to spring the trap."

"I get it," Sebastian said. "We've got to keep one sculpture in reserve."

Doug simply nodded. He was glad Sebastian and Martha were staying at Dinswood over the Christmas holiday. He was hoping the four of them would get a chance to look for the other two sculptures. There were still a couple of places within walking distance of the castle that he thought were worth checking out even though they weren't on the list they'd made. He wouldn't relax until he had the last two sculptures in hand. Only then would his dad and Lord Dinswood really be safe.

It still hadn't snowed by the time Saturday arrived. Thus far, the fall season had been unusually cold and dry. Emma had mixed feelings about the lack of snow. She was glad they would be able to make their last trip to Windland before winter set in, but she missed seeing the castle draped in winter white. *Oh well,* she thought, *there's still plenty of time left for a good snowstorm. After all, winter doesn't officially begin until the twenty-first of December.* With that happy thought,

Emma gathered the two afghans she needed to mail home and waited while Martha, Clarice, and Susie finished getting ready. The four girls then left the room together.

Dean Harwood had leased extra buses from a company in Benton so that any student wanting to take this final Windland trip could do so. As a result, the halls were crowded with noisy students—all headed in the direction of the castle's front entrance.

The buses were already idling out front, so the girls went on outside and boarded the second bus in the row. Emma got on first and took a moment to scan the faces of the other occupants to see if Doug and Sebastian might be on board. Not seeing them, she chose a seat near the front and, after stowing her gifts for her brothers under the seat, slid over to the window to make room for Martha. Clarice and Susie took the seat directly behind them. The bus was filled with the sound of excited voices. Everyone appeared to be in high spirits and looking forward to their last trip to Windland for a while. Emma wasn't paying attention though. She was watching out the window for Doug and Sebastian. Of course, it was possible that they were already on one of the other buses, but Emma hoped this was not the case. Emma's vigilance was rewarded when the two boys appeared a moment later. She began waving her hands to get their attention as they scanned the row of buses. Doug finally saw her and returned her wave. He and Sebastian boarded the bus a second later. As there were no seats available close to the girls, Doug led the way down the aisle to the back. Once the boys were settled, Emma turned back around and prepared to enjoy the ride to Windland.

They had all agreed that they would split up once they got to town so that they could Christmas shop for each other. Then they would meet for lunch at the Windland Inn.

The inn was designed like a ski lodge and was one of Emma's favorite places. One end of the inn was a good-sized restaurant; the other side was an enormous lounge area. The lounge area had a high ceiling that was supported by a network of crisscrossing wooden beams. Ceiling fans hung from some of the beams, and couches and comfortable-looking chairs were scattered around a large central circular fireplace. A carpeted hallway on the backside of the lounge led to the hotel rooms. The town of Windland had a regular restaurant on Main Street, but Emma much preferred the homey feel of the inn. The food was equally good at both places.

The foursome had made no plans beyond lunch, but Doug had mentioned that he was hoping for a chance to talk to Mr. Munsen. That meant a trip to the bookstore. Most likely, Mr. Munsen's daughter Becky would be working behind the counter today. Even though she was two years older, Becky showed too much interest in Doug as far as Emma was concerned. The truth of the matter was that Emma was jealous. Becky was a very pretty girl. Thus far, Doug hadn't paid her much attention, but things could change.

Emma frowned at the thought as the bus in which she was riding pulled into the inn's parking lot. Martha got off as soon as the doors opened. It took Emma a moment to get the afghans she'd stowed under her seat. Knowing of the plans they'd previously agreed to, she was surprised to see Martha waiting for her at the bottom of the steps.

"I know we're splitting up, but I wanted to tell you that Sebastian said he'd help us pick out a hockey stick for Doug before lunch. Can you meet us at the general store around eleven thirty?"

"Yeah, no problem," Emma answered. "You know I've been wondering how we're going to get Doug's present back to the school without him seeing it."

"Well, believe it or not, Sebastian has already thought of that. It seems that the store will deliver items to the school. Usually, they charge a small fee for the service, but because of the volume of items sold at Christmas time, they waive the fee," Martha explained.

"Problem solved then," Emma replied. Then she added with a sly grin, "It seems like Sebastian has thought of everything. I wonder who he's working so hard to please."

Martha simply smiled.

"See you at eleven thirty," Emma said with a wave.

A look at her watch told her she had an hour and a half to get her errands done. That should be plenty of time if she didn't dawdle. With a sense of purpose, Emma strode down the sidewalk to the Frame Shop to pick up the present for her parents.

Then it was on to the post office to get everything mailed home. Her arms were pretty full as she left the Frame Shop. She had the two blankets for her brothers and now the framed picture. Thankfully, she ran into Reggie who offered to help her carry everything to the post office.

"Thanks, Reggie," Emma said gratefully as she handed him the picture. "I just knew I'd drop the picture and break the glass before I could get it mailed."

"Gee, it looks great, Emma. Did you do the work yourself?"

"Yeah. It took me all semester, but I finally finished it," Emma answered.

Reggie only stayed with her until she was safely in the post office, and then he left to complete errands of his own. Emma thanked him again as he left.

After the post office, Emma looked at her watch. It was now ten thirty. She decided to get Martha's present next, so she made her way to the general store. Once inside, Emma took a quick look down each aisle to make sure that Martha wasn't in the store. Then she headed to the arts and crafts section. After much deliberation, Emma finally selected a small sketch pad and a large set of colored pencils. Martha was always sketching things, so Emma was sure she could use the extra paper. She wasn't as sure about the colored pencils though. As she was on her way to the front of the store to pay for her items, she passed through the photo section. One of the picture frames caught her eye. It was silver with scalloped edges, and at the top it said "best friends." Emma couldn't resist it. She picked it up before she could change her mind and made her way to the checkout counter. After she had paid for the items, a glance at her watch confirmed that she still had enough time to get Sebastian's gift at the candy shop.

Just as she had done before, she looked around the shop first to make sure Sebastian wasn't there. Then she picked out the biggest box of assorted chocolates she could afford and paid for them. By the time she was finished, it was time to meet Martha and Sebastian back at the general store.

Emma entered the store and headed back to the small sporting goods section. She scanned the area and was relieved to see that the store carried hockey sticks. It wasn't an extensive assortment by any means, but it was adequate for their needs. Emma was sure they could find something that would suit Doug from the sticks displayed. *Hockey must be a popular sport for the kids in town*, Emma reasoned. This would explain why the store carried the equipment. As she waited for her friends, she continued to look around the sporting goods area. She was disappointed, but not surprised, to see that the store did not carry ice skates of any kind. *That would have been too much to hope for*, Emma thought. Then she heard her name being called.

"Emma, have they got what we need?" Martha asked as she made her way over to Emma. Sebastian was right behind her.

"Yes, I think so," Emma answered.

Sebastian went over and stood in front of the rack of sticks. "I told you they did," Sebastian said to Martha. "We looked at them the last time Doug and I were in the store. There was one Doug really liked. If I can just remember which one it was."

Sebastian studied for a moment. Occasionally, he'd pull a stick out only to put it back. Just when the girls were about to conclude he'd forgotten which one Doug liked, Sebastian pulled one out and grinned in triumph.

"This is it," he said, holding it up for the girls to see.

"Are you sure?" Martha couldn't help asking.

"I'm sure," Sebastian answered. "This is the one."

"Well, we'd better pay for it and arrange to have it delivered to the school before Doug comes in," Emma urged Martha.

Sebastian kept watch while the two girls each paid their part of the expense.

"Do you want it wrapped?" the elderly woman behind the counter asked.

Emma gave Martha a questioning glance.

"There's not really any point, is there?" Martha asked. "I mean he's going to know right away what it is whether it's wrapped or not."

Emma couldn't argue with that. When they learned that there was an additional charge for wrapping, the decision was made.

"Just send it as is," Martha told the woman.

The woman nodded and then gave them a card to sign. Once the card had their names on it, the woman tied it to the stick along with a card that had Doug's name and the name of the school written on it. Then without further comment, she took the stick and disappeared into a back room where all of the items bound for Dinswood Academy were apparently being stored.

The two girls met up with Sebastian, who was waiting for them by the door, and together they stepped out into the cold. They were immediately struck with a blast of cold air. Emma hadn't noticed it earlier.

"Boy, it's gotten windy," complained Martha as they made their way to the Windland Inn to meet Doug for lunch.

"A front is coming in. It's supposed to start snowing later on this afternoon," Sebastian explained.

"I'm surprised the school still let us make the trip with snow on the way," Martha said.

Emma felt a growing excitement at the prospect of snow, but Sebastian's next words snuffed it out as quickly as a child's breath on a birthday candle.

"It's not supposed to amount to much—only a light dusting according to the weather report."

No more was said about the weather, but as they walked, they pulled their coats tighter around them and bent their heads into the wind. By the time they reached the inn, Emma's face felt frozen. Struggling against the force of the wind, she pulled open one of the double doors and stepped into the air lock. It wasn't much warmer in the air lock, but at least they didn't have the icy wind to contend with. Emma hurried to open one of the next set of doors and sighed with relief as the combined warmth of the restaurant and lounge fireplace hit her. She stood for a moment, absorbing the warmth and letting her shivers subside. Martha came in next, followed by Sebastian who was alternately rubbing and blowing into his hands in order to restore some feeling.

"Is Doug here yet?" Sebastian asked Emma.

"I haven't had a chance to look yet. I've been too busy trying to get warm again. I can't remember it ever being this cold last year."

"I know, and we had almost two feet of snow at this time last year. The weather sure is crazy around here," Sebastian agreed.

While Sebastian and Emma discussed the weather, Martha looked around the restaurant area for Doug. She finally spotted him sitting alone at a table in the far corner. The scowl he was wearing on his face turned to a smile when he saw Martha, Emma, and Sebastian by the entrance.

"Doug's over there at the back table," Martha said, giving a little wave to let Doug know she'd seen him.

As they threaded their way between tables, Martha worried about what had caused the expression she'd seen briefly on his face. He was definitely furious about something.

Martha couldn't wait to find out, so she asked Doug about it the minute everyone was seated.

"Doug, what's wrong?"

Sebastian and Emma looked at Martha in surprise and then looked at Doug, who in turn looked a little surprised himself.

"Sorry about that. The look on my face must have given me away," Doug guessed. Then with a shake of his head, he sighed and said, "It's nothing really. You'd think I'd know better by now. I shouldn't let Bobby Wilcox get to me, but I swear that guy really knows how to push my buttons."

"What's Bobby done now?" Emma asked as a feeling of dread crept over her.

"He's been following me all morning. I guess he wants to make sure that he's there to witness it if I should happen to break a school rule. It wouldn't matter at all except I was hoping to get a chance to talk to Mr. Munsen this afternoon, you know, to see if he's found out anything that could help us with the Reaper. I can't really do that with Bobby hanging around."

"We could keep Bobby busy for you," Sebastian offered.

"Bobby's too smart for that. I bet while he was tailing me, he had some of his buddies following each of you. Did any of you detect a tail?"

"You sound like a private investigator, and it's kind of creeping me out," Martha said with a shiver that had nothing to do with the cold. "No, I didn't notice anyone following me, but I wasn't really looking either." Then Martha turned to Sebastian and Emma. "How about you guys? Did either of you notice anyone hanging around?"

"I'm like you," Emma replied quickly. "I wasn't really paying attention."

"Me neither," Sebastian said.

"Well, I for one am glad that I didn't pick up on anything. It would have freaked me out, especially since I was shopping alone all morning," Martha exclaimed with another shudder.

"Sorry I creeped you out, Martha, but there's no reason to be afraid of Bobby or any of his goons," Doug replied. Then Doug looked at Emma and Sebastian. "Whether you guys noticed or not, I'd bet my last dollar you were being followed."

"That guy has serious issues," Sebastian commented with a shake of his head.

The waitress came just then, so all talk ceased for a moment as they each gave their order. After the waitress left to get their drinks, the topic of conversation shifted to the unusually dry and cold weather they'd been having. Doug sat quietly, only half listening to the conversation around him. He was still fuming about Bobby, and he was also trying to figure out a way to give him the slip this afternoon so he could talk to Mr. Munsen. Mr. Munsen probably didn't have anything new to tell him, but Doug wanted to speak with him anyway. The truth was Doug needed reassurance that Mr. Munsen was still working on a way to trap the Reaper.

It was then that Doug noticed the man sitting at the end of the counter no more than a dozen feet away. For some reason, the man seemed completely out of place. He looked to be in his early forties and was short and muscular with dark curly hair. He was wearing a plaid flannel shirt, jeans, and a pair of boots, which was pretty much the way all men dressed in Windland. What was unusual was that this man's clothes were all brand new—right down to the shiny scuff-free boots he was wearing on his feet.

The man was reading a newspaper and seemed to be totally unaware that he was being studied. This fact gave Doug the boldness to observe him even more closely. Doug noticed that he was clean-shaven and that his fingernails were clean and perfectly manicured. The man also had an expensive-looking watch on his left wrist. When he reached for his drink, Doug saw that he was wearing a big diamond ring on the third finger of his right hand. There was no doubt about it—this man was rich.

Doug began to wonder why a rich man would be in a little town like Windland. One explanation was that he was here to meet with the Reaper about buying the Mortals. This man could be the actual buyer, or he could be an employee of the buyer.

A little voice in Doug's head told him that he was jumping to conclusions. This man might have nothing to do with the Reaper or the Mortals. Then again, he might. Doug needed to know for sure.

As far as Doug knew, there weren't any other motels in Windland, so if the man was a visitor, he was most likely staying in one of the rooms at the inn. Doug decided he would wait until the man got up to leave, and then he'd follow him to see which room he was staying in. Then he would find Mr. Munsen and let him know what was going on. Maybe the guy planned to meet with the Reaper this afternoon, and they could catch him in the act. Of course, it was possible the meeting had already taken place. If that were the case, this man would be able to identify the Reaper. All they'd have to do is get him to talk. From the looks of the guy, that wouldn't be easy, but if anybody could do it, Mr. Munsen could, Doug reasoned.

The waitress came with their food, and for a while, everyone was busy eating their burgers and fries—everyone except Doug that is. Doug picked at his food absently while he continued to keep an eye on the man at the counter. About halfway through their lunch, the man stood up and laid some money on the counter to pay for his meal. Without a backward glance, he set off toward the lounge at a leisurely pace.

Doug stood up, startling Emma, Martha, and Sebastian.

"Sorry, guys. Nature calls. I'll be right back," Doug said in a rush. He hated lying to his friends, but there wasn't time for explanations. He left the table and hurried after the dark-haired man. When he got to the lounge, he saw that the man was headed toward the hallway leading to the hotel's dozen or so rooms.

Doug got to the hallway in time to see the man entering the third room on the right. All he needed to do now was see what the room number was. Then he could let Mr. Munsen know. Quietly and cautiously, Doug approached the door through which the man had just disappeared. A little brass plate identified the room as number five. Doug was just turning to leave when something totally unexpected happened. The door in front of him opened, and he found himself face-to-face with the dark-haired man. Before Doug could move, he was yanked inside and the door was kicked shut behind him. Then he was slammed and pinned against the inside of the door with all the force of a charging bull. The man simultaneously shoved his muscular forearm against Doug's neck and lifted him off his feet.

Doug struggled to get free but to no avail. All the wind had been knocked out of him when he'd hit the door, and he was having a difficult time breathing with the man's arm crushing his windpipe. He kicked his dangling feet uselessly against the door. His struggles only served to make the man increase the pressure on his neck.

"Why are you following me?" the man snarled close to Doug's face.

All Doug could manage was a croak in response. Just when Doug was convinced he was going to die of suffocation, the man loosened his hold slightly.

"I'll ask you again. Why are you following me?" the man repeated.

Doug's oxygen starved brain was unable to come up with a reasonable answer. Telling this man the truth would probably get him killed. As Doug continued to rack his brain for a lie that would work, he realized he wasn't going to leave this room alive no matter what he said.

The man grew impatient when Doug remained silent and doubled the pressure on Doug's throat. "Nothing to say for yourself?" he asked with a hiss, his mouth so close to Doug's face that he could smell his breath. "That's too bad."

Doug was beginning to lose consciousness when miraculously someone knocked loudly on the door. The sound surprised the man, and he released Doug.

"This is your lucky day, boy," he growled. Then he grabbed Doug roughly by the shoulders, opened the door, and shoved him through it. As Doug fell headlong into the hallway, he heard the door slam shut loudly behind him. Doug rolled over onto his back and lay there for a moment, taking in some much-needed air. Gradually, he became aware that someone was standing over him. He looked up to see none other than Bobby Wilcox staring down at him with a strange expression on his face.

"What's going on?" Bobby asked. "Who was that guy?"

"I don't know, but I think you just saved my life," Doug rasped painfully. His throat felt raw, and each intake of air was painful.

Bobby frowned at Doug but didn't say anything. It was obvious that he was still waiting for an answer to his question.

Doug sighed and ran a hand through his hair. "Look, believe it or not, I'd tell you what was going on if I could. But this isn't about breaking school rules. It's a lot bigger and a whole lot more serious than that."

Bobby studied Doug with narrowed eyes as if he were trying to gauge the truth of Doug's statements. Still he said nothing.

Doug realized he'd never get a better opportunity to try to mend things with Bobby. The two boys were alone in the hallway, and there wasn't anyone else within earshot. Bobby didn't have any of his friends around, so there was no need for him to put on a tough-guy act. He could be himself. Doug decided to give it a try. Looking Bobby in the eye, he began, "I know we've had our problems, but I'm asking you now for a truce—at least until the last day of school. Then I promise I'll tell you everything. You just saved my life, so I guess I owe you at least that much." Doug hesitated for a moment and a look of pain flashed briefly on his face. With a grim expression, he added, "It'll all be over then, one way or the other."

For a moment, Bobby didn't answer, and then the second miracle of the day occurred: Bobby held out a hand to help Doug to his feet and said, "We should probably get out of here."

Gratefully, Doug accepted Bobby's offer of help and realized that it was Bobby's way of agreeing to the truce. When Doug was upright once again, the two boys walked down the hallway side by side and entered the lounge together. Before they parted ways, Doug said quietly so that only Bobby could hear, "Thanks."

Bobby's only reply was a nod.

CHAPTER THIRTY-ONE
A SPECIAL CHRISTMAS PRESENT

obby walked away wondering why in the world he had agreed to a truce with Doug. In an effort to figure it out, he thought back over recent events. There was no doubt about it: Harwood had gotten in over his head this time. Doug was involved in something dangerous, and Bobby wanted nothing to do with it. If he continued to follow Doug around, he could be putting himself at risk. Bobby told himself that he had agreed to the truce as a matter of self-preservation. That might have been part of the reason, but if Bobby was being honest with himself, it wasn't the whole reason. Bobby had seen the look on Doug's face as he lay there gasping for breath, unaware of his presence. He had looked genuinely scared. That look had ignited a tiny spark of compassion in Bobby. In that moment, he had no longer envied Doug. He had felt sorry for him.

By the time Doug returned to his seat at the table, the others had finished eating. Although they looked at him curiously, he didn't tell them anything about what had happened. They would only give him a hard time for going off by himself, and he was in no mood for a scolding. No longer hungry, Doug told them that he was ready to go.

Emma knew that something was wrong, but she didn't want to question him in front of the others. Doug was back with them and he was safe. For now, that would have to be enough.

Later that afternoon, Doug got a chance to talk with Mr. Munsen without Bobby or his goons around. Bobby seemed to have given up on his quest to catch Doug doing something that would get him expelled from school. Emma didn't understand Bobby's sudden change in strategy, but she was grateful for it. While Doug talked with Mr. Munsen in the bookstore's back room, Emma, Martha, and Sebastian browsed the bookshelves.

The first thing Doug did was tell Mr. Munsen about the dark-haired man and what had happened when he'd followed him to his room at the inn.

"Boy, didn't I tell ya not to put yerself in harm's way?" Mr. Munsen began when Doug had finished. "Ya could've gotten yerself killed."

"I know it was stupid," Doug conceded. "I just wanted to find out his room number. I had no idea he knew he was being followed."

"Those kinda folks are real sly like. They pretend they don't see ya when all the while they know exactly what yer up to. That fellow sounds like a professional, a hired hand. I doubt he was the buyer. Most likely he works for him. I reckon he's long gone by now."

"That's what I figured," Doug agreed. "That's why I didn't rush right over here to find you. The guy probably skipped out right after he tossed me out of his room." Doug stopped talking for a moment and let the events in the motel replay in his mind. Then with a sigh, he told Mr. Munsen what he was thinking. "You know, that guy might not have had anything to do with the Mortals, but he sure acted like he was up to no good."

"We'll never know for sure, but I'm guessin' he's part of this mess. Listen, son. This here is gettin' mighty dangerous. I'll only help ya if ya promise to stop doin' stupid stuff," Mr. Munsen admonished.

"I've learned my lesson," Doug said quietly.

"Your job is ta find the rest of the Mortals. Let me take care of the bad guys. Okay?" Mr. Munsen smiled then and clapped Doug on the back with a big meaty hand.

"Okay," Doug said when he could breathe again.

Satisfied that Doug would do as he promised, Mr. Munsen's expression grew serious once again. "I was waitin' for ya ta come by and see me. I think I've figured out how the Reaper is gettin' the Mortals out of the castle. Not only that, but I think I know where he's storing them until he can find a buyer."

"That's great!" Doug began.

"Hold yer horses there, boy. I said I think I know. We need to be sure before we try ta spring our trap. That's why I need ya ta call me when you deliver the next Mortal. I'll be watchin' the castle, and I'll know for certain then. Can you do that?"

"Yes, sir, but I've only got one sculpture left," Doug answered uncertainly. What if he couldn't find the last two Mortals? He'd need at least one more to spring the trap.

Mr. Munsen must have understood Doug's dilemma.

"There are two more sculptures out there, son. Have a little faith that you'll find them. Seems like the Lord's been with ya so far. He's not gonna quit ya now. Remember you've got me ta help ya. I'll take ya anywhere ya need ta go."

After the day he'd had, Mr. Munsen's kind words of encouragement were almost Doug's undoing. Doug felt the sting of tears at the back of his eyes, but he was determined not to give in to them.

Mr. Munsen waited quietly as Doug struggled to get a hold of himself. He could only imagine how hard this was for Doug, and it wasn't over yet.

"Thank you, sir," Doug finally managed. "You don't know how much I appreciate your help."

"I think I do," Mr. Munsen replied. Then he put an arm around Doug's shoulders and led him out of the storage room and back into the store where his friends waited.

"Well, what did Mr. Munsen say?" Sebastian asked when Doug came over to join them. Emma, Martha, and Sebastian had gotten tired of wandering around the store and were now seated around the table in the bookstore's front window.

"I'll tell you when we get back to the school," Doug answered hastily. Without waiting for the others, he headed for the door. Doug didn't mean to be rude, but he was still trying to pull himself together. He was afraid that if he stayed to talk, he might break down completely and start blubbering like a baby.

Martha raised her eyebrows at Doug's curtness but didn't say anything. It was obvious from his behavior that he was not in the mood for conversation. Without comment, the others followed Doug out into the frosty air.

A look at their watches revealed that the buses would be leaving to return to the school in fifteen minutes, so they made their way to the inn's parking lot. Hunkered down in their coats in an attempt to protect themselves from the icy wind, no one spoke. The first flakes of snow began to fall as they boarded the bus. Normally, Emma would have been delighted, but at the moment she was too worried about Doug to enjoy the first snow of the season.

Once on board, Emma and Martha sat toward the front again, and Doug and Sebastian took the seat directly behind them. As soon as all of the buses were loaded and the dorm advisors had checked their lists to verify that each of their charges were present, the buses pulled out of the parking lot and began the thirty-minute trip to the academy. The bus was fairly quiet on the ride back to the school. It had been a long day, and most of the students were content to sit back and watch the snow falling outside their windows.

Emma glanced back at Doug every now and then with a worried expression. Doug had his head leaned against the back of his seat with his eyes closed. He didn't look relaxed though. His face was unusually pale, and the lines around his mouth were drawn tight. There was no doubt about it; something was very wrong. Emma closed her own eyes and began to pray for her friend.

All Doug could think about on the ride back to the academy was how stupid he'd been to deliver that last sculpture without first talking to Mr. Munsen. Now the pressure was on to find at least one of the two remaining Mortals. He'd need one sculpture so that Mr. Munsen could check out his theory about how the Reaper was getting the sculptures out of the castle, and he'd need another one to actually spring the trap that would hopefully capture the creep. Doug's stomach tightened into a hard knot every time he thought about what would happen if he couldn't find either of the last two Mortals. Images of his dad and Lord Dinswood kept floating across his mind. He worried so much that soon he began to feel physically sick. Afraid that he would embarrass himself by vomiting right there on the bus, he laid his head on the back of his seat, closed his eyes, and tried to breathe deeply through his nose. Suddenly into his troubled mind came the words of Mr. Munsen. *Have a little faith. The Lord's been with you so far. He's not going to quit you now.* Unaccountably, Doug felt himself begin to relax. A moment later, he was sound asleep.

When they arrived back at the school, Doug gave them a brief recap of his conversation with Mr. Munsen. Emma immediately understood why Doug was so worried. In order for Mr. Munsen's plan to work, they had to find another sculpture, and they were running out of places to look. Emma knew that for the last several weeks Doug had worried that they wouldn't be able to find the last two. He had been hoping that, with Mr. Munsen's help, they would be able to catch the Reaper before the deadline. Then it wouldn't have been necessary to find any of the other sculptures. Of course, they intended to continue to search, but the pressure to actually find one would have been off their shoulders. More importantly, with the Reaper in jail, Doug's dad and Lord Dinswood would have been safe from harm.

"Don't worry, Doug. We'll find another Mortal," Sebastian said in an attempt to ease his friend's obvious worry. It seemed even Sebastian had understood the ramifications of Doug's words.

"Yeah, Doug. We can start looking again over Christmas break," Martha chimed in. She could see now why Doug had seemed so curt back in the bookstore. He had been sick with worry. Her heart went out to him.

Doug said nothing but stood with his head bent in a posture of defeat, his gaze focused on the floor. While he appreciated his friends' attempts to console him, it didn't change anything. The lives of two people were in his unsteady hands.

Emma looked at Doug's pale face and found herself getting angry. It was all so unfair. Doug had done nothing to deserve the situation in which he now found himself. For the hundredth time, Emma hoped that someday the Reaper would get what he deserved for putting Doug through this torment, and the sooner the better. As these thoughts passed through her mind, Emma felt her resolve growing along with her anger. They were at the mercy of a madman, and it was time to take matters into their own hands. In a strong and determined tone, Emma said, "We can do it, Doug. We can do it and we will."

Surprised at the certainty in her voice, Doug looked up at Emma. He could see the light of determination in her eyes, and he drew strength from it. He realized that he'd been on the brink of giving up, and it was much too soon for that. Besides it wasn't like him. He was a fighter. Emma's words had reminded him of that. Grateful for the reminder, Doug straightened his shoulders and nodded.

THE WEEKS BEFORE Christmas flew by in a blur. The weather remained dry and uncharacteristically cold. The temperature never rose above freezing even during the day. The light dusting of snow they'd had the day of their trip to Windland remained on the ground—the temperature never warming sufficiently to melt it.

The end of the semester was approaching, and every evening the library, lounge, and even the dining hall were filled with students studying for the upcoming final exams. An almost audible sigh of relief could be heard at the conclusion of the last day of school before Christmas break. The somber atmosphere that had characterized the castle for the past two weeks lifted, and the castle became a frenzy of activity as students prepared to head home for the holidays.

The next day, Emma and Martha watched from the ballroom windows as the last bus, filled with departing students, left for the airport. Bobby, along with his girlfriend Natalie, had been the last to board.

"I'm glad to see the back of Bobby Wilcox," Martha commented. "At least we won't have him to worry about when we go looking for another Mortal."

"I don't know," Emma replied. "Ever since we got back from that last trip to Windland, Bobby doesn't seem to be as interested in what Doug is doing."

"I guess I didn't notice," Martha said thoughtfully as she pursed her lips. "But now that you mention it, I haven't seen him hanging around the last couple of weeks. What do you suppose it means?"

"I have no idea, but I'm not about to look a gift horse in the mouth."

"Maybe he's been spending more time with his girlfriend," Martha conjectured.

Emma shrugged her shoulders. She had a feeling that there was more to it than that. She suspected that Doug knew the reason behind Bobby's sudden disinterest, but Doug wasn't talking, and she hated to bring it up. It didn't really matter now anyway. Bobby was gone, and they had two weeks to find another sculpture.

The day before Christmas was spent making plans for their next hunting expedition. They looked over their dwindling list of locations and tried to brainstorm spots within walking distance of the castle where they might look. Satisfied that they had done all they could for the time being, they enjoyed their supper and spent Christmas Eve playing games in the lounge.

That evening while everyone slept, volunteers from the senior class delivered the presents that had been sent by the parents of those students staying at the academy over the holiday. Each student's presents were stacked neatly outside his or her door, waiting to be opened on Christmas morning. As was the tradition at the academy, the senior volunteers were then treated to a party in the lounge.

Emma and Martha awakened early, too excited to sleep any longer. Opening the door to their room, they discovered two stacks of brightly wrapped boxes. They made quick work of transporting their gifts to their beds, and when both girls had completed the task and were sitting on their beds, they tore in and began unwrapping with gusto.

Emma's gifts included some much-needed clothes along with a new winter coat. In her last box, she found a pair of gloves and earmuffs to match. Considering the cold winter they were having, Emma was thrilled. At least, she would be able to stay warm while they searched for the remaining sculptures.

Martha opened all of her smaller boxes first. As with Emma, her gifts were mostly clothes—a couple of pairs of jeans and some new sweaters. Emma noticed that Martha was saving her biggest box for last. Having finished with her own gifts, Emma watched as Martha eagerly tore the wrapping away from her last and largest present. Martha removed the lid with a flourish, and both girls laughed when they saw what was inside. The box contained a winter coat very similar to the one Emma had received.

"I think our parents must have gotten together to buy our Christmas presents," Martha said with another laugh.

"I think you're right," Emma agreed. "Or maybe they just know what a cold winter we're having around here. Anyway, considering that we're going to be spending a lot of time outside this next week, I'm glad to get a warm coat."

"Me too," Martha agreed.

After cleaning up the scattered wrapping paper and piling their new clothes neatly on their beds, the two girls got dressed. A little later, they met up with the boys in the dining hall for breakfast. As had become their tradition, the four of them planned to open their presents to each other after breakfast in the lounge. When they were seated comfortably in a semicircle around the lounge's fireplace, Sebastian began nagging the others to let him go first. For their own peace of mind, they quickly agreed. Once he was given the go-ahead, Sebastian wasted no time. He opened his present from Martha first.

"Thanks, Martha. I can't wait to read it!" he exclaimed upon seeing the cookbook. "There's a third book in the series too," he added, laying in a hint for next year.

Martha raised an eyebrow and said, "Maybe if you're good, Santa will get it for you."

Sebastian's only response was a laugh. He was too eager to open his other presents to delay long.

When he opened Emma's present, he told her that he'd been hoping she'd get him chocolates again. Then he proceeded to select one from the box and pop it into his mouth. He offered some to the others, but they each declined. Sebastian then eyed the box that contained his present from Doug.

"What is it, Doug?" he asked curiously as he shook the box.

"Open it and find out," Doug answered with a grin.

Sebastian tore the wrapping away and opened the box. With a smile of pleasure, he lifted the contents out so everyone could see. Doug had gotten him a jersey with the name of his favorite hockey player written on the back.

"Thanks, Doug. It's just what I wanted."

"I know," Doug said, laughing. "You've been hinting for the last three months."

"Yeah, but I didn't think you were paying attention," Sebastian said sheepishly. Then with another thank you to everyone, Sebastian sat back with a satisfied smile and prepared to watch his friends open their presents.

They talked Doug into going next. The girls had hidden his hockey stick behind the curtains of the nearest window. While he opened Sebastian's present, they went over to get it. When they got back to where the boys were sitting, Doug was holding up a hockey jersey similar to the one he had given Sebastian.

"Thanks, Sebastian. I really like it," Doug said sincerely. When he saw the hockey stick, he exclaimed, "This is great! Dad got me a new pair of hockey skates. Now with this jersey and the new hockey stick, I'm all set. I can't wait to give everything a try!"

"That pond you told us about has to be frozen solid by now," Sebastian said eagerly. "Maybe we can go skating this afternoon."

Emma didn't want to ruin the moment by pointing out that she and Martha didn't have any skates, so she remained silent.

Martha went next. The boys had gone together to get her an easel and canvas. She liked the sketch pad and colored pencils Emma had gotten her, but she let out a cry of pleasure when she opened the box containing the picture frame.

"I love it, Emma," she exclaimed. "We'll have to get a picture of the two of us to put in it."

"Okay now, Emma. It's your turn," Doug said with a conspiratorial wink at the others. It seemed as if they had intentionally planned it so that Emma would go last. Her curiosity was piqued when only one box was brought out and placed before her. The box was larger than a shoebox but smaller than the box that had contained her winter coat.

Emma hesitated for a moment, wondering what on earth it could be.

"Go ahead and open it," Doug urged. "We all went together."

Emma carefully unwrapped the box, purposely taking her time to prolong the moment. This was her last present, and she wanted to enjoy it. When the paper had been removed and set aside, she grabbed hold of the lid and looked at her friends. The expectant looks on their faces had her wondering once again what could possibly be in the box. Then she lifted the lid and looked down. Whatever was inside was covered with tissue paper. Quickly, she moved the top layer of paper aside and couldn't believe her eyes. Nestled in more tissue paper was a brand-new pair of figure skates.

"I love them! How did you do it?" she cried as she hugged each of her friends in turn. "Thank you. Thank you. Thank you," she repeated with each hug.

"I asked Dad to get them for us on his last trip to Benton," Doug explained. "I already knew what size you needed."

Emma realized then that Doug had been planning this surprise since Thanksgiving. He'd been paying attention when she'd gotten her rental skates that day in Benton, so he'd know what size to buy. Although she knew the skates were from all of them, she was certain that it had been Doug's idea.

"Merry Christmas, Emma," Doug said with a smile.

Blinking back tears of joy, Emma looked at his handsome face and said, "Merry Christmas, Doug."

CHAPTER THIRTY-TWO
A CHRISTMAS MIRACLE

D oug left them after that to spend some time with his Dad and
Lord Dinswood. He wanted to give Lord Dinswood the rocking
chair he'd made for him, and he was hoping that Lord Dinswood
would feel like playing a game of chess. Doug promised to meet up
with them again at lunch.

The others passed the rest of the morning relaxing in the
lounge. Sebastian began reading the cookbook Martha had gotten
him while the girls worked on a puzzle in front of the fireplace.

True to his word, Doug rejoined them promptly at noon. After a sumptuous Christmas dinner, which included ham and turkey
and all the fixings, Sebastian suggested they go to the pond and give
their new skates a try.

"I've already asked Dad if we could go, and he said it was okay,"
Doug told them. "He checked the pond out yesterday to make sure
it was safe."

"Martha doesn't have any skates," Emma pointed out. As much
as she'd like to go skating, she wasn't going to go without her friend.

"Actually, I do," Martha said quickly. Then she went on to explain. "I knew that we were getting you a pair for Christmas, so

I brought mine from home when I came back from Thanksgiving break. I got them last winter, but I've only worn them a couple of times, so they're practically new. I'm glad to finally get some use out of them."

"Where are they?" Emma asked, wondering why she'd never seen them.

"I hid them under my bed," Martha replied with a sly grin.

"Now I know your hiding place," Emma said, laughing.

"I guess now I'll have to find a new one," Martha answered.

"Well are we going or not?" Sebastian interrupted.

Although it was below freezing outside, the sun was shining in a cloudless sky. Anxious to get out of the castle for a while, the others agreed to Sebastian's suggestion. They split up then to go to their respective dorm rooms to get ready.

A few minutes later, they met in the lobby and left the castle by way of the main entrance. The girls were bundled up in their new winter coats. In addition to their coats, they wore earmuffs and gloves to ward off the cold. The boys were wearing down jackets, knit caps, and gloves. They had tied the laces of their skates together and slung them over their shoulders so they could carry their hockey sticks. Seeing the logic in this method, the girls did likewise. Then they stuck their gloved hands in their pockets for extra warmth.

"What are you guys going to use for a hockey puck?" Martha asked as Doug led them around the east side of the castle.

"I've got one in my pocket," Sebastian informed her.

"I should have known," Martha replied.

"How far is the pond?" Emma asked.

"Not too far," Doug replied. "It's about a half mile from the castle."

Doug was leading them in a southeasterly direction. They passed behind the bus barn and then began an uphill track following a narrow path through the trees. Gradually, the trees began to thin out, and they were walking in an open field.

Although the sun was shining, it provided little warmth. Plumes of fog formed in front of their faces as their warm breaths encountered the frosty air. Emma hoped that once they started skating, the exercise would warm them up. Her new coat was doing a good job of keeping her trunk warm, but her face and legs were cold.

"We're almost there," Doug informed them a few minutes later. "It's just beyond those trees up ahead."

They passed to the east of the stand of trees Doug had indicated, and the pond came into view. It was a good-sized pond, covering more than an acre, and just as they had anticipated, it was frozen solid. Several benches were scattered around the pond's perimeter.

"Did Lord Dinswood have these benches put out here?" Martha asked just as Emma was opening her mouth to ask the same question.

"Yeah, this was one of his favorite fishing spots," Doug told them.

"There are fish in this pond?" Martha asked in surprise. "Where did they come from?"

"Lord Dinswood said Darius had the pond stocked with fish shortly after the castle was completed. There are largemouth bass, perch, channel catfish, and crappie. Dad and I come here to fish a couple of times each summer."

When they reached the pond, they sat on the benches to put their skates on. The girls sat together on one bench and the boys on another. Emma took off her gloves so she could lace up her skates the way Doug had shown her on their trip to the rink in Benton. By the time she was finished, her fingers were frozen. She quickly put her gloves back on and stuffed her hands in her coat pockets while she waited for Martha to finish lacing her skates. By the time the girls were ready, the boys were already on the ice pushing a puck around with their new hockey sticks.

"Are you guys going to play a game?" Martha asked. "Because if you are, we'll wait here until you're finished." Martha had watched enough hockey games to know that a flying puck could cause a lot of damage to an unprotected face, and she intended to keep all of her teeth.

"No," Sebastian answered. "I only brought the puck, so we could practice moving it over the ice. If you guys are ready, we'll stop."

"We're ready," Martha said quickly. She stood up and began making her way to the edge of the ice. She looked at Emma, who was still sitting on the bench, and motioned for her to follow.

Suddenly, Emma felt nervous. It had been a while since she'd last skated, and she didn't want to make an idiot of herself in front of her friends. Martha must have sensed Emma's reluctance because she came back to where Emma was sitting and looped her arm through Emma's.

"Come on," she said, pulling Emma to her feet. "You can't get better if you don't practice. Nobody here is going to laugh at you. Every now and then, I still wipe out myself, so I'm not exactly an expert. The boys have both played hockey so they've had a lot more practice than we have. There is absolutely nothing to be embarrassed about."

All of this was said as Martha led Emma to the edge of the pond, and by the time she was finished speaking, both girls were standing on the ice. The boys had put their sticks on one of the benches and were now skating over to them. Without hesitation, Doug grabbed Emma's hand.

"We'll start off slow just like we did that day in Benton. Then once you get the feel of the ice, we can go a little faster," Doug told her.

True to his word, Doug led her around the pond's perimeter. Much to her delight, Emma quickly grew accustomed to the feel of the ice. Her new skates did a good job of supporting her ankles, and they hardly bowed in at all. As her confidence grew, she stopped watching the ice and began to enjoy the passing scenery. She had to smile when she saw that Sebastian was skating alongside Martha but lacked the courage to take her hand.

Despite what Martha had told her only moments ago, Emma could tell she was a skilled skater. She glided along with strong, confident strokes, and her ankles were centered over the blades as they should be.

Sebastian quickly grew tired of skating slowly around the edge of the pond. Suddenly, he stopped keeping pace with Martha and began racing along the ice. He zipped around Emma and Doug until he caught up with Martha again, and then he started skating circles around her.

"Come on, Doug. Let's show these girls some hockey moves," Sebastian yelled.

"Let's show off, you mean," Martha stated in a matter-of-fact tone.

"That's exactly what I mean," Sebastian admitted with a grin as he continued to do loops around Martha—much to her annoyance. A moment later, he turned and began skating backward. *He makes it look so easy*, Emma thought with envy.

"Go ahead, Doug, before he makes Martha mad," Emma whispered. "I'll be okay on my own. I'm used to the ice now."

"You're doing great," Doug complimented her. "I'll be back," he added over his shoulder as he sped off to join Sebastian.

Martha waited for Emma to catch up with her, and the two girls skated along together as the boys showed off their skating skills.

"I wish I could do that," Emma commented to Martha.

"From the looks of it, you'll be skating circles around them in no time," Martha replied. "Once you've had a little more practice, I'll teach you how to do some tricks."

"That'd be great! I can't thank you guys enough for the skates. They're really nice."

"It was Doug's idea," Martha told her, confirming what Emma had suspected earlier.

Just then Sebastian left the ice to retrieve his and Doug's hockey sticks.

"How about you girls learn to handle a hockey stick? Doug and I can show you how," Sebastian offered. As he was speaking, he began trying to get the puck out of his pocket, but his bulky gloves made what should have been a simple task almost impossible. Just as he worked the puck free from the confining material of his coat pocket, he started to drop the hockey sticks he was holding in his left hand. While he was trying to regain his hold on the sticks, the puck flipped onto the ice and rolled to the center of the pond before coming to a rest.

Emma was closest to it, so without hesitation, she yelled, "I'll get it."

"I'll race you," she heard Martha shout behind her.

Emma's competitive nature kicked in, and she started skating faster than she'd ever skated before. She could hear Martha close on her heels. All was going well until Emma leaned a little too far forward on her right skate. One of the teeth on the front of the blade grabbed the ice, stopping her right leg's forward motion and throwing her off balance. Unable to recover, she landed flat on her belly and continued to slide toward the center of the pond like a seal on a waterslide. Emma finally came to a stop within a foot of the puck. She lay there for a moment—too mortified to look at the others. She expected to hear laughter, but instead she heard, "Emma, are you okay?" from each of her friends.

"I'm okay," Emma answered with a sigh. *I'm just a big klutz*, she thought. She was pushing herself up with her arms when a glint of something under the ice caught her eye. She stopped trying to get up and leaned closer to the ice for a better look. What she saw had her blinking in amazement. The ice was acting as a sort of magnifying glass, and resting on the bottom of the pond, she could clearly see a metal chest. The chest exactly matched the ones in which they'd found all of the other sculptures.

"Guys, you're not going to believe this!" Emma cried excitedly.

"What?" Sebastian asked, skating over to her.

Emma waited until Doug and Martha joined her and Sebastian, and then she pointed to the ice. "Look and tell me what you see," she told them, trying to hide a smile.

They all looked where she was pointing, and it took only a matter of seconds for them to process the information their eyes were sending their brains.

"I can't believe it!" Sebastian exclaimed. "Emma, you've done it again. If there's not a Mortal in that chest, I'll eat my hockey stick."

"I'm going to hold you to that," Martha said without hesitation. "Although, I'm actually hoping that you won't have to eat your hockey stick for two reasons. First, you could get splinters. And second, for Doug's sake, I really hope there's a Mortal in that chest."

Doug stood there looking down with an incredulous expression. He was certain the chest contained a sculpture. He couldn't explain how he knew, but he did. It was nothing short of a miracle that they'd found it. If the pond hadn't been so low due to lack of rain, they wouldn't have been able to see the bottom. Emma falling and sliding to a stop directly over the spot where the chest lay could not have been a mere coincidence. Mr. Munsen was right: the Lord was with them.

"There's a sculpture in there all right," Doug told the others. "We'll have to wait until spring to get it though. There's no way we can get to it now."

"I don't understand," Sebastian said with a frown. "This pond wasn't even on our list."

"It should have been," Martha interjected. "In one of Rebecca's journal entries, I remember her mentioning how much she enjoyed going fishing with Darius. She didn't give a location, and I just assumed they fished in the river. At the time, I didn't know about this pond or that it had been stocked with fish. I'm sorry, Doug."

"It's not your fault, Martha. You couldn't have known. We've found it now, and that's all that matters," Doug told her.

"Who wants to skate?" Sebastian asked, breaking the somber mood that had fallen.

They skated a while longer, and the boys let the girls use their hockey sticks to practice moving the puck around on the pond's frozen surface. Of course, the boys provided lots of instruction on proper puck handling techniques.

When the sun began to drop behind the trees, they decided to call it a day, and after taking off their skates, they started the journey back to the castle.

Doug whistled merrily as he led the way. A great weight had been lifted from his shoulders today. Now he could enjoy the rest of his vacation knowing that the sculpture was safe and sound on the bottom of the pond. There, it would wait until the four of them came back to get it after the spring thaw.

Taking his cue from Doug, Sebastian began singing the words to the Christmas carol Doug was whistling. Without any shyness or embarrassment, Sebastian sang out in a clear tenor voice. After their initial surprise, the girls joined in. Doug stopped whistling and sang along with the others. Soon the castle came into view with a welcoming light shining from each of its many windows.

Once inside, they put their coats away in their rooms and then spent some time warming themselves in front of the fireplace in the lounge. New logs had recently been added, so the fire was blazing nicely and putting out plenty of heat to thaw their frozen limbs. They had just regained the feeling in all of their toes when it was time to head to the dining hall for supper. There were still plenty of leftovers from the Christmas feast they'd had earlier that day. When they'd had their fill of turkey, dressing, and pie, they returned to the lounge and played charades with some of the other students until it was time for bed. The best part of the evening was that Doug was more relaxed than Emma had seen him in a long time. He really seemed to be enjoying himself during the game.

Later that night, after preparing for bed, Emma laced her new ice skates together and hung them over the bedpost at the foot of her bed. As she climbed into bed, she thought back over the day and decided it had been a Christmas that she would never forget.

CHAPTER THIRTY-THREE
WAITING FOR SPRING

The rest of the Christmas break passed quickly. They went skating every day, and by the end of the week, Emma could skate backward and do some of the tricks that Martha had taught her. She still wasn't as good as Martha or the boys, but she was getting there.

The rest of the student body began returning on Saturday. The noise level around the castle rose substantially as the dorms were once again filled with chattering students.

On Sunday, after chapel, it began to snow. It began as big fat flakes drifting down lazily from a gray sky, but it soon turned into a full-blown blizzard. By the time it stopped snowing on Monday afternoon, more than two feet of snow covered the ground.

After classes concluded on Monday, excited students headed outside to enjoy the first real snow of the season. Some built igloos and forts and had snowball fights, while others worked on creating the most unique snowman. A number of sleds and toboggans had been purchased over the summer and stored in the bus barn for just such an occasion. These were brought out, and students took turns riding them down the steep hill on the west side of the school. Doug, Sebastian, Emma, and Martha chose a toboggan big enough for four and spent the hour before supper trying to get their best time down the hill. They pretended they were entered in the Olympics as a four-man bobsled team. Sebastian was hilarious as he assumed the role of coach for the team.

By the time everyone was called in for supper, the front lawn was dotted with a multitude of snowmen in various shapes and sizes, and the snow on the west side of the castle was packed down from all of the tobogganing.

Ravenous from the fresh air and exercise, students quickly put their coats away in their rooms and hurried to the dining hall where they feasted on turkey pot pie. Conversation was light while everyone concentrated on satisfying their hunger.

After the meal, Emma, Martha, Doug, and Sebastian collected their books and went to the library to do their homework. Mr. Criderman was sitting behind the counter, keeping a watchful eye on the studiers. Emma hoped he wouldn't start flirting with the senior girls again. It made her sick to watch it. She hadn't wanted to study in the library, but the lounge was full. Thankfully, there weren't any older girls in the library at the moment. As the evening wore on, Emma noticed that the majority of the students in the library were boys. Maybe Mr. Criderman's behavior had made the senior girls uncomfortable, so now they were avoiding him. Emma hoped so. It would serve him right. Mr. Criderman may be good looking, but he was way too old for high school girls.

The rest of the evening went without incident. They finished their homework and then retired to their respective dorm rooms. It had been a busy day, and everyone was tired. Emma fell asleep the minute her head hit the pillow and slept soundly the entire night.

The next day, Emma found herself looking forward to her PE class. The day before, they had begun the unit on English country dancing. Every year, students at Dinswood Academy were instructed in dances that were popular in seventeenth-and-eighteenth-century England. Then in the spring of their junior and senior years, they were invited to attend a ball. Those who attended wore costumes of the period and danced to music provided by a small live orchestra. The ball was held in lieu of a prom. Emma had loved the idea of a ball from the moment she'd learned about it and couldn't wait until her junior year so she could attend.

For the next several weeks, the boys and girls would have PE together. Doug and Sebastian did not have PE the same hour as Emma and Martha, so they could not be the girls' partners. Yesterday, Emma and Martha had stood in line as Mr. Dorfman had brought the boys' PE class in. Just like last year, the boys had been instructed to stand opposite the girl they wished to partner for the unit. Phil had quickly taken the spot opposite Emma. Emma was pleased because he had been her partner last year, and she knew he was a good dancer. Martha had waited nervously to see who her partner would be. Sebastian had been her partner last year, and although he'd been rather clumsy at first, he'd gradually gotten the hang of it. Since Sebastian wasn't an option this year, Martha hoped that at least she'd get someone who wouldn't stomp on her feet. Martha had been relieved when Tom had taken the spot across from her. She'd never seen him dance, but at least he was someone she already knew.

As Emma dressed for PE class later that day, she realized that Phil and Tom would probably rather be dancing with their girlfriends, but since Kim and Cindy didn't have PE in the same hour, she and Martha would just have to do. Emma tried not to think about whom Doug would be partnering during the dance unit. She found herself getting jealous just thinking about it. After some thought, Emma decided it would be better if she didn't know the girl's name, so she made a promise to herself that she wouldn't ask.

Emma and Martha entered the ballroom and waited with the rest of the girls in their class for the boys to come in. Last year, they had learned the steps to dances titled "A Trip to Highgate," "The Touchstone," and "The Barley Mow." Yesterday they had spent the hour reviewing these dances. Today, they would begin learning one of three new dances. The new dances were titled "Pleasures of the Town," "The Happy Captive," and "The Comical Fellow." Emma knew nothing about the new dances, but their titles implied that they would be bright and lively.

As the next couple of weeks went by, Emma's conjecture about the dances they were learning turned out to be true. The music for each dance had an upbeat tempo. This made the new dances more enjoyable for the boys and good exercise for everyone. On the last day of the dance unit, they were tested not only on the new dances, but also on the three they'd learned last year. At the end of the period, both Miss Krum and Mr. Dorfman complimented the class on how well they'd performed each dance. Emma hated to see the unit end but consoled herself with the fact that it would come around again next year.

It continued to snow off and on through the middle of March. Just when everyone began to think that spring would never come, the snow melted and the day-to-day temperatures started to climb. The first Saturday in April, Emma, Martha, and Sebastian accompanied Doug to check out the pond. The sun was shining, and the temperature had risen to the midfifties. It was the warmest day they'd had since last fall. When they got to the pond, they saw that it had completely thawed, but when they tested the water, it was ice cold.

"It's too bad we don't have neoprene dive suits," Sebastian said after sticking his hand in the water at the edge of the pond. "We'll have hypothermia for sure if we try to get the chest now."

Doug said nothing but nodded in agreement. The pond was deeper than it had been in the fall. The winter snows had restored it to its usual level. Not only did they have cold water to contend with, there was more of it.

"How are you going to bring the chest up?" Martha asked.

"I'll have to swim down and tie a rope around it," Doug answered. "Then we can pull it up." Doug hoped it would be as easy as he'd just made it sound. He sighed and ran a hand through his hair. The truth was he hated having to wait. With every passing day, he was getting more and more anxious to get this whole business over with. In that moment, he made a decision. He'd give it to the end of April. Then he would come for the chest regardless of how cold the water was.

"I'll help you, Doug," Sebastian quickly offered. As if he could read Doug's mind, he added, "Whenever you want to go for it, I'm in."

"Thanks," Doug replied. "As much as I'd like to get this over with, it's way too cold to try it now."

They wandered around the pond a while longer and then headed back to the castle. It had been good to get outside and get some fresh air. As they walked, Martha wondered yet again why Bobby Wilcox hadn't tried to follow them when they had left the castle. She decided it was time to ask Doug about it.

"Why isn't Bobby Wilcox spying on us anymore? Ever since Christmas, he's been leaving us alone. What gives?"

Doug hesitated for a moment before answering. He had no intention of telling the girls what had happened at the inn that day in Windland. He hadn't told Sebastian either. Choosing his words carefully, he said, "All I can tell you is that Bobby and I have worked out a truce of sorts. It's only temporary though—just to the last day of school."

"Why would Bobby agree to a truce?" Martha asked.

"I don't really know," Doug answered truthfully. "I'm just glad he did."

Martha continued to look at Doug with a frown. She wasn't satisfied with his answer, but she decided not to press the issue. It was obvious Doug wasn't going to say any more on the subject. Surely Bobby had demanded something in return for leaving Doug alone, but Martha couldn't begin to imagine what that might have been. She couldn't think of anything Doug had that Bobby would want. *Other than his good looks, great personality, and athleticism that is*, Martha thought with a wry grin. Thankfully, these were not things that Doug could give away.

Emma listened to the exchange between Doug and Martha with interest. Like Martha, she suspected that Bobby had demanded some kind of payment in return for agreeing to the truce. She hadn't asked Doug about it herself because she had been certain that he wouldn't tell her. His answer to Martha just now confirmed her suspicions. It seemed that at least for now, the terms of the truce would remain a secret.

CHAPTER THIRTY-FOUR
DISTURBING NEWS

The temperature remained mild the next couple of weeks, some days even rising into the sixties. Doug began making plans to get the sculpture from the pond.

Trips to Windland had resumed at the end of March, and the freshman class would be going the last weekend in April. Even though Bobby had been keeping to the truce, Doug decided it was best not to take any chances, so he planned to get the sculpture on the Saturday that Bobby would be in Windland. The water would still be pretty cold, but they couldn't wait any longer. The Reaper's deadline was fast approaching.

The Monday before the planned excursion to the pond, Martha, Emma, and Sebastian were sitting in the dining hall having their breakfast. Doug had gone upstairs to his dad's suite to see if he could get a couple of things they would need that Saturday, namely a couple of diving masks and a dive light. He had told Sebastian to go on to breakfast, and he would meet everyone in a few minutes.

Emma was halfway through her bowl of cereal when Doug came in. He was carrying an envelope in his hand and was visibly upset. Not wanting to attract the attention of the other diners,

Emma waited until he got to the table before asking, "Doug, what's wrong?"

"I went upstairs to get some stuff for Saturday and then took it to our room. On my way here, I decided to check my mail. This was in my box," Doug explained with a grim expression. Saying nothing more, he handed the envelope to Emma.

With shaking fingers, Emma pulled a folded piece of paper from the envelope. After some fumbling, she finally managed to open the note and immediately recognized the handwriting as that of the Reaper. The first thought that went through Emma's mind was that the Reaper had decided to move the deadline up, but after a quick scan of the note, she realized he was demanding something far worse than an earlier deadline.

"Can you believe it?" Doug asked furiously as he took a seat next to Sebastian.

"One of you guys wanna fill us in?" Sebastian asked, looking back and forth between Emma and Doug. "I'm guessing the note was from the Reaper, but what did he ask for now—the Crown Jewels?"

"He might as well have," Doug replied.

"He wants Doug to get the sculpture that Lord Dinswood already has in his possession," Emma told the others when Doug didn't elaborate.

After a shocked silence, Martha blurted out, "And just how are you supposed to do that? It's locked in a safe in his room. That guy is completely insane! Does he think you're a professional safecracker or something?"

"It's bad enough that I've been lying to Lord Dinswood all this time, telling him there are no more sculptures out there. Now I guess I'm supposed to steal from him too," Doug exclaimed angrily.

"How soon does he want it?" Sebastian asked.

"The note doesn't give a specific deadline, so I'm assuming he wants it along with the others before the last day of school," Doug answered.

"No problem then. With the sculpture we found in the pond, we've got all we need to catch him. He'll be in jail before the end of school," Sebastian reasoned.

"You're right," Doug agreed, surprising Sebastian. He had no intention of stealing from Lord Dinswood. The only other option was to catch the creep before it became necessary.

"Why do you suppose the Reaper has suddenly decided he wants the sculpture Lord Dinswood has?" Martha asked, breaking the brief silence that had fallen.

"My guess is that he's found a buyer, but the buyer wants the complete set," Doug responded. It was one of the things Doug had been worrying about since receiving the Reaper's very first note. Why would anyone be satisfied with only six of the seven sculptures Marnatti had so skillfully crafted?

"That makes sense," Martha said. "But I still don't understand how the Reaper expects you to get it."

"It's simple. Lord Dinswood trusts me."

"It doesn't hurt that he treats you like his grandson. He'd probably just give you the thing if you asked for it," Sebastian chimed in.

"That's exactly why I can't do it," Doug countered. There was no way he could break Lord Dinswood's trust. In his weakened state, it might very well kill the old man, and that's exactly what Doug was trying to prevent.

"Well then I guess it's time to reap the Reaper," Sebastian quipped.

Doug didn't say anything but nodded his agreement. After they got the sculpture from the pond on Saturday, Doug would call Mr. Munsen and set the plan in motion. It just had to work!

CHAPTER THIRTY-FIVE
DIVING FOR BURIED TREASURE

After a week that seemed, at least to Doug, to last an eternity, Saturday finally arrived. As soon as the buses left for Windland, Doug, Sebastian, Martha, and Emma set out for the pond. Thankfully, the weather was cooperating. The sun was out, and the temperature was supposed to rise into the midsixties by noon. Doug and Sebastian carried backpacks containing their diving masks and towels. They were wearing their swimming trunks under their jeans. The girls carried a coil of rope, a crowbar, and a small shovel so the boys could dig around the chest if necessary.

When they got to the pond, the boys hurriedly stripped down to their swimming trunks. Before entering the water, they tied a branch about a foot long and an inch in diameter around the end of the rope hoping it would make it easier to slip it under the trunk. Then they put their diving masks on and waded into the water.

Both boys sucked in their breaths at the coldness of the water.

"This water is seriously cold," Sebastian exclaimed with a shudder.

Emma noticed goose bumps had appeared on the arms and upper bodies of both Doug and Sebastian. She felt sorry for them having to swim in such cold water. She just hoped it didn't make them sick.

"There's no way to ease into it," Doug said. "We're better off to just dive right in."

Neither boy spoke as they contemplated the unpleasant task ahead. Then taking a few deep breaths, they disappeared beneath the water. The initial shock of the cold water breaking over his head nearly took Doug's breath away. With conscious effort, he ignored the cold and kicked strongly down toward the center of the pond where the water was approximately eight feet deep. The water was a little murky, but the sunlight penetrated all the way to the bottom, and as Doug got closer, he could see the chest without difficulty. Doug had the end of the rope with the branch tied to it, and Sebastian was following close behind with the little shovel. The first thing they had to do was loosen the chest from the mud in which it had settled so they could slip the rope beneath it.

The girls watched anxiously from the bank while the boys worked. Every now and then, one or the other of their heads would break the surface, as they came up for air. After several minutes, Sebastian swam to the edge of the pond with the end of the rope. Doug was right behind him. Once on shore, both boys began pulling on the rope. In moments, the chest appeared, and the boys were able to drag it onto dry land.

It was then that Emma noticed both boys were shivering uncontrollably and that their lips were blue.

"You guys better dry off and get dressed before we open this thing. You both look positively frozen," Emma told them.

"I think you're right," Doug agreed. Up until then, he'd been too busy to notice how cold he was.

"Even my g-goose b-bumps have g-goose b-bumps," Sebastian stammered between frozen lips.

A sudden breeze had both boys grabbing their backpacks and disappearing behind a thick stand of cedar trees where they quickly shed their wet swimming trunks and dressed in the dry clothes they'd brought.

"Whew, I feel much better!" Sebastian exclaimed as they made their way back to the girls wearing jeans and hoodies once again.

"Yeah, me too," Doug replied absently. He was already thinking about what might be in the chest they'd just recovered.

When they rejoined the girls, Doug wasted no time. He grabbed the crowbar and began working on the padlock. After a few attempts, the padlock broke, and Doug knelt down to open the chest. Most of the water in the chest had drained out when it had been drug on shore, but the contents of the chest were still pretty soggy. The chest was filled with wet hay, and in the middle of all of the wet hay was an object wrapped in strips of linen cloth. Carefully, Doug lifted the object from the chest and began removing the linen wrappings. The strips of cloth were soaked, making them a little harder to unwind. Gradually, a form began to take shape, and there was no longer any doubt. They had successfully recovered another one of Marnatti's Mortals.

Emma held her breath as the last linen covering was removed. In Emma's view, the sculpture in Doug's hands was the most beautiful they'd seen thus far. Emma smiled to herself when she realized that she had thought the same thing about every single one of the Mortals they'd found. "This time it's true," she told herself.

The woman Marnatti had sculpted was kneeling and had her hands folded in prayer. A long scarf covered her head and fell nearly to her waist in the back. The woman's head was bowed, and although her features were beautiful, it wasn't her beauty that had Emma gasping in awe. There were tears on the woman's cheeks and tracks of tears as if some had already fallen. If Emma hadn't known better, she would have sworn that the sculpture was actually crying.

"I don't know how Marnatti did it," Martha said excitedly beside Emma. "It really looks like she's crying."

"That's just what I was thinking," Emma agreed.

"Who is it?" Sebastian asked.

Doug turned the sculpture over and looked at the underside of the base. "It's Hannah."

"That explains why she's crying," Emma said.

"Who is Hannah, and why is she crying?" Sebastian asked.

Martha was tempted to give Sebastian a hard time for not remembering the story, but she wisely held her tongue and left it up to Emma to answer him.

Emma was more than happy to relate the tale of Hannah. "In the beginning of 1 Samuel in the Old Testament, it tells of a man named Elkanah who had two wives. One wife was Peninnah, and the other was Hannah. Peninnah had children, but Hannah did not. Every year when Elkanah would go to Shiloh to worship and to sacrifice to the Lord, he would give portions of meat to Peninnah and to each of her sons and daughters, and he would give a double portion to Hannah because he loved her even though she was barren. And every year during this time, Peninnah would take great delight in taunting Hannah about her childless condition. Hannah would become so upset and miserable that she wouldn't eat. Year after year this went on until I guess Hannah had had enough. After the meal, which of course Hannah didn't eat, she went to the temple. As she wept, she prayed to the Lord for a son and vowed that if the Lord would grant her request, she would give this son in service to the Lord. The Lord answered her prayer, and in due time, Hannah had a son and named him Samuel."

"Did she keep her vow?" Sebastian asked totally engrossed in the story.

"Yep, as soon as he was weaned, she took Samuel and left him with the priests," Emma answered. "Every year she would make him a little robe and take it to him when the family went up for their annual sacrifice."

"Did she ever have more children?" Doug couldn't help asking. Then he looked a little embarrassed. "I mean I kind of forgot the story too."

"Well, the answer to your question is yes. She had three more sons and two daughters," Emma replied, trying to hide her smile. "It's one of my favorite stories, so that's why I know it so well."

"You can see how that story would relate to Rebecca," Martha pointed out. "Rebecca waited nine years for a child. Then finally the miracle happened. Darius probably commissioned the sculpture of Hannah shortly after they found out she was pregnant."

"It was the last sculpture she ever received," Doug said quietly. "Remember, Lord Dinswood told us Rebecca died before he could give her the last one."

Doug shook his head, as if to clear it, and then stood up and began wrapping the sculpture in his towel. When he was finished, he put it in his backpack. "We'd better get back to the castle. I've got to give Mr. Munsen a call and set up a time to deliver the next sculpture to the Reaper."

"So Mr. Munsen thinks he knows how the Reaper is getting the sculptures out of the castle?" Martha's question was more of a statement. Doug had already told them that much. She was probing to see if Doug knew more than he had previously shared with them.

"Not only that, but he thinks he knows where the Reaper is hiding them all until he can sell them." Doug stopped talking then and looked at each of them in turn before continuing. "And before any of you ask, he hasn't told me anything other than that. He thinks it's best if I don't know all of the details."

"He's probably afraid you'll try to go after the guy yourself," Sebastian hypothesized.

"Maybe," Doug replied with a shrug.

It didn't escape Emma's notice that Doug hadn't denied Sebastian's allegation. Sebastian was right. It was obvious from Doug's expression that he wanted to be more involved in the plan to capture the Reaper. Mr. Munsen had been wise not to give Doug too much information.

When they got back to the castle, Doug went to his room to hide the sculpture, and then he went up to his dad's suite to return the items he'd borrowed. He planned to call Mr. Munsen on his dad's private line. He knew his dad had gone to Benton on school business, so he wouldn't have to worry about being overheard.

After a short conversation with Mr. Munsen, everything was set. Doug would hang the school banner in his dorm window next Friday morning and deliver one of the sculptures that evening. Mr. Munsen promised he would be ready and waiting.

Doug spent the next week in an almost constant state of anxiety. Concentrating on his schoolwork was nearly impossible. All he could think about was the possibility that Mr. Munsen's theories were wrong. Then they'd be back to square one. If they didn't catch the Reaper before the deadline, they would be forced to steal the sculpture of Ruth from Lord Dinswood, and they would have to find Marnatti's last Mortal. Doug's stomach knotted painfully every time he thought about either eventuality. The other sculptures had been discovered mostly by accident. In Doug's view, it had been a string of miracles. He didn't know if it was possible or even proper to expect another one.

Friday evening finally arrived. Doug snuck the sculpture of Mary into the storage room beneath the kitchen and put it in the barrel. Then he returned to the lounge where Emma, Martha, and Sebastian waited.

"Well, my part's done," Doug reported as soon as he saw his friend's anxious faces. "Now it's up to Mr. Munsen."

"When will you know something?" Martha asked.

"I'll call him in the morning, but we don't really have any way of knowing when the Reaper will try to move the sculpture. Mr. Munsen is assuming he'll try to get it out of the castle tonight."

"That makes sense," Sebastian said. "The Reaper would want to move it at night under cover of darkness, and he wouldn't want to leave it in the barrel too long and risk it being discovered by someone else."

"That's not likely considering we're probably the only other people in the whole castle that know about the little room behind the refrigerator," Doug replied.

"You don't know that for sure though, do you?" Sebastian countered. "And neither does the Reaper."

"Sebastian makes a good point," Martha said, surprising Sebastian. It wasn't often that she agreed with him. "I think the Reaper will try to move it tonight."

"Well, we'll know soon enough," Doug said with a sigh.

CHAPTER THIRTY-SIX

A NEW TRADITION AT DINSWOOD

Doug spent the night with his dad so he could call Mr. Munsen the moment his dad left for breakfast in the morning. As soon as the door closed behind Dean Harwood the next morning, Doug dashed to the phone and dialed Mr. Munsen's number. While he waited impatiently for someone to answer on the other end, it occurred to him that it was only seven thirty. He didn't know how late Mr. Munsen normally slept. He might very well be getting the man out of bed. Surely Mr. Munsen would forgive him under the circumstances.

"Hello," a male voice answered on the third ring.

Doug was relieved to hear Mr. Munsen's voice and not that of his wife or daughter. Taking a deep breath, he asked the million-dollar question. "What happened last night?"

"Doug, I figured it was you," Mr. Munsen said in a voice much quieter than his usual booming tones. It was obvious he was trying to make sure he wouldn't be overheard.

"I'm sorry if I woke you, sir," Doug began.

Mr. Munsen interrupted before Doug could go on. "No need to apologize, son. I understand how anxious you are to hear how things went last night, and I won't make you wait any longer. Everything was exactly as I'd figured. All we need to do now is set a time to spring the trap."

Doug was so relieved that for a moment he couldn't speak. His legs went weak, and he had to sit down. After a few deep breaths, he finally managed to pull himself together.

"Mr. Munsen, I can't thank you enough!"

"Don't thank me yet, boy. We've still gotta catch this bum. I was thinkin' I could have everything in place next Saturday. That sound okay to you?"

"It sounds great," Doug agreed quickly. He couldn't believe that the nightmare he'd been living the last several months was almost over.

Mr. Munsen must have understood some of what Doug was feeling because he said, "It's almost over, son. Hang in there."

"I will," Doug replied after a moment. Mr. Munsen was right; it wasn't over yet. He needed to stay strong for just a little while longer.

They talked a minute or two more to finalize their plans for Saturday. It wasn't until Doug hung up the phone that he realized that next Saturday was the night of the junior-senior ball. Things couldn't have worked out better. While the entire school was focused on the dance, he would be focused on trying to catch a thief. The net would be cast, but what if the Reaper somehow managed to slip through the net? A plan began to form in Doug's mind—a way he could make sure that the Reaper didn't elude Mr. Munsen. He was sure neither Mr. Munsen nor his friends would approve of his idea, so he decided to keep it to himself. He knew what he was planning was risky, but if it would guarantee the capture of the Reaper, it was well worth the risk. With his decision made, Doug left his dad's suite and headed downstairs to breakfast. He knew his friends would be in the dining hall waiting eagerly to hear the results of his conversation with Mr. Munsen.

"Mr. Munsen was right about everything," Doug told them as soon as he had taken a seat across from the girls and next to Sebastian. "Now we can get this guy."

Emma could only imagine how relieved Doug must be. He hadn't been himself all last week. When they had met to study in the evenings, it had been obvious that his mind was somewhere else. Emma knew how worried he was. She had tried to reassure him on several occasions and so had Martha and Sebastian, but their words of encouragement had fallen on deaf ears. Emma really couldn't blame him. She'd have been just as worried if she were in his shoes. All she could do was pray that Mr. Munsen would come through. Emma knew that Doug had been praying the same thing, and now it looked like their prayers would be answered.

"When are you going to set the trap?" Martha asked, breaking into Emma's thoughts.

"This coming Saturday."

"That's the night of the junior-senior ball!" Martha exclaimed.

"I know," Doug said with a nod.

Everyone was quiet for a moment as they remembered what they'd been doing the same night last year.

"Boy, it seems like everything happens on the night of the ball," Sebastian said finally, putting voice to what the others had been thinking.

"Well, things turned out okay last year. Maybe they will this year too," Doug replied. He didn't tell them about the plan he'd come up with to make sure that things turned out okay. They would try to talk him out of it, or worse yet, they would insist on being a part of it. Doug knew that what he was planning was dangerous, and he didn't want to put his friends' lives at risk.

———— ❧ ————

THE JUNIOR-SENIOR BALL was traditionally held on the evening of the first Saturday in May. This year was no different. As Doug, Sebastian, Emma, and Martha ate breakfast that Saturday morning, the noise level in the dining hall was almost unbearable as students chattered excitedly about the night ahead.

Even though she was too young to attend the dance, Emma was looking forward to it almost as much as the juniors and seniors. Those who attended the ball were required to dress in the clothes of the period, and Emma loved seeing the girls in their fancy gowns. Every year, a couple of hairstylists came from Benton to fix the girls' hair in styles that were popular in eighteenth-century England. Sometimes the transformation from present-day to the eighteenth century was so complete that even the senior girls Emma knew were difficult to recognize. Emma had to admit the boys looked pretty impressive in their formal wear too.

The underclassmen were always allowed to watch the proceedings in the ballroom from the terrace. Then at nine o'clock, they were shooed to their dorm rooms by the chaperones. Both Emma and Martha planned to stay on the terrace as long as possible tonight. Doug and Sebastian weren't all that keen on watching the dancers, but as there was nothing much else to do, they agreed to accompany the girls.

"When are you going to deliver the sculpture of Hannah?" Sebastian asked Doug as he raised a spoonful of cereal to his mouth.

"I thought I'd do it a few minutes after curfew. I'm gonna spend the night with Dad, so I figured I'd take care of it before going upstairs. The coast should be clear then, and if anyone stops me, I can say I'm headed up to Dad's suite."

Doug looked into his cereal bowl as he spoke. He was afraid that if Sebastian could see his eyes, he'd know he was lying. Only part of what he'd just told Sebastian was true. Doug planned to make his delivery after curfew, but he was not going to spend the night with his dad. Doug was going to put the sculpture in the barrel and then hide out in the room beneath the kitchen until the Reaper came to claim his prize. Then Doug would follow him.

If Sebastian thought he was spending the night with his dad, he wouldn't know what Doug was really up to. Doug hated lying to his friend, but he didn't feel like he had a choice. There was too much at stake.

"Do you want me to go with you?" Sebastian asked.

His offer of help made Doug feel even worse.

"No thanks. I'd better do it myself. If we got caught, you wouldn't have a good reason for being out after curfew."

"And you would," Sebastian finished for him. "I guess you're right. I just don't like you going down to that creepy room alone."

"It's not so bad. I'm used to it by now," Doug responded, trying to sound casual. Tonight of all nights, he didn't want Sebastian tagging along, but he also didn't want to hurt his friend's feelings. Thankfully, Sebastian didn't insist and let the matter drop.

As soon as breakfast was over, Doug hurried to his room. He wanted to get everything ready for the night ahead. After making sure that he was alone, Doug took the sculpture of Hannah from its hiding place in his closet and wrapped it in a towel. Then he put it in his backpack along with a flashlight. He patted his pocket to make sure he had the Swiss Army knife Emma had given him the Christmas before last. It had saved his life last year, and ever since then, it had been sort of a lucky charm for him. Once Doug was satisfied that he had packed everything he'd need, he returned the backpack to his closet and went to rejoin his friends.

While the older students spent the day preparing for the evening's big event, most of the underclassmen spent the day outdoors enjoying the fine weather. It was a beautiful spring day—sunny and warm with only a slight breeze. Doug, Sebastian, Emma, and Martha spent the morning playing croquet, and in the afternoon some of the sophomores organized an impromptu badminton tournament. The day passed quickly, and by suppertime everyone was famished.

The dining hall was less crowded than usual as the juniors and seniors weren't present. They would be treated to a separate, more elegant meal in the ballroom.

Even though the eleventh and twelfth graders were missing, the dining hall was just as noisy. A general feeling of excitement could be felt throughout the room.

"From the sound of it, you'd think we were all going to the ball," Sebastian said loudly so he could be heard over the din.

"I know," Martha shouted back.

Sebastian nodded to indicate he'd heard her.

They didn't try to converse anymore after that but instead concentrated their efforts on finishing their meal. As soon as they were finished, they emptied their trays and left the dining hall.

"Whew, it's good to be out of there. I thought my head was going to explode from all the noise," Sebastian exclaimed.

"I think mine did," Emma agreed with a laugh.

"What do you guys wanna do until the dance starts?" Sebastian asked the group.

"Why don't we play cards in the lounge?" Martha suggested.

The others agreed, and the next couple of hours were spent companionably in the lounge. Finally, the strains of the little orchestra tuning up could be heard drifting down the hall from the ballroom.

"It's getting ready to start!" Martha cried excitedly. "Let's go outside."

"Oh joy," Sebastian said with a sour expression that didn't match his words.

"We might as well go," Doug said, laughing. "The girls won't leave us alone until we do."

"I'll go, but I don't have to like it."

"Stop fussing, Sebastian, and come on," Martha urged as she grabbed his arm and began pulling on it.

"Okay. Okay," Sebastian said with an exaggerated sigh.

Dutifully, the boys followed the girls outside to the terrace. There was already quite a crowd gathered when they arrived. It was hard to see what was going on inside the ballroom with so many students milling about.

"This is crazy," Sebastian complained. "We can't even see."

"Be patient," Martha said as she stood on tiptoe in an effort to see over all the heads between her and the ballroom's French doors.

Sebastian tried to be patient, but it wasn't long until he'd had all the standing around he could take. He was just about to tell the girls that he was leaving when he was struck by a sudden idea.

"Hey, I just had a great idea," Sebastian told the others.

"Uh-oh. Here we go," Martha said, rolling her eyes.

"No really. I think you'll like this idea."

"Okay, let's hear it," Martha responded in a tone that indicated she was fully prepared to totally dislike Sebastian's idea.

"We can hear the music from the ballroom, right?"

"Right," Martha agreed. She had no clue what he was getting at, but at least he had succeeded in arousing her curiosity.

"Well, instead of standing around here gawking, why don't we have a little dance of our own? We know these dances just as well as the seniors do, and we've got the whole lawn to dance on. What do you think, Martha? Are you game?"

"Sebastian, I think that's a great idea, but there are only four of us."

"I bet if we start, others will join in," Doug said. He liked the idea of getting a chance to dance with Emma.

Emma felt a little thrill of excitement at Doug's words. She had expected him to be against the idea, but it seemed just the opposite was true. Could it be that she was finally going to get an opportunity to dance with Doug?

"I see Phil and Kim and Tom and Cindy over there by the rail," Sebastian said, really warming to his idea. "I bet they'll dance with us. I'll go over and ask them. Be right back."

In a minute, Sebastian returned with a big grin on his face. "They're in. Come on."

Without another word, Sebastian led the way down the stairs, around the fountain, and onto the front lawn. The music was fainter here, but it was loud enough for their purposes. They took up the positions for the Barley Mow and began the dance just as they'd learned it in PE class. At first, those on the terrace just looked on in astonishment, but it wasn't long until others began to drift down to the lawn and either join their group or start a group of their own. Susie and Daniel appeared a few minutes later, and Emma wondered briefly where Clarice and Reggie were. She didn't have to wonder long because Clarice came down the steps just then with Reggie in tow.

"There's nothing else to do," Clarice explained as she and Reggie took places next to Susie and Daniel.

After she had recovered from her initial shock, Emma was glad that Clarice had decided to join in the fun. She was especially happy for Reggie who appeared to be enjoying himself immensely.

Miss Jennings, who was out on the terrace to supervise the onlookers, watched the spontaneous lawn dancers with a big smile. In a moment, she went over and opened some of the ballroom's doors so the music could be heard outside more clearly. Miss Grimstock was inside chaperoning the ball. When she saw Miss Jennings open the doors, curiosity drew her outside. Emma could have sworn she saw her smile when she saw what was going on.

That night, a new tradition was started at Dinswood Academy. Every year, from that night on, while the juniors and seniors were enjoying their ball in an exquisitely appointed ballroom, the underclassmen enjoyed a ball of their own under the stars.

Emma couldn't remember when she'd had so much fun. It was wonderful dancing with Doug. Although the type of dancing they were doing rarely called for couples to be in a proper hold, she at least had the pleasure of holding Doug's hand and promenading beside him when the dance required it. As she had suspected, he was an excellent dancer. He knew all the steps and had perfect timing. Even more satisfying was the fact that he seemed to be enjoying himself just as much as she was.

A collective moan arose from the lawn dancers when the teachers announced that it was almost curfew. Emma hated to see the night end.

Before leaving, Doug took both of her hands in his and said, "It was a pleasure dancing with you, m'lady."

"I found it equally pleasurable, m'lord," Emma answered with a smile.

"Regretfully, I must take my leave of you. Until we meet again." Doug bowed formally and lightly kissed the back of her right hand. Then with a wave, he turned to go. Emma watched him go in a haze. She vaguely registered that Sebastian caught up to him just before he disappeared inside the castle.

Emma walked to her dorm room, barely aware that Martha was beside her. It had been a night she would never forget. Much later, she would think to ask Martha if she'd had a good time.

As he and Sebastian headed to the dorm room they shared with Phil and Tom, Doug's thoughts grew serious. Now it was time to get down to business and set his plan in motion. With any luck, by the end of the night, the Reaper would be in custody.

CHAPTER THIRTY-SEVEN
TO CATCH A THIEF

Doug waited until just after curfew, and then he grabbed his backpack.

"I'm going to spend the night with Dad," he explained to Phil and Tom on his way out. "See ya later," he said to Sebastian.

After making sure that Phil and Tom weren't looking, Sebastian gave him a thumbs-up signal for good luck. Doug returned the sign before closing the door behind him.

As Doug left Bingham Hall, he saw that the main hallway was clear. He could hear the music coming through the closed doors of the ballroom. Doug had just taken a few steps down the hall when the ballroom door closest to him swung open. Even though he had a legitimate reason for being out after curfew, instinct told him to hide. It occurred to him that if a teacher stopped him, he or she might get suspicious and decide to call his dad to check on his story. Doug couldn't take that risk. Quickly, he stepped behind the door so that, as it swung all the way open, he was between the door and the wall. He could hear some girls talking and laughing and assumed they were on their way to the restroom. The girls' restroom was across the hall and a little further down from his position. With any luck, the door would shield him from view until they were gone. The door swung forward, exposing his hiding spot just as the last girl entered the restroom. Doug let out the breath he'd been holding and hurried on his way before anyone else from the dance decided they needed to use the restroom. The rubber soles of Doug's tennis shoes made barely a sound on the marble floor, and in no time, he was turning left down the short hallway that led to the kitchen. Now that he was no longer in sight of the ballroom, Doug relaxed a little. Before entering the kitchen, Doug took a moment to listen at the door. Usually, the kitchen would be empty at this time of night, but because of the ball, this wasn't a normal night. It was now only a little after nine o'clock, and the cooks might still be cleaning up dishes. Doug had already made a plan for just such an event. If the cooks were still working when he arrived to deliver the sculpture, he would hide out in the janitor's closet until the coast was clear. The door to the closet was just a little further down from the kitchen door. The cooks had their own supply closet somewhere in the kitchen so Doug knew he wouldn't be discovered.

Doug pressed his ear to the door. All was quiet on the other side. Cautiously, Doug pushed the door open and peeked inside. He stepped back in alarm when he saw Mrs. Bertram and Mr. Sutton standing side by side at the counter to the right of the sink. Fortunately, they had their backs to him and didn't see him. As Doug carefully closed the door, he heard Mrs. Bertram say, "I'd better take Lord Dinswood his tea."

Doug hurried to the janitor's closet and squeezed in next to the mop bucket. He closed the door as quietly as possible and waited. A moment later, he heard the kitchen door open. He could hear the teacup rattling on the tray as Mrs. Bertram carried the tea service down the hall in the opposite direction. Mr. Sutton's boots clomped past him, and then Doug heard the outer door open and close. Mr. Sutton had gone outside—most likely to the trailer that was serving as his temporary living quarters while he worked on the gymnasium. Doug waited a couple more minutes just to be sure the coast was clear, and then he left the janitor's closet and slipped into the kitchen. *Whew, that was close*, he thought as he made his way over to the stairs leading to the basement storage room. Once there, he went straight over to the refrigerator covering the secret door and pulled it out. Then he turned on his flashlight and entered the musty room beyond. When he got to the barrel at the back of the little room, he set the flashlight and his backpack on the floor. In the flashlight's diffuse glow, Doug unzipped the pack and carefully removed the wrapped sculpture of Hannah. Then he took the lid off the barrel and laid it gently inside. He put the lid back on the barrel and was turning to leave when he noticed the old wooden door behind the barrel. He wondered yet again where it led. He had tried the door on several occasions, and it had always been locked. He couldn't leave without trying it one last time. Maybe tonight would be different. With his flashlight in hand, he quickly stepped around the barrel until he stood in front of the door. Taking a deep breath, he grasped the brass knob and tried to turn it. The door was locked. Even though it was the result he'd expected, Doug experienced a moment of disappointment. With a sigh, he left the room and pushed the refrigerator back into position.

Now he needed a place to hide until the Reaper appeared. It was then that he noticed several boxes piled in the corner to the right of the door. The school must have received a delivery yesterday, and with the extra work caused by the ball, the staff hadn't yet had a chance to unpack the boxes.

Not knowing how soon the Reaper would come, Doug quickly set to work, moving boxes and stacking them so that he could hide behind them. He even managed to make a peephole so that he could see the door to the barrel room without the Reaper seeing him. Once he was satisfied that his hiding place was ready, he climbed over the wall of his makeshift fort, turned off his flashlight, and hunkered down. The room was totally dark. The only sounds were the humming of the freezers and refrigerators. Doug settled himself more comfortably. Now all he had to do was wait.

Every now and then, Doug would check his watch. The hands of his watch glowed in the dark, so he didn't have any trouble seeing it. Time seemed to be passing at a snail's pace. An hour later, Doug yawned and realized he was getting sleepy. The room was warm, but not uncomfortably so, and the low humming from all of the appliances was having a soothing effect. Doug shook his head and shifted his position in an effort to remain alert. A few minutes later, he was sound asleep.

Doug awoke with a start. It took him a minute to remember where he was. Gradually, he became aware that he was lying on the concrete floor of the storage room. His head was resting on his backpack. Apparently, he'd been using it as a pillow. He sat up rubbing his stiff neck and tried to figure out what had awakened him. The storage room was dark, and except for the sounds of the appliances, all was silent. When he looked through his little peephole, he saw that the refrigerator blocking the door to the barrel room was right where it should be. Something wasn't right though.

Doug cocked his head and listened. For a moment, he heard nothing, and then he detected a faint scraping noise. It sounded like it was coming from the barrel room. Quickly, he left his hiding place and hurried over to the barrel room door. With great care, he began slowly pulling the refrigerator away from the wall, trying not to make any noise that would alert whoever might be on the other side. When the refrigerator was finally clear, he stepped behind it and put his ear to the door. The scraping noise was unmistakable now. Someone was in the barrel room.

For a moment, Doug was confused. How had the Reaper gotten into the barrel room? Then it hit him. *How could I have been so stupid?* Doug thought, mentally kicking himself. The barrel room had two doors. The Reaper had simply used the other door.

Determined not to let the Reaper get away, Doug pressed his ear to the door again. He heard the creak of the door on the other side, followed soon after by a loud click. Doug assumed that the Reaper had left the room, but he wanted to be sure. He forced himself to wait two interminable minutes before opening the door on his side. Then he opened it just a crack and peered inside. The room beyond was dark and silent. Hesitantly, Doug stepped into the room and turned on his flashlight. Quickly, he swept the light around the room. Once he'd confirmed that he was alone, he hurried over to the barrel and lifted the lid. As he had suspected, the sculpture was gone. Taking a deep breath, Doug stepped around the barrel and put his hand on the brass knob of the other door. Then he sent up a brief prayer and tried the knob. It turned easily in his hands. Beads of sweat popped up on Doug's upper lip as a tingle of fear and anticipation snaked its way down his spine. He hesitated only a moment before pushing the door open and stepping into the unknown.

Doug found himself standing in a fairly wide passage. He was surprised to see brightly blazing torches in brass holders staked along the walls at regular intervals. The torches provided plenty of light, so Doug switched his flashlight off. Doug noticed the walls were made of limestone and realized that the passage must be part of the cave system that lay beneath the castle. The floor of the passage consisted of hard-packed dirt. It was clear that at least at some point in the castle's history, this passage had been frequently traveled.

Treading lightly, Doug started off along the passage. It ran level and straight for about twenty-five feet before making a sharp turn to the left. There, Doug encountered a set of stone steps leading downward. The passage was a little narrower here but was still wide enough to allow two people to walk comfortably side by side. The downward slope was gradual at first but became steeper as Doug descended. To accommodate the greater incline, the stairs became shorter and more closely spaced. Doug had to slow down to keep from slipping on the smooth stones. It was then that he began to worry he'd given the Reaper too much of a head start. With that thought in mind and heedless of the risk, Doug picked up his pace once again. At least he wasn't having any trouble finding his way. Torches continued to line the walls all the way down.

Doug didn't slow until he came to the end of the passage. He could see that it opened into a larger room, but before leaving the shelter of the stairway, Doug stopped to listen. He could hear the gentle lapping of water but nothing else. Cautiously, he stepped out into the open. Doug was surprised to find himself in an enormous cavern. The ceiling was at least thirty feet above him. A large opening opposite where he was standing revealed the stars in the night sky. He could see ripples of reflected moonlight in the water flowing beyond the huge cavern opening and realized he was looking at the Hyaline River. It was then that he remembered Mr. Munsen telling them about another cave along the river. He had mentioned it the day he had given them a boat ride to Cathedral Cave. All of the puzzle pieces finally clicked into place, and in that instant, Doug knew how the Reaper had been getting the sculptures out of the castle.

The light from the passage behind him didn't illuminate the interior of the cavern very well, so Doug switched his flashlight on again. He swept the narrow beam around the walls of the enormous room in which he was standing. Seeing nothing out of the ordinary, he directed the beam downward. Water filled most of the cavern's interior and gently lapped at the surrounding rocks, which sloped upward to within a few feet of Doug's position. The water looked fairly deep, and the opening was big enough to accommodate a good-sized boat.

It was then that Doug noticed a small motorboat floating on the water just inside the cave's entrance. No doubt the boat belonged to the Reaper, and if that were the case, the Reaper hadn't left with the sculpture yet. The thought that he was in big trouble had just begun to crystallize in his brain when he was struck hard on the back of the head. He experienced a moment of intense pain, and then everything went dark.

When Doug came to sometime later, the first thing that registered was that he had a pounding headache. He kept his eyes closed and was on the point of moaning when he remembered being hit on the head. Firmly, he closed his mouth and made an effort to lie perfectly still. If his attacker was still around, he wanted him to think that he was still out. Slowly, he lifted one eyelid just enough to take a quick peek of his surroundings and was alarmed when he couldn't see anything at all. In a panic, he opened both eyes and was greeted by total darkness. Doug willed himself to remain calm. With his eyesight gone for the moment, he began paying attention to the information his other senses were sending him. He was lying on his left side on a cold hard surface. Although he couldn't see it, he heard the familiar purr of an outboard motor. He realized he was lying on the bottom of a boat, and it seemed to be moving through the water at a pretty good clip. Doug's hands were tied behind his back, and a slight shifting of his feet revealed that his ankles were also bound. He could feel something rough scratching his face, and the air he was breathing was warm and humid. He could also feel something that felt like a rope rubbing the hide off his neck. Putting it all together, Doug understood why he couldn't see. The Reaper had tied a cloth bag over his head.

His assessment complete, Doug continued to play dead while he tried to figure out what to do next. No one knew where he was, so he was on his own. He realized too late how foolish it had been for him to try to follow the Reaper. The Reaper must have heard Doug coming down the steps of the passage and hidden somewhere in the cavern until Doug stepped out into the open. Then he'd simply snuck up behind him and bashed him on the head. Doug had made it all too easy for the Reaper to get the drop on him, and now he could pay for that mistake with his life. With that realization, Doug tried to ignore the persistent pounding in his head and think of a way out of the mess in which he now found himself. Just then the boat hit a rough patch, and Doug was lifted completely off the floor of the boat. He came down hard on his left shoulder and hip before hitting his head on the hard metal. His head began pounding even worse, and a wave of nausea washed over him. Against his will, a groan escaped his lips. Doug just hoped the loud roar of the boat's motor had covered the sound.

Doug swallowed hard and waited for the nausea to pass before turning his thoughts once again to the problem at hand. This nightmare of a boat ride would be ending soon, and he needed to be ready.

Doug reasoned that the Reaper was probably taking him to his hideout—the place where he had been stashing all the sculptures he'd been getting from Doug. Most likely his hideout was one of the houses along the river. The Reaper would dock the boat and then have to carry Doug and the sculpture into the hideout separately. With any luck, the Reaper would take him in first. Then he would be left alone while the Reaper returned to the boat for the sculpture. That's when Doug would make his move. Everything depended on his being able to free his feet. When he'd tested the bonds around his ankles, they'd seemed a little loose. Doug just hoped they were loose enough.

All too soon the boat began to slow. Doug tried to slow the pounding of his heart and relax. For his plan to work, the Reaper had to think he was still unconscious. A moment later, he felt and heard a bump as the boat made contact with the dock. The Reaper cut the engine, and then Doug felt the boat tip and sway as the Reaper secured the boat to the dock. Doug held his breath and waited. The next instant, he was grabbed roughly underneath his arms and hauled upright. Then he was hefted up and slung over the Reaper's shoulder like a sack of potatoes. *Whoever this guy is, he's pretty strong,* Doug thought as he celebrated inwardly that the Reaper was doing just as he had hoped. He was taking him up to his hideout first.

The Reaper walked along the dock and then grunted with the strain of carrying Doug up a flight of stairs. When he reached the top of the stairs, the Reaper took a few more steps before coming to an abrupt halt. Doug understood why a moment later when he heard a click and then the creak of a door being swung open. The next instant, Doug was dumped unceremoniously on a smooth floor. Doug waited until he heard the retreating steps of the Reaper, and then he set his plan in motion. Alternately using the toes of one foot on the heel of the other, he managed to kick off his shoes. He was then able to slip his feet free from the ankle restraints. His hands were tied behind his back, so he began working them down over his bottom. It took a lot of squirming, and with the bag over his head, he began to get overheated. Sweat beaded up on his forehead and began pouring down his face. The air inside the bag was becoming stifling, and he was having a hard time getting his breath. He felt like he was suffocating. Gasping for air, he scrunched his legs up and maneuvered them through the circle made by his arms until his hands were in front of him. Exhausted by the effort, he would have liked nothing better than to lie down and rest, but there wasn't time. He had to get the bag off his head so he could make his escape. The bag had a drawstring that the Reaper had tied around his neck. Doug set to work on the knot, but it was being stubborn. The more frantically he worked on the knot, the less progress he made. He had just gotten one loop of the knot pulled free when he heard footsteps approaching. The Reaper was returning. Doug hadn't been fast enough.

Doug heard the door swing open. It was all over now. The Reaper would know that he was conscious and had tried to get away. Doug's hands were still tied together, and he was essentially blind.

He was at the mercy of the Reaper. It occurred to Doug that he was going to die never knowing what the Reaper looked like. His dad and friends would never know what happened to him. All of these thoughts ran through his head in quick succession as he waited help-lessly on the floor. Then he heard the unmistakable sound of a round being chambered in a rifle. *So that's how I'm going to die*, he thought. The Reaper was going to shoot him. Doug steeled himself for the feel of a bullet tearing into his flesh, but the sound of a rifle shot was not what he heard next.

"Hold it right there, mister," a familiar voice ordered. It was Mr. Munsen! Doug sagged in relief. That knock on his head must have made him loopy. How could he have forgotten about Mr. Munsen?

Doug was still processing the fact that he'd been miraculously saved when he felt hands at his neck.

"We'll have you free in a sec," a female voice said. "Just hold still."

"Somebody turn the lights on," a male voice Doug didn't rec-ognize commanded.

The lights came on just as the cloth bag was removed from Doug's head. He blinked in the sudden brightness. When his eyes had adjusted to the light, Doug saw that there were several people in the room with him. A dark-haired woman wearing a deputy's uni-form was kneeling in front of him, working on the bonds around his wrists. Mr. Munsen was standing across the room, watching Doug with a look of concern. A short, stocky man wearing a sheriff's uni-form was standing next to Mr. Munsen. Both men were holding ri-fles. Another deputy, younger and well muscled, was handcuffing the man Doug assumed was the Reaper. The man was turned away from him at the moment so Doug couldn't see his face.

"Are ya okay, son?" Mr. Munsen asked once Doug's hands were free. "How in the world did ya end up here?"

Doug struggled to his feet. He knew Mr. Munsen was not going to be pleased with his answer. Doug was just opening his mouth to explain when the young deputy turned the Reaper toward him. Doug gasped in surprise as he looked into the face of Mr. Criderman.

"You!" Doug shouted. Never in a million years would Doug have suspected that Mr. Criderman was the Reaper.

"You know this guy?" the sheriff asked.

"He's the librarian at school," Doug answered in a tone of disbelief. Disbelief was quickly replaced by confusion. "How did you even know about the sculptures?"

Mr. Criderman stared at Doug but didn't answer. Just then another man entered the room. He was tall and thin with a balding head, and his deputy's uniform was covered in dirt and cobwebs.

"I found four more sculptures in the crawlspace under the house," the deputy announced. "They're all wrapped up good and tight in bubble wrap."

"Well let's see now," the sheriff began. "We've got you on kidnapping and theft. Anything else we can add to the list?" he asked the still silent Mr. Criderman.

"Nothing to say, eh?" the sheriff prodded. Then with a sigh, he said to the deputy who had cuffed Mr. Criderman, "You and Dodds take this scum back to the station and make sure you read him his rights on the way. Fitch and I will wrap things up here and be along in a bit."

Dodds must have been the name of the woman who had freed Doug because she nodded and left with Mr. Criderman and the young deputy. Now in addition to Doug, only the sheriff, the tall, thin deputy, and Mr. Munsen remained.

"Now do you want to explain what you're doing here, son?" the sheriff asked. His tone was stern, but his expression was sympathetic.

"The Reaper threatened to kill Lord Dinswood and my dad. I just wanted to make sure he didn't get away," Doug answered.

"The Reaper, eh?" the sheriff asked with a raised eyebrow.

"That's what we started calling him." Doug then went on to explain how the nickname had come about.

"Well, the *Reaper* won't be causing any more trouble for a while. At least not in the foreseeable future," the sheriff added reassuringly. "Mr. Munsen filled me in on what's been going on, but I'll come by the school tomorrow to take you and your friends' statements. I'll also want to talk to your dad and Lord Dinswood."

"What about the sculptures?" Doug asked. "Can we give them back to Lord Dinswood now?"

"Not just yet. They're evidence in a crime." Then seeing the look of disappointment on Doug's face, the sheriff added, "I'll see to it that Lord Dinswood gets them back as soon as we're finished with them."

Then the sheriff left the room with Deputy Fitch, presumably to retrieve the sculptures from the crawlspace and get them loaded into his car for transport back to the station.

When they were alone, Mr. Munsen turned to Doug. "What were ya thinkin', boy? Ya could've gotten yourself killed," he scolded. "I told ya I'd take care of things. Ya should've trusted me."

"I know," Doug agreed solemnly. "I'm sorry, Mr. Munsen. I do trust you, and I should have let you handle it like you said, but I just couldn't sit by and do nothing."

Mr. Munsen pondered Doug's words for a moment, then said, "Takes a real man ta admit when he's wrong, and I guess I understand ya feelin' like ya needed ta do somethin'. Ain't nothin' worse than for a man ta feel helpless."

Grateful that Mr. Munsen understood, all Doug could do was nod. His head was still pounding, but the pain had lessened a bit. It had been a long stressful night, and all he wanted to do now was get back to the castle and get some much-needed sleep. The Reaper was caught; his dad and Lord Dinswood were finally safe. He knew that for the first time in months, he would sleep like a baby.

While they waited for the sheriff to return, Mr. Munsen explained how he'd figured everything out. "When ya told me where ya was leavin' the sculptures for the Reaper, I had a pretty good idea how he was gettin' 'em out of the castle. Ya see in the castle's early days, supplies were brought by boat down the river to the mouth of that cave. From there, they were carried up to the castle using that passage ya found tonight. Not too many people know about that cave nowadays, and they sure don't know where it leads. I'm not sure how the Reaper learned about it, but he did."

Although Doug's head was hurting, his curiosity got the best of him. "How did you know about this house?"

"Ah, now that took a bit of investigative work. Once I figured out he was using the river and that he had a boat, it made sense that he'd have ta have a place to dock it along the river. He'd also need somewhere ta stash the goods until he could sell 'em. I've got a friend in real estate. A couple of months ago, I paid him a visit and asked if any of the houses along the river had been rented recently. My friend acted like he was surprised by my question. He told me that this house had been rented in September and that the entire thing had been arranged through the mail. He'd never actually met the client face-to-face."

"Didn't your friend think that was odd?" Doug asked.

"Not really. I guess that kinda thing happens all the time. The guy claimed he was from out of town and that he was plannin' on moving ta the area. He said he wasn't sure exactly when he'd be arrivin', but he wanted a place waitin' for him when he did. None of that sounded suspicious ta my real estate friend, but it did ta me. Anyway, once I had it pretty well figured out, I had ya deliver a sculpture, so I could make sure I was right."

"And you were," Doug said, nodding his head.

"Yep, I sure was. I rounded up some of my buddies ta help me. I stationed them along the bluff overlooking the river while I staked out this house. We were able ta watch the guy's progress along the river, and then he stopped at this very house. He didn't know I was watchin' through the window while he hid the sculpture in the crawlspace." Mr. Munsen paused in his narration and smiled at the memory. Then he shook his head and continued, "Anyway, once you and me had decided ta set the trap tonight, I went ta the county sheriff and told him the whole story."

"Let me guess. The sheriff is a friend of yours too," Doug said with a wry grin.

"It pays ta have friends, son," Mr. Munsen acknowledged.

Just then, as if on cue, the sheriff returned. "Well, let's get this young man back to the castle. We can sort everything out in the morning."

CHAPTER THIRTY-EIGHT
EXPLANATIONS

Doug and Mr. Munsen rode with the sheriff back to Dinswood Academy. Mr. Munsen waited in the car while the sheriff took Doug into the school. The sheriff had a brief conversation with the school's head of security and then instructed Doug to go to his room and try to get some sleep.

"I'll be back in the morning," the sheriff called on his way out.

Doug nodded his understanding and looked at his watch. It was two o'clock. Technically, morning had already arrived. When Doug got to the room he shared with Sebastian, Phil, and Tom, he slipped in quietly and hastily removed his shoes and jeans. With a yawn, he pulled the covers back on his bed and climbed in. Despite the dull throbbing in his head, he was asleep within minutes.

Doug was awakened the next morning by the sounds of his roommates getting ready to go to breakfast. With a groan, he opened his eyes. Sebastian came over as soon as he saw that Doug was awake.

"I thought you were spending the night with your dad," he said, looking at him curiously. "What happened?"

"It's a long story," Doug replied. Then he looked meaningfully in Phil and Tom's direction and added in a whisper, "I'll tell you later."

Sebastian got the message. Doug didn't want to talk about it until Phil and Tom had left the room. Although he was dying of curiosity, Sebastian managed to contain himself until the other two boys had gone to breakfast. As soon as the door closed behind them, he sat on his bed, which was across from Doug's, and leaned forward expectantly.

Doug told him the whole story, ending with, "I'm sorry I lied to you about where I was going last night, but I knew you'd want to come with me, and I didn't want to risk your life too."

"Next time let me decide whether or not I want to risk my life," Sebastian said with a frown. "If there'd been two of us, the Reaper would never have gotten the drop on you like that."

"You're right, Sebastian," Doug admitted. "I guess I never thought of it like that."

Deciding he'd made his point, Sebastian changed the subject. "I still can't believe Mr. Criderman is the Reaper."

Grateful that Sebastian seemed to have forgiven him for lying to him, Doug gladly took up the new topic. "I know. If I hadn't seen him with my own eyes, I wouldn't have believed it myself."

"How did he even know about the sculptures?" Sebastian asked.

"That's exactly what I wondered," Doug said with a shake of his head. "The sheriff will be here sometime after breakfast. Maybe he'll know."

Doug had already told Sebastian that the sheriff was coming back to get his and the girls' statements. Sebastian had been a little nervous at first, but Doug had told him there was nothing to worry about, that all he had to do was tell the truth.

The boys went on to breakfast after that, and while they ate, they filled Martha and Emma in on everything that had transpired the night before. Doug knew the girls would be upset with him for going after the Reaper by himself, but there was no point in trying to keep it from them. It was all going to come out anyway when the sheriff arrived. Emma was just as upset as he'd anticipated.

"You could have gotten yourself killed," she began and then surprised even herself when she stopped and closed her mouth. She had intended to say more but realized there wasn't really any point. What was done was done, and nothing could change it now. The truth was she understood why Doug had followed the Reaper, and she also understood why he hadn't asked Sebastian to go with him. Thankfully, it had turned out all right, and the Reaper was finally in custody. Deciding to focus on the positive, Emma said, "At least it's all over now. You don't have to worry about your dad or Lord Dinswood anymore."

As it would later turn out, Emma was only half right.

The sheriff arrived shortly after breakfast and met with each of the kids individually in Dean Harwood's office to take their statements. When it was his turn, Doug gave the sheriff all the notes the Reaper had written and took a seat. The sheriff, who was sitting at Dean Harwood's desk, took a moment to read each one. Then he laid them down on the desk. "Well, it's pretty clear from these that Mr. Criderman threatened to kill your father and Lord Dinswood. I suppose you checked out the chess piece mentioned in one of the notes?"

"Yes," Doug answered. "It was just as he'd said. I don't know how he did it, but he managed to get into Dad's suite. I figured if he could get into Dad's room, he could get into Lord Dinswood's too."

"You should have come to us when you got the very first note," the sheriff told him sternly.

"I was afraid he'd carry through on his threat. I didn't have any idea who the Reaper was, but I figured he was watching my every move. I just couldn't risk it," Doug explained.

"Well, that's all water under the bridge now," the sheriff said. "Mr. Criderman has confessed to everything."

"He did?" Doug asked in amazement.

"His lawyer recommended that he come clean, especially since we caught him red handed so to speak. His lawyer explained to him that the judge was more likely to give a reduced sentence if he pled guilty and spared the county the expense of a jury trial."

"Something's been bothering me ever since I found out that Mr. Criderman was the Reaper."

"What's that?" the sheriff asked.

"How did he find out about the Mortals in the first place?"

"I asked him that very question. He said he came to the school over the summer to interview for the librarian's position. Your dad offered to put him up for the night and gave him one of the empty suites on the third floor. He says he was watching out the window when two guys from the construction crew unearthed the first sculpture. Later, he overheard you kids in the library and put two and two together. I guess you know the rest." The sheriff sat back in Dean Harwood's chair and regarded Doug solemnly. "Sorry you had to go through this, son."

Doug swallowed hard as the realization that the nightmare was finally over really began to sink in. Then something else occurred to him. "How did the Reaper know I was following him last night?"

"He said he was on his way back up the passage to lock the door to the storage room and extinguish the torches when he heard you coming down the stairs. He says he hid and waited for you to come out into the open. If it's any consolation, I don't think he was planning to kill you. He swears he was going to let you go later. That's why he put the bag over your head and why he never spoke in your presence. He did it so you couldn't identify him. He said your appearance last night complicated everything and that he'd decided to cut his losses and get what he could for the five sculptures he already had."

"What about my dad and Lord Dinswood? Do you think he would have killed them?" Doug couldn't help asking.

"My gut tells me no, but you can never be sure what a guy will or won't do if he gets desperate enough. I think you were right to take the threat seriously. Your mistake was not going to the law right away."

The sheriff was silent for a moment as he let his last statement sink in. Doug had been very lucky in the way things had turned out. He might not be that lucky next time—if there ever was a next time. The sheriff hoped not for Doug's sake. The boy had been through enough.

"Well, I guess that's all I needed," the sheriff said, breaking the silence, "unless you have any other questions."

Doug shook his head in the negative and got up to leave. He was almost to the door when the sheriff called after him.

"Oh, I forgot to tell you. Since Mr. Criderman confessed to everything, we'll be able to return the sculptures to Lord Dinswood within the week."

That was good news. As Doug left his dad's office, he just hoped it wasn't too little too late.

That afternoon, after all of the interviews were over, Doug was summoned to his dad's office again. Only this time, the meeting was with his dad. He knew his dad was extremely upset with him. Doug couldn't really blame him. After all, Doug had lied to his dad on numerous occasions and willfully deceived him into believing that the other Mortals no longer existed. Of course, he'd had good reasons for his actions, but somehow he doubted that his dad would see it that way.

When he entered the office, his dad was sitting behind his desk just as the sheriff had been earlier. Doug took a deep breath and sat in one of the chairs facing his dad's desk. Dean Harwood looked tired, making Doug feel even worse.

As soon as Doug was seated, Dean Harwood, his face expressionless, looked at his son and said quietly, "I want to hear the whole story from the beginning. The sheriff's told me what he can, but I want to hear it from you."

Doug took another deep breath and began. Dean Harwood listened quietly, only interrupting now and then to ask a clarifying question. Doug explained the significance of the chess piece on the mantle and told his dad that that was when he'd realized he needed to take the Reaper's threats seriously. When Doug was finished, he said, "I hated lying to you and Lord Dinswood, Dad, but I didn't feel like I had any other choice."

"There's always a choice, son, and I'm not totally convinced you made the right one," his dad replied.

Then Doug asked the very question that Dean Harwood had been asking himself throughout his son's rather lengthy narration. "What would you have done, Dad, if the Reaper had threatened me?"

Dean Harwood was silent so long that Doug was just about to decide that he wasn't going to answer. Finally, Dean Harwood cleared his throat and said, "I guess I would have done exactly what you did." Dean Harwood hated to admit it, but he wasn't going to lie to his son. He loved his son very much, and the truth was that if the roles had been reversed, he would have done exactly as his son had done.

Doug looked at his dad in surprise.

"That wasn't what you expected me to say, was it?" Dean Harwood asked, smiling for the first time since Doug had walked in.

"No, sir, it wasn't," Doug replied with a grin of his own.

"I guess I'm finally starting to realize that you're not a little boy anymore. I need to let you grow up and become a man. I can see that these last few months that's what you've been trying to do."

Not trusting himself to speak, Doug simply nodded. He could hear the love and pride in his dad's voice. It occurred to him then that his dad was exactly the kind of man he wanted to become.

"I guess I owe Mr. Munsen a huge debt of gratitude," Dean Harwood said, breaking into Doug's thoughts. "He sounds like a good man."

"He is," Doug agreed.

"In fact, he sounds like someone that I'd like to get to know," Dean Harwood added almost to himself.

"Well, I found out last night that he has lots of friends," Doug said, grinning widely.

Doug and his dad continued to talk a little longer, and then Doug left to return to his friends. He found them in the lounge. Emma and Sebastian were involved in a game of chess, while Martha watched from the sidelines. Martha had to struggle to keep from grinning at the rashness of some of Sebastian's moves. She would have offered her help, but Sebastian had made her promise to stay out of it before beginning the game. As time went on, she realized that, although some of his moves were rather unusual, they more often than not produced the desired result. At any rate, Emma was having a hard time figuring out his strategy. *I feel your pain*, Martha thought with a smile.

The game was temporarily called to a halt when Doug came in. They were all curious to hear what Doug had found out from the sheriff. Doug quickly filled them in, describing in detail how Mr. Criderman had first learned about the existence of the Mortals.

"So he was watching out the window when the construction guys dug up the first one," Sebastian said, recapping what Doug had told him.

"Yep, and when we were in the library doing our research, he was spying on us."

Emma couldn't help the shudder that went through her as she remembered the night she'd seen him dressed as the grim reaper. She'd had nightmares about that night several times since it had happened.

"I know he's been caught, but just the thought of him lurking around gives me the creeps," Martha said with a shudder of her own.

"Well, thankfully it's all over now," Doug replied. With a sigh, he ran his hand through his hair. "The sheriff says Lord Dinswood should get his sculptures back this weekend."

"Good. Maybe he'll perk up once he sees them," Martha suggested.

"I hope so" was all Doug said in reply.

CHAPTER THIRTY-NINE
A LAST RESORT

True to his word, the sheriff returned the following Saturday morning with the five sculptures recovered from the Reaper's hideout. Doug was in the library with Sebastian, Martha, and Emma when he happened to look out the window and see a couple of cars with the words *County Sheriff* stenciled on the sides, pulling up in front of the school.

"The sheriff's here," he informed the others. "He must be returning the sculptures."

By mutual consent, they all left the library and hurried to the lobby. They were just in time to see the female deputy and the tall, thin deputy Doug had met the night of the Reaper's capture come in. They were each carrying a sculpture wrapped securely in several layers of bubble wrap. Deputies Dodds and Fitch stepped into the school's only elevator and smiled at Doug when they saw him. Then the doors closed, and they disappeared from view. A moment later, two more deputies and the sheriff himself came in with the last three sculptures. Just as Dodds and Fitch had done, they entered the elevator. It looked like the sculptures were being taken directly up to Lord Dinswood's suite. Doug wished he could be there to see the look on Lord Dinswood's face as he gazed upon them for the first time.

Doug hadn't been up to see Lord Dinswood for several weeks, but the last time he'd seen him he hadn't looked well at all. Nowadays, he never left his suite, and lately Doug's dad had taken to checking on him at regular intervals throughout the day. As he had almost daily since the beginning of school, Doug said a silent prayer for Lord Dinswood.

Shortly after lunch, they were sitting around in the lounge playing cards when Dean Harwood came in and told them that Lord Dinswood wished to see them. They gave each other questioning looks as they quickly put the cards away and followed Dean Harwood to the elevator.

"What's he want, Dad?" Doug asked once the elevator doors had closed.

"He didn't tell me, son," Dean Harwood answered with a smile. Fully aware that the four youngsters were dying of curiosity, he added, "If you'll be patient for one or two minutes more, you'll find out."

Just as Dean Harwood finished speaking, a soft pinging sound signaled their arrival on the third floor. The elevator doors slid open, and there was a slight traffic jam as all four youngsters tried to exit at the same time.

"Why don't we let Doug's dad go first," Sebastian suggested after trying unsuccessfully to squeeze past everyone.

"I think that's a fine idea, Sebastian," Dean Harwood said with a raised eyebrow. It was clear from his expression that he was doing his best not to laugh. Before knocking on the door to Lord Dinswood's suite, however, his expression grew serious once again. "I want you to be prepared," he began quietly. "Lord Dinswood's health has deteriorated drastically in the last couple of weeks. I've been trying to get him to go to the hospital, but he refuses. I'm telling you this because I don't want you to act shocked or surprised when you see him.

He's very weak so don't tire him with endless questions." This last was said with a pointed look in Sebastian's direction.

Doug's heart sank at his dad's words. It was just as he feared. The sculptures had been returned too late to have any positive effect on Lord Dinswood's health. Doug's earlier curiosity was replaced with a profound sadness. As the door to Lord Dinswood's suite swung open, Doug steeled himself for what he was about to see.

Lord Dinswood was lying on the couch in the living room. He was covered with a light brown blanket and had several fluffy white pillows propped behind his head. His white hair was frizzy and pointing in all directions. Doug was reminded of the picture of Albert Einstein he'd seen in his science book. Lord Dinswood's face was pale and gaunt, but his blue eyes were clear and lucid.

"Come in. Come in," Lord Dinswood invited, waving his right arm weakly.

Doug hated seeing him this way and had to look away before he broke down and started crying right then and there. It was then that he noticed that all six of the recovered Mortals were sitting on the kitchen counter where they could be seen from Lord Dinswood's current position.

Following the direction of Doug's gaze, Lord Dinswood smiled weakly and said, "They're a beautiful sight, aren't they?"

In unison, all of the others turned to look at the sculptures.

"They're exquisite," Martha said, answering for the group. "This is the first time we've seen them all together." She stopped for a moment and then added quietly, "I just wish we could have found the last one."

"There's always the hope that someday you will," Lord Dinswood said with a tired smile.

Although, he hadn't actually said it, the implication was clear. Lord Dinswood did not expect to be around if and when the last Mortal was found.

Doug tried to keep his outward expression calm, but on the inside his heart was breaking. He wanted nothing more than to get away and find a quiet place where he could be alone. His dad must have known how Doug was feeling because he was looking at his son with an expression of concern. Thankfully, Doug was unaware of it. Sympathy from his dad in that moment would have been his undoing. With an effort, Doug took a deep breath and tried to concentrate on what Lord Dinswood was saying.

"I brought you all up here for two reasons. First, I wanted to hear how you found each of the missing Mortals, and second, I wanted to thank you personally for finding them," Lord Dinswood explained. "From the moment the first one was found, I've harbored a certainty in my heart that the others were out there somewhere just waiting to be discovered. Of course, I understand that the Reaper, as you call him, threw a bit of a kink in the works. Despite his interference, you four came through and once again succeeded far beyond my expectations. I want to thank you from the bottom of my heart."

"You don't have to thank us, sir. We were glad to do it," Doug said quickly.

Sebastian, Martha, and Emma murmured their agreement. They had begun the job simply because someone they cared about had asked them to do it. Unfortunately, finding the sculptures had quickly become a matter of life and death. Looking back over the last several months, none of the four youngsters felt the need for any thanks. Their sole motivation had been to keep Doug's dad and Lord Dinswood safe.

At Lord Dinswood's prompting, the four youngsters then took turns describing how they had found each of the five sculptures.

Although it was obvious he wasn't feeling well, Lord Dinswood listened with rapt attention, and when they had finished, he once again expressed his gratitude.

"I have been trying to decide on a suitable reward," Lord Dinswood said after a brief moment of silence. "And I think I've finally hit on the perfect thing."

"Really, sir. That's not necessary," Doug objected. For the past several months, Doug had been deceiving Lord Dinswood by leading him to believe that they hadn't found any of the other sculptures. He certainly didn't feel like he deserved a reward. Doug was just opening his mouth to object further when Lord Dinswood forestalled him.

"I'm not taking no for an answer. I've decided that from now on none of you will have to pay tuition to attend the academy."

Emma sat there in stunned silence. She couldn't believe what she was hearing. Keeping her grade point average high enough to maintain her scholarship had always been a major concern for her. Now, although she planned to continue to do her very best in all of her classes, she wouldn't have to worry so much about her grades. Emma felt as if a great weight had just been lifted from her shoulders.

Doug, who was also attending the academy on a scholarship, was experiencing a similar relief.

Although their families were well able to afford the academy's yearly tuition, Sebastian and Martha were just as appreciative of Lord Dinswood's gesture as Emma and Doug.

"I don't know what to say," Emma finally managed. "Thank you!"

The other three echoed Emma's thank you.

"You're very welcome," Lord Dinswood replied with a smile. "Now I'm afraid I have one last request to make." Lord Dinswood laughed softly when he saw the look of concern that crossed the faces of all four youngsters simultaneously. "Don't worry," he hastened to reassure them. "Compared to what you've been through recently, this will be a piece of cake. There's an item I need from my ship. I was hoping you four would be willing to navigate the underground passages one more time and retrieve it for me."

"We'll be glad to," Sebastian piped up. Then he happened to notice the stern look Dean Harwood was giving him. Swallowing nervously, he added, "That is, if it's okay with Dean Harwood."

"Is it okay, Dad?" Doug asked. He really wanted to see the amazing ship Lord Dinswood had built again, but he wasn't going to do it without his dad's approval.

Dean Harwood smiled then. "It sounds safe enough. Yes, you may go."

"What is it you want us to get?" Sebastian asked excitedly the moment Dean Harwood had given his okay.

Lord Dinswood smiled at Sebastian's enthusiasm. "Well now, there's a little black box in the top drawer of the dresser in the captain's cabin. I want you to get that box and bring it back here to me."

"What's in the box?" Sebastian chimed in again before any of the others could ask the very same question.

"I would like that to remain a mystery until we can open the box together," Lord Dinswood replied with a mischievous grin. "Do you think you can keep your curiosity in check that long?"

Emma had to keep herself from laughing at the disappointment on Sebastian's face. They would have to make sure they didn't put Sebastian in charge of carrying the little black box. It would be too much of a temptation for him.

"We can do it this afternoon," Doug volunteered before Sebastian could reply.

"Good, good," Lord Dinswood said with a nod. "You can go through the passage that runs beneath the chapel." Lord Dinswood then went on to explain how to find and open the secret entrance in the chapel's basement.

They had stumbled upon Lord Dinswood's two-masted schooner last year when they were looking for the treasure. They had found it floating on a huge underground lake after swimming through a submerged passage. That short swim had been the most frightening experience of Emma's life, so she was relieved to hear that she wasn't going to have to do it again. Thankfully, there was another way to get to the ship.

After a few more instructions, Lord Dinswood sent them on their way. The others filed out obediently behind Dean Harwood, but Doug stayed behind. There was something he needed to say to Lord Dinswood. Lord Dinswood looked at Doug expectantly as he struggled to find the words that would adequately express what was in his heart.

Finally, after clearing his throat, Doug began, "I'm sorry I lied to you, sir. I hated keeping the truth from you, but I was really scared that the Reaper would hurt you or Dad."

"There's no need to apologize, son. You did what you felt you had to do," Lord Dinswood replied with a solemn expression. "I understand completely. Learning to make tough decisions is a part of growing up, and I must say that I'm very proud of the man you are becoming."

For a moment, Doug was overcome with emotion. "Thank you, sir," he finally managed to say.

Trying to lighten the mood, Lord Dinswood smiled broadly and, pointing to the sculptures on the counter, said, "I'd say things turned out all right, wouldn't you?"

Doug looked at the six Mortals and couldn't help thinking that the set wasn't complete. "We'll keep searching until we find the seventh Mortal, sir," Doug promised.

"I'm counting on it," Lord Dinswood replied.

CHAPTER FORTY

THE LITTLE BLACK BOX

When Doug left Lord Dinswood's suite, he saw that, with the exception of his dad, the others were waiting for him by the elevator. Although they all gave him questioning looks, no one asked him what had delayed him. Doug was grateful because he didn't feel like explaining. What had transpired moments ago was between him and Lord Dinswood.

"I can't believe we actually have permission to go back to Lord Dinswood's ship!" Sebastian exclaimed excitedly while they waited for the elevator to return to their floor.

"I know," Doug agreed. "When we get downstairs, I'll get some flashlights and extra batteries for us."

"We probably ought to take some bottled water too," Martha suggested.

"Good idea," Doug said.

"What else should we take?" Sebastian asked.

"I'd say the flashlights and water should be all we need," Doug answered. "We're not going to be down there that long."

Sebastian looked disappointed. "I was hoping we could do a little exploring while we're down there. This might be our last chance to look around."

Although Emma and Martha didn't say anything, the excited looks on their faces said very clearly that they agreed with Sebastian.

Doug looked at his friends and smiled. "Who says we can't?"

Sebastian let out a little whoop of joy. "This is gonna be great!"

When they got off the elevator, the girls and the boys separated to get the things they needed from their rooms. A short while later, they met back up in the lobby. Doug was carrying a backpack, which contained four flashlights, extra batteries, and some bottled water.

"Everybody ready to go?" Doug asked after explaining what was in the backpack.

"You bet," Sebastian answered.

Eager to get started, Sebastian led the group out the front doors and down the steps. From there, they headed over to the chapel and entered through the back door. Directly in front of them was a long hallway that led to the chapel area. Further along on the right side of the hall were doors that opened into the pastor's office and the chapel library. Immediately to their right was a set of old wooden stairs that led to the chapel's basement. They took the stairs and stopped at the bottom to get their bearings. Small rectangular windows set high up on the walls to their right and left let enough light in for them to see by. Lord Dinswood had told them that there was a secret panel in the wall directly across from the stairs. The walls of the room had all been covered with old-fashioned paneling in a dark brown color. Doug counted ten panels from the corner on their far right. Once he had located the correct panel, he pushed on it. It sank in about an inch and then, with a click, swung outward. Doug stepped back quickly to get out of the way.

"It must be some kind of a magnetic latch," Doug commented as he peered inside. Another set of stairs led downward. Doug opened his backpack and gave everyone a flashlight.

"You lead the way," Sebastian suggested. "I'll close the door as soon as everyone's in."

"Okay," Doug agreed. Then he switched on his flashlight and started down the stairs.

Emma went next, followed by Martha and Sebastian. The narrow stairway had stone steps and was bordered closely on both sides by walls made of cement bricks. Emma's claustrophobia began to kick in, and she took several deep breaths in an effort to calm her rising panic. When they got to the bottom, they found themselves in a section of the castle's underground cave system. This passageway was a good deal wider than the stairway they'd just come down and was surrounded on all sides by limestone; all man-made materials had been left behind. The sound of water dripping could be heard echoing off the walls up ahead. Now that there was more room, Emma's claustrophobia began to subside.

Doug waited until everyone had made it down the stairs and then set off at a brisk pace.

"What's the hurry?" Sebastian complained.

"Sorry. I guess I'm just excited about seeing Lord Dinswood's ship again," Doug said.

After that, he forced himself to slow down so that everyone could keep up. It was pretty easy going for a while because the ground was level and the ceiling of the cave was high enough for them to walk upright. When they came to a fork in the passage, Doug took the left fork as Lord Dinswood had instructed. This section of the cave required that they go single file for a while. Then it widened out again, but the ceiling was lower, so they had to walk stooped over. Just when they thought their backs would break, the passage opened up into an enormous cavern. The afternoon sun was shining through a large opening in the opposite cave wall, its rays reflecting off the smooth surface of the lake. Sitting on the water, looking just as it had the last time they'd seen it, was the two-masted schooner that had taken Lord Dinswood twenty years to build.

"There she is!" Sebastian exclaimed when he spotted the ship. "I still can't believe there's something that awesome hidden way down here."

As there was plenty of light, Doug collected everyone's flashlights and put them in his backpack.

Sebastian handed his flashlight over first and then, without waiting for the others, hurried over to the ship's gangway. About halfway up the wooden ramp, Sebastian paused and let his gaze travel over the ship from bow to stern—a look of reverence on his face. The last time they'd been on board, they'd been in a hurry, but now there was no need for haste. Sebastian planned to look around to his heart's content. By the time Sebastian was ready to board the ship, he had been joined by the others.

"Let's get the box from the captain's cabin, and then we can look around the ship," Doug suggested.

The others agreed and followed Doug down a short flight of stairs and along a hall that ended in Lord Dinswood's cabin. The room was just as it had been the last time they'd visited. The bed, dresser, and table were all constructed of a dark cherry wood. In addition to building the ship, Lord Dinswood had also made all the furniture in the room.

"That guy is amazing," Sebastian commented as he looked around the room. "I'd never be able to make anything as fine as this." This last was said as Sebastian ran his hand over the footboard of the king-size bed. As Lord Dinswood had not been able to return to the ship in quite some time, the furniture in the room had accumulated a thin coating of dust. Sebastian's action swept enough dust aside to reveal the smooth polished wood beneath. Even covered in dust, there was no mistaking the expert craftsmanship exhibited by every piece of furniture in the room.

While the others continued to poke around the room, Doug opened the top drawer of the dresser and looked inside. He was a little disconcerted to see that the drawer contained T-shirts and underwear. Doug hesitated for a moment. He didn't feel right about sifting through Lord Dinswood's personal things. Deciding that it had to be done, Doug shoved his hand into the drawer and began shifting the contents around in search of the black box. He found it in the back corner on the drawer's right side. With a sigh of relief, he grabbed the box and quickly shut the drawer. He looked over at the others then. If they had seen what was in the drawer, they didn't let on.

Sebastian noticed Doug holding the box. "Let's have a look inside. Lord Dinswood will never know."

"Absolutely not!" Martha exclaimed. "He specifically asked us to wait, and that's exactly what we're going to do."

"Aren't you the least bit curious?" Sebastian needled.

"Of course I am, but unlike you I have some self-control," Martha replied.

"I have self-control," Sebastian began indignantly.

It was then that they heard it—a low rumble that grew in magnitude until it echoed loudly off the cavern walls around them. Wide-eyed, they looked at each other for a second and then ran for the stairs. The rumbling continued and had just began to subside when they reached the deck. Dumbfounded, they looked around trying to pinpoint the source of the sound.

"There," Doug shouted, pointing.

The others looked where he was pointing and saw an enormous cloud of dust issuing from the passage they'd just come through.

"What's going on?" Martha all but screamed as she looked at the others in panic.

Doug put the black box in his backpack and pulled out one of the flashlights. "Stay here," he ordered the others. "I think I know what just happened, but I have to make sure." Without another word, he raced down the gangway and over to the opening to the chapel passage. The others watched as Doug disappeared inside the tunnel. He reappeared a moment later with a grim expression.

The others waited anxiously as he made his way back to them.

"Well, it's just as I thought," Doug called out as he walked up the gangway. "There's been a cave-in. The passage is completely blocked."

There was a shocked silence as the others digested this information. Considering her earlier panic, remarkably it was Martha who was the first to find her voice.

"We were just in there. If that had happened just a few minutes earlier, we would have all been killed."

No one spoke for a moment. Emma assumed that everyone was doing what she was doing—sending up a prayer of thanks that they hadn't been in the tunnel when the roof had suddenly decided to come crashing down.

"What do you think caused it?" Sebastian asked, breaking the silence. "I mean these caves have been here for ages, and nothing like this has ever happened before. Why now?"

"I think I might have the answer," Doug replied. "It's all the new construction. When they were digging the foundation for the gym, they hit a big section of rock. They had to use dynamite to break it up. The explosions might have made part of the cave system unstable."

"But that was last summer," Martha objected. "Surely, it would have caused cave-ins before now."

"Maybe it did. We don't know for sure because we haven't checked out all the passages."

"You mean other passages could be blocked?" Emma asked in surprise.

"It's possible," Doug answered.

"But what caused this cave-in?" Martha asked, reiterating Sebastian's initial question.

"I don't know for sure, but I think the stuff they did last summer must have weakened the passage. For the past couple of months, big trucks have been coming up to the school every day to deliver more materials for the gym. Maybe the trucks produced enough vibration in the ground to cause the already weakened passage to collapse."

"Sounds reasonable to me," Sebastian said, nodding.

Listening to the others, Emma became very frightened. If the entire cave system was unstable, none of the passages were safe. Deciding it was time to point out the real problem to the others, she said, "It's not important how it happened. What's important now is how do we get out of here?"

CHAPTER FORTY-ONE
MICE IN A MAZE

Martha and Sebastian looked at Emma with wide eyes. It was clear from their expressions that they hadn't considered the seriousness of their current situation. Doug, who had been thinking along the same lines as Emma, didn't answer immediately. With a frown, he began running through their options in his head. Gradually, he became aware that the other three were all looking at him— waiting for him to come up with a solution. Although he was flattered that his friends viewed him as their leader, he also felt the weight of the responsibility. It didn't help that they were all down in the cavern, their lives in danger once again, because of him. With a sigh, Doug ran a hand through his hair and made a decision.

"Well one thing's for sure. We can't stay here," Doug began. Then he went on to explain his plan for getting them to safety. "Most likely, only the passages immediately surrounding the construction site are unsafe. I think we'll be okay if we head away from the castle, and that means taking the passage that leads to the underground river."

A shiver ran through Emma at the thought. Last year, when they'd been searching for the treasure, Doug had broken his arm and nearly been washed away by the rushing water as he tried to cross the river by jumping on the tops of some exposed rocks. She didn't want him to have to try that again.

"There's got to be another way," Emma said, shaking her head. "You nearly got yourself killed last year."

"Yeah," Sebastian agreed. "Besides, I remember last year Mr. Hodges telling us that there were a lot more passages than the ones we found."

"And Mr. Hodges would know because he had a map showing the maze of passages down here," Martha added.

"I wish we had that map now," Doug commented wryly. Still, he had to admit the others had a point. Considering the size of the lake cavern, there was a very good chance that more passages opened into it. They would just have to search more carefully. To the others, he said, "Well, the only way we'll find another way out is to look for it, so I suggest we get started."

Without another word, Doug turned and led the way down the gangway, followed by Emma and Martha. Sebastian, however, hesitated on the deck of the ship. He had been so looking forward to getting to explore it more fully. Now, with the stability of the underground passages in question, Sebastian realized he might never get another opportunity. With a wistful expression and a sigh, Sebastian gave one last look around and then joined the others where they were waiting on shore.

Doug must have known how disappointed Sebastian was because he said, "We'll see her again, Sebastian. I promise."

Inexplicably, Sebastian believed him, but all he said was "Right now, I'm only interested in getting out of here in one piece."

Doug nodded his agreement. "I think our best approach is to spread out and start feeling along the walls of the cavern," he told the others. "We should be able to find even a camouflaged opening that way."

Given the enormous size of the cavern, even with the four of them searching, it was most likely going to take a while to find another way out—if another way out even existed. The opening that led to the underground river was clearly visible, so Doug started his search immediately to the right of it. Emma saw what he was doing and began searching from the river passage's left side. Martha and Sebastian started on the opposite wall directly across from where Doug and Emma were. Initially, they stood side by side and then began moving away from each other, so they could be certain that every section of wall was examined. It was a good system, and everyone worked in silence for a while.

Emma didn't know how much time had passed when Sebastian finally began to lose patience. Every few seconds, he would utter some complaint. Just when Sebastian's constant complaining was beginning to get on Emma's nerves, Martha shouted that she'd found an opening. Immediately, everyone ran over to where Martha was standing.

Emma gasped in shock when she saw what Martha considered an opening. It was a vertical slit, approximately two feet wide. It was positioned next to an outcropping of rock along the cavern wall. Emma could see why they hadn't noticed it before. You had to be practically standing in front of it to see it.

"That's not an opening," Emma said, shaking her head. "That's just a crack in the wall. We can't fit through there."

"We can if we turn sideways," Martha replied. "It opens up and gets wider as you get farther in. I checked it out before I called everyone over."

"I'm not going in there," Emma said in a state of panic. All she could think about was being buried by tons of rock in that tiny passage. "Besides, it looks like it goes back toward the castle."

"It's bound to branch somewhere along the way," Martha pointed out. "We won't know which direction it will take us until we get in there."

"I'm not going," Emma said, her eyes wide with fear. "I'll just wait here, and you can send someone back for me when you get out."

"We're not going to leave you here," Doug stated in no uncertain terms. "We're going to stay together."

"Maybe there's another opening that we haven't found yet," Emma suggested. Just the thought of having to squeeze through that narrow gap made Emma's heart pound. Suddenly, she felt hot all over, and beads of sweat began to form on her upper lip.

"We've been searching for over half an hour, and I'm tired of looking," Sebastian said.

"There's not much of the cavern wall left to search, so I'd say this opening is our best option," Martha argued in an effort to persuade Emma to come along.

"I guess we could swim through the underwater tunnel we used last year, but that would take us back toward the school for sure," Sebastian added when it looked like Emma still wasn't convinced.

"We'll save that as a last resort," Doug said to Sebastian. "I think we should see where this passage takes us first." Then Doug looked over at Emma. All of the color had drained from her face, and she was as white as a ghost. Up until this moment, she had been able to control her claustrophobia, but it was clear from her expression that it had a firm grip on her now. "It'll be okay," Doug told her softly. "Just take my hand and close your eyes. I'll lead you through the tight spots. You won't know how narrow the passage is if you can't see it."

"You've got to try," Martha urged.

Emma looked at each of her friends in turn. They were determined to enter Martha's passage, and they were equally determined that she would go with them. Doug had a hand extended, waiting for her to take it. Emma knew when she was beat. She sighed in resignation, then took a deep breath and swallowed in an effort to slow her rapid heartbeat. Then she took Doug's hand and closed her eyes.

"You guys go first," Doug instructed Martha and Sebastian. "Emma and I will follow."

Emma heard shuffling as Martha and Sebastian started through the opening. Then she felt Doug's tug on her hand, and she began moving forward. Suddenly, Doug let go of her hand. Emma was just opening her mouth to protest, when she felt his arm encircle her waist.

"It will be easier to guide you this way," Doug told her. "Just stay by my side."

Doug pulled Emma along as he began moving sideways, and she matched her steps to his.

"Keep your eyes closed," he reminded. "I'll let you know when it's okay to open them."

Emma momentarily forgot her claustrophobia as she concentrated instead on the warmth of Doug's arm on her waist and the feel of his body next to hers. She couldn't help the little pang of disappointment that went through her when, a few minutes later, Doug let go of her and told her to open her eyes.

The others had their flashlights on, so Emma could see that the passage had opened up considerably. The ceiling was at least ten feet above her head and thirty feet or more separated the walls.

"Are you okay?" Doug asked with concern.

"This is much better," Emma answered with a smile. "Thanks for your help."

"No problem," Doug responded with a smile of his own. Then his expression turned businesslike. "Now let's find a way out of here."

For the next couple of hours, they wandered around the underground passages like mice in a maze. When given a choice of paths, they would make a choice and follow that path until it came to a dead end or another fork. It wasn't long before they lost all sense of direction. They could no longer tell whether they were headed toward or away from the castle. Doug had been marking their path by scratching an X on the cavern walls with a rock, but all that did was keep them from retracing their steps.

When their flashlight batteries began to give out, Doug declared it was time for a break. He opened his backpack and gave everyone a bottle of water. While the others sat on the rocky floor sipping their water, Doug put new batteries in the flashlights.

"Boy, I sure am glad you brought extra batteries along," Sebastian exclaimed. "It'd be impossible to find a way out in the dark."

"That's what I'm worried about," Doug answered. "I never dreamed it would take us this long. If we haven't made it out in the next half hour, I think we should go back to the lake and take the underwater passage."

The others agreed, and when everyone had satisfied their thirst, they set off again. It wasn't long before they came to another fork in the passage.

"Which way do you guys think we should go?" Doug asked, consulting the others for the first time.

"Well, we've been taking the right fork up till now, so I say let's go left this time," Sebastian offered.

"It doesn't make any difference to me," Martha commented with a shrug.

"Me neither," Emma agreed.

"Left it is then," Doug said in a surprisingly cheerful tone. Emma knew Doug was worried, but he was making an effort to hide it from the others. Emma wasn't fooled, and she was pretty sure Sebastian and Martha weren't either. Still, she appreciated Doug trying to keep things light for the benefit of his friends.

They hadn't gone very far when the passage made a sharp turn to the left. They all stopped in surprise as they rounded the corner. A faint light could be seen up ahead. With fresh hope, they hurried toward the light. They were stopped short of their goal by a pile of rubble lying right in the middle of the passage. Above the mountain of rubble and directly ahead was a large hole. The light they had seen was coming through the hole. Thinking that there must have been a cave-in, Emma shone her light on the rubble and was surprised to see that it was composed of red bricks, and not rocks as she'd expected.

"What is all this?" she asked in confusion.

"It looks like part of a brick wall has caved in," Doug answered.

"But what's a brick wall doing down here?" Sebastian inquired just as confused as Emma.

Instead of answering, Doug began scaling the pile of bricks, slipping and sliding until he was able to stick his head in the opening. The light was coming from somewhere to his right. Doug swept his flashlight around to get a better look.

"Guys, you're not going to believe this," Doug exclaimed after a moment.

"What?" the others asked in unison.

"I think this is the castle's basement," Doug answered. Then he climbed down the other side of the mound and disappeared from view.

Emma, Martha, and Sebastian looked at each other for a moment. Then Sebastian began climbing after Doug. With a shrug, Emma and Martha followed. Soon they were all standing in a long hall. The floor and walls were of the same brick that comprised the pile of rubble. Spaced along the walls at regular intervals were brass holders with torches in them. Of course the torches weren't lit at the moment, so Doug was using his flashlight to look around. Several wooden doors could be seen on both sides of the hall, and on the end of the corridor closest to them was a set of stairs leading upward. The meager light was coming from the stairwell.

"Are we in the dungeon?" Sebastian asked with a look of surprise.

"Why would Darius and Rebecca need a dungeon?" Martha huffed. "They weren't at war you know."

Before Sebastian could come up with a witty retort, Doug spoke up. "This whole area was probably used for storage or something."

"Do you think the stairs lead to a way out?" Emma asked. The light coming from above was a good sign.

"Only one way to find out," Doug answered, heading to the stairs. The others quickly followed.

At the top of the stairs, they found themselves in a large circular chamber. A spiral staircase wound upward around the chamber walls and ended several stories above them. There were several windows spaced unevenly around the outer perimeter of the structure. These accounted for the light spilling down the lower stairs into the basement. Although the first window was a couple of stories above where they were standing, it provided enough light to make their flashlights unnecessary.

"Do you know where we are?" Martha asked excitedly. When she received only blank stares as a reply, she continued. "We're in one of the castle's towers, and by the looks of it, we're in the west tower."

"I thought the towers were sealed off a long time ago," Sebastian argued.

"They were, but we came in through the basement. I'm guessing access to the basement has been closed for ages too, but thanks to the collapse of the basement wall, we got in." Martha stopped her narration for a moment to draw breath. Then her eyes widened as something else occurred to her. The others didn't have to wait long to find out what that something was. Martha grabbed hold of Emma's hand and blurted out, "Emma, do you remember the night of the hayride?"

Martha barely gave time for Emma to nod before she started talking rapidly again, her excitement almost a palpable thing. "Remember we saw a strange light coming from the tower that night, and we didn't know what it could be?"

Again Emma nodded, finally realizing the cause of Martha's excitement.

"With everything that happened after that, I totally forgot about it," Martha went on.

Emma knew that Martha was referring to the Octoberfest dance—or as Emma had come to think of it—the Preston Danvers fiasco. Emma looked over at Doug to see if he had caught Martha's meaning, but she couldn't tell anything from his expression. He continued to watch Martha with a slight frown.

Seeing the direction of Emma's gaze, Martha looked over at Doug too and said, "I meant to ask you about it. Do you know what's up there? I thought maybe Lord Dinswood might have mentioned it."

"No," Doug replied. "All he told me was that at some point in the castle's history the towers were sealed off because they'd become unsafe."

Nothing was said for a moment as everyone looked around in alarm, half convinced that the tower walls were about to come crashing down on them. It was then that Emma noticed a large rectangular area of brick that didn't match the color of the original brick.

"I bet that's where the entrance to the tower used to be," Emma said, pointing to the newer looking brick.

"I bet you're right," Doug agreed.

"We've got to find out what's up there," Martha urged. "The light coming through the tower window that night was so bright it was positively creepy."

"This tower is supposed to be unsafe," Sebastian pointed out. "The last thing we should do is climb to the top of it. The stairs are most likely the problem."

"They look solid enough to me," Martha said, running over to where the stairs began. Before anyone could object, she climbed the first several steps.

"Martha, get down!" Sebastian commanded. "What are you trying to do, get yourself killed?"

"The staircase is in perfect condition," Martha answered back.

Sebastian didn't reply but instead went over to the stairs to see for himself. "You're right," he said to Martha after a moment. Then he frowned and scratched his head. "I don't get it. If the tower is safe, why did they seal it off?"

"If I wanted to hide something priceless at the top of the tower, I'd seal it off and tell everyone that it was unsafe," Martha answered, sharing the hypothesis she had come up with the night of the hayride many months ago. Seeing that the others weren't quite convinced, she added, "It's the perfect plan. Nobody would think to question it."

Martha stopped talking then and gave Doug a pleading look. "We've got to see what's up there. We might never get another chance."

Doug didn't answer Martha immediately but instead looked at Sebastian and Emma. "What do you two think?"

"I'd like to see what's up there," Emma answered without hesitation. Like Martha, she had forgotten all about the strange light, but now her original curiosity had returned full force.

"Me too," Sebastian seconded Emma.

"Okay, we'll do it," Doug said. In truth, he was just as curious as the others to see what was up there, but he wanted the decision to be a unanimous one. Before anyone could move, Doug added, "But

I think we should take it slow. The stairs farther up may not be in as good a condition as these at the bottom. I'll go first and check them out as we go."

Sebastian, Martha, and Emma nodded their agreement and watched eagerly as Doug started up the spiral staircase.

CHAPTER FORTY-TWO
TOWER OF TERROR

The staircase was made of some kind of hard wood, probably oak, Doug guessed. As Martha had said, it seemed to be solid and in good condition, which was surprising considering its age. Doug looked up and saw that the stairs continued to a dizzying height. He began to worry that Martha, who had a fear of heights, wouldn't be able to make it to the top. Doug was also concerned because there were no handrails.

"Stay close to the wall," he cautioned the others as he continued to climb.

Only a short while later, Martha stopped climbing. "I don't think I can do this."

"I'd tell you to close your eyes," Sebastian joked, "but under the circumstances, I don't think that'd be a good idea. You might stagger over the edge."

Martha gasped in fright.

"Sebastian!" Emma yelled. "You're not helping!" Emma looked at Martha's pale face and said quietly, "You can do this, Martha. Stay close to the wall and look only at the steps. Don't look up or down.

Just look at the steps and put one foot in front of the other. Before you know it, you'll be at the top."

Martha nodded her understanding but still hesitated, so Emma came down a few steps until she was standing next to Martha. "I'll stay beside you, and we'll take the steps together. That way I'll be between you and the edge, okay?"

"Okay," Martha agreed, taking a deep breath.

Even though the staircase was fairly wide and there was plenty of room for the two girls to climb side by side, Doug didn't like the idea. But since he didn't have a better solution, he said nothing. Instead, he turned back around with a frown and began climbing once again. Doug led the way, followed by Emma and Martha with Sebastian bringing up the rear. Because Martha and Emma were taking it slow and Sebastian was stuck behind them, it wasn't long before Doug was quite a bit higher than his friends. So far, the staircase had proved structurally sound, so Doug decided to wait for the others. The trouble began when they were only about twenty feet from the top. Doug noticed a little bit of movement and some creaking sounds as he moved from one step to the next. He turned back to caution the others when the staircase swayed alarmingly. Martha screamed and grabbed hold of Emma, causing her to lose her balance. She would have gone over the edge if it hadn't been for the quick action of Sebastian, who grabbed her hand and pulled her back.

They all stood as still as statues. The staircase stopped swaying, but the creaking sounds continued to grow louder with each passing second.

"It sounds like the supports are giving way," Doug shouted to the others. "We have to get off this thing fast!"

At this point, they were closer to the top than the bottom, so Doug urged them upward. "Come on!" he shouted again. He came down a few steps, grabbed Emma by the arm and began pulling her along.

Martha was frozen in fear. Sebastian had to literally push her from behind. Emma and Doug made it to the top first, then turned and watched anxiously as Martha and Sebastian climbed toward them. A huge splintering sound echoed off the tower walls as the top section of the staircase started to separate from the wall. Sebastian practically threw Martha up the last few stairs. Doug reached out and pulled her to safety. Sebastian had just set a foot on the landing when the upper portion of the staircase dropped completely away. Emma grabbed his hand and pulled with all her might to keep him from falling backward.

"Whew! That was close!" Sebastian exclaimed as he collapsed on the floor next to Martha, who was on her knees sobbing quietly.

"It's okay, Martha." Emma knelt down beside Martha and put an arm around her. "We're all safe."

"At least for the time being," Sebastian said.

Martha sobbed louder, and Emma gave him a look that would have killed if looks could kill.

"What?" Sebastian asked Emma innocently.

Emma didn't bother to answer. Sebastian knew exactly why Emma had given him the "shooting daggers" look. Instead, she began looking around. They were sitting on what looked like a wooden bridge that spanned the entire diameter of the tower. The bridge was at least fifteen feet wide and had rails on both sides. It felt solid and secure. Emma could only assume it had a support system separate from that of the spiral staircase. On the end farthest from where they were sitting was a large wooden door with a brass knob and brass fittings. The end closest to them led to a door-sized opening in the tower wall. Inside the opening, Emma could see a set of stone steps leading upward.

Emma gradually became aware that Doug was leaning over the rail, examining the underpinnings of the bridge.

"Boy, it's a good thing this bridge has its own support," he commented. "Looks pretty sturdy too."

"Glad to hear it," Sebastian commented with an uplifted brow. Then he pointed to the wooden door and asked, "Where do you think that goes?"

"I'm guessing it leads to the roof of the castle," Doug replied. "There's one way to find out though."

While the others watched, Doug crossed the bridge and tried the door. "It's locked," he said. It was apparent from his tone that this was exactly the result he'd expected.

Before Sebastian could ask where the stone stairs led, Doug said, "Those stairs probably lead to the turret."

"What's a turret?" Sebastian asked.

By this time, Martha had stopped crying and was listening with interest to the exchange between Sebastian and Doug.

"It's a small tower that projects from a building," Doug answered.

"That's where the light was coming from," Martha told them as she wiped tears from her cheeks with the back of her hands.

"Well, since we're stuck up here for the time being, we might as well take a look," Sebastian suggested with a grin at Martha. Then he came over to help her up.

"Sorry for giving you a hard time. I thought if I made you mad enough, you'd forget your fear," Sebastian told her once she was on her feet.

"Considering that you just saved my life, I'd say you're forgiven," Martha said, smiling weakly.

"I think Martha should go first this time," Sebastian proclaimed. Then he bowed down and made a big sweeping gesture with his right hand to indicate that Martha should lead the way.

Martha didn't have to be asked twice. Without hesitation, she started up the short flight of stairs. Since there were walls on both sides of the steps and the steps were made of stone, Martha felt secure and proceeded without fear. Anxious to see what the turret might contain, the others followed right on her heels. When they reached the top of the stairs, they found themselves in a small circular room. There were tall windows all around; and in the center of the room, sitting side by side, were two sarcophaguses. The tombs were made of stone and were elaborately carved and ornamented. A large golden cross stood at the end of the tomb on the right, and set in the cross's center was an enormous ruby cut in the shape of a rose. The arms of the cross were studded with numerous diamonds and gems of every shape and color. Inscriptions at the foot of each tomb identified the occupant of the one on the right as Rebecca Rose Dinswood and the one on the left as Darius Bartholomew Dinswood. Amazing as this discovery was, it was the object sitting on Rebecca's tomb that had them all staring in awe.

Sitting at the head of Rebecca's tomb was the last of Marnatti's sculptures. Tears sprang to Emma's eyes as she realized the significance of the last Mortal. Marnatti had sculpted Mary holding baby Jesus. Mary was looking down at the baby she had cuddled in her arms with an expression of love. Emma remembered that Darius had intended to give this final piece to Rebecca after the birth of their first child. Tragically, Rebecca had become ill and died before he'd gotten the chance.

There might be some who would argue that a piece of marble could not possibly convey an emotion such as a mother's love for her child, but Emma would argue that they had never set eyes on any of Marnatti's work.

Emma noticed how quiet everyone had become. She looked over at Martha to see her reaction. Tears were streaming down her face as well. When she saw Emma's look, she said, "That is the most beautiful thing I've ever seen, and to think Rebecca didn't even get to see it."

"And it looks like Darius wanted to be sure that if Rebecca didn't get to see it, no one else would either," Doug commented as he realized that the four of them were probably the first people to set eyes on the sculpture since Darius's death.

"Except for himself and Marnatti," Martha corrected quietly.

"Why are Darius and Rebecca entombed way up here?" Sebastian asked, changing the subject. The girls were getting too emotional for comfort.

Emma, who had gone to the side of Rebecca's tomb to get a better look at the sculpture, happened to glance down just then. "I think I have the answer to your question, Sebastian. There's an inscription here." Emma began to read out loud.

> A view of the land you held so dear, season to season and year to year, from this high tower is yours to see, henceforth throughout eternity. While in death your flesh doth sleep, I pray the Lord your soul to keep. Though I know not why we were forced to part, you'll live forever within my heart.

"It's signed D. D.," Emma informed the others when she had finished reading. Then she grew silent as she imagined Darius writing this message—the last words of a grieving husband to his beloved wife.

"D.D., Darius Dinswood," Sebastian needlessly explained for everyone.

Instead of giving Sebastian a hard time for stating the obvious, Martha stood unmoving with a far-off look. She was busy putting all the pieces of the puzzle together in her mind. When she felt she had a satisfactory explanation for everything they had just seen, she shared it with the others. "Darius probably had Rebecca entombed up here with instructions to have him placed by her side at his death. Then the tower was sealed, and everyone was told that it was because the tower was unsafe. But of course that wasn't the real reason."

"I don't know. Given what we just went through, I'd say it's pretty unsafe," Sebastian said sarcastically.

"It's not safe now," Martha argued. "But I'm sure it was perfectly fine back when Rebecca and Darius died."

Thinking that this was probably a good time to change the subject, Doug spoke up before Sebastian could say something he'd regret later. "Martha, when you and Emma saw the light coming from this turret the night of the hayride, I bet it was the moonlight reflecting off the diamonds and gems in the cross."

"And it was probably especially bright that night because it was a full moon," Sebastian added.

"Do you suppose it shines like that every night, and we just never noticed because we're usually not outside the castle at that time of night?" Emma asked.

"Maybe, but I'm guessing it doesn't shine the way you guys saw it unless there's a full moon," Doug answered. "Conditions must have to be just right for it to happen, or lots of people would have seen it before, and we'd have heard rumors about it."

Emma nodded, glad to have that particular mystery solved. It was then that something else occurred to her. "You know, I always assumed that Darius and Rebecca were buried in the Dinswood family cemetery."

"Me too," Doug said. "But then I've never actually looked for their graves. I'll ask Lord Dinswood about it when we get back."

"Speaking of getting back, how are we supposed to do that? Half of the staircase is gone and we're like a jillion feet up," Sebastian pointed out.

"What about the door on the other side of the bridge?" Emma asked.

Doug was already shaking his head in the negative. "That door's made of solid oak, and it's locked. There's no way we're going to break it down."

"So we're stuck up here forever?" Martha asked with a note of panic in her voice.

Doug didn't answer immediately; instead he began looking around the room as if it might provide the answer. Then his eyes brightened as they lit on the drapes hanging at the chamber's windows. "I think I have an idea."

Emma was already pretty sure she wasn't going to like Doug's idea. His ideas usually involved him risking his life. Curiosity forced her to ask anyway. "Okay, what's your idea?"

Before answering, Doug walked over to the nearest window and pointed to the tieback on one of the drapery panels. The tieback was a gold color and looked like a length of thick rope. Emma looked at all the windows then and saw that every drapery panel had an identical tieback.

"We can tie all of these together to make one long rope. Then I can climb down it," Doug said casually as if it would be no big deal.

"That's crazy!" Emma blurted out. "First of all, those things have to be almost three hundred years old. They've probably dry rotted by now. Not only that, even if we do manage to tie them all together, the rope won't be long enough."

"It only has to be long enough to lower me to the part of the staircase that's still intact," Doug pointed out patiently. He understood that Emma was afraid he'd get hurt or possibly killed, but they had to do something. They couldn't just sit at the top of the tower hoping someone would eventually find them. He looked at Emma then and smiled slightly. "And we'll make sure the rope is strong enough to hold me first. Okay?"

Emma nodded reluctantly. She still hated the idea, but as she had no other solutions to offer at the moment, she kept her mouth shut.

It didn't take them long to get all the tiebacks gathered. Then, Sebastian's sailing knowledge came in handy—specifically his knowledge of how to tie knots. In no time, he had the tiebacks all securely joined together. When he was finished, the rope looked like it would be just barely long enough to reach the very top of the intact portion of the staircase.

"Now, it's time to give this thing a test," Sebastian said, standing up from where he'd been sitting on the floor tying the knots.

The test consisted of performing a tug-of-war with Doug and Emma on one side and Sebastian and Martha on the other. They stood across from each other on the bridge, and when Doug gave the signal, each team pulled for all they were worth—putting their full weight into it. Much to everyone's relief, the rope held together.

"Okay, that's it then. Looks like we're ready," Doug said when the test had been completed.

"I think I should be the one that goes," Sebastian volunteered suddenly.

"You failed rope climbing in PE last year," Doug quickly reminded him. "Besides, I'm lighter. We don't want any more weight than necessary on that rope."

Sebastian hated to admit it, but Doug was right. In seventh grade, he'd been shorter and plumper than he was now, and he hadn't been as strong. Back then, no matter how hard he'd tried, he hadn't been able to climb the rope. Although he was pretty sure he could do it now, this wasn't the time to learn. With a sigh of reluctance, he nodded.

"I'm a good rope climber, and I'm the lightest one here. It should be me that goes," Emma said suddenly, surprising even herself. The thought of dangling a hundred feet above the ground by a rope made of tiebacks scared her to death, but if it would keep Doug from getting killed, she would do it.

"No," Doug said, firmly shaking his head. "There's more to this than just getting to the bottom of this tower. Whoever goes also has to find a way out of the passages and bring help back. Emma, are you sure enough of your sense of direction that you could lead someone back here?"

Emma nodded hesitantly. "We marked the way we came."

"Those marks will lead you back to the underground lake. The only ways out of there are the underwater passage and the one that leads to the river. I was going to try some of the other passages and only go back to the lake as a last resort," Doug explained. Although everything Doug was telling her was true, what he didn't tell her was that under no circumstances would he even think about letting her do something so dangerous. But he knew if he just told her no, she would get mad and insist on going. He had to give logical reasons why she shouldn't be the one to go for help.

When he put it like that, Emma wasn't all that keen on going anymore. Once again, he was right. Her sense of direction was terrible, and even if she marked her path, she would most likely get turned around. Her bouts of claustrophobia wouldn't help things either. The idea was to go for help—not end up needing help herself.

Sensing her inner struggle and admiring her courage more than she would ever know, Doug grinned at her and said, "I really appreciate you offering to go, but I need you to take care of these two." With a laugh, he pointed at Sebastian and Martha. "Make sure they don't strangle each other before I get back."

CHAPTER FORTY-THREE
TRAPPED

N o more was said as Doug began making preparations for his descent. He didn't want to wait too long. If he had too much time to think about the danger involved, he might be tempted to change his mind. Added to that was the fact that it would be starting to get dark soon. The task ahead was going to be difficult enough in the light of day. It would be nearly impossible in the dark.

Doug took all the flashlights and put them in his backpack. He wanted to leave one for the others, but they insisted that he take them all. There weren't any more extra batteries, and there was no way of knowing how long it would take him to find a way out.

"We don't need a flashlight," Sebastian had told him. "When the sun goes down, we'll have light from the moon. You don't know how long you'll be wandering around down there, and you don't want to be left in total darkness."

Doug had to concede that this time Sebastian was right, so he quickly loaded the backpack and put it on his shoulders.

The plan was to tie one end of the rope around the wood railing of the bridge and then let Doug climb down, but when they finally had the rope secured to their satisfaction, the other end didn't quite reach the top of what was left of the stairs. From their position, it was hard to tell how much distance there was between the end of the rope and the stairs. Also, the end of the rope wasn't directly over the stairs; it was off to the side a bit. Unfortunately, because of the position of the stairs in relation to the bridge, there wasn't anything they could do about it.

"You guys will probably have to swing me over and then it looks like about a two- to three-foot drop," Doug estimated as he peered over the rail. "It shouldn't be a problem." Doug's tone was light as if this was something he did on a daily basis. He knew that if he showed the slightest bit of fear, his friends would keep him from going.

Emma felt sick. She tried not to think about what would happen if Doug's hands slipped off the rope. Taking a deep breath, she said a quick prayer and tried to pull herself together.

"Are you sure you want to do this?" Martha asked him for what must have been the tenth time. "You don't have to go you know. We can wait here. Help will come eventually." Even when they were searching for the treasure last year, they'd never tried anything this dangerous. Like Emma, Martha was sick with worry for Doug.

"We can't count on that," Doug replied, his jaw set in a firm line. "I'll be careful. I promise." Then he turned to Sebastian. "Sebastian, get set to swing me over to the staircase."

"I'll be ready," Sebastian promised.

Doug looked at the worried faces of his friends and smiled in an effort to reassure them. Then he turned toward the railing and climbed over it, grabbing the rope on his way over. Quickly, he wrapped his legs around the rope and began to lower himself.

Almost immediately the rail the rope was tied around began to creak loudly under the force of Doug's weight. They had tested the strength of the rope but hadn't really had any way to test the strength of the bridge's railing.

"Hurry, Doug!" Sebastian shouted. "I don't know how long this rail's gonna hold!"

Doug was already going as fast as he dared. He was gripping the rope so tightly his knuckles were white. There was no safety net below him. If he lost his grip on the rope, it wasn't going to be pretty. Doug could hear the rail creaking above him. With an effort, he blocked the sounds out and concentrated on the task at hand. Sweat popped out on his forehead, and his hands began to sweat and slide down the rope. As it turned out, the knots Sebastian had tied every couple of feet were his salvation. His hands slid to one of the knots and stopped. Doug hung there for a moment and took a deep breath. Supporting his weight with only his legs, he carefully removed his hands from the rope one at a time and wiped them dry on his jeans. When he was finished, he started down again.

The others watched anxiously from above. All the while, the rail continued to creak alarmingly.

Doug was almost to the end of the rope, when everything began to fall apart at once. The wooden rail started making splintering sounds as one by one the nails holding it to the bridge began to pull loose.

"It's coming loose!" Martha screamed.

"Start swinging me!" Doug yelled simultaneously. What the others didn't know and couldn't see was that the rope was beginning to fray as well. Doug knew he was running out of time.

Sebastian was lying down on the bridge on his stomach with his arms extended between the rail's vertical slats. Grabbing the rope, he began trying to swing it back and forth. He soon realized that what he was doing was having absolutely no effect. Doug was hanging directly below him unmoving.

"I'm trying, Doug, but nothing's happening," Sebastian shouted in frustration.

"Maybe I can get it going," Doug called. Gripping the rope firmly with his hands, he let his legs hang free and began pumping them as if he was on a swing. This action put even more strain on the rail, and it began creaking louder than ever. In the meantime, the rope was slowly coming apart in his hands.

At first, his efforts produced only a slight back-and-forth movement. But Doug didn't give up; he continued to pump his legs—his progress agonizingly slow. Because his legs had to be free so he could swing them, he had to support his entire weight with his arms. It wasn't long before his biceps began to burn painfully. Doug wasn't sure how much longer he could keep going.

Above him, Sebastian was doing his best to brace the rail, but he knew he wouldn't be able to hold it once the nails finally worked loose. "Hurry, Doug, hurry!" he urged frantically.

Gradually, Doug's swings began to widen. He looked down and saw that he was almost there—the stairs tantalizingly close. The next swing should bring him directly over the stairs. He had just reached the top of his next swing when the rope broke. Doug felt himself falling, and then he landed with bone-jarring force on the top stair. His momentum carried him forward, and he collided with the tower wall. Thankfully, he got his head turned in time so that his left shoulder took the brunt of the collision.

Sebastian watched helplessly as Doug fell, giving a huge sigh of relief when he saw that Doug had miraculously managed to land on the stairs. He had been so focused on Doug that it took him a moment to realize that Martha was screaming something at him. In sudden comprehension, he let go of the rail just in time to keep it from dragging him over the edge with it. The nails had finally pulled free. With a loud splintering sound, a large portion of the rail disappeared from view and fell to the tower floor a hundred feet below.

Down below, Doug's troubles weren't over just yet. The force of his landing started a chain reaction, and the remainder of the staircase began to collapse. Wasting no time, Doug got to his feet and started racing down the stairs, barely managing to stay one step ahead of the destruction. He was halfway down the last flight of stairs when he realized that he wasn't going to make it. Without giving himself time to think, he jumped the rest of the way and rolled clear just as the entire structure came crashing down. For the next several seconds, he lay there on the floor breathing heavily, thankful that he was still in one piece.

From somewhere far off, Emma heard someone screaming hysterically. Gradually, she became aware that someone was shaking her shoulders. A second later, she realized that she was the one doing the screaming. Her eyes focused, and she saw Martha kneeling in front of her with an anxious look, her hands on Emma's shoulders.

"He's all right. He made it," Martha kept repeating over and over in an attempt to get through to Emma.

When Martha's words finally sank in, Emma collapsed on the floor and began sobbing. The last few minutes had been the worst of her life, and she knew she would never forget the sight of that rail breaking free. She hadn't really seen what happened after that. Her mind had immediately conjured an image of Doug lying on the tower floor in a mangled heap. The last thing she remembered before she'd started screaming was the thunderous sound of the collapsing staircase. Emma looked at Martha now with a hopeful expression. "He's alive?" she asked. She was half afraid that Martha was lying to her just to calm her down.

"Yes," Martha answered with a nod and a sigh. "I don't know how, but he made it. See for yourself."

Emma scooted to the edge of the bridge and cautiously peered over. The first thing she saw was a huge pile of splintered wood. Then, she saw Doug standing by the basement stairs looking up at her.

He waved and shouted, "I'm okay."

All this did was make Emma cry even harder.

"I'm really okay," Doug tried again, but Emma was making so much noise she didn't hear him.

While Emma continued to sob in relief, Sebastian began whooping and hollering and pumping his fists in the air. "Wow! That was awesome! I can't believe you made it. That was the coolest thing I've ever seen!" He would have gone on, but he happened to glance in Martha's direction. Her icy stare stopped him cold. It was clear she didn't consider Doug nearly getting himself killed either awesome or cool.

With a shrug of his shoulders, he said defensively, "He's okay, you know. We don't have to act like we're at a funeral."

Martha didn't respond but continued to glare at him. Knowing when to give up, he turned away from Martha and looked back down at Doug. He saw that Doug was in the process of opening his backpack.

"Did the flashlights make it okay?" Sebastian called down.

"Yep." Miraculously, none of the flashlights appeared to be broken. Doug tried each one in turn to make sure they all worked. When he was finished, he yelled, "I'll be back with help as soon as I can." He kept one of the flashlights out; he would need it once he left the tower. Then he slipped the backpack over his right shoulder and started down the stairs leading to the basement.

Sebastian watched Doug leave and then turned to the girls. "Well, we might as well make ourselves comfortable. This might take a while."

"I don't think we should stay on this bridge," Martha said, "especially not with half the railing gone."

"We don't have a lot of options," Sebastian pointed out.

"We can stay in the turret. At least it has a stone floor." In the last few minutes, Martha had grown to distrust anything constructed of wood. The turret was made completely of stone with no wood to splinter and no nails to pull loose. In her book, that made it the best choice as a place to await their rescue.

Sebastian knew better than to argue. In fact, he found that he actually agreed with her. The bridge seemed to be solid but then so had the railing. "Okay then. After you, m'lady," he said with an exaggerated bow.

He waited while Martha pulled Emma to her feet and then followed the two girls up the stairs. Once they were in the turret room, Martha couldn't resist the urge to examine the sculpture of Mary and Jesus more closely. When she was finished, she began looking around for a comfortable spot to sit.

"I've got an idea," Sebastian said suddenly. "We can make a pallet on the floor with the drapes."

Martha had to admit that it was a good idea. The drapes were made of a heavy material, and it would certainly beat sitting on the cold hard floor. The only problem was going to be getting them down. The tops of the windows were well above their reach, so there was no way they could unhook the drapes, and although they were nearly three hundred years old, the drapes appeared to be in good enough shape that they couldn't be torn down either.

"How are you going to get them down?" Martha asked dryly after she'd had a moment to consider the logistics of Sebastian's suggestion.

"I have this," Sebastian answered with a triumphant grin as he pulled out his pocketknife.

"You want to cut the drapes?" Martha asked in disbelief. "They'll be ruined."

"Who cares? No one's been up here to see them for three hundred years. Besides, don't you think it's time for some new ones?"

Martha didn't respond, but Sebastian could see that she was close to giving in. She just needed a little more persuading before agreeing to ruin the drapes.

"I'm sure Lord Dinswood will understand. He'll be glad we tried to make ourselves a little more comfortable, and he can certainly afford to buy new ones."

"Well, I guess it's okay," Martha said slowly.

Sebastian quickly began cutting drapery panels before Martha could change her mind. Then with the girls' help, he piled several on the floor. It was already starting to get dark, and they were most likely going to have to spend the night, so Sebastian cut a couple more panels to use as blankets. Once their pallet was made, they all found a spot and settled down to wait.

"I'm hungry," Sebastian said a few minutes later. "I wish Doug had packed some food in that backpack of his."

"He had no way of knowing that this was going to happen," Emma said, speaking for the first time since the whole rail incident. "At least we have water."

Before Doug had started down the rope, he had taken all the water bottles out of his backpack saying they'd add too much weight. Emma had felt bad that he wasn't taking any water for himself, but as it turned out, they needed it more than he did. Doug could always make his way back to the ship if he needed something to drink or eat. Lord Dinswood kept plenty of supplies on board his ship. The tower, on the other hand, had no food or water to offer.

"That's true," Martha agreed. "Things could be a lot worse."

"Tell that to my stomach," Sebastian muttered.

CHAPTER FORTY-FOUR
THE RESCUE

With flashlight in hand, Doug quickly found the collapsed portion of the basement wall. He climbed back into the cave and picked up a fist-sized piece of brick from the rubble so he could mark his path. Before they'd found the tower, they'd been marking the walls of each passage they traveled with an X. Doug planned to mark any new routes he took with an O. He smiled to himself when he realized that when writing notes, X's and O's meant hugs and kisses. Then his expression sobered as he realized that his friends were counting on him to get help. Rubbing his sore left shoulder, he set off down the passage.

Now that he was by himself, Doug was able to move along a lot faster. It wasn't long until he came to a place where the tunnel forked. Without hesitation, he picked the passage they hadn't chosen previously. He followed this same procedure every time the passage branched. Doug found it more than a little ironic that after they'd left the lake—when they were trying to choose tunnels that led away from the castle—in every instance, they'd taken the ones that led back to it. He must have gotten completely turned around. His friends had been depending on him, and he'd let them down.

On the other hand, if he hadn't gotten turned around, they never would have found the last Mortal. Doug couldn't wait to tell Lord Dinswood about it, but a visit with the old man would have to wait. First, he needed to find help.

Doug couldn't say how long he'd been walking when suddenly the passage opened up into a huge cavern, as high as it was wide. He stopped for a moment in surprise. Then he swung his flashlight around to get a better look and saw that the ceiling of the cavern was literally covered with sleeping bats. He quickly lowered his flashlight beam so as not to disturb them. In that instant, he knew where he was. They'd come through this same room last year. Sebastian had called it the "bat room," and Martha had been terrified. Doug remembered it all like it was yesterday.

The good news was that now that he knew where he was, he also knew how to get out. He looked around until he saw it: the tunnel that opened out next to the stream that ran on the west side of the castle. Doug wanted to shout with joy, but he was pretty sure the bats wouldn't appreciate the noise, so he kept quiet.

A few minutes later, he was standing beside the stream. It was nighttime now, but the half-moon provided enough light for him to find his way, so he turned off his flashlight. Whistling as he went, he followed the stream back up to the castle.

EMMA SAT UP and rubbed her eyes. Light was just beginning to filter in through the tower windows. She yawned and looked over at Sebastian and Martha, who were both still sleeping. Emma continued to watch her friends as she wondered where Doug was. Martha must have sensed that she was being watched because she rolled over a moment later and peered groggily at Emma, her eyes barely open.

"What time is it?" she asked, her voice thick with sleep.

"I don't know. Probably around six."

"Has Doug made it back yet?"

Emma was about to say no when the faint sounds of people talking began to drift up from below. The girls quickly got to their feet and left the turret room, leaving behind a still sleeping Sebastian. When they were standing on the bridge, Emma walked over to the edge and looked down. Martha's fear of heights prevented her from going anywhere near the edge, especially with most of the railing gone.

"It's Doug, isn't it?" Martha asked. Then before Emma could answer, she asked another question. "Who's with him?"

"I can't really tell. It's still kinda dark down there," Emma answered. She could make out Doug's form because she knew it so well. The two people with him were still a mystery, but she was pretty sure neither one of them was Doug's dad. Her brow furrowed in confusion. She had been certain that Doug's dad would come with him, not only for Doug's sake, but also for the sake of three of the academy's students. The fact that he hadn't, meant something else must have happened, most likely something bad. Emma had just begun to worry about what that something could possibly be when Doug called up to her.

"Sorry it took me so long to get back. Mr. Dorfman said we couldn't really do anything until it got light outside anyway."

Well, that explained who one of the two people with Doug was, Mr. Dorfman. The other person appeared to be a woman. A few minutes later, the sun came up, and Emma could see that her assumption was correct. The third person was Miss Krum.

The three of them were carrying ropes and backpacks full of clanking equipment of some sort, and they were all dressed similarly in what looked like biker shorts, tight-fitting short-sleeved shirts, and some special type of shoes. As they began pulling things out of their backpacks, it finally dawned on Emma what they were preparing to do. The clothes and the equipment were for rock climbing. With a gasp of surprise, she realized that one of the three of them, most likely Mr. Dorfman, was going to scale the tower wall.

The next moment, she chided herself for being surprised. How else were they supposed to get to the top of the tower? They couldn't exactly use the stairs.

While preparations for the climb continued below her, Emma backed away from the edge and thought about whether or not she could ever do what Mr. Dorfman was about to do. Even though she wasn't afraid of heights, Emma had a healthy respect for gravity. She finally decided that rock climbing might be something she would actually like to try sometime.

Emma quickly figured out how they planned to get her, Martha, and Sebastian down to the tower floor. The procedure would undoubtedly involve harnesses and ropes. Martha, who did have a fear of heights, would freak out if she knew what Doug's rescue team was planning, so Emma kept quiet about what was going on down below her.

"Hey, looks like they're gonna climb up here and then lower us down," Sebastian said directly behind Emma, making her jump. She'd been so engrossed in her own thoughts that she hadn't heard his approach. Thankfully, she was no longer standing near the bridge's edge, or he might very well have caused her to fall. That wasn't the reason, however, for the glare she was currently giving him.

"What?" Martha shouted in a panic. She'd heard what Sebastian had said.

"When will you learn to keep quiet?" Emma hissed. "I wasn't going to tell her how they were planning on getting us down until it was absolutely necessary."

Martha's face had drained of all color, making her normally pale complexion even paler, if that was possible. She looked like she was about to faint. Fearing that her friend might actually pass out,

Emma went over and gently advised her to sit down. Martha didn't even argue. She immediately plopped down in the middle of the bridge and put her head between her knees. Then she began taking deep breaths, all the while muttering, "I can't do it. I can't do it."

Emma gave Sebastian a scathing look and mouthed the words, *thanks a lot!* She got even madder when Sebastian merely shrugged.

"She would have found out sooner or later," he said.

"Later would have been better!"

While the drama continued up above, down below Mr. Dorfman calmly walked over to inspect the wall more closely. He needed to get an idea of what type of protection devices he'd be able to use on his climb. The wall was in poor condition; the mortar between the stones had deteriorated. In some spots it had crumbled, and in others large chunks of it were missing. This was actually a good thing. He would have plenty of places to wedge the nuts and cams he had with him.

Nuts were small blocks of metal attached to a loop with a cord. The metal ends were jammed into cracks and crevices, and the climbing rope was then attached to the loop on the other end using a carabiner. Carabiners were common devices with multiple uses, including rock climbing. They consisted of a metal loop with a spring-loaded gate. Cams were similar to nuts except that the end placed in the crevice would spring open once it had been inserted, providing a secure hold. As he climbed, Mr. Dorfman would place these devices in the wall at regular intervals along his route and connect his climbing rope to them. Then, if he should happen to lose his footing, he wouldn't fall all the way to the bottom. The last protection device he'd placed would stop his fall.

Mr. Dorfman took a step back from the wall and viewed it from a broader perspective. Three hundred years ago, when the wall was being constructed, the builders had used quarried rock. This meant that the rocks were not uniform in size or shape; and, unlike the quarried rock of today, they weren't perfectly smooth or flat either. The result was numerous ridges, which a climber could grip with his hands, and numerous projections upon which a climber could rest his feet.

Satisfied that it wouldn't be too difficult a climb, Mr. Dorfman went over to where he'd laid his equipment and stepped into his harness. Emma watched from above as he attached several nuts and cams to the harness's numerous loops. Then he strapped on a small helmet and adjusted it until it rested comfortably on his head. After one last check of his equipment, Mr. Dorfman tied in and nodded at Miss Krum.

Miss Krum was going to act as the belayer. Her job entailed keeping the slack out of the rope and preventing any additional rope from playing out in the event Mr. Dorfman fell. The protection devices Mr. Dorfman placed would do him no good if Miss Krum didn't do her job properly.

Although Miss Krum weighed quite a bit less than Mr. Dorfman, this was not a problem. Miss Krum was using a belaying device called a GriGri. All she had to do was remain alert and use the device to arrest the movement of the rope if Mr. Dorfman lost his footing.

Emma watched with fascination as Mr. Dorfman stepped up to the wall again—this time to begin his climb. He had a slight build, but as Emma was about to find out, he was very strong. Sebastian came up to stand beside her then. Martha was still sitting in the middle of the bridge, rocking back and forth nervously.

"Belay on," Mr. Dorfman called to Miss Krum.

"On belay," Miss Krum replied.

"Climbing," Mr. Dorfman said.

"Climb away," Miss Krum answered.

"Communication is very important in rock climbing," Sebastian told Emma. "Mr. Dorfman was making sure Miss Krum was ready, and she was letting him know that she was. Climbers can be seriously injured, or even killed, if there's any miscommunication between climber and belayer."

"What's a belayer?" Emma asked then.

While they watched Mr. Dorfman's progress, Sebastian began to explain the basics of rock climbing. Whenever Mr. Dorfman stopped to place a nut or cam, Sebastian told Emma what he was doing and why.

"How do you know so much about it?" she asked Sebastian when he had finished.

"I've gone rock climbing with Doug and his dad before."

"You mean Doug climbs too?" Just when she thought she knew everything there was to know about Doug, she learned something new.

"Sure. We did a little climbing early last summer. There are a lot of good spots around the academy, it being situated in the mountains and all. I'm still a beginner, but Doug's pretty good."

"I didn't know Mr. Dorfman and Miss Krum were into the sport," Emma mused. "Mr. Dorfman must really enjoy it. He's got a lot of equipment, and he's climbing that wall like he's Spider-Man."

"Yeah, he and Miss Krum are exceptional climbers. Mr. Dorfman told me once that climbing was one of the reasons they both took jobs at the academy. They like to go on the weekends, and there are some pretty challenging rock faces nearby."

Emma and Sebastian grew silent then and continued to watch as Mr. Dorfman climbed higher and higher. Emma began to appreciate just how much upper body strength Mr. Dorfman had. He also seemed to have a very strong grip and amazing agility. Although she'd meant it as a joke earlier, he really did remind her of Spider-Man.

It wasn't long until Mr. Dorfman was climbing onto the bridge. "Everybody okay up here?" he asked as he walked toward them.

Sebastian looked at Martha before answering. "We're all okay." Then he nodded in Martha's direction and whispered, "But Martha's afraid of heights."

Mr. Dorfman nodded his understanding but didn't say anything. There was only one way down from their current position. Martha may not like it, but they were out of options. He would do his best to make Martha feel as secure as possible when it was her turn to be lowered. Other than that, there wasn't much else he could do.

"We'll have you down from here in no time," Mr. Dorfman told them. He then began looking for a good place to set the anchor. When he had found a suitable crevice in the wall, he inserted a cam and hooked the rope to it using a carabiner. He repeated the procedure with three additional cams. When he was satisfied with his anchoring system, he fed the end of the rope down to Miss Krum. Then he stepped up to the edge of the bridge and hollered down to Doug.

"Okay, Doug. You can tie in now. Miss Krum has you on the other end. Start climbing when you're ready."

Emma was both surprised and dismayed. She hadn't realized Doug would be doing any climbing today. She was also more than a little confused. "Why does Doug need to climb up here?" she asked Mr. Dorfman.

"He's going to remove all the protection devices I placed. Don't worry. Doug will be perfectly safe. I've got him anchored up here now, and Miss Krum has him on belay."

Emma didn't ask any more questions but instead stepped to the edge of the bridge and watched anxiously as Doug started up the wall. She could tell right away that she had nothing to worry about. Doug didn't seem to be having any problems and had a strength and agility matching that of Mr. Dorfman.

While Doug climbed, Miss Krum watched alertly from below. When Doug reached the bridge, Mr. Dorfman went over to give him a hand. The next moment, he was standing on the bridge smiling at them all as if their current situation was an everyday occurrence.

Emma's head was spinning with all the questions she wanted to ask Doug, but she decided all but one could wait until later. "Where's your dad, Doug?" Emma realized as soon as the question was out that it sounded more like an accusation. In an attempt to soften her tone, she added quietly, "I thought he'd come with you."

Doug stepped close to her before he answered. He didn't want the others to hear what he was about to tell Emma. "When I got back to the castle, I couldn't find Dad anywhere. I ran into Miss Grimstock and she told me that Lord Dinswood had collapsed. Dad found him lying unconscious on his living room floor. Lord Dinswood's been rushed to the hospital in Benton, and Dad's there with him. That's all I know."

Emma's heart sank at the news. She could see how upset Doug was, and she understood completely why he didn't want to share the bad news with everyone right now. It must be hard on Doug not knowing what was going on with Lord Dinswood. Emma prayed silently that Lord Dinswood would be all right.

Doug left her then to rejoin Mr. Dorfman. Together, they got everything set for the descent. Mr. Dorfman and Doug had each brought additional harnesses with them so there would be enough for everyone. The harnesses were made of a lightweight nylon and, like Doug's and Mr. Dorfman's, were the kind you put your legs through.

Once everything was set, they put a harness on Emma and prepared to send her down. They had decided Emma should go first so that Martha could see how easy it was going to be.

Before he let Emma go, Mr. Dorfman shouted down to Miss Krum, "Ready to lower!"

"Lowering!" Miss Krum yelled back.

Emma hung there for a moment and then began to descend at a slow but steady pace. Emma found herself enjoying the ride down. All she had to do was sit in her harness and let Miss Krum do the work. "This is a piece of cake, Martha," Emma shouted up to her friend. She couldn't see from her position that her words were having absolutely no effect. Martha was terrified, and nothing anyone said was going to change that.

Once Emma was safely down, it was Martha's turn. Incredibly, she allowed Mr. Dorfman to put the harness on her and get her set. It wasn't until they began walking her to the edge of the bridge that she balked and began screaming her head off.

"Let me talk to her," Sebastian suggested.

Doug and Mr. Dorfman readily agreed. Their only other option was to forcibly drag Martha to the edge and then push her off. Neither of them wanted to have to resort to force. If Sebastian could reason with her, they were all for it.

"It'll be okay, Martha," Sebastian began in a soothing tone, but Martha wasn't listening. She just kept shaking her head and mumbling. Not knowing what else to do, he grabbed her shoulders and squeezed hard. Martha was so surprised by the sudden pain that she stopped what she was doing and looked at him. Sebastian spoke quickly while he had her attention. "Listen, Martha. There's no other way down. You're going to have to do this. I know you. You're brave. Now suck it up and get going. Just close your eyes and think of it as a ride, okay?"

To his amazement, she nodded her agreement. He wasn't sure which of his rather harsh statements had gotten through to her. He was just glad she was back to herself. He'd apologize later for hurting her shoulders. Right now, they needed to get her going before she had any more time to think about it.

As Sebastian had suggested, Martha closed her eyes and let Mr. Dorfman swing her over the edge of the bridge. She sat back in her harness and kept her eyes closed the whole time she was being lowered. When she felt her feet touch the floor, she stood up and then nearly fell over as Emma threw her arms around her and hugged her tightly.

"You did great! I knew you could do it! It was kind of fun, wasn't it?"

Martha smiled weakly. "I don't ever want to do that again. If I even think about climbing to the top of anything ever again, you stop me. Deal?"

"Deal," Emma answered with a laugh.

Now that the two girls were down, it was Sebastian's turn. He'd been climbing before, so it was no big deal for him. Doug went next, followed by Mr. Dorfman. As soon as everyone was safely on the ground, Mr. Dorfman and Miss Krum began packing the equipment away in their backpacks while Doug dealt with the rope. As she watched Doug expertly coil the rope, Emma thought about the seventh Mortal still sitting up in the turret room. They had decided it was too risky to try to bring it down with them. Sadly, it would remain where it was, watching over Rebecca until someone figured out a way to get it down safely. As they left the tower, Emma couldn't help wondering if Lord Dinswood would ever get to see it.

CHAPTER FORTY-FIVE
A SURPRISING CONFESSION

Once they were out of the cave, walking along the stream on their way back to the castle, Doug told Sebastian and Martha about Lord Dinswood's collapse. They were just as shocked and dismayed as Emma had been.

"He'll be okay, Doug. He's a tough old guy," Sebastian said in an attempt to comfort his friend.

"At least now maybe the doctors will be able to figure out what's wrong with him," Martha added. It occurred to her that Lord Dinswood's illness might not be treatable, but that wasn't what Doug needed to hear right now.

No more was said as they neared the castle with Mr. Dorfman and Miss Krum in the lead. The second they stepped through the front doors, they caught the tantalizing smell of bacon and realized they were just in time for breakfast. Their stomachs reminded them that they hadn't had anything to eat since lunch the day before. After heartily thanking Mr. Dorfman and Miss Krum for coming to their rescue, they separated to go to their rooms and wash up. Doug and Sebastian were already filling their trays when the girls arrived back at the dining hall. Conversation at the table was light as they stuffed themselves with scrambled eggs, bacon, sausage, biscuits, and blueberry pancakes. When they had eaten their fill, Sebastian and the girls went to the Sunday morning service in the chapel, while Doug headed to his room for some much-needed rest.

The first thing Doug noticed when he got back to his room was his backpack. It was sitting on his bed where he'd hurriedly dumped it earlier. Inside the pack was the little black box. Doug ran a hand through his hair and sighed. Then he picked the backpack up and set it gently on the floor in his closet. He would not open the box until Lord Dinswood told him to. Tiredly, Doug lay down on his bed. Unlike his friends, he hadn't gotten any sleep the night before. Doug said another quick prayer for Lord Dinswood, then closed his eyes and immediately fell sound asleep.

The next day, Doug finally got a chance to tell his dad everything that had happened down in the passages, including the discovery of the last Mortal. Dean Harwood's expression grew grim as Doug told about being lowered on a rope made of drapery ties. Doug ended by telling how Mr. Dorfman and Miss Krum had rescued everyone.

Dean Harwood sat quietly for a moment as he digested everything his son had told him. It was hard to believe that Rebecca and Darius Dinswood had been entombed in the west tower all this time, and the discovery of the seventh sculpture was great news. But the part of the story that disturbed him the most was the part where his only son had once again risked his life.

"Son, why didn't you wait for someone to find you when you were stranded at the top of the tower?" Dean Harwood finally asked. "Why did you feel you needed to risk your life?"

"Nobody even knew we were in the passages except you and Lord Dinswood. I was afraid you wouldn't be able to find us, what with the passage blocked and all. We didn't have any food, and we only had a little bit of water. We wouldn't have lasted very long on that," Doug answered.

Dean Harwood sighed in frustration. "Why didn't you trust me?"

Doug sat back in surprise, temporarily speechless. How could his dad think that he didn't trust him?

"It's not that, Dad. I do trust you. I knew that you would come for us and that you wouldn't rest until you found us. I just didn't know how long that would take. It's like a maze down there."

"And you had your friends to think of," Dean Harwood added for Doug. "You felt responsible for them. Is that right?"

"Yeah," Doug admitted. Then he realized that the story he'd just told his dad had not portrayed his friends in a very positive light. To correct any wrong impression his dad might have of his friends, he filled in some of the details he'd left out the first time through. "When I came up with the rope idea, they tried to talk me out of it. Sebastian and Emma even offered to go in my place, but Sebastian failed rope climbing in PE, and Emma gets turned around too easily. I knew she wouldn't be able to find her way out of the cave, even if she somehow managed to make it down the rope. Then there's Martha. She's afraid of heights. So you see, there was only me. I had to do it."

"You didn't have to, son. You could have waited and then risked your life on that so-called rope only when the situation became desperate."

"But by then, I might not have had the strength to climb down the rope," Doug pointed out.

Dean Harwood had to admit that in this instance Doug had a valid point. Once again, he tried to picture what he would have done if he'd been in Doug's position. He finally concluded that he and his son were too much alike. "I'll give you that one," he conceded. "But it wouldn't have hurt you to at least wait until the next morning. Promise me that next time, if heaven forbid there is a next time, you'll at least give me a chance to come to your aid before doing something reckless."

Doug realized that his dad was only worried about him, so he grudgingly agreed. Then he made a concession of his own. "I'm sorry, Dad. You're right. I shouldn't have been in such a hurry to play the hero."

Now it was Dean Harwood's turn to be surprised. When he'd recovered from his shock, he smiled and, with a slight nod, said, "Finally. Progress."

Doug smiled back. Then he remembered something. "Dad, I'd like to be the one to tell Lord Dinswood that we found the last Mortal. I mean when he's feeling better." Doug didn't even want to consider the possibility that Lord Dinswood might not get better.

"I promise, I won't say a word," Dean Harwood replied. "Thanks, Dad."

"No problem."

Doug was just getting up to leave when his Dad remembered something else he'd wanted to tell his son.

"By the way, I called Mr. Munsen to thank him personally for everything he did for you. We had a good conversation. Turns out we have some interests in common, namely hunting and fishing. Anyway, he's invited us to do some fishing with him this summer. What do you think?"

"Sounds like fun," Doug answered sincerely. He was glad his dad had talked to Mr. Munsen. He hoped the two men would become friends. As Doug left his dad's suite, he couldn't help thinking that his dad and Mr. Munsen had more in common than just fishing and hunting.

IT WAS TUESDAY before they heard anything about Lord Dinswood's condition. Sebastian, Martha, and Emma were at breakfast when Doug came in and told them he had some news.

"Dad gave me permission to tell you guys, but he doesn't want the other students to know just yet," Doug began seriously.

"Okay," the others agreed in unison.

Judging by Doug's expression, Emma figured that Lord Dinswood must be seriously ill, so she was greatly relieved by Doug's next words.

"Lord Dinswood is going to be all right. The doctors seem to think he'll be able to come home on Saturday."

Just as Emma was wondering why they couldn't share the good news with the other students, Doug went on.

"Apparently, he was suffering from some type of poisoning."

"Poisoning!" Sebastian exclaimed.

"Sebastian, be quiet!" Martha hissed before looking around to see if anyone else had heard his outburst. All the other students appeared to be involved in their own conversations, and no one was looking in their direction. This was one time Martha was actually glad that the dining hall was always so noisy.

"Sorry," Sebastian apologized with a shrug. "I couldn't help it. That was the last thing I expected Doug to say."

Although they didn't say it, Emma and Martha couldn't have agreed more. It wasn't every day that you heard about someone being poisoned, and it certainly wasn't something you expected to happen to someone you knew.

"How could that have happened?" Emma asked. "Is there something wrong with the castle's plumbing?" Even as she asked it, Emma knew that if that were the case, they'd all be sick.

Doug shook his head in the negative. "No. It turns out he was intentionally being poisoned by Mrs. Bertram and Mr. Sutton."

"What?" Martha asked. She was thoroughly confused now. None of this made any sense. Why would Mrs. Bertram or Mr. Sutton want to poison Lord Dinswood?

"Well, we only know about it because Mrs. Bertram confessed to the whole thing. She came forward when she found out that Lord Dinswood had been rushed to the hospital. She said she's been putting a sleeping pill in Lord Dinswood's tea every evening since last summer and that she never meant to make him sick. She says she got the sleeping pills from Ray Sutton. Apparently, he's the one who put her up to it."

"So how did Lord Dinswood get poisoned?" Sebastian broke in. The story was getting stranger and stranger by the minute.

"They weren't sleeping pills like Mrs. Bertram thought. Sutton was actually giving her tablets laced with poison to put in the tea."

"Why would Ray Sutton want to kill Lord Dinswood?" Emma asked.

"He didn't want to kill him. He just wanted to keep Lord Dinswood out of the way in case he came across any other priceless objects while he was working on the new gym. He thought it was Lord Dinswood watching from the third-floor window the night the first Mortal was discovered."

"That wasn't even Lord Dinswood. It was Mr. Criderman," Sebastian said with disgust. All this time Lord Dinswood had been paying the price for a case of mistaken identity.

"You and I know that, but Ray Sutton thought the old man was spying on him. He figured he could keep anything else he might find as long as Lord Dinswood didn't know about it."

"And Lord Dinswood wouldn't know about it if he was too sick to keep an eye on Sutton," Sebastian finished for Doug.

"That's it exactly," Doug said with a shake of his head.

"Sutton had to know that the poison would eventually kill Lord Dinswood," Emma pointed out.

"Apparently, Sutton was only giving him a very small dose, enough to make him sick but not enough to kill him."

"That's just crazy," Martha said with a shake of her head. It was disturbing what people would do in the name of greed. Low dosage or not, Ray Sutton had almost killed a sweet old man. She hoped Sutton would get what he deserved. That thought prompted her to ask, "What's going to happen to Mrs. Bertram and Mr. Sutton now?"

"Sutton's been arrested."

"What about Mrs. Bertram?" Emma asked before Martha got the chance.

"It seems Sutton may have actually cared for Mrs. Bertram because when she confessed, he corroborated her story. He told the sheriff that Mrs. Bertram truly believed she was only giving the old man sleeping pills."

"Well, that was decent of him," Martha said with a snort. She felt nothing but disgust for Ray Sutton, but she couldn't help feeling a little sorry for Mrs. Bertram. Sutton had misled her and used her. "Mrs. Bertram probably thought he really loved her."

Doug nodded his agreement and then continued. "Anyway, Lord Dinswood decided not to press any criminal charges against her. Mrs. Bertram won't go to jail, but she's been fired from her job. She no longer works at the academy."

"Come to think of it, I haven't seen her these last couple of days," Martha said after a moment.

"She left with all her stuff Monday morning," Doug said grimly.

"But Lord Dinswood's really going to be all right?" Emma asked, getting back to the heart of the matter. It was hard to believe that a man of eighty could survive a case of poisoning. She needed to hear Doug say it again.

"Yep. Crazy as it sounds, he's going to be okay. Of course, it's going to be a while before he gets all his strength back, but Dad says he's already looking a lot better. He's got color in his cheeks again, and he seems to have more energy. Dad says he's keeping the hospital staff on their toes."

"Good for him," Martha said with a smile. "I'm really glad he's going to be all right, Doug."

"Me too," Doug agreed.

CHAPTER FORTY-SIX
GIFTS AND GOODBYES

L ord Dinswood was too feisty and stubborn to stay down long. By Thursday, he was feeling so much better that he began trying to bully the doctors into letting him go home. On Friday morning, he finally wore them down, and they agreed to release him. The nurses on his floor hated to see him go. They'd grown rather fond of him. Although he was gruff with his doctors, he never said a harsh word to the nurses. To them, he was sweetness personified.

The next week, he continued to improve. And the following Saturday afternoon, eight days after his release from the hospital, Doug, Emma, Martha, and Sebastian were once again summoned to Lord Dinswood's suite with instructions to bring the black box. Doug couldn't wait to see him and tell him they'd found the last Mortal. He had wanted to visit the old man earlier, but the doctors had insisted that he have no visitors for at least a week. In fact, they had made it a condition of his release. Lord Dinswood had been so anxious to get out of the hospital that he would have agreed to anything.

This time when they entered Lord Dinswood's suite, he was sitting in the recliner. Doug couldn't get over how much better he

THE MISSING MORTALS | 481

looked. He'd put on some weight, and his previously pale cheeks had a nice blush of color. He looked much as he had the first time they'd met him in the bookstore in Windland.

"Come on in and have a seat," he called in a strong voice when he saw them. The full-time nurse who was currently caring for him had let them in.

Doug had been concerned upon seeing the nurse, but his mind was relieved when he saw how well Lord Dinswood looked. It didn't look like the old man would need a nurse much longer.

Emma, Martha, and Sebastian took seats on the couch, and Doug sat in the room's only other chair.

Lord Dinswood waited until everyone was settled before speaking. "You're probably wondering why I called you up here."

"We're glad to see that you're feeling better, sir," Doug said in the brief silence that followed.

Doug's statement broke the ice, and his three friends all began speaking at once.

"You look so much better," Martha said.

"We're just glad you're all right," Emma said sincerely.

"It's good to see you, sir" was Sebastian's comment.

Lord Dinswood smiled at the four youngsters. They really were good kids, and he had the feeling that they genuinely cared about him. Until recently he'd never been around kids much, so this was new for him. He found that he was enjoying the attention immensely. He took time to savor the moment and then got down to business. Looking at Doug, he asked, "Did you remember to bring the black box?"

Doug nodded as he handed the box to Lord Dinswood. He was turning to go back to his seat when Lord Dinswood startled him by grabbing his hand. "You might as well stay here, son. I want you to have what's in this box." He gave the box back to Doug and instructed him to open it.

Surprised, Doug slowly lifted the lid and looked inside. Lying on a piece of black velvet was a gold ring bearing the Dinswood Crest. For a moment, Doug didn't know what to say.

"I wore that ring when I was your age. It hasn't fit me for a long time, but I'll wager it'll work for you. If it doesn't, I'll have it sized for you," Lord Dinswood offered.

"I don't know what to say, sir. I'm honored, but I can't accept something this nice," Doug finally managed to say.

"After all you've done for me, it's the least I can do. I've already talked with your dad, and he said it was all right for you to accept it."

"Then I guess all I can say is thank you, sir." Doug took the ring from the box and tried it on the third finger of his right hand. "It fits just fine."

"I thought it might," Lord Dinswood said with a smile. Then he turned to the other three youngsters. "I have something for each of you as well, just small tokens of my appreciation for your help with the Mortals." He then turned to the table next to his chair. Three little boxes, which Emma hadn't noticed when she first came in, were sitting there. Lord Dinswood passed a box to each of them and told them to open them.

Emma's box contained a necklace with a charm that looked like a shield. She immediately recognized the red and green colors on the shield as those of the Dinswood family crest. Martha opened her box to reveal a charm bracelet, its only charm a red and green shield. Sebastian was the last to open his box. He was pleased to find it contained a small pocketknife with the Dinswood family crest embedded in the handle.

"I'm making you all honorary members of the Dinswood family. Please accept my gifts with my thanks," Lord Dinswood told them when they'd all opened their boxes.

"I love it, thank you," Emma said as she put her necklace on,

Martha echoed Emma's thanks and then had Emma help her put her bracelet on.

"This is great! Thanks!" Sebastian exclaimed as he examined each of the knife's blades.

"I'm glad you like them," Lord Dinswood said as he watched them with a satisfied smile.

"We've got a surprise for you too, sir," Doug said.

Lord Dinswood looked at them all with raised eyebrows. He couldn't begin to imagine what the surprise might be.

Doug didn't wait for Lord Dinswood to ask what he was talking about; he plunged right in. "We found the seventh Mortal."

Doug let the news sink in for a moment before going on to relate the events that had taken place while they were down in the cave. He told about discovering the west tower and how they'd found the tombs of Darius and Rebecca along with the sculpture of Mary holding the baby Jesus. "We didn't bring it with us, sir. We were afraid something might happen to it if we tried to bring it down. It wasn't worth the risk," Doug explained when he had finished his story.

Lord Dinswood was quiet while Doug spoke. Emma noticed his eyes growing misty. She suspected that he never expected the last Mortal to be found, at least not in his lifetime. His next words confirmed Emma's suspicions.

"I didn't think I'd ever get to see it," Lord Dinswood began softly. "I can't believe you found it. A simple thank you doesn't quite seem adequate, but I'll say it anyway. Thank you all."

"You don't have to thank us, sir," Doug said. "We found it totally by accident."

"In my experience, son, there are no accidents," Lord Dinswood told him gently. He thought back to the youngsters' stories of how each piece was found. He could see the Lord's hand in each of the discoveries, and he was grateful. Lord Dinswood grew quiet then as he struggled to get ahold of his emotions. Doug's description of the last Mortal had affected him greatly. It had been the final gift of a doting husband to his beloved wife, and it had a sentimental value far beyond its monetary worth. To his knowledge, excluding the four youngsters before him, only two other people had ever laid eyes on the seventh Mortal: Marnatti, who sculpted the piece, and Darius Dinswood, who commissioned it.

Although he was anxious to see it, it didn't appear that that was going to be possible for quite some time. The tower would have to be repaired first and then some sort of lift installed so he wouldn't have to climb any stairs. All the repairs and modifications would take time. Still it gave him something to look forward to.

"Sir, I was curious about something," Doug began, after giving Lord Dinswood a moment to collect himself.

"What's that?"

"Well, I always just assumed that Darius and Rebecca were buried in the Dinswood family cemetery. It seems like somebody would have noticed their absence before now."

Lord Dinswood looked at Doug with a raised eyebrow. "Now that you mention it, there are crypts bearing the names of Darius and Rebecca Dinswood in the family mausoleum. I know because I've seen them. After what you've just told me, we can now assume that those crypts are empty, mere decoys. It seems Darius wanted to make sure that the actual tombs were never discovered."

"That's what I thought," Martha exclaimed. "Before he died, Darius must have left instructions that upon his death he was to be laid to rest next to Rebecca in the west tower. Then the tower was to be sealed and declared unsafe to keep it all a secret."

"I'd say that's exactly what happened," Lord Dinswood agreed. "And for nearly three hundred years, his ruse worked. If you four don't mind, I'd like to honor Darius's memory by keeping his secret a little while longer. What I mean is, I'd like this information to stay just between us."

"Dad knows," Doug informed Lord Dinswood. "But he won't tell anyone."

"I'm sure I can trust your father," Lord Dinswood said with a smile. He had a lot of respect for Jacob Harwood. These last several months, as his illness had progressed, Jacob had cared for him more like a son for his father than an employee for his boss. Between them, there had grown a mutual admiration and affection. Lord Dinswood had no doubt that Jacob would respect his wishes in this matter.

With that settled, Lord Dinswood talked with the youngsters a little longer. He asked them how their classes were going and if they were excited about the new facility that was nearing completion.

"Even with the delays caused by recent events, it should be ready for the start of the next school year," Lord Dinswood told them. Then he went on to explain that although Sutton was no longer in charge of the project, the work was progressing and would be completed on schedule.

When the youngsters noticed that Lord Dinswood was beginning to tire, they thanked him for their gifts and said their goodbyes. The two girls each gave him a hug, and the two boys shook his hand. It was a good thing they left when they did, or they would have seen an old man cry.

THE LAST DAY of school came all too quickly. Every student went to homeroom to receive final report cards, and then they were dismissed to go do their packing.

The four youngsters had agreed to meet in the lounge as soon as they were dismissed. Emma and Martha were the first to arrive, but Doug wasn't far behind. Eagerly, they shared the results of their hard work. Emma and Doug had both made straight A's again. Martha had gotten an A in everything except math. While they waited for

Sebastian to make an appearance, Martha chewed her lip nervously. She knew he'd been working harder these last several months so he could get into the Alpha-O's next year. Martha hoped his hard work had paid off. It just wasn't any fun doing things without Sebastian along.

A few minutes later, Sebastian came in waving his report card proudly. Martha grabbed it from him, and as she scanned it, her eyes widened in amazement. He had received an A in every class except Miss Grimstock's. In her history class, he had miraculously managed a B.

"I bet I get into the Alpha-O's next year," he told her with a satisfied grin.

"I bet you do too," Martha agreed, laughing. Then she surprised even herself by giving him a hug. "Congratulations!" she said into his shoulder. "I knew you could do it!"

When she finally let him go, Sebastian was blushing with pleasure. To cover his friend's embarrassment, Doug punched him lightly in the arm and said enthusiastically, "Way to go!"

"Good job, Sebastian," Emma said, adding her congratulations. "I can't wait until next year when we're all Alpha-O's. It's going to be so much fun!"

They talked a little while longer about some of the activities the Alpha-O's were planning for next year and then split up to go to their dorm rooms. Emma, Martha, and Sebastian were leaving for the airport later that afternoon and still had some final packing to do. Doug went along with Sebastian to keep him company while he got ready to go.

Later, they ate their last lunch of the school year together in the dining hall, and then the buses began pulling up in front. Doug helped them get their luggage out to the buses. After they'd loaded their things in the bus's lower compartment, they stood back and watched solemnly as the other students did likewise. This was the part of the school year Doug hated the most—saying goodbye to his friends.

Clarice and Reggie came out a moment later, and Sebastian and Doug helped them get their things loaded too. Emma wondered briefly where Susie was; then she saw her with Daniel a few buses down. When Doug and Sebastian finished with the luggage, Clarice murmured her thanks, and Reggie shook their hands.

"Thanks, guys. I guess I'll see you next year. The new gym's going to be great," Reggie said brightly as he climbed onto the bus behind Clarice.

Emma knew that she, Martha, and Sebastian should be boarding as well, but she couldn't bring herself to leave Doug just yet.

They were still standing on the terrace when Emma saw Preston Danvers emerge from the school. Emma tensed as he walked toward them. She was certain he would say something nasty to either her or Doug. Emma couldn't prevent the small sigh of relief that escaped her lips when he walked right past them without even glancing in their direction. She looked up at Doug to see if he'd noticed Preston going by. He had noticed all right. His whole body was tense as he stared at Preston's retreating back with an unreadable expression. Doug didn't relax his stance until Preston had boarded his bus.

A moment later, all students were instructed to board their respective buses by none other than Miss Grimstock. She was wearing her usual no-nonsense look, the look that dared any student to disobey. Emma saw Sebastian shiver and smiled. Martha's fear of heights was nothing compared to Sebastian's fear of Miss Grimstock.

Martha and Sebastian boarded first so that Emma and Doug could have a moment alone. As usual, Emma found herself feeling awkward and shy. Angry with herself for being such a goof, she looked up at Doug. He was smiling at her with that special smile that he reserved just for her. As she smiled back, she felt her embarrassment melt away.

"I'm going to miss you most of all," Doug said as he continued to smile down at her. Then his expression sobered. "I don't think I would have made it through this last year if it hadn't been for you."

Emma leaned back and looked into his dark eyes. He was just as handsome as ever, but the stress of the last year had taken its toll. He seemed older somehow. Not knowing how to respond to his statement, she hugged him instead.

Immediately, he put his arms around her and drew her close, resting his chin on the top of her head. They stood there like that until they heard the sound of someone loudly clearing their throat. They both looked around to see Miss Grimstock standing only a few feet away from them. She was staring at them, her eyes narrowed in what Emma recognized as her most severe look.

Embarrassed, they parted, but Miss Grimstock remained where she was. Their chance at a private farewell had come to a sudden and unexpected end.

Not knowing what else to say under the watchful eyes of Miss Grimstock, Emma murmured, "I'll see you." Then she looked at Doug's handsome face one last time and boarded the waiting bus.

"I'm counting on it," Doug replied softly after she had gone. He stood on the steps and watched until the bus bearing his friends turned onto the main road and disappeared from view. The rest of the buses soon followed. Doug was just turning to go back into the school when Bobby Wilcox came strolling through the main doors as if he didn't have a care in the world.

"You're too late, man. The buses have all gone," Doug told him.

"Dad's coming to pick me up," Bobby replied. "Should be here any time now."

Doug nodded his understanding thinking that Bobby would go on about his business, but instead he walked up to Doug and stopped directly in front of him.

Bobby didn't waste time but came straight to the point. "Just so you know, Harwood, the truce is now officially over."

Doug had been hoping that, after all this time, Bobby had forgotten about the feud, but apparently that was not the case.

Bobby didn't wait for a reply or the explanation Doug had promised him when they'd both first agreed to the truce. Instead, he turned abruptly and went back the way he'd come. Doug stayed where he was, mulling over what Bobby had said. Compared to the year he'd just had, the feud with Bobby seemed pretty trivial. Doug shrugged his shoulders and grinned ruefully. For the past several months, he'd been praying that things would get back to normal. Everything concerning his dad and Lord Dinswood was finally back to normal, and just now he'd learned that Bobby Wilcox still hated him. It seemed his prayer had been answered.

EPILOGUE

Two months later, Lord Dinswood stood in the turret of the west tower viewing the tombs of Darius and Rebecca for the first time. Repairs to the tower had gone very quickly, but installing the elevator had been more of a problem than he'd anticipated. Although there had been some snags along the way, the work was finally finished and Lord Dinswood was pleased with the results.

The first-floor entrance to the tower had been reopened and was now guarded by a sliding metal door. A keypad to the right of the door insured that only those who knew the access code could enter. Once through the door, it was only a short walk to the lift. The lift was similar to the kind you would find in some of the fancier hotels. Its walls were transparent so that the occupants could look out as they ascended. The doors of the lift opened onto the bridge that connected the turret to the castle's roof. The bridge and its supports had been totally reconstructed with new wood.

The turret had also been inspected and had been found to be in excellent condition, needing only some minor repairs and, of course, some new drapes. Other than the new drapes, it remained much as it had been when the kids had seen it, and the stone steps leading up to it were the only ones Lord Dinswood had been required to climb. Fortunately, there weren't very many of them, and Lord Dinswood had made it into the turret room without any difficulty.

He had requested that all seven of the Mortals be placed in this room. Each one now rested on top of its own marble pedestal. The pedestals were approximately five feet tall and were arranged in a semicircle at the heads of the tombs of Rebecca and Darius. Lord Dinswood was seeing the seventh Mortal for the first time. The sculpture of Mary and baby Jesus was more beautiful than anything he could have imagined. This mother and child had been intended for another mother and child, Rebecca and her son. Lord Dinswood could understand why Darius had chosen to place it on Rebecca's tomb. It had been meant only for her, and with her it would stay.

Lord Dinswood's eyes grew misty as he looked at the seven symbols of Darius's love for his wife Rebecca. Although the story of Darius and Rebecca was a sad one, Lord Dinswood had recently come across some information indicating that the ultimate ending had been a happy one.

A few weeks ago, he had found an old family Bible in the secure section of the library. In that Bible, he had found the baptismal record of one Darius Bartholomew Dinswood. According to the date on the document, Darius had been an old man at the time of his baptism, but Lord Dinswood knew from experience, that as long as one had breath, it was never too late to change one's eternal destiny. He could only imagine Rebecca's joy when she saw her husband coming through heaven's pearly gates.

Lord Dinswood looked at his watch and realized he needed to get going. He had been invited to go fishing with Frank Munsen. Jacob and Doug were going along too. Lord Dinswood hadn't been fishing in a very long time, and he was really looking forward to it. He was also looking forward to seeing Frank again. It had been a long time since he'd last seen him.

Frank's wife and daughter had been working in his bookstore in Windland for the past couple of years. During that time, he had gotten to know Frank. Lord Dinswood had a high regard for Frank Munsen and knew him to be a good and honest man. As a result, he hadn't been at all surprised to learn how Frank had helped Doug when he had needed it the most and had even saved Doug's life. As a token of his gratitude, Lord Dinswood had signed over ownership of the bookstore to the Munsen family. Frank had initially refused the gift, saying it was too much and that he hadn't helped Doug expecting a reward. But Lord Dinswood was not a man to be denied, and the Munsen family now owned a very lucrative business in the small town of Windland.

Before leaving the turret, Lord Dinswood let his gaze wander over the seven Mortals one more time. In their current arrangement, they looked like guardian angels silently watching over the remains of Rebecca and Darius. Lord Dinswood smiled with satisfaction. A year ago, the Mortals had been nothing more than a story, treasures from the past believed to have been destroyed in a moment of grief. Incredulous as it seemed, they had survived the centuries, and now here they were before him, all seven Mortals together. After nearly three hundred years, they were home at last.

ABOUT THE AUTHOR

Ellen Alexander was born and raised in Springfield, Illinois. She attended the University of Illinois and graduated with a bachelor's degree in microbiology. After graduation, she and her husband Jim moved to Dixon, Missouri, where they raised their three sons. Ellen taught high school chemistry in Dixon for twenty-six years. Now retired, Ellen spends her time writing and enjoying her grandchildren.